W9-AGH-011
04/2021

PALM BEACH COUNTY
LIBRARY SYSTEM
3650 Summit Boulevard
West Palm Beach, FL 33406-4198

"*The Moonlight School* wraps around you like a colorful quilt, planting you soul deep in turn-of-the-century Kentucky. Suzanne Woods Fisher pens an unforgettable story about love and the transforming power of words and community in this remarkable Appalachian-inspired novel. Deeply moving and uplifting!"

Laura Frantz, Christy Award–winning author
of *Tidewater Bride*

"*The Moonlight Schools* by Suzanne Woods Fisher is a captivating story with rich history and engaging characters who pull at your heartstrings. Readers will gladly ride up in the hills with Lucy to get to know the local folks. They'll cheer on Cora Wilson Stewart as she finds a way to open up the world of reading to people who missed out on proper schooling as children. That the story shares the true historical beginnings of the first Moonlight Schools makes it all that much better. If you like fascinating history mixed with great storytelling the way I do, you'll love Fisher's *The Moonlight Schools*."

Ann H. Gabhart, bestselling author of *These Healing Hills*
and *An Appalachian Summer*

DISCARDED

Novels by Suzanne Woods Fisher

LANCASTER COUNTY SECRETS

The Choice

The Waiting

The Search

SEASONS OF STONEY RIDGE

The Keeper

The Haven

The Lesson

THE INN AT EAGLE HILL

The Letters

The Calling

The Revealing

AMISH BEGINNINGS

Anna's Crossing

The Newcomer

The Return

THE BISHOP'S FAMILY

The Imposter

The Quieting

The Devoted

NANTUCKET LEGACY

Phoebe's Light

Minding the Light

The Light Before Day

THE DEACON'S FAMILY

Mending Fences

Stitches in Time

Two Steps Forward

THREE SISTERS ISLAND

On a Summer Tide

On a Coastal Breeze

The Moonlight School

The Moonlight School

A NOVEL

SUZANNE WOODS FISHER

Revell

a division of Baker Publishing Group
Grand Rapids, Michigan

© 2021 by Suzanne Woods Fisher

Published by Revell
a division of Baker Publishing Group
PO Box 6287, Grand Rapids, MI 49516-6287
www.revellbooks.com

Printed in the United States of America

All rights reserved. No part of this publication may be reproduced, stored in a retrieval system, or transmitted in any form or by any means—for example, electronic, photocopy, recording—without the prior written permission of the publisher. The only exception is brief quotations in printed reviews.

Library of Congress Cataloging-in-Publication Data
Names: Fisher, Suzanne Woods, author.
Title: The moonlight school : a novel / Suzanne Woods Fisher.
Description: Grand Rapids, Michigan : Revell, a division of Baker Publishing
    Group, [2021]
Identifiers: LCCN 2020035383 | ISBN 9780800735012 (paperback) |
    ISBN 9780800739652 (casebound)
Subjects: LCSH: Appalachian Region—Fiction.
Classification: LCC PS3606.I78 M66 2021 | DDC 813/.6—dc23
LC record available at https://lccn.loc.gov/2020035383

Scripture used in this book, whether quoted or paraphrased by the characters, is taken from the King James Version of the Bible.

This book is a work of fiction. References to real people, events, establishments, organizations, or locales are intended only to provide a sense of authenticity and are used fictitiously. All other characters, and all incidents and dialogue, are drawn from the author's imagination and are not to be construed as real.

Published in association with Joyce Hart of the Hartline Literary Agency, LLC.

21 22 23 24 25 26 27   7 6 5 4 3 2 1

The brightest moonlit night
the world has ever seen.

~CORA WILSON STEWART

Cast of Characters

Cora Wilson Stewart: first female superintendent of schools for Rowan County, Kentucky

Lucy Wilson: second cousin to Cora Wilson Stewart

Brother Wyatt: raised in the mountains, educated in the city, now a singing school master

Finley James: mountain boy, aged fifteen, works at the livery, attends Little Brushy School only when he has no choice

Angie Cooper: mountain girl, grade 8 at Little Brushy School

Arthur Cooper: father to Angie, trustee of Little Brushy School, owner of the livery in Morehead

Andrew Spencer: sales agent for Valley View Lumber Company

Charles Wilson: father to Lucy, husband to Hazel, first cousin to Cora, owner of the Valley View Lumber Company

Hazel Wilson: Lucy's very young stepmother

Mollie McGlothin: elderly mountain woman

Sally Ann Duncan: young mountain wife

Glossary

The accents and pronunciation of mountain talk can seem simple, quaint, or uneducated, but it's far more complex than one might think. It resembles a Scottish-flavored Elizabethan English dialect spoken long ago. Many of the words, expressions, the phrasing and framework date all the way back to the time of the first great English poet Geoffrey Chaucer, who wrote *Canterbury Tales* in the fourteenth century.

afreared: afraid

ahr: hour

a mite: a little

a'tall: at all

bar: bear

book red: educated

cousined to death: nepotism

deef: deaf

far: fire

haint: ghost

heered: heard

holp: help

idn't: isn't it

if'n: if only

jolt wagon: a farm wagon, like an oxcart

laht: light

nary: none *or* never

nigh: near

nothing never stop: unending

parts: neighborhood

pert-near: almost

pizen: poison

poke: bag

retched: reached

scald: used to describe
    "exhausted" land

tolable like: pretty good

wampish: wiggle

And just to keep things interesting, there are words that seem to have been invented out of thin air:

si-goggling: something that isn't
    straight

jasper: stranger

gaum: all cluttered up

Prologue

January 1901
Train Depot, Louisville, Kentucky

Lucy Wilson shifted on the wooden bench, hardly aware of the afternoon chill as she waited for Father to return to the station. She was halfway through Louisa May Alcott's *Little Women*, and she sensed a niggling worry about sister Beth's fragile health.

Whenever Lucy finished a chapter, she restrained from turning the page and made herself put down the book to check on her own sister, two-and-a-half-year-old Charlotte, who was curled up like a cat on Father's coat, napping soundly, arms wrapped around a favorite stuffed bear she called Mr. Buttons. Lucy stroked one of her sister's chubby little white hands and tucked a blonde ringlet away from her round cheek. At moments like this, when Charlotte was sleeping, she could see so much of Mother in her sister's little face. She pulled the edge of Father's coat over Charlotte's woolen stockings and picked up her book, only to put it down again when she heard the railroad clock chime.

Two o'clock. Father had been gone for over an hour. He didn't say when he might return from his business meeting, only that Lucy must keep close watch on her sister. Charlotte was a curious little girl and had an annoying tendency to wander off. Just yesterday, Lucy had caught Charlotte in Mother's writing room, playing with her jewelry box. She scooped up Charlotte in one arm and gathered the jewelry with her free hand, but when she looked through the jewelry box later, one ring was missing. An anniversary gift Father had given to Mother, a ring of small ruby chips. As soon as they returned home to Lexington, Lucy would resume the hunt for the ruby ring before Father realized it was gone.

Father had forbidden Lucy and Charlotte to play in Mother's writing room, though that didn't stop the girls. One time when cousin Cora had come for a visit, Lucy had overheard Father say it was the one place in the house he could still sense his wife's presence.

Lucy felt the same way about the writing room. She could almost smell her mother's scent, a lavender perfume that she liked to dab behind her ears. The writing room had been left virtually untouched since Mother had died, right down to the quill pen left in the same inkpot, as if she were going to return soon from an errand and pick up a story where she had left off.

Lucy and Charlotte often sneaked into the writing room after Father had left for work and the housekeeper was busy with the day's tasks. The room was actually Mother's dressing room, but she had used it for her writing room because she liked how the corner windows let light stream in all day long. The girls would sit on the floor together, and Lucy would show Charlotte each piece of jewelry and tell stories about Mother. She wanted Charlotte to have memories of their mother, even if imagined ones.

Lucy missed her mother with all her heart, missed everything about her; her gentle ways, her sparkling laugh, her joy of life. Her mother used to tell Lucy stories, and together they would come up with plot twists or surprise endings. Someday, she told Lucy, they would write a book together. But someday never came.

Charlotte squirmed in her sleep, and Lucy wiggled her back against the cold bench. When would Father return? He felt the girls were safer waiting here at the station than at a lumberyard, with big saws and horses and wagons and hardened tree fellers.

She glanced once more at the clock and sighed. Only a few minutes past three, though it felt like hours since Father had left. As long as Charlotte napped, she didn't mind waiting for Father because she was able to read to her heart's content. Father didn't approve of novels, not after Mother died. He said such twaddle softened the brain.

A train came into the station. Lucy watched dozens of people, all kinds—rich and poor and everything in between—stream out its doors. A young woman stood at a distance, looking at them with a peculiar expression on her face. Lucy realized the woman's attention was focused on Charlotte. She glanced down at her napping sister and saw her blue eyes open briefly, blinking, before drifting shut as she fell back to sleep. Lucy turned the page to the next chapter in *Little Women* and was immediately transplanted into the world of Jo and Beth and Meg and Amy, upstairs in their bedrooms, Marmie downstairs in the kitchen with the cook.

She read a chapter, and then another and another, sobbing as she came to Beth's tragic death. She knew it! She *knew* Beth was going to die.

"Lucy!" Her father's fierce shout broke through her shell of absorption. "Lucille!"

She snapped the book shut and stuffed it in her bag before turning to see her father stomp toward her, all buttoned up in his dour black suit, gesturing wildly at her.

"Lucille!" he shouted again. "Where is your sister?"

Lucy jerked around to where Charlotte had been sleeping. Father's coat remained, all bunched up, Mr. Buttons the bear tucked under a sleeve. But her sister was gone. She placed her hand on the spot to see if it was still warm. Stone cold.

A fear rose in Lucy, a greater fear than she'd ever experienced in her nine years, including that terrible day her mother lay dying.

ONE

The train jerked and jolted as it rumbled out of the station. Lucy Wilson stared out the window, watching her neat and tidy world fade into the distance. Watching her well-ordered life, if a bit pedantic and predictable, disappear.

She placed a hand over her heart and waited for its clamor to calm. Only six months, she reassured herself. She was expected to work for her father's favorite cousin, Cora Wilson Stewart, for only half a year, then back home she'd go.

But back home to what?

To her father's new wife, Hazel? A young, vivacious woman, scarcely older than Lucy. Hazel wanted to make a home that didn't cling to the past.

Back home to Lucy's charity work among the Lexington matrons, most of whom were twice, if not thrice, her age?

Back home to Father? Her presence only evoked his sorrow.

Lucy squeezed her eyes shut. Cora needed stenography help, Father had said, and wouldn't listen to her objections about a move to Morehead. Cora was superintendent of education for Rowan County, an impoverished area full of—how had Father phrased it?—moonshine and dulcimer pickers. Having grown up

15

there, he should know. But what exactly did a stenographer for a superintendent of education do? Lucy had no idea. She had many accomplished skills from her education at the Townsend School for Girls: from mastering the art of embroidery to conjugating Latin verbs. And so she had dissected the word *stenography*: from the seventeenth century, Greek roots. *Stenos* meant "narrow," *graph* meant "writing." The process of taking dictation. That, Lucy thought she could do.

Outside the window, the landscape had started to change. The train made fewer stops; its tracks wound through rolling green hills, thick with trees. Now and then she would spot a house with a sagging laundry line, but even those were becoming rare.

Think of this as an adventure, Hazel had suggested. A time to spread wings and gain confidence. Six short months, she reminded Lucy.

Hazel's enthusiasm was contagious. Lucy had gone to bed last night with a vow to herself that she would be brave today. Strong and courageous.

Her bold resolve weakened at the station this morning, and dissolved completely with her father's last words, said as the train to Morehead arrived: "Don't disappoint me." When had she not?

Then she saw his eyes soften, grow shiny with tears. She'd never been entirely sure he loved her until that moment.

Perhaps knowing *that* was worth *this*. Whatever *this*—working for Cora—might be. After all, it was only six short months.

Lucy turned her gaze away from staring out the window and faced forward, ready for what lay ahead.

MOREHEAD, KENTUCKY

AS LUCY LIFTED HER HAND to knock on her cousin's office door, she paused to take in the nameplate: CORA WILSON STEWART, SUPERINTENDENT OF ROWAN COUNTY SCHOOLS. She hadn't seen much of her father's favorite cousin in the last few years since she'd been elected as the first female superintendent in eastern Kentucky. Voted in by a substantial majority. Lucy would have voted for Cora, if women could vote. Father wouldn't have.

Lucy drew in a deep and satisfying breath, at least as much as the tight strings in her corset would allow. She hadn't felt this sense of freedom, this sense of possibility, for a very long time. She was excited. Nervous! She had *butterflies*.

"She's not there."

Lucy spun around to see a man sitting on a chair on the other side of the hall, one leg crossed over the other, his eyes focused on an open leather-bound book that rested on his knee. A hole was on the sole of his worn-out shoes, and his clothes were shabby. She'd been so focused on finding the right door to Cora's office that she'd only been dimly aware of him as she walked down the hall. "Are you waiting to see Mrs. Stewart?"

"Miss Cora? Indeed I am."

"How long have you been waiting?"

He gazed out the window at the end of the hall. "'Bout an hour." He set his book—a Bible—on the empty chair next to him, rose to his feet, removed his hat, and folded it to his chest. "When Miss Cora does return, I promise to be quick about my errand." He extended his hand. "Folks around here call me Brother Wyatt."

Lucy took his hand, which had strength to it. She blinked, regarding this man: he was younger than she first assumed, his nearly black hair flowed in ill-kempt waves in need of a cut. His face was etched, with sharp, angular cheekbones. Gray downturned eyes crinkled at their edge in crow's-feet. Unlike the young men in Lexington, he wore no trimmed mustache. No muttonchop side whiskers. "Are you a circuit preacher?" Father was not a fan of what he derisively called saddlebag preachers. Always looking for handouts and free meals, he said.

"Not intentionally, though there are times the Lord has asked me to preach his Word. But my true vocation is a singing school master."

She'd never heard of such a thing and wondered if he was making it up.

"I didn't catch your name." He gave her a smile, his first. She thought it an oddly poignant one.

"My name? Lucy. Lucy Wilson."

"And what brings you to Miss Cora's door today?"

Lucy never liked to give a quick answer to anything. She mulled it over and came up with a clear response that she hoped would discourage more questions. "I've come for an employment opportunity with Mrs. Stewart. She's desperately in need of assistance."

Brother Wyatt's smile faltered, but then he found it again. "Well," he said, trying to recover from his surprise, but his skepticism was hard to miss. "Well"—he cleared his throat and tried again—"this should be quite . . . an adventure for you."

"What makes you say that?"

His gaze swept her from head to toe. "Miss Cora is not known for coddling her teachers."

Coddling? "I'm not here to teach, but to assist Mrs. Stewart," she said, sounding much braver than she felt. "Short term. Only six months." Six short months.

"Two of my favorite people!" came a shriek down the hall. "Lucy! Dear girl!" Striding toward her came Cora, arms outstretched to give her a maternal embrace.

Cora Wilson Stewart was a good-sized woman, well-endowed in all the right places, and her presence filled the narrow hallway. Whatever size room she was in, she had a way of filling it. Lucy allowed herself to be swallowed up in Cora's arms.

Cora released her, though still gripped her forearms. "How was the trip? I'm sorry I wasn't there to meet your train. I tried, I truly did, but something came up, like it always does. Were you able to locate the boarding house? I hope Miss Maude was accommodating. It's nothing fancy, but it's decent and clean. Goodness, you must be famished. Exhausted! And how is that Victorian father of yours? Has his young new wife redecorated the palace yet?"

Sentences came out in rapid fire, one after the other, with no time or space for Lucy to respond. "Just look at you. You've gone and grown up on me. You certainly don't take after the Wilsons, do you?" She paused at last to let Lucy answer.

"I suppose not," Lucy said, after taking a moment to interpret what Cora meant. The Wilsons were bold, handsome people in personality and appearance. In her midthirties, Cora's angular face and piercing brown eyes made her seem older than her years, though her dark hair had no sign of gray. In a way Lucy had never understood, Cora seemed ageless.

Cora released the tight grip on Lucy's forearms and said, "Come in. Come in to my office and let's catch up before my next meeting. I'll send someone for tea. Wyatt, have you met my cousin? Of course you have. Have you been waiting long? I do apologize."

Hands behind his back, Brother Wyatt lifted his shoulders in a mild shrug. "Not so very long."

"Over an hour," Lucy said, thinking he was being overly kind. "I'll wait outside while the two of you talk."

"Better still, come in, Wyatt, and join us for tea."

"Wish I could, but I've much to do today. It won't take long, Cora, but I do need a minute of your time."

Some kind of silent exchange passed between the two that Lucy picked up on, suddenly aware Brother Wyatt's errand required privacy. "I'll go see about finding some tea," she said. Working as Cora's stenographer, she assumed she'd be making quite a bit of tea.

Cora seemed relieved. "Thank you, Lucy. Down the hall."

Lucy came to a modest ladies' room that seemed to double as a kitchen, including a small electric stove. She rummaged through a cupboard and found cups and a tin of teabags and a small teapot. Tea always seemed to calm her—not the tea, just the fixing of it. As she waited for the water to boil, she started to rearrange the contents of the messy cupboard. It actually cheered her to discover a task she could do to serve Cora. First role: tea making. One thing Lucy was well trained in. Not much else, but tea she could make.

Father, being a staunch traditionalist, wouldn't consider educating a woman beyond finishing school. Then came marriage. According to Father's thinking, anyway. There were a few boys who tried to court Lucy, but they were just that. Boys . . . with very little on their minds. She gradually fell off invitation lists and sat at home, working halfheartedly at embroidery; her only outings were to visit the elderly or attend church or a charitable event.

And then Father turned everything upside down when he married Hazel, a beautiful, charming debutante who'd been Lucy's peer all through finishing school.

Father and Hazel had scarcely returned from their grand honeymoon, following their even grander wedding, when he informed Lucy that cousin Cora had pleaded for her help as a stenographer. As Father muttered while writing the acceptance letter to Cora, "It's impossible to say no to the Little General." That was Cora's childhood nickname. "But just for six months," he added. "Then back to Lexington."

All these thoughts rumbled through Lucy's head as she returned to Cora's office carrying a tray of three steaming cups of tea. She stopped short in the hallway as she heard Cora mention her name. "Lucy is my cousin's daughter. She's come to help with them."

Them? Who was them? Lucy leaned closer to the door left ajar. She strained to hear Brother Wyatt's response, but his voice was low and deep and gentle. She thought he said something like, "It's happening more and more often."

"I know. The drought doesn't help." Cora's voice, unlike Brother Wyatt's, could be heard clear and loud.

"It's so much more than that."

"I know, I know. They're so vulnerable. But change comes slowly to the people of the mountain." Cora let out a loud sigh. "Have faith, Wyatt. You're always telling me that very thing. 'For with God, nothing is impossible.'"

When there was a long moment of silence, Lucy gave up being the bug on the wall and used her elbow to push the door all the way open. "I brought tea."

"Thank you, Miss Lucy, but I mustn't tarry." Brother Wyatt smiled, though this time it didn't reach his eyes. In fact, he seemed rather preoccupied. He gave Cora a meaningful nod, and then he left.

Cora sat behind her desk, an enormous oak piece, ornately carved, and riffled through papers as if looking for something.

Lucy gazed around the office. A richly colored oriental rug covered the floor. One wall had three standing bookshelves, with books jammed in every spare inch of space. "Cora, where shall I work?" There wasn't a surfeit of room, and every horizontal inch was taken up with books or papers. "Perhaps I could locate a small desk and set it out in the hallway. Even a table would work."

Still hunting for something on top of her desk, Cora didn't even look up. "You can share my desk. It's double-sided."

"But I'll get in your way."

"Not at all. You'll hardly be here."

"Pardon me?" Still holding the tea tray, Lucy walked toward her cousin's stately desk. "Where *will* I be?"

"Out in the field." Cora lifted a pile to reveal a fat brown envelope. "There it is!" She set the envelope on top of a stack of books. "These are letters that need answering. Precious letters."

"But surely I could do that from here. Take your dictation."

"Surely not. These letters aren't to me. Or from me."

"I don't understand."

"There are people in the rural areas who need someone to dictate to. They come all the way into town to have me help them with their correspondence." She let out a happy sigh. "Oh, Lucy. I can't tell you how glad I am that you're here. These good people work so hard. You can go to their homes and save them a trip to town." She inked her quill as if that was all there was to say and she had other matters to attend to.

"Why don't they write their own letters?"

Cora's head snapped up. "Because they never learned to read or write."

"So they're imbeciles?"

Cora's swift and stern reaction reminded Lucy of her father's disapproving looks. "Not in the least." She set the quill in the inkpot. "Mountain people aren't stupid, Lucy. They haven't had an opportunity for an education, but they're not stupid."

"Mountain people? Um . . . just where are their homes?"

"Up in the hollers."

A cold chill trickled down Lucy's spine. "Oh. I see." Though Lucy didn't see at all. She had come to Morehead to help her cousin with secretarial work, not tromp into the hills of eastern Kentucky. "I assume there's a car and driver to hire?"

Cora looked up in surprise. "A car?" She gave Lucy a patient smile. "Dear girl, I'd daresay that most everyone you'll meet up there has yet to lay eyes on an automobile. In fact, there's not much of any road to speak of into the hollers other than a few logging roads, and you should stay clear of those."

Lucy paused. "Then, uh, perhaps I could hire a hansom cab?"

Cora leaned back in her chair, eyes crinkling with amusement. "A dray? A hackney?" Then Lucy had a startling revelation. "Oh, you can't possibly mean . . ."

"Horseback. There's a livery stable down the road. Horses for hire."

Oh my stars and garters. Lucy's newfound courage, so thin and fragile and untried, began to shatter. The teacups clattered, and she set the tray on her cousin's desk before she dropped it. "Cora, I'm not trained to ride a horse." She was well trained in making tea.

Cora's eyes lit up at the sight of the tray, as if it just occurred to her that she'd sent Lucy out to make tea. "Why, Lucy! You remembered I like honey in my tea." She properly loaded her cup with honey and took a sip, then gave Lucy a satisfied smile. "Perfect. Just perfect."

Not so fast. "I've never been on the back of a horse in my life." Taking another sip, Cora peered over the cup's rim at Lucy. "You're not serious."

"But I am. Father felt it was unladylike."

"Your father"—Cora set the teacup back on the tray with a frown—"likes to forget where he came from. When we were children, we rode bareback all over those hills and hollows." She lifted her eyes to the ceiling, as if lost in a pleasant memory.

"Father would never allow me to go into those hills and hollows unchaperoned."

Cora shifted to peer out the window. "There's a boy named Finley James who works over at the livery. Tell him to choose a horse that gives a nice gentle ride and doesn't shy at snakes."

"Snakes?" Lucy sucked in a gasp of air. "Even if I could ride a horse, which I can't, I have absolutely no idea where to go. I don't know my way around these parts. It's not sensible."

Cora seemed astounded by Lucy's objections. "Just follow the creek. Triplett Creek. When there's a ford in the creek, cross over to the opposite bank and head up the trail. It'll take you straight up to Mollie McGlothin's."

Ford? Cross a creek? On a *horse*? Lucy barely had time to digest this, to explain that she had no ability to do any of those things, when Cora added, "As for the rest, you've got the names on those letters. Everybody knows everybody else. They'll point you in the right direction." She tucked her chin and started to write something.

"Cora . . . I can't."

She looked up, surprised. "Lucy, there's nothing to be afraid of."

Nothing? What about snakes? Or falling off a horse? This was crazy! "I can't ride any kind of four-legged creature into the woods, all alone. What if something happens?" An encounter with a wild beast? A fall off the horse? "Where do I sleep? Or eat?" Lucy had a stomach-sinking feeling that she already knew the answers to those questions. She was on her own.

"You'll be back to town in a wink." Cora tugged at the time-piece pinned to her shoulder and glanced at it, frowning. "Maybe two."

"Why would anyone let me in their home? I'm a stranger."

"Now that's easy. Just let them know you're a Wilson. Tell them you're my kin and you've come to do work for me. Once they know we're related, they'll give you the shirt off their backs, and most only have one shirt to speak of."

Lucy's father rarely spoke of his childhood, but the stories he told described a very foreign place inhabited by jelly-making hillbillies. "Father only gave me permission"—she paused as she saw Cora cringe at that word—"to come to Morehead because you told him you needed a stenographer."

"And I do."

Lucy was having serious doubts. This job wasn't what she had expected. "But, Cora," she pleaded, feeling a little teary, "Father would be outraged if he thought I was riding into those hills alone."

Cora peered at Lucy. "Your father always overprotected you. He's not here to make decisions for you. You're a grown woman, Lucy."

Lucy felt like a mouse cornered by a cat. There was no way out and it wasn't going to end well. "I'm not . . . very brave."

"You're stronger than you think. Every woman is, even if she doesn't know it."

Cora sounded so final that Lucy felt a growing sense of desperation. "But I . . ."

Palms on her desktop, Cora leaned forward, like a judge delivering the verdict. "Lucille Wilson, *this* is your chance. To release you from the terrible burden of losing Charlotte."

Lucy looked down at the tips of her boots. Would she ever be free of that burden?

"Oh dear girl," Cora said, her voice growing tender. "After Charlotte went missing, I saw you change from a happy child, full of curiosity and adventure, into a shell of a girl buried under an enormous weight. It was as if the sun was hidden behind a cloud. You lost interest in everything, as though the very idea of curiosity about life belonged only to the past. I hoped that with time, you'd return to your old self, but when I saw you recently at your father's wedding, I thought my heart was going to break. It must be so hard to breathe with a heavy stone on one's chest." Cora let out a weary sigh. "It's time, dear girl. High time to rejoin the living."

Lucy kept her head down, blinking back tears. She hated being the object of pity. "I admit," she said softly, "that a change might be needed."

"That's my girl!"

She chanced a look at Cora and saw a big smile wreath her face.

"This is the time to discover just how brave you really are." Cora clapped her hands, as if the matter was settled. "Off to the livery."

Lucy's head snapped up. "I can't. I just . . . can't go up in those hills. Not alone. And especially not on a horse. I've never had much of a sense of direction."

"That's understandable. Your father never gave you a chance to think for yourself."

Lucy swallowed past the lump in her throat. "I just can't do it *alone*."

Cora stared at Lucy for a long while, then dropped her pen, jumped up, and knocked on the window. She waved to someone down below, beckoning whoever it was to come to her office. She turned back to Lucy with a smile. "I do believe I've found you a suitable chaperone."

Not two minutes later, a skinny barefoot teenaged boy dressed in bib overalls stood at the open door. "You needing somethin', Miss Cora?"

"Finley James, why aren't you in school this morning?"

"Teacher's ailin' agen."

Cora frowned. "You telling the truth?"

"Cross my heart." He made a big X over his chest. "But, Miss

Cora, I do believe Miss Norah is playin' possum. She only gits sick on days when the postman comes through these parts. I think she's sweet on him."

"Now you're twisting the yarn."

"I ain't lying. I wouldn' nary tell a lie."

"Don't say ain't. Say isn't." Under her breath, Cora muttered, "Norah is absent far too often." She looked straight at Finley James. "In the meantime, how'd you like to earn two bits?"

His eyes brightened. "You need me to fetch and carry agen?"

"Better than that. I need you to take Miss Lucy to a few cabins in Deerlick Hollow. She's got some letters to read and ones to write." She pointed to Lucy, whom the boy had yet to notice. When he turned to see her, he startled, staring wide-eyed and openmouthed.

"Stop gawking, Finley James."

He snapped his mouth shut, then opened it again. "Pardon me for saying, Miss Cora, but she don't look like she'd last long on a mount. Even on Jenny."

"Yes! My sentiments exactly," Lucy said. "Who's Jenny?"

They ignored her. "You need to stay with her, Finley James, and bring her back in one piece. Just head to Mollie's and Sally Ann's and back down to town." Cora felt the thick envelope. "Perhaps a few more, if time allows. Lucy just needs a little help learning the trails. She'll get a nose for it soon enough."

Lucy fanned herself a little more vigorously. She would never get a nose for *this*.

"In fact, Finley James, you can be even more than a trail guide. Lucy is new to our ways. Teach her about the mountain people. Interpret for her."

"Interpret?" Lucy said. "Don't they speak English?"

"In a manner of speaking, yes."

Finley James stroked his unwhiskered chin. "All that for jest two little tiny bits?"

Eyes twinkling in amusement, Cora released a longsuffering sigh. "Fine. Four bits."

26

"Hmm, that does shed a new light on the matter." He tapped his chin, a gesture that made him look much older than his years. "But I'll need new bullets in m'gun. That'll cost y' some."

Lucy's eyes went wide. "Gun? Whatever for?"

As if quoting someone, he said, "There ain't nothing more important to a Rowan County man than his gun."

"But . . . ," Lucy looked to her cousin, "what does he need a gun *for*?"

Once again, she was ignored. Cora's eyes were fastened on the boy's. "No need for bullets. There will be an extra two bits if you get her back to town in one piece. So, then, do we have a deal?"

Finley James stuck his hand out to shake Cora's. "I'm your man," he answered without another moment's hesitation.

And with that, the bargain was sealed, and Lucy Wilson's new life in Rowan County began.

Two

N ow and again, Finley James would lean back in his saddle to see how Miss Lucy was faring on ol' Jenny. His heart beat a little faster each time he got another look at her. There was something entirely different about this fine city lady than any other female he'd knowed. Something sweet and shy. Something refined.

He hoped Miss Cora knew what she was doing when she brung her here. Miss Lucy sat on the oldest, gentlest pony in all Kentucky, but she was shaking in her fancy shiny black boots and her eyes looked all glittery, like she was trying hard not to cry. It took every ounce of Fin's self-control not to double over in laughter as she stood on the mounting block and tried to climb up on Jenny. Three tries—first as a side saddle, which only tangled her up—then she finally figured out it was best to hitch up her skirts a wee bit and swing a leg over the pony's back.

"Miss, you ought not to feel so squirrelly," he said. "Jenny ain't gonna hurtcha none."

"What if she rears and tosses me off?"

"Don't reckon that's possible," Fin said. The ol' pony jest plodded slowly along the path, but the city lady sat stiff-backed, gripping the saddle horn with both hands, and her pretty face was all tight and tense and pale.

"This pony doesn't seem very happy to have me on her back."

"Jenny can git sulky. She's a touch moody." He rubbed an eye and yawned.

"Do we have much farther to go?"

Mid-yawn, a laugh nearly burst out of Fin. They were still ambling along the creek, slow as molasses in January. He rolled his eyes, wondering how long these errands might take. It was his own fault; he knew better than to let Miss Cora catch sight of him in town. She always had things for him to do, and whilst she paid him a fair wage, Fin would ruther call his own shots on his rare day off. But how did a man say no to the likes of Miss Cora? He never could. He shoulda known better than to sit at the livery in her line of vision. Fin sat down in the sun to rest a spell, and that was when Miss Cora spotted him from her window, rapped on the glass, crooked her finger, and beckoned him to her office. Something about Miss Cora made his back go straight as an arrow. Eyes on the back of her head. Eyes everywhere. He was more than a little afreared of her. Everyone with half a brain was.

But he was smart enough not to tell this city lady anything more than she needed to know. "Pert-near. Jest up yonder a bit. Deerlick Holler." He glanced at her. "Don't suppose ya know why we call places hollers and not valleys."

"I have no idea."

"Cuz ya can holler across and still be heered. Cain't do that in a valley."

She didn't respond. "Tell me again to whose house we're going?"

He snorted. To whose house? Such fancy talk. Nobody talked like that. "Mollie McGlothin. She's as old as the hills. Older. Her great-grandpappy was one of the first settlers 'round these parts. Mollie claims he was kin to Daniel Boone, but it's best not to ask her to prove it. She can git tetchy." He turned back to check on Miss Lucy and thought her face seemed a little less drawn, so he decided to keep on talking. He liked to talk and tell stories. "Mollie McGlothin's birthed hundreds o' babies. Thousands, maybe."

"That's impossible."

"It's the gospel truth. She'll tell ya 'bout it. She birthed pretty nigh on everybody in the county."

"Oh! Now I see. You meant she's trained in midwifery."

He turned to look at her. "No. She helped the womenfolk have their babies." He noticed Miss Lucy had loosened up her grip on the saddle. She still held on tight, but she wasn't clenching quite so much. He didn't think so, anyhows. She was wearing gloves.

"I didn't expect it to be such a circuitous trail."

"Huh?" He frowned. Angie Cooper was always showing off by throwing them fifty-cent words at him. "What's cir . . . cir . . . cue . . ."

"Circuitous. Circular. It appears we're going in circles through the trees." She let out a deep sigh. "It's so dark and shady. More of a forest than I'd expected, as well."

Going in circles? Well, how else did a body get hisself up a steep hillside? *Oh brother.* Fin had a heckuva lot better things to do with his time than this. But he did like the feel of them bit pieces clinking in his pocket. He pointed to a fork in the path. "We're going down that way. Coming up to Ghost Crick. Jenny'll cross nice and easy. She's done it thousands of times afore. Crick used to be a good bit wider and deeper, but we've had a real bad dry spell this year."

"Ghost Crick?"

"Yes indeed, Miss Lucy. Thar's a haint that lives in the water. Long time ago a feller crossed the creek on his horse and the horse began to sink in the middle. The feller called for holp and folks ran to holp him, but afore they could git to him, this feller and his horse plumb disappeared. Never to be seen again." He paused and shifted around on his horse so he could see Miss Lucy's face as he delivered the rest of the story. "Except on full moons. Folks say there's a man on his horse swimmin' down the creek, calling out for holp." He cupped his mouth to mimic the haint's shouts. "Holp! Holp me! I be drownin'!"

Her eyes went wide, jest as he'd hoped.

"Finley James, by any chance are you telling me that tale just to spook me?"

"No, miss. That tale is the gospel truth. And you can call me Fin. Everybody does except Miss Cora. She says it holps to put the fear of the devil in me." Angie Cooper called him Finley James, too, which annoyed him to no end.

"Tell me what my errand is with Mollie McGlothin."

"Mollie's got herself a daughter Jane up there in Chicagy who sends her letters. She be wantin' to know what Jane sez. Miss Cora does the readin' and writin' for her." He glanced back. "And now you be doin' it." They ambled along the narrow bank of the creek. Little by little, the creek widened, then joined another branch, until it had become one large stream. When he didn't hear another question aimed at him, he looked back and realized Miss Lucy wasn't following behind him. Way back, Jenny had stopped to snack on some grass, and Miss Lucy looked like she was scared half to death. He turned Sheila around. If'n he lost the city lady, Miss Cora would never let him hear the end of it. "Shake the reins, Miss Lucy."

She jiggled the reins and Jenny kept munching on the grass.

"Harder. Give her a kick."

"But I don't want to hurt her."

"Not to fret. Ponies got thick hides." Fin watched Miss Lucy give Jenny a feeble kick in the girth, which the ol' pony ignored. He turned Sheila back and leaned over to grab Jenny's bridle to yank the pony away from her snack. They plodded along for several minutes, then he turned to give her fair warning. "We're heading acrosst Ghost Crick."

Miss Lucy stared at him.

"What's wrong?" What's wrong *now*, he wanted to add.

Her gaze was fixed on the crick. "There's absolutely no way I can cross that."

"Jest grab on to Jenny's mane and hang on tight." He kicked his horse and took Jenny's reins to lead her down the bank. The pony huffed and snorted as they went, hooves skidding at times, which made Miss Lucy yelp. As they waded into the water, he said, "Best not to look down." He held tight to Jenny's reins so the pony wouldn't balk.

"I'm not looking down. I'm not even looking."

He glanced back to see Miss Lucy's eyes squeezed shut, her arms clinging around poor Jenny's neck for dear life. He grinned. One thing he had to admit about this little city lady—she looked and acted like a fish outta water, and he'd half expected her to turn tail and head back to town. But she sure as heck weren't giving up.

Heck was the sole cussing word his maw would allow him, so he tried to use it as often as he could.

LUCY WOULD HAVE screamed as the pony picked her way through Ghost Creek, but she was terrified that any movement or sound she made might cause the pony to miss a step and she would nosedive into the creek.

As soon as Lucy returned to the town of Morehead today, she would have to explain to Cora that she simply couldn't do this job. She faintly wondered if there was a train running back to Lexington tonight or if she'd need to wait until tomorrow.

The pony tripped, caught itself, stopped, until Finley James yelled at it to keep going, and thankfully, it started to move again.

This was too much. It was all too much. She wanted to collapse on her lumpy bed at Miss Maude's boarding house and weep, but she could do no such thing. She had made a vow to herself to be brave in this new venture. But this? She hadn't expected *this*.

What had ever possessed Father to agree to Cora's request for Lucy to move to Morehead? And why hadn't she been more force-ful in her objections? Perhaps she hadn't felt as if she had a place in Father and Hazel's life, but at least she wasn't in danger of tumbling right over a pony's big ears and plunging to her death in a haunted creek!

Breathe, Lucy, breathe. In and out.

Now and then the pony would just stop short, but Finley James would make a clicking sound and urge it on. At long last they made it to the other side and Lucy thought she was safe. So wrong.

"Hang on tight," Fin said. "We be going straight up this hill."

"Wait! I'm going to slide right off the back of this beast."

"Lift your bee-hind up and lean forward. But drop the reins a bit. Hold 'em loose so Jenny can stretch her neck."

Lucy cringed, holding on to the saddle horn until her hands ached with tension. Hours passed, or possibly minutes, as they snaked up the steep hill. Finley James sat loose-limbed in the saddle, practically sashaying up the hill along with the horse. Lucy had been gripping the saddle with the inside of her knees so tightly that they burned from the constant rub. As they climbed higher and higher, plunging deeper and deeper into the woods, it grew dark. Tall trees crowded out the sun. Even the sound of the pony's hooves was hushed, plodding on top of a carpet of pine needles. When the boy came to a level place where the path was wide enough that they could ride side by side, he reined his horse until Lucy caught up. He reached out to hold back a low-hanging branch so it didn't hit her in the face.

"Finley James?"

"Call me Fin, Miss Lucy. I prefer it."

"Yes, sorry. Fin, what kind of shrubs are these?"

"What. Them showy flowers? That's red buckeye."

She looked up. "What about that tree? The leaves look similar to the shrub."

"Yellow buckeye. Pretty to look at but the wood ain't no good. Too weak, real soft. There's lots of trees up here." He swung his arm, pointing at one tree, then another as he talked. "Birch and beech, sugar maples, lindens. And that one . . . that's the loblolly pine. Best tree in the world. Finest lumber you'll ever find. And the best turpentine from the pitch too. Them trees are wanted the world over." He lifted his chin. "Hear that?" He pointed halfway up a pine tree. There was a persistent *tap tap tap* sound that Lucy followed until she saw a bird, about nine inches long, knocking its head against the tree. "That be a red-cockaded woodpecker. They peck little cavities in the loblollies for their nests. If you work in the timber, like my paw did, you shoot 'em."

"Why?"

"Cuz they damage wood meant for lumber. But if you asked my opinion, I'd tolerate a few holes in the wood. I'm rather fond of 'em."

"Your father works for the lumber company?"

A shadow passed over Fin's face. "He passed on a while back. But Paw didn't work for no one but hisself. Wouldn't have it no other way."

It took every effort for Lucy to not wince at his horrible grammar. *Didn't* he pronounced as *dint*. *Wouldn't* was pronounced as *wooden*. Fin didn't speak again for a long while. Had she overstepped? She felt a bit concerned, wondering what she'd said that hit some kind of sore spot. From what her father had told her, the lumber companies in Morehead had tried to bring economic prosperity to this impoverished county. "Do you intend to work for the lumber company after you graduate from school?"

Fin gave her a sharp look. "I'd quit school now, if Maw would let me." He fell quiet again, and Lucy sensed she shouldn't ask more. She wanted to, though. She was grateful for his knowledge of the mountain. She couldn't believe Cora thought she could handle this trip alone. Just what kind of a person did she think Lucy was? Because whatever it was, she wasn't.

The trail forked off to a level area, though trees still surrounded them on all sides. And then, through the trees, there sat a little one-room schoolhouse with a bell tower topping its roof.

Fin stopped in front of it. "That's Little Brushy School. That's where I go, so long as the teacher ain't ailin' or moonin' after the postman."

"It looks new." The simplicity, the beauty of the little roughly hewn building shone through.

"It shorely is. Old one burnt down. I built this one m'self." He rocked his hand in the air. "Mighta had a little holp."

A young girl wearing a large floppy calico sunbonnet came out of the schoolhouse carrying a bucket, and Lucy thought she heard Fin utter a mild profanity.

The girl's face broke into a beaming smile when she saw Fin. "Hey there, Finley James."

"Hey yourself, Angie." He sounded much less enthusiastic than the girl.

Her smile dissolved as she sized up Lucy. She took in her face, then her eyes traveled slowly to her boots and lingered there. Lucy glanced down at the clothes she wore—traveling clothes. A well-tailored overcoat that covered a white shirtwaist, tucked into a charcoal-gray woolen split skirt borrowed from Cora. And her boots—something this young girl seemed particularly fascinated by—were new, a gift from Hazel and Father. She suddenly felt acutely aware of how finely dressed she was, and it almost shamed her. No wonder this barefoot country girl couldn't stop staring at polished boots.

The girl seemed just as aware of her own plain appearance. With the palms of her hands, she tried to smooth the wrinkles out of her dirty pinafore. "Finley James, your horse wantin' some o' this here water?" She held up the bucket.

"Nope."

"Did you come for your lessons? I could try and holp you with 'em. I noticed you made a dreadful mess of your 'rithmatic yesterday."

He scowled. "Heck no."

All this time, the girl continued to eye Lucy suspiciously. She was right on the cusp of leaving girlhood behind for good, with bright blue eyes, unruly blonde hair, and a turned-up nose. Not pretty, exactly. But she had presence. "Then," she said, turning her gaze to Fin, "whatcha doing up here?"

"Angie Cooper, you keep your beak outta my business."

Angie's eyes narrowed, as if wounded by his curtness. "I'll tell your maw I seen you gone off fishing this morning."

His chin jerked up. "I'm doing a favor for Miss Cora," he said defensively. "Escortin' this fine lady here to meet some folks."

"Who's she?"

"I'm Lucy." She lifted a hand in greeting. "Lucy Wilson."

"She's kin to Miss Cora. Came from the big city to holp with her work."

Angie's face clouded. "You teachin' school in place of Miss Norah?"

"No, no. Goodness, no," Lucy said quickly. She had no desire to teach school. None.

"Good. Because that's what I'm supposed to do, soon as I pass my grade 8 exam. I jest passed my grade 7 exam. With flying colors, Miss Norah sez. Not a single mistake."

"Biggerty. She brags on herself all the livelong day." Fin turned to Lucy. "See what I have to deal with?"

Angie scowled at Fin before she turned back to Lucy. "So why're you here?" There was an edge to her voice.

Lucy had to fight back a smile at this girl's direct ways. Her face gave away every feeling she had. "I'm employed as Cora's stenographer."

Angie's face crinkled into a question. "What's *that*?"

"It means she's working for Miss Cora. And today, so am I. We gotta go." Fin gave Sheila a kick and started along a thin trail that wound through the grass behind the schoolhouse.

Lucy waved a gloved hand at Angie and squeezed Jenny's sides with her legs to urge her forward. The pony didn't budge. She dropped her neck to chew on some grass. Jiggling the reins, Lucy could feel Angie's amused eyes on her. The pony still didn't move.

By now, Fin realized she wasn't following and circled back to grab the reins to yank Jenny along. "Ya gotta be the boss with her."

"I'm trying my best," Lucy said.

"Try harder," Fin said, sounding irritated.

Lucy had a feeling his sudden bad mood had something to do with Angie. "She's a very attractive girl."

"Angie Cooper?" He shrugged, as if the thought had never occurred to him. "Her paw is the trustee for Little Brushy."

"Don't like her much?" Because Angie was obviously smitten with Fin. Besotted.

"She's a know-it-all. Betcha by now she'll get word to my maw that she seen me. She's been tattling on me since as long as I can remember. Prickly as a thistle, that girl."

Lucy grinned, glad Fin was facing forward. No wonder he emphasized to her that Miss Cora had asked him to work for her today. "She seems quite knowledgeable."

"Angie's been known to give advice," he warned. "Most any time, you don't gotta ask for it." He thought for a moment. "That's pretty much true of everybody here."

This boy was good company. "Fin, how old are you?"

"Almost sixteen."

"Oh? When's your birthday?"

"February."

Lucy choked back a laugh. Today was the fifteenth day of March. "So, you must be in grade 8?" She could see his back stiffen and wondered what she'd said now to make him bristle. Goodness, he could turn fractious fast. "That's how it is in Lexington. Boys your age were in grade 8 or 9." Actually, more like grades 9 or 10.

"Different here," he said gruffly. "I'm needed to work. Cain't be bothered to waste time in school."

"School isn't a waste of time. It's important to know how to read and write well, and to use arithmetic."

He stopped Sheila abruptly and turned to face Lucy, a cross look on his boyish face. "My paw didn't need learnin', his paw didn't neither. I'd ruther be outside any day of the week than stuck inside a stinkin' schoolhouse." He turned Sheila back around and continued along the trail, as if to signal the conversation was over.

But not for Lucy. "Then, why do you bother to go to school?"

Fin led Sheila through a shallow rock-strewn stream of water that looked clear and cold, and took his time answering, so long that Lucy thought stalling was his way of not answering. "Miss Cora," he said as they reached the other side of the stream and waited for Jenny to plod along. "Since she's been superintendent, she's been chasing after every boy and girl in the county to git to school. No chance to escape."

"Angie seems to like it."

He shrugged. "She's the only one in Little Brushy who's had straight-through schooling, on account of her paw being the trustee. She's planning on being a schoolteacher for Miss Cora as soon as she can. She tries to practice on everyone. Thinks she's boss of everybody in the whole holler."

"The Little General."

"Exactly." Fin pronounced it *egg-zackly*.

"That's the nickname Cora's father gave her when she was a girl."

"Well, that makes sense. Angie tries to walk like Miss Cora and talk like her and boss people around like—"

He stopped abruptly, glancing at Lucy, as if he just realized to whom he was griping. Lucy had to bite on her lip to keep from laughing.

Fin spotted another woodpecker, which seemed to cheer him up. He chatted companionably for what seemed like a long stretch on a thin dirt trail, though it was difficult to get any sense of time in the thick woods.

"Up that ridge is by Sam Stamper's place. You oughta stay clear of Sam's place."

"Why's that?"

"He's a whiskey maker. He ain't here but his son is working

in his place till he gets out of jail. If'n he ever gits out. I think he likes the pokey. Three meals a day." Fin grinned, rubbing his stomach. "He had his chance to git out. Last February, four prisoners escaped from the county jail. Sam coulda made a break for it along with them prisoners, but he decided he'd jest ruther stay put."

"How did they escape?"

"They'd been sawing the bars on the window for months and the sheriff never caught wind of it. Middle of the night, out they climbed, free as birds."

"Why were they in jail in the first place?"

"Well, let's see. Grant Gilkerson, he was in for cutting Marshall Moore."

"Cutting?"

"Murder." Fin made a slashing movement with his hand. "He's known for being good with the knife. I figure he's the one who got the ideer of cutting the bars. Now, Jess Adkins . . . I do believe he was arrested for forging checks. Cooper Alley and Nora Byron . . . hmm, I can't remember what they was in the pokey for."

"After the escape, were they ever caught?"

"Naw. Sheriff's still workin' on it." He glanced at Lucy. "You might hear about mountain folks catching glimpses of Grant Gilkerson roaming the hollers on moonlit nights, slashing away. Practicin'." He brandished his arm like a sword. "Grant left a note on his jail bunk that he's out for revenge on the town for lockin' him up."

Lucy couldn't quite tell if Fin was making stories up to frighten her or if this was the strange new world she had come to. And if it was the latter, she had no one to blame but herself. Her father had tried to warn her.

Just ahead of Fin, in the gloom among the thick shelter of trees, she could barely make out the bones of a tiny dilapidated cabin.

When they came to the clearing of the yard, Fin hopped off his horse in one seamless move. He cupped his hand around his mouth. "Miss Mollie? Mollie McGlothin? It's me. Finley James." He turned to Lucy. "Some folks say she's as mad as the moon, but don't believe a word o' it." He shouted out to her again. "Always best to let her know who you be. She's a little deef and she may be older than dirt, but she still got good aim."

THREE

FINLEY JAMES WALKED past a rusty iron kettle and hopped over a large ax in a chunk of tree stump, then jumped up to the porch to rap on the door. "Miss Mollie? You in there? I brung you a visitor." He put his ear to the door, then turned to nod at Lucy. "She's a-comin'."

The door creaked open and a small cloud of gray grizzled hair poked out.

"Hey, Miss Mollie," Fin said. "How y' doing today?"

"Tolable like."

"Well, that's good t' hear."

"Oh, I got me a touch of the collywobbles." The door opened a little wider to reveal a wrinkled face, crackled as an old mixing bowl. "Who you got there?"

"This here's Miss Cora's second cousin. On her paw's side. She's a Wilson. Goes by Lucy. Miss Cora sent her to write yor letter so ya don't have to travel to town this week."

The door opened wide to reveal a bent figure as old as Methuselah. Near her feet, a chicken pecked. Then another.

"Chickens!" Lucy burst out. "There's chickens in the cabin. Fin! Do something! Help her collect them!"

"Mollie likes 'em inside."

She looked at him in astonishment. "Whyever for?"

41

"To keep 'em safe. They's like pets to her."

"But . . . safe from what?"

"Foxes. Bobcats. The occasional wolf or bar."

"What kind of animal is a bar?"

"Ain't ya ever met up with a grizzly bar?"

"Bear?" He meant bear?!

His eyes twinkled and she hoped he was teasing her again. He waved to her. "Come on down off that pony and be friendly."

Lucy lifted a leg over the pony's head and caught her dress on the saddle cantle, nearly toppling headfirst. She hung on to the saddle horn for dear life.

"No, no! Not that way." Fin jumped off the porch and ran to untangle her dress and hold her steady as she slid clumsily down the side of the pony. "Thunderation! Ain't ya ever got off a pony afore?"

Lucy swayed on her feet. Her backside was completely numb. Smoothing out her skirt, she said, "I told you. Not a horse. Not a pony. Not any kind of beast."

"How'd you git places?"

"By carriage, of course."

"Y' mean, a jolt wagon?"

"What's that?"

Fin looked at her as if she were from another world. "An ox cart."

"Oh misery me! No! Never!"

Exasperated, Fin started toward the cabin. "Come on and meet Miss Mollie."

Picking her way gingerly through the weedy yard, Lucy reached Miss Mollie and put her hand out to shake. The old woman didn't take it, only peered at Lucy through milky pale blue eyes, rimmed red, sunken deep. "You don't look much like Cora. I've knowed her since she was jest a girl." She looked past Lucy. "Where's yor pony off to?"

Lucy spun around to see Jenny's hindquarters trot down the

path toward the woods. "Oh no! No! Stop!" She'd had to nudge and kick that pony all the way up that mountain, and now Jenny seemed to be in a hurry to get home. She started to chase after the pony, but Fin got to her first and grabbed the reins.

"Ya didn't tie her up!"

"Tie her up? To what?"

Fin shook his head in disbelief. "If ya don't have something to tie a horse to, ya never leave it facing home. Always turn yor mount around. Everybody knows that much."

"I didn't."

He seemed appalled at her ignorance. "I'm gonna water them horses. You go read and write for Miss Mollie afore she needs her afternoon nap." He lowered his voice to add, "She'll offer you food but don't take it."

"Why not? I'm quite hungry."

Fin rolled his eyes. "Cuz then she might not have no supper for herself."

Lucy went to the porch where Miss Mollie continued to eye her with suspicion. "Shall we get started?" She wanted to get back down that mountain and into a hot bath at Miss Maude's boarding house. At least, she hoped there was a bathtub at Miss Maude's.

"Jest how be you kin to Cora? You shore don't look like her."

"Miss Mollie," Fin said firmly, leading the horse and pony to a rusty trough filled with dirty rainwater. "Cora said to tell you she's kin. That'd be all that matters."

"Cora said you needed help writing a letter," Lucy said.

Mollie scratched her chin. "Mebbe I'll jest wait on Cora."

"No, ya cain't," Fin shouted, though he was far on the other side of the yard.

He must have ears like an owl, Lucy thought.

"You know as well as I do what Miss Cora tol' you," he yelled.

Gingerly, Lucy climbed the porch steps, stepping around rotted boards and who knew what else. "What exactly did Miss Cora tell you?"

"She sez that from now on, you'll be doing the reading and writing chores."

From now on? Lucy had no such intention.

Miss Mollie called down to Fin. "I don't want no jasper knowin' my business."

Fin had left the pony and horse at the trough and picked up the axe that had been jammed in a tree stump. "Miss Mollie, Miss Cora sent along a letter from Jane. How 'bout if Miss Lucy reads it to ya? Then you can decide if ya want to let her know yor business."

Fin had found just the right words to soften the old woman. "Come on in then," she said, still eyeing Lucy.

As Lucy followed her into the one-room cabin, she was slapped in the face by a mélange of strong, heavy smells: cooking fat, tobacco smoke, and something sour and musty and tangy. Chicken dung? She nearly lost her breakfast from the rank stink. She took a handkerchief out of her skirt pocket and covered her nose as her eyes adjusted to the gloom. She could see nothing at first, other than the glow of coals coming from a fireplace. When she realized the floor was made of dirt, she gasped.

Miss Mollie didn't notice. She hobbled over to a rocking chair in front of an open stone hearth, so large it nearly took up the full wall. She took a clay pipe that was resting on the hearth and settled into the rocking chair, stuck the pipe between her lips, and sucked in air so that her cheeks disappeared. She exhaled, coughing, and pointed to a stool. "Sit down by the far. Better laht."

Far? What did she mean? *Oh . . . fire! Laht. Light.*

"Lemme hear what m' girl has to say."

Stalling to cover her shock at the condition of the cabin, Lucy pretended to blow her nose behind her handkerchief. There was a small rope mattress bed tucked against the wall near the fireplace, and a large blackened kettle hung on a hook in the open hearth. Besides the rocking chair and the stool, there was no place else to sit or to eat. And chickens strutted about, making discontent squawks, leaving feathers and other remains behind. The only heat came from the coals in the fire, and they gave off more sooty smoke than warmth. It all seemed so . . . primitive. How could anyone live like this?

Swallowing a groan, Lucy tucked the handkerchief away, eased her aching bottom onto the little stool, and opened the large envelope to find the letter meant for Mollie McGlothin. Lucy cleared her throat and began.

Dear Maw,

It was wonderful to hear from you. We are settling into Chicago and getting used to the bustle and noise. Clive is happy with his job as a meat packer and wants to stay put. I miss the peace and quiet of the mountains, and the people, but I think he is right about cities and opportunities. He says to tell others who want to stop working in the timber. He says he will help find them work, so long as they can cipher numbers and write their own name.

Maw, I have some good news. My Eliza and her Bobby are going to have a baby come summer. How many great-grandchildren will that make for you?

Please ask Miss Cora to write again for you soon.

Fondly, Jane

Lucy put the letter down and took a fresh piece of stationery out of the large envelope. "Shall I take dictation for you?"

Mollie's sparse eyebrows shot up. "Y' take the drink?" She pointed to a mason jar on the hearth. She smiled then, eyes twinkling, a lovely smile except for her missing teeth. "Go on. Holp y'self."

Confused, Lucy tried again. "Shall I write down what you'd like to say to your daughter?"

"Oh shore, like Cora does." She settled back in her rocking chair and folded her arms against her and closed her eyes. "Dear

Jane. It was a real treat to git yor letter and hear another baby is a' coming. I do believe this will make eight great-grans for me, but each one is mighty special soz I don't like thinking about them as if they was jest numbers . . ."

Lucy wrote as fast as she could, not wanting to interrupt Mollie's stream of consciousness. One page was filled, then another, then another. Lucy's hand started aching at the sheer volume of Mollie's soliloquy. Finally, the old woman slowed down to a drizzle. "One more thing, dear Jane. Do not neglect yor Bible reading each and every day. The mighty Word of God has a way of working its way into yor soul. Love, your Maw."

Lucy paused, pondering that last phrase. She'd never considered the Word of God to be much more than a list of dos and don'ts.

"Read it back to me, soz I know you done right."

Lucy cleared her throat and read Mollie's letter just as she'd dictated it. She thought the old woman nodded off during page 2, as her chin dropped to her chest. Then she realized that tears were trickling down the old woman's parchment-like cheeks. "Mollie, what's wrong?"

"If only I could read and write m' own words."

"But . . . I took care to write down just what you said." In the exact way she'd spoken. Lucy didn't even try to correct her shocking grammar.

"You done jest fine. But it ain't the same."

Considering Mollie McGlothin had spent most of her life without reading and writing, it seemed a little silly to fuss over it now.

"Mebbe you can teach me." The old woman leaned forward in her rocking chair. "Cora's too busy, but you gots time. What else ya gots to do?"

The eagerness in her voice caught Lucy by surprise. "Oh my goodness . . . I'm no teacher. I'm here to help Cora with her work as superintendent of the county schools. And I'm sure that will keep me quite busy." Lucy wasn't really sure what work that might be, but she hoped it would be significant. For a moment, she forgot she wanted to leave Rowan County as soon as possible.

Clearly disappointed in Lucy, Miss Mollie leaned back in her rocker. "I'm feeling a little tarred."

"Tarred?"

"Tarred," Miss Mollie repeated with a yawn. She turned away from her to stare into the coals, and it wasn't long before Lucy heard a whiffling snore.

Lucy folded Jane's letter and tucked it in an envelope to mail from the Morehead post office. Quietly, she tiptoed to the open door, longing for fresh air. Mollie's snoring deepened and Lucy suddenly realized what "tarred" meant. *Tired!* Outside, she took several gulps of cold, clean air, eager to get the smelly stink of chickens out of her nose. She felt as if she had stepped off the train this morning into another country, separated from the world she had known.

Fin was tossing wood up on the porch and had taken his shirt off, sweating from the labor. Lucy was startled to see the boy was bone thin, ribs sticking out. But then Mollie McGlothin's living condition shocked her too. It shamed Lucy to realize she'd had no idea this kind of poverty existed, just sixty-five miles from Lexington. She cringed as she thought of how she must have sounded in Cora's office earlier today, wondering where her next meal might come from. Lucy had never gone hungry a day in her life. Watching Fin work so hard for a meal and a few bits, she wondered how many meals he'd gone without.

She set down Cora's large envelope and got to work to help Fin finish the stacking. She noticed that under the porch were rows of mason jars, like the one on the hearth that Mollie had offered to her. She bent down and took one out, unscrewed it, and got a whiff of strong liquor. "Pew!"

Fin stopped stacking wood and put his hands on his hips, eyes dancing with amusement. "Why, Miss Lucy, ya didn't strike me as a gal with a taste for moonshine."

Moonshine? "I'm not! Truly, I'm not. There were so many jars lined up and I wondered what was in them."

"Don't ya worry none. I won't tell nobody. It'll be our little secret."

As she started to sputter away, defending herself, he doubled over in laughter, and she realized he was teasing her again, and she found she didn't mind so much. They smiled at each other then. Their first moment of affinity.

When all the wood was leaning against the wall, Fin shielded his eyes to see how low the sun was dropping. "We'd best be off."

They stopped beside the creek to rest. Fin broke his corn bread in half and shared it with her. Sunlight dappled through the trees; a gentle breeze rustled the leaves. It was peaceful here with the creek gurgling and the birds chirping in the treetops and the soft sound of the horses' tails as they swished. Every now and then the birds would grow quiet, and she had never experienced such stillness.

Such a deep, deep quiet.

Without realizing it, she let out a soft sigh.

He grinned. "It's even nicer when the weather warms some and the leaves finish comin' out. But I think fall's my favorite time. All them colors in the leaves, and the way they rustle under the horse's feet . . . it's real nice."

Lucy tilted her head. So this boy had a bit of poetry in him. "Do others live like Mollie?"

"How's that?"

The dirt, the poverty. Mason jars full of home-brewed alcohol under the porch. "Chickens wandering in and out of the house."

He bit off a piece of corn bread and took a moment to chew. "Them chickens, they be good company for Mollie. She don't have no family around no more."

"Why didn't she move to Chicago with her daughter and son-in-law? Or her other children? Why doesn't she go live with them?"

"This holler is her home. She don't know nothin' different."

Lucy cringed at his grammar but took care not to show it. Oh, it was awful! It hurt her ears to hear him butcher the English language so. "It must be lonely for her."

He shrugged. "Folks look out for each other. They's good to each other."

"Mollie's son-in-law . . . his name is Clive?"

Fin nodded. "Yep."

"Jane wrote that Clive wanted to encourage workers to leave the timber. He said to tell others he'd help them get jobs, so long as they can read and write."

Fin chewed thoughtfully. "Most cain't."

"I thought the lumber companies needed workers." Lumber was king, her father always said. Other eastern Kentucky counties had coal reserves, but for Rowan County, their treasure was their trees. She waited for him to chime in, but he was peering up at the treetops.

"Fin?"

He dropped his chin and gave her a long, steady look, and she caught a fleeting glimpse of the man he would become, strong-willed and determined. "Yor paw owns Valley View Lumber? Ain't that so?" Then he glanced away, as if deciding not to say more.

She hadn't realized he had made the connection to her father and Valley View Lumber. Father rarely traveled to Morehead because a foreman managed the timber crews. More significantly, there was a sales agent, Andrew Spencer, who handled the contracts to harvest lumber from privately held properties. Her father spoke highly of Andrew Spencer; Hazel was, Lucy thought, overly eager for her to meet him. Just a year or so ago, Valley View was going to abandon Rowan County. Its lumber heyday in the 1890s was long gone, its virgin timber harvested. According to Father, Andrew Spencer had foreseen the demand for pitch from loblolly pines, a natural resource for Rowan County, and talked Father into the concept of selective harvesting. It had been a tremendous success for Valley View, and Father felt beholden to Andrew Spencer's farsightedness. "Yes, that's right."

"Jest ask yor paw 'bout it, then."

There was an edge to his voice that startled Lucy, making him sound older than his years.

"Where else is Miss Cora sendin' you today?"

Lucy pulled out the next envelope and held it up to him.

Fin peered at it, scowling. "Cain't read that chicken scrawl."

"It's not chicken scrawl. It's an elegant cursive, as clear as can be—" and then she had a startling revelation. *Oh my stars and garters.* Fin couldn't do Cora's reading and writing errands because he couldn't read or write. Lucy tried to hide the shock she felt. This boy—a bright, clever, funny boy edging up to manhood, a boy full of potential—couldn't read. It must be humiliating for him to be stuck with a primary grade in a one-room classroom. No wonder he didn't want to go to school.

"Sally Ann Duncan."

Fin smiled and jumped to his feet. "Duncan place be right over yonder. Let's go."

"Oh good," Lucy said, laughing weakly with relief. Over yonder was about all her aching legs and bottom could handle.

OVER YONDER, Lucy was quickly discovering, meant anything from a few feet to a dozen miles. She rode silently behind Fin for another half hour or so of plodding through vines and branches, crossing creeks, twisting around shrubs, before they reached a clearing in the woods.

This property was vastly different from Miss Mollie's. The log cabin with stone chimney sat not on stilts but on the highest point, sheltered by a strand of tall pines. The yard and garden were tidy and cared for; even the henhouse had a cheerful coat of red paint. Firewood was neatly stacked on the porch. A cow and two sheep grazed in the pasture behind a whitewashed rail fence. Long ago, someone with experience had chosen this site with care.

The empty hillside in front of the cabin had been plowed sometime in the past, though the field looked fallow as if waiting for spring. The remnants of last autumn's cornstalks littered the field like broken arrows.

"Shouldn't the corn be plowed under by now?" Lucy asked, but Fin only frowned at her. She didn't know much about farming, but on the train ride here, she'd seen farmers plowing and planting their fields. She waited for him to answer her, but he only shrugged.

"Lots of things should be different, but that don't make it so."

What did that mean? Lucy couldn't figure out half of what Fin was talking about, or not talking about.

He cupped his hands around his mouth. "Hallo! It's me, Fin! And I brung someone!"

Almost immediately, a young girl came out of the cabin. Shielding her eyes to peer at the visitors, she waved and shouted to come on up.

As the horses walked toward the cabin, Lucy noticed two baskets of flowers hanging from the porch. The girl looked as neat and tidy as her house and yard, with thick coils of brunette hair wreathing the back of her head. Drawing near, Lucy was shocked to discover this girl had a very round belly. Why, she couldn't have been much older than Fin!

He swung a leg behind him and slipped to the ground next to Sheila. "Sally Ann, I brung along Miss Cora's new letter writer. This here's Miss Lucy. She's kin to Miss Cora." This time, he came to the left of Jenny and helped Lucy down.

The look on Sally Ann's face was like Christmas had come. "Have you got a letter for me from Roy?"

"I do believe so," Lucy said. Seeing the pure delight in the young woman's eyes made the long ride almost worth it. "You're Sally Ann Duncan?"

Her face lit with joy. "That'd be me."

Lucy opened the saddle bag and took out the letter from Cora's big envelope. "Roy Duncan. Is he your husband?"

"Shore is. He's real good about sending word to me."

51

"He's got fine penmanship."

Sally Ann gave a shy smile. "He shorely does."

"Where is he?"

"He's looking for work in Lexington, seeing as how we gotta move." She pointed to the open door. "Would ya have time to come in? Sit a spell?"

"Naw," Fin said, his tone a bit doleful. "We can't stay, Sally Ann. Jest the letter reading and writing and then we gots to be on our way."

Happily, Fin's dolefulness did not have any impact on her. "Come on, Fin," Sally Ann said. "You can spare a few minutes. Besides, I jest made some fresh bread."

Fin brightened. "Oh, well, that changes things."

Suddenly famished, Lucy's stomach rumbled at the sweet aroma as it wafted through the door. Following Sally Ann into the cabin, Lucy was transfixed by the feeling of welcome she received. The cabin was bright and cheery, the light streaming through the windows and open door, shining rays onto the oak floor. A wooden floor! Not dirt.

She took a few steps inside and saw a corner hutch was filled with china. A small lantern sat in the middle of the tabletop, surrounded by pieces of bright cloth. When Lucy looked closer, she saw that Sally Ann had been working on a quilting project when they interrupted her. Spread over the table were small cut pieces of fabric, shades of pink and blue, arranged like puzzle pieces. "What are you making?"

Sally Ann reached out to gently caress a triangle cut of pink cloth. "A crib blanket. Jest a little somethin' for the baby."

When Lucy spotted the needle and thread Sally Ann had been working with, she felt an urge to sit down at the worktable, to pick up where Sally Ann had left off and complete the seam. Such a thought astonished her. Never, in Lucy's entire life, had she wanted to do needlework. It was always a dreaded chore, something she considered to be a tiresome social pastime. Her gaze swept in the tidy little cabin, filled with the sweet aroma of freshly baked bread. "How could you bear to leave this home? Why, it's charming!"

Gently, Sally Ann closed the door, and turned to exchange a look with Fin. Lucy sensed she'd said something wrong, though she wasn't sure what. Cautiously, Sally Ann said, "If you're kin to Miss Cora, don't that make you kin to Valley View Lumber?"

"I, um, well . . ." Lucy stumbled on what to say next. She'd never felt anything but pride to be connected to her father and his business.

"Yeah," Fin said, "but try not to hold that against her."

The door swung open. Sally Ann looked over Lucy's shoulder and smiled broadly. "Angie!" she said, as Fin let out a loud groan. "You snuck up on us as quiet as a bobcat."

Angie Cooper stood at the open door with narrowed eyes fixed on Lucy. "I can read that letter t' my friend. And I'll write one in return for her and post it m'self."

"Good," Fin said in a cross voice. "We'll be off, then."

Lucy felt pinpricks of disappointment. She would have liked more time at Sally Ann's. Despite how radically different their lives were, she sensed they could be friends. She hadn't had many true friends in her life. Most girls considered Lucy far too serious, too quiet, too dull. She didn't add much to their circle and was included in gatherings only out of necessity, only because of her father's social status.

"Finley James," Angie said in a sweet voice, very different than the one she used for Lucy. "You be goin' to the singing school on Sunday next? I'll be makin' my fried chicken."

He was on his way out the door and barely responded. "Too busy."

Angie's appearance brought back Fin's earlier prickliness. He seemed in a hurry to go and had already gathered the animals' reins. "Miss Lucy, I cain't take you on any more of Miss Cora's errands this afternoon. It's gettin' late and I gotta git home. Got chores of m' own to do."

Lucy wasn't a bit sorry that more afternoon errands were cut short. Her backside burned red hot, sorely chaffed from the saddle. "I couldn't have managed the day without you, Fin."

Fin held Jenny steady while Lucy struggled to mount the pony. And struggled. Finally, Fin heaved her up from behind. Thoroughly unladylike. She thought she heard Angie snickering from the porch.

"Jest follow the creek to get back to town." He grabbed Sheila's rope reins and hoisted a leg over the horse's back. "Pleased to meetcha, Miss Lucy."

"I'm starting to realize that you're quite the tease. I know you wouldn't leave me here."

He circled back. "Jenny'll see you home. In half the time too. Every horse knows their way home." He didn't wait for Lucy to respond. He gave Sheila a kick and Lucy a wave, and soon the woods swallowed him up.

Lucy stopped dead in her tracks, grabbed her blouse over her heart, and gasped long and loud. *Oh my stars and garters*. He was gone. She would have to find her way back to town all alone.

Jenny wiggled her sizable ears as if trying to decide whether to follow Sheila or head home. She must have decided to go home because, with no prompting from Lucy, she turned and headed toward the creek. Lucy clutched the saddle horn, her breath tight in her throat, her heart pounding, trusting the pony's sure feet as she picked up its pace and began to trot. Lucy squeezed her eyes shut, praying the first desperate prayer she'd prayed since losing Charlotte: *Please God, please God, please God*. But he hadn't answered her then, and she wasn't at all sure he would answer her now.

Four

EVERY INCH OF LUCY'S BODY ACHED, from her toes to her fingertips, from yesterday's horseback excursion up and down a mountain. Even lifting her arm to comb her hair hurt. Her hip joints ached like she was ninety, not nineteen. She felt sore muscles she never knew existed! She smelled coffee brewing, ran the brush through her hair one last time, and looked in the mirror. She should do more with her hair, but the best she could manage this morning was to tie it back with a ribbon. It looked all right. Maybe not for Lexington, but good enough for Morehead.

She tossed her brush on her bed in the small room in Miss Maude's boarding house, a corner room with two windows so, she discovered today, the morning light streamed in from two angles. Those corner windows reminded her of her mother's writing room, but nothing else. This room was bare: a small desk with a lone chair, a braided rug, and a shiny brass framed bed, covered by a cheery quilt. Bare but clean, and more than adequate, considering Lucy didn't expect to be here for long.

She had slept like a bear in hibernation, exhausted, and woke famished. Gingerly, she bent down to put on her shoes and groaned. Never again would she get on a pony, nor a horse. Father was so right. There was nothing ladylike about riding on a beast of burden.

She checked her hair one more time in the mirror, smoothed her skirt, and went downstairs for breakfast. Miss Maude, the keeper of the boarding house, bustled between the kitchen and the dining room with a ceramic pitcher, filled with what Lucy hoped was hot coffee. Widowed in midlife, Miss Maude had a cushiony bosom, a merry face with soft downy cheeks. And she was amply blessed with the gift of conversation. Lucy discovered just how blessed last night, when she arrived at the boarding house bone-tired, reeking of horses and trail dust, longing for a hot bath, and Miss Maude cornered her on the stairs. An hour later, she finally managed to wedge a word into the conversation to excuse herself and hurry up the rest of the stairs.

This morning, Miss Maude spotted Lucy coming down the stairs and pointed to an empty chair. "Come in, come in, Lucy, and sit there. From now on, that'll be your chair for every meal. When you're done with breakfast, fold your napkin and leave it at your place setting. I have a girl who comes to do washing but only once a week." She strode to the door. "I'll be back in two shakes of a lamb's tail."

Lucy stopped abruptly at the doorjamb, surprised to discover a nearly full table of boarders peering back at her. It had seemed so quiet last evening. Miss Maude had volunteered much about herself, her entire life history, but nothing about other boarders.

Eyes followed her as she made her way to a chair at the opposite end of the table. Gingerly, she eased herself into the chair, trying not to moan from sore muscles. She took her time spreading the napkin over her lap. When she looked up, she found four people staring at her: two older ladies, one middle-aged woman, and then a man whom she recognized. Brother Wyatt.

"Good morning," he said in that low, deep voice of his.

The kitchen door swung open and in burst Miss Maude, still talking as if she'd never left the room. "Have you all met Lucy Wilson?" Miss Maude paused for formal introductions. "Lucy's kin to our Cora."

She poured coffee first into Brother Wyatt's cup, then she turned to fill the two elderly ladies' cups, talking a swift stream like the dark liquid she poured. Lucy picked up her cup, hopeful that it would be filled soon.

"Her father is Charles Wilson, Cora's first cousin. He left Rowan County to go make something of himself in the big city, and he did right for himself, didn't he, Lucy?" She didn't give Lucy a chance to answer but shook the pitcher and realized it was empty. "Goodness, I'll have to get a larger coffeepot if my boarding house stays full." Pleased, she spun around and disappeared into the kitchen again.

Brother Wyatt must have noticed the disappointed look on Lucy's face as the coffeepot disappeared. He rose and brought his coffee cup to her, eyes softening in sympathy. "Please take mine. I haven't touched it. Hope you don't mind, but I added sweet milk."

She gave him an appreciative smile as she accepted his offer and took his cup. There was a natural dignity about the man, almost courtly. She took a sip of coffee, thinking sweet milk meant sugar or honey had been added, but it tasted like just cream.

Brother Wyatt turned to the other women. "Allow me to introduce you. These two are the Hicks sisters. Miss Lettie on the left, Miss Viola on the right. They're longtime boarders for Miss Maude."

"Miss Hicks," Lucy said, nodding to both.

"Do call us by our first names," Miss Viola said. "Otherwise we feel like two old ladies."

Lucy swallowed a smile at that, because they *were* old ladies.

He pointed across the table to the middle-aged woman whom, Lucy noted, did not return her smile but only a cautious appraisal. In an odd way, the wary look reminded her of the way Angie Cooper had gazed at her. As if Lucy had committed a crime. "And this is the late Judge Klopp's wife."

"You may call me Mrs. Klopp." One of her sharp eyebrows arched. "How exactly are you related to Mrs. Stewart?"

"Cousins," Lucy said, and by the look on Mrs. Klopp's face, she could tell that wasn't a good thing. "Second cousins, to be exact." That was as much information as she wanted to provide.

"Don't mind Mrs. Klopp," Miss Viola said. "She eyes the world with suspicion."

Mrs. Klopp sniffed. "A result of being the town's only librarian, married to the town's only judge." She shuddered. "You discover everyone's secrets."

"A library?" Lucy hadn't seen a library yet, though she hadn't had a spare moment to wander. Perhaps today, she thought. "Where is the library, Mrs. Klopp?"

"Nowhere," she said with a sorrowful sigh.

"She means," Brother Wyatt said, "that the library burned down recently."

"One year," Mrs. Klopp said, coffee cup held in midair, "two months, and three days ago."

"I'm so sorry," Lucy said.

Mrs. Klopp nodded. "My house went up in flames along with it."

"Her residence housed the library," Brother Wyatt explained. "Mrs. Klopp's late husband, the honorable Judge Klopp, bequeathed his home and library to the town when he passed."

"And a fine home it was." Mrs. Klopp exhaled mournfully, and took a sip of coffee.

"Will you rebuild?" Lucy asked. "Start a new library? Every town should have one."

"The judge," Mrs. Klopp said, "was the only one in this town with a love for books. He had hundreds of them."

That wasn't true. Lucy knew that much about Morehead. Cora loved to read, and her office had two full bookshelves, brimming with books. "Perhaps I could ask for donations from my . . . from friends in Lexington." She was going to say her father, but she didn't want to be known in Morehead as the daughter of a well-to-do man. She'd lived long enough under that shadow.

Mrs. Klopp stiffened her spine. "We don't need charity."

"Yes, we do," Miss Viola said.

From the far end of the table, Brother Wyatt had been listening. "Mrs. Klopp, most libraries begin with accepting book donations. Not the judge's, of course, but most. And Rowan County has a great lack of reading material. Perhaps you should reconsider Miss Lucy's offer. Might be just what this town needs. Losing your husband's library was a great blow. I know I have sorely felt its absence."

Mrs. Klopp sweetened at his words.

Brother Wyatt wiped his mouth with his napkin and tucked it back at its place. He struck Lucy as a man who took care with manners, as if they were newly taught to him and required conscious effort. "Please excuse me. I must be off." He rose and nodded to everyone, his eyes resting on Lucy. "Have a good day, ladies."

Miss Viola watched him go, then patted her heart with both wrinkled, liver-spotted hands. "If I were only thirty years younger."

"Fifty," said her sister. It was the only word Miss Lettie had uttered throughout the breakfast conversation, and Lucy instantly loved both sisters.

Ignoring the sisters, Mrs. Klopp turned to Lucy. "So you've come to visit Mrs. Stewart?"

It surprised Lucy to hear Cora referred to as Mrs. Stewart. No one called her by that name. "Actually, I've come to work for her. As her stenographer."

Mrs. Klopp's lips pursed in disapproval. "Well, I'm surprised your father would want you associating with such a woman. She's divorced, you know. Three times. Twice to the same man. Divorced him one month, married him again the next. Only to divorce him all over again!"

Lucy knew.

"The judge," Mrs. Klopp said, sitting straighter in the chair, "campaigned vigorously against Cora Stewart in the election for the superintendent position."

"An election that Cora won by a substantial majority, as I recall,"

Miss Viola said, eyes narrowed and voice firm. "The first woman elected to be superintendent in the county."

"We helped," Miss Lettie said.

"Oh, we did indeed. We came up with Cora's campaign slogan, didn't we, Sister?"

"The Children's Friend," Miss Lettie said.

"Yes! That's it. Good for you, Lettie. The Children's Friend. And Cora won by a landslide. Imagine! A Democrat winning a Republican county." She slapped her fragile, birdlike hands on the table. "And a woman, to boot!"

The judge's wife was not impressed. "Cora's politics have only added to our county's many troubles."

"Cora Wilson Stewart," Miss Viola said, all fired up, "is the best thing that's ever happened to our county. In fact, she's becoming a powerful public figure in the entire state of Kentucky."

"I don't know about that," Mrs. Klopp said, glowering at Miss Viola, then picked up her knife to butter a piece of bread.

"I do," Miss Viola said. "And I'm always right." She relaxed in her seat and sent a wink to Lucy. She smiled back. Mrs. Klopp harrumphed.

Lucy felt better after coffee and breakfast, better about being here, better about her aching body. She hated riding, hated Jenny, but it pleased her to no end to hear about the impact Cora was making, and she felt a tiny glimmer of renewed enthusiasm about coming to Morehead.

ANGIE COOPER ATTACKED the floor of the Little Brushy school-house with her broom, peeved at Miss Norah for ailin' so often. Days were wasting away and she was *this* close to her final exams for grade 8. Once she passed them, she could teach. But she needed Miss Norah to give her the exam, even though she knew twice as much as her teacher did.

And then there was Finley James. She wouldn't marry him until he could read, at least up to grade 6. Maybe grade 4. He was plenty smart, but he needed proper schooling if'n he was ever to catch up with Angie. If Angie were the cussing type, she would cuss out Miss Norah for being such a no-good worthless teacher.

She swept the dirt out the door and off the porch. While she was outside, she looked around the corner at her troublesome little brothers. She'd sent them out to take turns on the swing that hung off a big oak tree. They weren't near the oak tree. They'd found a big mud puddle and were stomping and splashing around in it, both of them covered in mud.

Angie sat down heavily on the edge of her porch and, in case either of her brothers bothered to note her reaction, did her level best to look calm and not, in any way, agitated. Inside, however, she was seething, simmering anger over Miss Norah's slothiness. Was that a word? *Laziness*. She knew that was a genuine one.

She heard the sound of rustling leaves, then the rhythmic clomping of an approaching horse, so she jumped off the porch, dusted her skirt, straightened her bonnet, all in hopes the rider would turn out to be Finley James. But it was only Brother Wyatt riding past the schoolhouse on his beautiful black horse. She called to him and waved, then walked through the yard to greet him as he came through the trees.

"Looking for Paw? He's over yonder, getting ready for the brush arbor." She stroked Lyric's black velvet nose, wishing she had a bit of carrot for this fine horse. The finest horse in Rowan County, Paw said.

"I am indeed. Thought I'd come up to help."

"Paw said you're welcome to stay at the farm."

"Thank you, Angie. I might take you up on that, if I'm not any trouble."

"You're no trouble. Them boys," she said with an eye on those two little brothers, "they's nothing *but* trouble."

"No school again today?"

"No. It's a worry. Twice this week." She glanced up at him. "Say, mebbe you could do the teaching, if Miss Cora fires Miss Norah." She bit her lip. "Oh, Paw warned me to keep quiet about that and not tell anyone." But Brother Wyatt wasn't jest anyone. He was . . . about as close to a holy man as a man could get.

"I won't tell a soul." Then he shook his head. "But I can't teach at Little Brushy. Too much to do."

Her brother Mikey had started toward the schoolhouse, but Angie saw and cut him off. "Oh no . . . no, you don't. I jest swept dirt out of that schoolhouse that you brought in. You two git. Go worsh off."

His twin Gabe was jest as muddy. He lifted up brown palms, as if he was surprised to discover the dirt. "Where?"

"Oh good grief. At the well." She sighed. "I gots to do everything for them boys." She turned back to Brother Wyatt, who was watching the scene, amused. "It's only funny if you ain't the one to scrub their clothes."

"I suppose so," he said with a laugh. "Don't be too hard on them. Mud puddles are a favorite pastime for little boys. I well remember." He pulled on Lyric's reins to turn her back to the trail. "I'll see you later tonight, Angie."

She smiled, despite her annoyance with her brothers. It was always a treat when Brother Wyatt stayed with them. Paw would get out his fiddle and Brother Wyatt would sing and Angie and her brothers would clog to their hearts' content.

Later that afternoon, Angie baked two loaves of fresh bread and took one over to Miss Mollie.

Next to her paw and them brothers, Angie Cooper loved Miss Mollie best. Everybody did. Her lap was always big enough for a crying child, and she always had something sweet to spare from her pantry. Folks in the holler knew to go to her for all their troubles. Collywobbles, heebie-jeebies, colic, too-much celebratin'. Miss Mollie might not be learned, but she knowed most everything worth knowin'.

Angie was particularly fascinated with the love potions and charms concocted by Miss Mollie, all kept in her head. She claimed credit for every love match in the holler, which Angie's paw said was jest an old woman's muddle-mindedness.

But Angie thought her paw was wrong on that. Once she'd asked Miss Mollie why her love potions hadn't done right by Miss Cora. Thrice divorced! No one in the holler ever got themselves divorced. They might hate each other with a fiery passion, but they wouldn't nary think of divorcing. One holler over, there was a maw and a paw who had said naught a word to each other for years and years and years. They couldn't remember what they was mad at, but they stayed good and mad.

"Well, there you see," Miss Mollie had sniffed. "Cora didn't ask for my holp."

That settled things for Angie. Miss Mollie was the one to go to for love and everything else.

"I recollect a surefire one," Miss Mollie said. "If a man wipes his hands on a woman's apron, he's shore to fall in love with her."

Angie looked down at her clothing. "Does that work for a pinafore? Or does it have to be an apron?"

"Apron," Miss Mollie said firmly, and then, "I think."

ON SATURDAY, Finley James came to till Arthur Cooper's field so he could spend the whole entire day at the livery, its busiest day. Angie took a jug of cold water down to the field. She offered the jug to Finley James, then made a point to accidentally-on-purpose pour water all over him. She held out the corners of the apron she wore, her mother's blue one, for him to wipe his hands on, but he refused.

"You're all gaumed up," he said. "And you stink awful bad too." He grabbed the jug, drank down the rest of the water, handed it back to her, raked his hands through his hair and plopped his hat back on, then returned to plowing.

She looked down at her apron, streaked with chicken dung after mucking out the henhouse. She sniffed her underarms and realized she did smell a little ripe. Miss Mollie shoulda told her to clean up first. Sometimes she thought the old woman's wits were growing addled.

Bother!

AS THE DAYS PASSED, it wasn't difficult for Lucy to find practical ways to help ease her cousin's immense workload. Cora's day, Lucy had quickly discovered, would start in one direction and veer off into dozens of small distractions. So Lucy's main objective would be to handle as many of those distractions as she could. She set to work to organize the chaos. Scattered all over the office were notes—meetings, reminders, invitations to speak, and an abundance of to-do lists. She pinned a calendar to the wall, an attempt to keep Cora tethered, to try and create some semblance of order for her.

This morning Lucy found a file full of neglected correspondence from teachers and principals who applauded Cora's work as superintendent of schools, including many invitations to speak. Lucy found one letter from Kentucky's Christian Women's Board of Missions, asking Cora to speak at their convention in Louisville about Progressive Reform. She was a gifted orator and would love to make more time for speaking engagements, but she was bent on improving the fifty-one little one-room schoolhouses sprinkled throughout the county. An education, she believed, was the great equalizer, the answer to all of life's injustices.

Lucy hoped Cora was right about that. She was astounded at the abject poverty, the enormous gulf between townspeople and hillbillies. She corrected herself. Cora disdained the term *hillbillies*. She was a fierce advocate for the mountain people, speaking of them almost as if they held on to characteristics fading away in the rest of America: honesty, pride, ambition, reverence for God, a simplicity that she described as a purity of heart. She felt that the barriers between mountain people and city people were geological, not intrinsic. The mountains isolated them and kept them from the opportunities that were due to them. Educational ones, mostly.

A gentle knock on the door interrupted Lucy. An older man opened the door and looked around. "Morning," he said, hat in hand. "I came hoping to see Miss Cora."

"She should be back soon. She had a meeting to attend, but it will be over soon. Would you like to wait?"

The man wasn't really listening, he was looking past Lucy toward the books on the wall.

"Would you like to borrow one? I'm sure Miss Cora wouldn't mind." Lucy knew Cora loaned books out to others. In fact, on Lucy's to-do list was to start a record of those who borrowed Cora's books.

The man walked up to the bookshelves, eyes as wide as a child in front of a candy shop. He gently fingered the back of one book's spine as if touching pure gold. "Can't read. Can't write." He turned back to Lucy and she noticed his eyes were shiny. "I'd give twenty years of my life if I could read jest one of them books." He put his hat back on and said, "I'll come back later for Miss Cora."

After the door shut, Lucy looked over at the narrow bookshelves that lined the walls. Seeing the hunger for knowledge written all over that man's face left her feeling unsettled, disturbed.

It reminded her of a buried memory from her childhood— walking down a busy Lexington street, past a beggar, as she and Charlotte ate ice cream cones. Father held both girls' hands and kept them moving along, ignoring the beggar's pleas. But even at age eight or nine, it didn't seem right.

FIVE

I T TOOK SOME DOING for Angie to coax more love potions
out of Miss Mollie since last Saturday's blunder with Fin. The
old woman said it had been a long time since she used her magic
and she'd forgotten most of it, and besides, potions were a mighty
powerful tool and oughtn't be used by bossy girls who might marry
too soon. *Hardly!* At thirteen or fourteen—she wasn't quite sure
which—Angie was no girl.

After she swept out Miss Mollie's dirt floor one afternoon, the
old woman was in a more pliable mood. "I got a good one for
you." Miss Mollie held up a threadbare sock she was darning.
"This knot I knit, will true commit, to know the thing I know not
yet, that I may see, who shall my husband be."

Angie wrote it down. "So each time I sew, I say that chant?"

"Jest on the nights when you want to be dreaming of who he
be." Mollie stroked her whiskered chin. "Mebbe 'twould holp to
put a sock or two under yor pillow."

That night, Angie tried it. She dreamed only of socks.

As soon as school let out, Angie hurried to Miss Mollie's to
tell her the love charm hadn't worked, and that she dreamed not
of her beloved but of darning socks.

Miss Mollie took the news unfazed, as matter-of-fact as if
she were making a pot of soup. "I recall something else about

that love charm. There's a second verse that's shore to work. 'This knot I knit, will true commit, our hearts entwined, our love aligned.'" She took in a big draft from her pipe, then coughed and coughed.

"You shore about this one, Miss Mollie?"

"Try sticking the needle in the feller you're sweet on. Guaranteed to work."

Oh, Angie could jest imagine how that would turn out. Finley James would likely kill her. "That sounds like a heap of nonsense."

Offended, Miss Mollie wouldn't talk to Angie for the rest of the visit, so she gave up and went home.

FIN WAS AT THE LIVERY, fixing a loose board in Jenny's stall, when he saw Miss Lucy walk down the road toward the boarding house. As his thoughts wandered off to Miss Lucy, how delicate she was, how graceful-like she walked, he got a little sloppy with the knife and sliced his finger. A thick scarlet river spurted down his hand and arm. He screamed bloody murder and Miss Lucy came running.

"What's happened? Oh, Fin, you've cut yourself!"

"I'll be fine," he said bravely, and then promptly passed out.

Miss Lucy shook him back to the living by making a tourniquet with her dainty lace handkerchief. He saw the red stain soaking the handkerchief and passed out again.

The next thing he knew, those two little Cooper twins were staring down at him. "Is Fin dead?"

"No, no," Miss Lucy said. "He just fainted from the sight of his own blood."

"I done nothing of the kind," Fin said in a weak voice.

Suddenly there was Angie Cooper, peering down on him. She took hold of Fin's hand to examine it, unwrapping the blood-soaked handkerchief.

"I think it might need a stitch or two," Miss Lucy said.

"It's a mighty bad cut," Angie said, sounding like she knew everything. "Finley James, what were you thinkin' that you didn't pay no attention to what you were doing?"

One of those little boys—Fin was never sure which was which—shouldered his way in to peer at the bloody hand. "Yeah, Fin. What was you thinkin'?"

What was Fin thinking? He'd been thinking about how Miss Lucy always smelled as sweet as a flower, and how she always looked fresh and neat, like she'd jest had a spring bath. But heck if he would say any of that out loud. All his feelings would come tumbling out and he might embarrass hisself.

Arthur Cooper saved the day. "Boys, get back and give Fin some air. Angie, go in the tack room and get the needle and thread." He tipped his head toward the back of the livery.

"I'll be fine," Fin said, even though nobody paid him any mind.

"Let's get him up on one of them barrels." By the time Fin got settled on top of a barrel, Angie had returned with a big sewing needle threaded with black thread.

"What are ya gonna do with that?" Fin asked.

"I noticed a button was off yor shirt and figured I'd jest sew it back on." Arthur Cooper chuckled, mopping away the blood to find the cut. "What do ya think I'm going to do with it?"

This was no time for making fun. Fin squeezed his eyes shut. "Take yor time with it. I want a tidy scar."

"If'n it's tidy ya want, then Angie should do the stitching."

Fin's eyes popped open to see Angie grin and wave the needle up in the air.

"I'll be glad to," she said, with a vicious glint in her blue eyes. Such a big sharp point on that needle. "Go ahead. I can take it."

Those twins crowded in on him again. "Paw," Angie said, "take them boys out of here while I do the surgery."

"She's right, boys. Let's get the horses fed."

Angie tied a knot on the end of the thread. Fin wanted to swat her off, but then he caught sight of the needle coming close and he felt faint again. The last thing he remembered was Angie handing the needle to Lucy and saying, "Hold this a second. I gotta find something first."

As Fin struggled back from the darkness, he felt Angie's hair brush his face. She was whispering a poem in his ear, something under her breath, something about knots and knitting and husbands and hearts entwined. "This knot I knit, will true commit, our hearts entwined, our love aligned."

Then Lucy turned and smiled down on him, and Fin thought she looked a little like an angel.

Suddenly Angie let out a yelp. "YOU SEWED HIM UP?"

"He'd fainted," Miss Lucy said, in her singsongy voice. "I thought it would be better for him to get stitched up while he was unconscious."

"YOU STUCK A NEEDLE IN HIM?" Angie was outraged. "YOU DID IT WITHOUT ME?"

"It just took two little stitches. I used to sew up my sister's stuffed animals. It seemed like the same kind of thing, considering Fin was temporarily lifeless."

If Fin wasn't mistaken, Miss Lucy seemed rather proud of herself. He lifted his head to look at his hand. It was bandaged up, no blood seeped through. She'd done herself a fine doctoring job, and he thought it was especially sweet that she took care of it while he was unaware.

But something about it made Angie madder than a hornet.

EARLY ONE MORNING, a particularly cold and gray day, Lucy was alone at the breakfast table. Two weeks had passed since she had first stepped off the train in Morehead. Miss Maude bustled in and out, bringing her a cup of coffee. Just as she reached out to pick up her coffee, the front door opened and in came Cora.

"Good morning, dear girl. It's all over town that you sewed Finley James up after he nearly lopped his hand off. Well done."

"It wasn't quite so serious as that." Still, Lucy was quite proud of having the confidence to stitch his cut after he'd fainted. When Angie had thrust the needle at her and disappeared, Lucy wasn't sure if she was coming back. With Fin out cold, she took matters into her own hands. It seemed the right thing to do, to stitch his cut before he came to, and Lucy was pleased that all those years of embroidery work at the Townsend School for Girls had not been for naught. But stitching Fin up sent Angie Cooper into a snit. She had come back with a piece of paper, bent down to whisper in Fin's ear, looked at his hand, and started to yell. Glaring at Lucy, she'd torn up the paper she'd been holding and left the scene without another word.

Cora pulled out the chair next to Lucy, then eyed the cup of coffee held in her hands. Smiling, Lucy handed the cup to her. She knew Cora loved coffee even better than tea and honey. "Take it. I'll get another."

"I'm glad to know you're an early riser. I thought as much." She raised the coffee cup to her lips, closing her eyes as she sipped, as if sampling a taste of heaven. "I'm catching the train to lead a teacher training institute, and I wanted to be sure you knew where you're going today."

Going? Lucy froze. "Cora, you don't mean to send me back up that mountain on that horrid pony?"

"Horrid pony? Why, Jenny's a sweetheart." Cora took her time to swallow down the last of Lucy's coffee. "I'm sorry Finley James isn't available as a guide. He's in school, where he belongs. Miss Norah promised no more absences this term." She patted Lucy's hand. "Each time you go out, I guarantee you'll learn more about peoples' ways."

Each time? Lucy's jaw dropped, then she snapped it shut. "Without Finley James as a guide, I can guarantee I will get lost and never return."

"Dear girl, you *must* stop underestimating yourself."

That might be true about most things, but when it came to riding a horse into those hollows alone, she was certain she had predicted the situation accurately. She would never be seen again.

The kitchen door swung open and in walked Brother Wyatt, a look of quiet pleasure on his face when he saw Cora.

Cora returned his warm smile. "Good morning, Wyatt. I didn't realize you were in town."

Lucy hadn't either. She hadn't seen him since that first breakfast, two weeks ago.

"Came in on the train last night. Heading up to the hills today." He set a basket of warm hoe cakes near them and sat at the far end of the table, the same place as before. "Miss Maude was just telling me how Miss Lucy saved Fin's life."

This story was growing bigger with each telling. Lucy opened her mouth to object, but he gave her a wink, and she realized he was teasing.

"Two tiny stitches," she said, and he grinned.

Cora reached out for a hoe cake, lathering it thickly with butter, then topped it off with a huge spoonful of peach jam. She did everything with gusto. Talking, walking, eating. She noticed Lucy watching her chew and, between bites, said, "Eat up, dear girl. You'll need your energy today."

Now that was just the kind of comment that made Lucy's stomach swirl into a tight knot.

Cora finished the hoe cake in three bites, then turned to Brother Wyatt. "Lucy's heading up to Blacklog to Barbara Jean Boling's. She sent word there's an important letter she needs written."

"I'm going near there myself," he said. "I'll see Miss Lucy gets to Barbara Jean's in one piece. Then I'll have to keep on going, but Jenny'll see her home."

Lucy gasped. "Not again! What if she takes a wrong turn?"

Brother Wyatt's eyes lit with amusement. "No need to worry. God gave horses the know-how to get back to their own barn."

The entire scenario was unacceptable to Lucy. Father would disapprove of her being in the company of a young man without a chaperone, and she was not at all willing to put her life in the hands of that long-toothed pony, trusting the beast to return home. Not that Miss Maude's boarding house in Morehead was *home*. In fact, at this moment, she was seriously considering hopping the train to return to Lexington.

Into the dining room walked Mrs. Klopp, just as Miss Maude bustled into the room with a bowl of scrambled eggs. She set the bowl in front of Mrs. Klopp, who scooped a large spoonful unto her plate. Two scoops, then three.

By now the elderly Hicks sister had come down the stairs to join them at the table, delighted to see Cora. Mrs. Klopp passed the bowl of scrambled eggs to Miss Lettie, then Miss Viola, to Cora, to Brother Wyatt, to Cora, and by the time the bowl reached Lucy, there was just one teaspoonful left. Lucy scooped it up with her fork and straight into her mouth. Father would frown, but it was clear to see that if you didn't look out for yourself in this boarding house, you'd go hungry.

Brother Wyatt wiped his mouth with a corner of the cloth napkin. "Let's be off, then, in five minutes." He left the dining room without waiting for Lucy's response.

Did no one wait for an answer in this town? They just swept along on their agenda, assuming Lucy was on board. And she wasn't! "Cora," Lucy whispered, dropping her voice lower still as she noticed that Mrs. Klopp and the Hicks sisters stopped eating to lean forward and eavesdrop. "It just isn't proper for me to travel alone with Brother Wyatt."

"Oh Lucy," Cora said with a dismissive wave of her hand. "That sounds like something your father would say."

"For good reason! It's poor form."

"I heartily agree with the girl," Mrs. Klopp said, as if she'd been asked.

"Brother Wyatt is a preacher!" Miss Viola said. "You've no need to worry. We've known him since he was a boy. We'd travel with him anywhere, wouldn't we, Lettie?"

Lettie smiled, chin jutting out, lips drawn tight like a wrinkled apple doll. Lucy had to grin. Where in the world would those two elderly sisters travel? They were so thin and frail that a gust of wind could blow them away.

"Maybe sometime soon, Brother Wyatt will treat us to a song or two," Miss Viola said. "And we could dance, couldn't we, Lettie?"

"Dancing is the devil's tool," Mrs. Klopp added. "The judge never approved of it."

Miss Viola rolled her eyes. "The judge never did approve of anyone having a good time."

Mrs. Klopp's eyebrows furrowed together as she opened her mouth to object, but at just that moment, Brother Wyatt popped his head into the open door. "Miss Lucy, are you ready to go?"

"But . . . I haven't eaten."

Cora grabbed a hoe cake right off Mrs. Klopp's plate and handed it to Lucy. "Here you go, dear girl. That should hold you for a while. All that butter and jam." She turned to Brother Wyatt. "Take good care of her. She's still making friends with Jenny."

Lucy cringed. She hated riding. She hated Jenny.

Six

Jenny didn't seem any happier about getting saddled up than Lucy did about riding her. The pony let out a mournful sigh as Brother Wyatt tightened the girth. *My feelings exactly*, Lucy mused, as she dragged a mounting block over to Jenny to climb onto the saddle. Her arms and legs trembled so badly she could barely pull herself onto the pony's back.

Brother Wyatt untied the reins and handed them to her with that amused look in his eyes. "Haven't ridden much?"

Lucy huffed. "Not until I arrived in Morehead."

He swung a leg over a large black horse with a black mane and headed toward the creek. Lyric, he called his horse, and she danced on her hooves as if walking on hot coals. Jenny the pony plodded behind, so slowly that he kept circling Lyric back so they could ride side by side.

"Beautiful day," Brother Wyatt said, gazing up at the sky as a flock of small birds passed overhead. "A bluebird carries the sky on its back."

"That's a lovely phrase."

"Wish it were mine. It's a quote from Henry David Thoreau."

Lucy shot him a curious look. "You've read Thoreau?"

"A few books. I'd planned to read them all until Judge Klopp's library burned down."

"I wish Mrs. Klopp would consider my offer to help start a new library." After just a few days at the boarding house, she wished Mrs. Klopp had more on her mind than her late husband. The judge was all she spoke of, and he sounded every bit as pedantic and fault-finding as his wife. Lucy hoped Brother Wyatt might volunteer more about the Klopps, but like Fin, he was closemouthed.

As the trail narrowed, they moved into single file. Brother Wyatt kept his face forward, so Lucy struggled to hear his low voice. At a ford in the creek, Brother Wyatt motioned toward a different direction than Fin had taken her the other day.

"Excuse me, but I believe we're to go in the other direction."

Leading the way, he called back to her, "We're heading up toward Blacklog Holler."

"I thought the creek went that way."

He stopped and waited for Jenny to catch up. "There are streams and creeks all over these mountains."

"But . . . Fin said that I could never get lost if I followed the creek."

"He's right. All creeks flow downstream, and all the routes follow the creeks. So eventually, you'll end up down in the valley."

"Yes, but which valley?"

He laughed, a low rumble. He had a good laugh, like church bells.

"Tell you what. I promise that you'll make it back to Miss Maude's. Safe and sound." His eyes began to smile; his mouth was soon to follow. "Today."

Lucy relaxed slightly at that promise. Perhaps she was influenced by Miss Viola's swooning each time Brother Wyatt left the room, but she sensed she could trust this man. She rode silently behind him for a while. "What exactly is a singing school master?"

Over his shoulder, he said, "I suppose you might call me a music teacher. I teach folks how to sing."

"Seems like nearly everyone here can sing, dance, or play an instrument."

"Yes. We've a rich culture I'm trying to preserve."

"In spite of the isolation?"

"Because of it, I think. Not only do we have to rely on each other for survival, but also for entertainment."

"Brother Wyatt, could you tell me a little about the schools here?"

"What about them?"

"According to Fin, Cora is on a mission to chase down every school-aged child she can find and march them like prisoners into school. He didn't seem at all happy about it."

Brother Wyatt pulled Lyric to a stop and turned in his saddle, grinning. "Fin's assessment isn't too far from the truth. Miss Cora is a mighty force to reckon with, especially when it comes to her beliefs in the power of education. I'm living proof of that. She talked a sponsor into providing funds to send me off to Louisville for proper schooling."

"But you came back. Why?"

"Why? This is my home. These are my people." He gave up a slight grin. "But ever since I came back, they've tagged me a halfback. Some are leery of my city schooling."

"Yes, but . . . why didn't you stay in the city?" It seemed like a lonely life that Brother Wyatt led. As far as Lucy could tell, he had no real home or family, and she wondered if he was entirely dependent for meals and lodging on the kindness of others.

He didn't answer right away. She wasn't sure if it was just his style to be slow to speak or if he felt reluctance to answer her nosy question and wished she would stop. Of course she was being nosy. She wanted to know more about him, and if she didn't ask questions, she would never find anything out.

Finally, he said, "Aren't there plenty of other music teachers in the cities?"

"Yes, of course."

"If there are others to fill the roles, then I'm not needed. But out here in these hollers, there isn't anyone else to preserve the tradition of mountain music." He clucked his tongue and Lyric started again. "So what is your calling, Miss Lucy?"

"Me? I don't suppose I have one."

"Happy are those whose purpose has found them."

"Is that in the Bible?"

"No," he said, laughing. "Not word for word, anyway. But everyone has a purpose in this world, if they only ask the Lord for it. What did you want to do as a wee lass, before the world wrung the dreams out of your grasp?"

She hesitated. Why had he phrased that question the way he did? "I fancied myself a writer. A novelist." She smiled. "Of fairy tales."

They came to a level spot and he stopped Lyric until Jenny came up by his side. "Whatever happened to that fancy?"

How to explain losing Charlotte to this man? Lucy could barely understand it herself. "My father didn't believe in fairy tales for children. Or any other kind of stories. Too fanciful. He wanted me to spend my time in other pursuits."

Again, his eyes remained on her. But he must have noticed her discomfort because he changed the subject. "If you look through those trees," he said, pointing straight ahead, "you'll see a shiny object. That's a still. Best to stay clear of those. Give them a wide berth. You might be mistaken for a trespasser and get yourself shot."

"A still? You mean . . . moonshine? Surely you jest." She thought her father had been exaggerating about the whiskey stills scattered throughout the hills, until she had seen Miss Mollie's jars under that rickety porch. Could Miss Mollie, that tiny toothless old lady, have a still? It seemed ludicrous to think so, yet so many things seemed incredulous in these hills.

Again, Brother Wyatt grinned, and she found she rather liked his rugged face with its squared-off jaw, especially when he smiled. "Most everyone in these mountains either drinks whiskey, makes it, sells it, or runs it. But the higher up you go, the more ornery the moonshiner. They're up there for a reason. They want to be left alone, and don't want anyone telling them what to do or how to do it."

"Why is Kentucky known for its whiskey?"

"Ideal conditions. And, of course, it's in our blood. They say that when the English emigrated to the New World, first thing they did was to build a church. The Germans came and built barns. The Scotch-Irish came and built whiskey stills." He glanced at her. "All jesting aside, the highlanders do get tetchy about their stills. I'm dead serious about staying clear of them. They've been known to shoot first and ask questions later."

"Duly noted," she said, though she didn't expect to come up in these mountains again. She was going to have a long talk with cousin Cora about her job description. Clarify things. Agree on parameters.

They followed the creek upstream for nearly half an hour, and Lucy was wishing she had eaten more breakfast. And wishing she'd worn warmer clothing too. Though the morning fog had burned off, whenever the sun was blotted out by the thick trees, the temperature would markedly drop. And it was dark, gloomy. What must it be like in these hills at night when the moon was but a sliver? She shivered at the thought.

Brother Wyatt stopped to point out a dry creek bed, and a gigantic stump of a tree. "There's the landmark to turn off to Barbara Jean's house."

"That tree stump. It's . . . enormous!"

"Aye. Virgin timber. All gone now. When I was a lad, those giant, ancient trees covered the hills."

He said it without accusation, but Lucy felt it, all the same. In the 1890s, lumber companies had poured into Rowan County to harvest an abundance of virgin timber. Her father's company was one of them. The boom lasted less than a decade.

Brother Wyatt led her down a narrow trail and into a clearing. The moment he rode into the open yard, a swarm of children—all boys, towheaded and tan—poured out of a cabin, surging toward him like wasps from a hive, greeting him with joyful shouts. Then they stopped abruptly when they saw Lucy. Stopped and stared.

"Why are they staring at me?"

"Not many strangers venture into the hollers. You're a bit of a curiosity."

Brother Wyatt slid off Lyric and held Jenny's reins while Lucy dismounted. She heard the children chuckling and snickering at the ungainly way she lifted her leg up over Jenny's head, slid to the ground, then tripped over her own feet and landed on her aching backside. It felt like her first day all over again.

As Brother Wyatt helped her up, Lucy kept her eyes on the ground. Her cheeks burned hot with embarrassment as she brushed herself off and followed behind him. He exchanged howdies with each boy before introducing Lucy to their mother, Barbara Jean, who remained on the porch. This woman might have been attractive in another place, another setting, but her face was too thin, her cheeks too hollow, her high forehead exaggerated by hair parted severely in the middle and pulled back into a bun. Everything about her projected a weariness, all but her eyes. Those eyes, they were strangely compelling. There was a fierceness in those dark eyes. A determination.

"How ya makin' out, Barbara Jean?" Brother Wyatt's tone was tender, caring. And Lucy noticed his careful enunciation fell away in an instant.

"Fine, jest fine. Now, children, you hush. Let Brother Wyatt hear hisself think."

"Oh, they mean no harm. Barbara Jean, this is Miss Cora's kin. She goes by Miss Lucy. Cora sent her to help write that letter."

Barbara Jean scratched the back of her head, looking Lucy up and down. "Yep. Mollie tol' me t' expect ya. Can I git ya somethin' to drink? Some coffee, mebbe?"

That sounded heavenly to Lucy, but Fin's warning to not accept anything circled in her head. Yet she was thirsty after the ride. "Just water, please."

"Willie, git some water for the lady."

One of the boys shot off to a bucket and brought back a tin cup full of gray water. He seemed so pleased as he held it out to Lucy, giving her a big gap-toothed smile, and she tried not to notice how dirty his hands were, or that he was scratching the back of his head so fiercely. She took a small dainty sip, trying not to gag, and held the cup out to Brother Wyatt, who drained it.

Lucy turned to Barbara Jean. "You can tell me what you'd like to say in the letter and I'll write it all down for you."

Barbara Jean squirmed a little, scratching behind her ear. In fact, all the children seemed to be scratching their heads. "I don't got no paper or pen."

Lucy held up her satchel. "I brought some from Cora." She opened the satchel and dug around to find paper and her inkpot. "I seem to have forgotten a pen."

"That I can help with," Brother Wyatt said. "Willie and Sammy, do ya happen t' have a spare feather? A big 'un?"

Sammy darted into the house and came out again with a long black-and-white striped feather in his hand. He handed it to Brother Wyatt, who examined it with a pleased look on his face.

"Wild turkey. Well done." He pulled a pen knife from his duster pocket and started to whittle the end of the feather to a sharp point. "Will this do, Miss Lucy?"

Impressed with his resourcefulness, Lucy sat down on the porch step and tugged the cork off the ink pot. "Let's find out." She made a small six-pointed star on the paper. "Why, it's better than my forgotten quill. It'll do just fine." The children crowded around her so tightly to see the star that she could barely move her elbows. And how badly they smelled! Sorely in need of a good soapy scrubdown, each one. Lucy tried to breathe through her mouth instead of her nose.

Thankfully, Barbara Jean shooed them away. "Boys, let her be! Give a body room." She pointed to the yard and the boys sprang off the porch to stand in a long row like little soldiers, all eyes fastened on Lucy.

Brother Wyatt scooped up the reins of Lyric and Jenny. "While you two are working, I'll get the horses out of the sun and maybe find some water for them, if you don't mind." He paused, waiting for Barbara Jean to give him the go-ahead, but she had something else on her mind besides watering the animals.

"Willie, you take them horses fer him. Ollie, go git yor paw's fiddle for Brother Wyatt. I'm hoping you're in a mind for a little fiddling today."

"We can't stay too long, Barbara Jean." But even as he spoke, a violin and bow were thrust in his hands by a small boy in overalls. He smiled down at him. "Well, maybe jest one song."

The children moved in a half circle around Brother Wyatt. He had one foot up on the porch step and tuned the strings one by one. Then he cleared his throat and started to play a plaintive tune, slowly at first, then he picked up speed, his nimble fingers going so fast they blurred. As he did, the children started swaying, swinging their arms, and then they burst into movement. Their arms stayed by their sides, their faces, though flushed pink, remained serious, and their legs moved so fast that Lucy couldn't peel her eyes away from them. Heel, toe, over a knee, step back, step forward, a whirl of rhythmic beating of the feet. All too soon, Wyatt drew the song to a finish and dropped his bow.

Everyone clapped, but he shrugged off the praise and shifted it to the boys. "Miss Lucy, you've just seen some of the finest cloggers in the county. And that's sayin' a lot."

Embarrassed, the boys elbowed and jabbed each other, their eyes glowing from the compliment.

"So that's clogging?" Lucy had heard of clog dancing but had never seen it. "I've never seen feet fly so fast!" And Brother Wyatt's violin skills were impressive. "A violin only has four strings, yet you made it sound as if you were playing chords on a piano."

"Double stops," he said. "Two notes played at once. Like so

much in life, it works as long as they're in harmony." He grinned, and she couldn't help but smile in return. He handed the fiddle to Ollie. "Now I'd better get some water for the horses."

A shadow passed over Barbara Jean's face. She scratched her bun vigorously. Or nervously? Lucy couldn't tell. "Thing is, Brother Wyatt, we been having some trouble gettin' water. On account of that pond going in."

Brother Wyatt's back straightened, and he cast a glance at the bucket. "How about if the boys and I fill up some buckets of water in the creek?"

A sigh of relief came from Barbara Jean. "If it ain't no trouble."

Wyatt turned to Lucy. "By the time you finish the letter writing, we'll be back."

Lucy wondered how long that errand might take, because the last creek with running water that she remembered crossing was quite far from this cabin. But then she remembered that he had told her creeks and streams and rivers crisscrossed these mountains.

Sammy and Willie scurried to keep up with Wyatt's long strides. How could anyone run over dirt and rocks in bare feet? But they were all barefoot, even Barbara Jean.

"How do you manage so many children?" Lucy asked. She got the impression that there was no husband or father around.

Barbara Jean shrugged. "Ain't so many. Jest six."

In Lexington, families were small. Many of Lucy's schoolfriends were only children. Once she had asked the housekeeper why that was so, and she had responded coolly, "There's no need for a houseful." Lucy was left with the impression that having children was not particularly valued or desired. At least not among the well-to-do.

Yet look at the happiness that poured out of that house, like honey from a jar. She thought back to her silent home, the quiet supper table, the empty rooms. From deep inside Lucy rose that familiar longing for Charlotte, her sister, for family, for all that had been missed.

The four remaining boys surrounded her again, enclosing her

in a tight circle, waiting for her to begin to write. And they were all scratching. Had they been in poison ivy? Could it be eczema?

"Back away, boys," Barbara Jean said, "afore you tip the ink pot all o'er Miss Lucy."

"Yes, boys, please do give me a little space to write."

The little boy named Ollie peered solemnly at Lucy. "You talk funny."

Barbara Jean slid down on the porch step, a few feet away from Lucy, and pulled the boy onto her lap. "That's cuz Miss Lucy comes from the city."

"Where's that at?"

Lucy smiled. "In a place called Lexington. Lots and lots of people live there in houses close together."

"Cheek and jowl? Oh, there's a pity," Ollie said, and his elfin face looked worried for her.

On Lucy's lap was the satchel and paper. "Barbara Jean, you just go ahead and tell me what you'd like to say, and I'll write it down."

Barbara Jean nodded, like she'd rehearsed this moment. She straightened her back and said loudly, "To whom it may concern. The creek has dried up. It jest ain't right, what you done. Yours truly, Barbara Jean Boling."

Lucy looked up. "That's it?"

"That's it."

Lucy set the feather in the ink pot. "To whom shall I deliver this letter?"

Barbara Jean looked at her as if she might be dim-witted. "To the lumber company, o'course."

"Why do you say that?"

"They scalded m' land."

"Scalded?"

"Ruined."

Lucy looked around. "I'm confused. How did they spoil this farm?" Surrounding the small, hilly farm were thick woods.

"They stopped up the creek."

"Stopped it up?"

Exasperated at Lucy's inability to understand, Barbara Jean tried again. "They stopped up the creek"—she pointed uphill— "to make a pond up yonder. Soz they could send the logs down the mountain. That creek used to come right along the farm. We counted on it, especially with this drought. Now we gotta go a long way to git water."

"Didn't they inform you of what they intended to do? The contract should have spelled it all out."

"Lots of fancy language in it." Barbara Jean looked away, pushing a stray lock of hair back from her face, and Lucy nearly gasped when she saw something small and white move by her ear. Lice! She jumped up, nearly toppling the ink pot. So *that's* why these children kept scratching their heads. Trying to recover her horror at the lice discovery, she held up the letter she'd written. "Barbara Jean, what's the name of this lumber company? I'll post the letter as soon as I return to town this afternoon." Which couldn't be soon enough! She felt an itch in her hair. Down her back. Below her chin.

Barbara Jean looked away. "Valley View."

Lucy stilled. Her father's company.

SEVEN

MERCIFULLY, Brother Wyatt came chugging up the hill, carrying a large trough of water, followed by Sammy and Willie, carrying buckets. He set it down against the house with a large exhale, his face red from exertion. "It's past noon. We must be on our way."

Lucy marveled at how he, and Finley James as well, seemed to know how to tell time without a timepiece. She tucked Barbara Jean's letter in her satchel. "I'll deliver it myself, Barbara Jean. And I'll make sure you get an answer from the lumber company."

Weary relief sprang to the woman's face. "You'd do that?"

"It's a promise."

Barbara Jean gave her a broad smile, her first. Lucy tried not to show her shock at the gaps of missing teeth in her mouth. The boys ran alongside them as they rode back toward the trail, stopping to turn back when they reached the dry creek bed.

Lucy and Brother Wyatt rode for a long distance without speaking. As they came to a creek with flowing water, he slowed Lyric to a stop and loosened his reins to let her drink. Lucy followed his lead and slackened the reins so Jenny could lap up the clear, cool water.

"Let's rest a bit," he said. As Lucy started to slide down off Jenny, he stopped her, startled. "Hold it! Wrong side."

"Horses have a wrong side?"

"Left side. Always." This time, he hopped off his horse to help her so she didn't tumble in her dismount, like she'd done at Barbara Jean's and made the boys double over in laughter. "We can have a bite to eat before we carry on."

"What is there to eat?"

"Miss Maude always packs me a lunch. More than one man could possibly eat."

Lucy doubted that, but she was famished. That lone hoe cake hadn't done much to stave off hunger.

Brother Wyatt hooked the reins of Lyric and Jenny to low hanging tree branches, so they could drink all they pleased. Then he crossed the creek by leaping from stone to stone, and jumped on to a grassy spot on the bank, nimble as a gazelle. He turned in a circle, hands on his hips. "This looks like just the spot for a picnic."

Stepping cautiously, she followed his path across the creek, but stopped at the last stone.

"What's wrong?"

"It's rather far." It would take a large leap to reach the bank, and she could just see how it would unfold: she would end up plopping into the water, bottom first.

He reached a hand out to help her make the leap and her cheeks grew warm, but whether it was from feeling a little embarrassed by needing his help or from the touch of a man's fingers, she couldn't tell.

He sat down and patted a place in the soft grass for her to sit. "I checked. No snakes."

"Snakes?" It came out in a croak.

"Not to worry," he said, laughing. "Sit."

There was that nice laugh again, like a low rumble. He didn't laugh often enough. Stiff, chafed, and saddlesore, she eased down on the ground, trying not to grunt and moan. She avoided his eyes, because she was sure he was laughing at her like everyone else, but when she cast a sideways glance at him, his head was lifted up.

A gentle breeze was causing a tree in bloom above them to shower petals down, like a rainfall of confetti. He picked up a blossom and held it out to her on his open palm. "Flowering dogwood. One of my favorites."

She lifted it to her nose to sniff the sweet scent. "I've seen a few of these trees along the trails."

"There used to be more. When I was a lad, the woods were full of them."

"What's happened to them?"

"The lumber companies found out that dogwood is the best wood for tools. Mallets and hammers and such. The wood doesn't crack or split. So they've cut most of them down."

She noticed he had reverted back to a more formal, crisp diction. One she could sense took effort for him.

He passed a thick slab of corn bread to her. "Lumber companies call it harvesting, like a renewable crop. But they're wrong. 'Tis a pity, for the splendors of spring aren't the same without those native trees." He lifted his head to gaze again at the flowering tree. "Glad this one is still here to provide a canopy of blossoms for us on this fine spring day."

A canopy of blossoms. This man was a phrase maker, an artist with words, and it triggered her long-buried love of language, something she was born with, and nurtured, until that terrible day. "Brother Wyatt . . ."

"Call me Wyatt. The mountain people tagged that label on me when I started the singing schools. Now I'm known by it."

It was a term bestowed in honor, that much Lucy knew. "I'll drop the moniker only if you'll call me Lucy. Not Miss Lucy. Makes me feel like I'm as old as the Hicks sisters." He grinned, and she couldn't help but smile back. "Speaking of lumber companies, Barbara Jean seems to feel that a lumber company had taken advantage of her. That was the purpose of the letter she had me write." Just thinking of Barbara Jean made her feel itchy. She scratched the back of her neck, wondering if she had caught a louse or two, as she waited for Wyatt to say something.

He sobered, but volunteered nothing. He took an apple from the sack and his knife from his trouser pockets. He rubbed the apple against his shirt before carving a slice for her, holding it out to her on the tip of the knife.

As she took the apple slice, she said, "Does your silence mean you agree with Barbara Jean's suspicion?"

He lifted his head, eyebrows creased in a frown. "Suspicion?"

"Did the lumber company intentionally take advantage of her?"

Overhead, a hawk let out a screech as it whizzed past. "Have you ever noticed that birds of prey do not sing?"

Goodness, it was hard to get a straight answer out of him! Unless that *was* his answer? Was he trying to hint that the lumber company was a predator? She waited for him to explain, waited and waited.

"When a person can't read," he said at last, "they are quite . . . vulnerable."

Vulnerable. Something she had never considered. But did the lumber company agent know that Barbara Jean couldn't read the contract? Was he culpable? Or ignorant of that fact? "Are there others? Like Barbara Jean?"

"Illiterates, you mean?" He scoffed. "Most. Nearly all the mountain folks can't read nor write."

Lucy thought of the man who came into Cora's office and stared at her bookshelves like a thirsty soul stared at a glass of water. "But . . . there are schools in the hollows. Lots of them. Fifty-one, I think Cora said."

"For the children. And that's if parents can afford to let them go."

"It doesn't cost money to go to school, does it?"

"By afford, I meant to go without their help on the farm or in the timber for a day or a week or a month. Or in many cases, for years."

"But it's every parent's obligation to see that their children are educated. It just seems wrong to not make their children a top priority."

He gave her a sharp look. "Keeping the farm going is a man's top priority. That's how he'll feed his family." He tossed the apple core across the creek to Lyric and she caught it with her teeth. Reaching into the sack, he pulled out two hardboiled eggs and handed her one. "If you don't mind a bit of advice, be careful not to judge mountain folks by city standards. We're all human beings and have thoughts and dreams like everybody else. You'll find that we're all alike in the end."

She'd been given a similar scolding by Cora when she first arrived. As she cracked the eggshell, her mind traveled back to Barbara Jean's children. It occurred to her that they should've been in school. Should've, but couldn't. They had to drag buckets from a far-off creek to provide water for the family and animals. It must take them all day long!

How naïve Lucy felt. In just a short time, her eyes were getting opened wide to another world. One that her father knew well.

As she popped her last bite of egg into her mouth, she wondered if Wyatt's roundabout way of answering her question was because he was aware, like everyone apparently, that her father owned Valley View Lumber. "But did the lumber company do something wrong?" She just couldn't believe her father would allow such a thing. He was as honorable as a man could be. Straight as an arrow, that was her father.

He lifted his chin to gaze over the creek. "If it's not wrong, does that make it right?" He rose to his feet and brushed on his trousers.

Sitting where she was, she noticed how shiny the cloth over his knees had become, how seams sprouted messy threads, how scuffed his shoes, how thin the soles. Those shoes wouldn't last much longer. She thought of the clique of girls in her finishing school, and how they would scorn such a man. Cracker poor, they would snicker behind his back.

With a decent haircut and fashionable clothes, Brother Wyatt could be a good-looking man. He had a certain appeal. But she had a hunch that he cared not a whit for such a shallow measure of a man.

He picked up his saddlebags and leapt over the creek to feed a cut-up apple to the horses. Then, as if remembering himself, he turned back to offer Lucy a hand and help her onto that first stone. On the other side, he took Jenny's reins, tugged them under his arm, then cupped his hands so Lucy could step up onto the pony. A groan slipped out of her as she heaved herself onto the saddle. Her bottom hurt. Everything hurt.

Patting Jenny's whiskery nose, he glanced at Lucy. "Come to the brush arbor on Sunday's fortnight." He paused, realizing she might not understand him, which she didn't. "Two Sundays from now."

"What's a brush arbor?"

"It's church, held outdoors." Gracefully, he swung a leg over Lyric like she was just another stepping-stone. "Some of the men work together to create a little sanctuary, right in the midst of God's creation. We'll have the worship service, and in the afternoon comes the singing school."

"Right in the woods?"

He gave her that patient look. "'Hope can be found even in the darkest of forests,'" he quoted. Then added, "As the psalmist says, 'Let all the trees in the forest sing for joy.'"

"What if it rains?"

"I always say a prayer that the weather smiles upon us."

"Does that work?"

That brought an easy smile to his lips. "So far, so good. In fact, we've had naught but glorious Sundays, the sky as blue as a jay's wing, a light breeze chasing through the trees. It's as if the Lord lays a hush over the world. Join us."

"I can't," she said uneasily.

He acted as if she hadn't said no. "There's picnicking afterward. Some of the best fried chicken this side of the Big Sandy."

"Really, I don't think I could even find my way to wherever it is you're holding the brush arbor."

"Ask Cora to join you. She'll come." He pointed toward a thin trail between trees. "There's the trail that leads straight back to town." He glanced up at the tree tips, and she followed his gaze, noticing for the first time that afternoon was swiftly falling to dusk. "Sunset comes early in these mountains. Best not t' linger." He tipped his hat. "Good day, Lucy."

And once again she was left alone to find her way home. Jenny wiggled her ears back and forth, as if she was waiting for orders, and then finally gave up. She turned around and plodded toward the downstream trail that led home. At least, Lucy hoped the pony was homeward bound.

THERE WASN'T MUCH SPARE TIME for Angie Cooper to read her beloved novels, but whenever Paw took the boys into the livery with him, she claimed the time for her own. The cabin was overly hot from a morning of bread baking, so she went outside to lie on the hammock hung between two big shade trees. She brought her book, fetched from deep under her mattress, far from snooping brothers and Paw's watchful eye.

Angie loved to read. There weren't many books available to her, especially after Judge Klopp's library burned down. Though that wasn't a great loss to Angie; most of them books was dull as dishwater.

Now *these* books, they be excitin'.

As Angie settled into the hammock, a gentle breeze stirred the leaves around her, and as thrilling as the story was, her eyelids grew heavier and heavier, and soon she drifted off.

"Oh my stars and garters! Don't tell me you're reading *that*."

Angie jerked awake, so violently that the hammock flipped her right out and she landed facedown on the ground. She pushed herself up to see Miss Lucy holding her paperback novel.

Angie jumped up, brushed herself off, snarled, "That's mine!" and grabbed the book out of her hands.

"Does your father know you're reading such . . . such . . ."

Angie looked at the book. "Such what?"

"A book of such dubious literary worth."

"Huh?" This lady spoke another language.

"Where did you get it, anyway?"

"Miss Norah done give it to me."

That admission caused Miss Lucy to gasp.

Glory be! What a fussbudget. Angie hugged the book to her chest. "She give me lots of books to read."

"Books like that one? Cheap dime-store novels?"

Angie frowned. "She knows I like reading."

Miss Lucy gazed at her for a long while, so long it made Angie squirm.

She glanced at her bare toes. "I skip over the racy parts." Sometimes. Not always. "What are you doing up in these parts, anyhows?"

"Apparently, I'm lost. Or rather, Jenny is lost. I was told she would take me straight to town, but she ended up here. So much for a pony's instinct to return to the barn for her oats and hay."

"Jenny's instincts ain't wrong. The trail to town goes right by our land." Angie pointed to an opening in the trees. "You'd best be on yor way."

"I was hoping I could trouble you for a drink of water. For Jenny too."

Now it was Angie's turn to sigh. She hardly ever had time alone, and the last thing she wanted to do was to give it up for this la-di-da lady. But Paw was always drilling into her to be good to others, even ones ya didn't like. "Fine," she said, aggrieved. "Wait here." She took a few steps, then turned, lifting the book in her hand. "I suppose yor plannin' to tattle to Paw on me about this."

"Of course not," Miss Lucy said. "We'll keep it between ourselves." Jest as Angie turned around to head to the water pump, she added loudly, "However!"

Angie froze.

"However, I am going to find a book for you to read that will expand your horizons. I promise that you'll no longer be satisfied with such common fare."

Angie rolled her eyes to heaven. There she went again, into her foreign language. Why couldn't she talk like a normal person? "My fare is jest fine, thank you very much." And she darted off to fetch the bucket and fill it at the pump. The sooner she gave her the water, the sooner the city lady would be gone.

LUCY FELT DRAINED by the time she arrived at the livery. She found Finley James cleaning a saddle, a bucket of warm water by his side, and handed Jenny's reins to him. "Fin, what's Miss Norah like?"

He scrunched up his face. "How do ya mean?"

"Is she a good teacher?"

"Like . . . how so?"

"Does she challenge the students?"

He shrugged. "She's a heckuva lot better than the one we had afore her. That one kept a jug of liquor under his desk and nipped at it all the livelong day. Slept most of the afternoon with his head on his desk." He rubbed his chin. "As soon as he started to drool, then we knowed he was out cold and we all slipped out the door. All but Angie Cooper, o'course."

Lucy thought of her schooling, of the discipline and high standards, and the dedication of the teachers.

"Don't be lookin' so woebegone, Miss Lucy. School don't matter much in the mountains. No need for it."

"But there is, Fin. There's tremendous need for it. And Cora's making sweeping changes. She's working hard to make school matter to everyone."

"Don't I know it." He hung his head in defeat. "A man cain't hardly go to town no more without Miss Cora chasin' him back to school." He made a whipping motion with his hand.

"Is Miss Cora back?"

He nodded. "Jest got off the train. Tol' me she was thinkin' 'bout startin' Saturday school to make up for lost days." He shook his head. "Ain't that a frightful thing to tell a man at the end of a hard day at work?"

Lucy didn't know how to answer that, so she left Jenny with Fin and headed up the road to the office. Cora was at her desk, head down, scribbling away on a paper pad. She raised a finger (*One minute*), then lowered a palm (*Please sit*). Lucy pulled her chair from her little makeshift desk and placed it in front of Cora's large one, then she sat down and waited. And waited. And waited.

Finally, Cora set down her pen and turned her attention to Lucy. "Dear girl. You look upset."

"I'm . . ." Lucy scratched her head, convinced lice were crawling through her hair. "I'm . . ."

"Overwhelmed? Shocked by the poverty? Horrified by the deplorable living conditions?"

"All that, yes, and more." She tried to let it all out as concisely as possible. Chickens in Mollie's cabin, lice in Barbara Jean's hair, barefoot boys who should be in school, the lumber company diverting the Bolings' creek.

Cora listened without expression. "Did your father not tell you about life in the hills and hollers?"

"He did. But not all of it, only his version. There's another side—Sally Ann, for example. Her farm is picturesque. And the forests . . . they fill me with awe and wonder. I suppose that's why I feel so overwhelmed. There are such stark contrasts here. Serenity and beauty, filth and squalor. It's hard to put it all together."

"Well said. There is a surprising amount of diversity in the mountains."

Lucy let out a sigh. "There's one thing they all seem to have in common. They can't read or write." Leaning forward, her hands cupped her knees. "Fin claims you're chasing down every child in Rowan County to get them into school. Now I can see why that's so important to you."

"Absolutely critical. It'll take a generation."

"A generation? How can a young man—like Finley James—prepare for the twentieth century when he can barely read?"

"You're preaching to the choir, Lucy."

"Wyatt says you've been having trouble getting the parents to send their children to school. He said that many parents just don't consider an education to be important."

"They don't always see the need for an education since the boys will all work in the timber someday. And some folks genuinely do need their children to stay home and help out with the farm work. Barbara Jean's oldest boys, Willie and Sammy, for example. She's a widow."

"Do you happen to know of a man named Andrew Spencer?"

Something flashed through Cora's eyes. Here and then gone. Hmm . . . what was Lucy missing here? She couldn't quite catch its meaning. "I know him," Cora said.

"I want to speak to this Andrew Spencer about diverting the creek away from Barbara Jean's cabin. She's having a terrible time of it. The boys have to go a long distance to bring back water."

Cora rose and looked out the window. "Well, now's your chance. He's over at the railroad station."

Lucy joined her to see where she was looking. Over by the train station was a man standing with his back to them, holding a clipboard, walking beside a wagon filled with logs. As if he sensed he was being watched, he turned to look in their direction.

Eight

S O, THIS WAS MR. ANDREW SPENCER. He was surprisingly young, and startlingly handsome. No wonder Hazel had oohed and aahed over him. "I'm Lucy Wilson. I'm new to town. I work for Miss Cora."

His eyebrows lifted when she said her name, and he whipped off his bowler hat with a flourish. "I've been keeping one eye peeled for you, Miss Wilson. Why, you're the hottest topic in town. Everyone's been talking about you. I heard you were a real looker, but I didn't expect you to be the prettiest little thing I ever laid eyes on."

Lucy knew her face was turning scarlet, because she could feel its radiating heat. She hadn't expected Andrew Spencer to be a flirt. Nor did she expect him to have such a strong mountain accent, though his words actually had consonants on the end, unlike Fin's. She turned away from him and ran a hand on the VV brand seared into the rough cut of the sawed-off logs.

"I want to extend a warm welcome to this humble little town, Miss Wilson. Indeed, you are a sight for sore eyes."

"I hope you'll think so after I give you this." She handed him Barbara Jean's letter and waited as he read it.

With barely a glance, he skimmed the letter and tucked it in his pocket. "Thank you for the hand delivery."

"Mrs. Boling claims that Valley View Lumber diverted the creek away from her farm to create a pond."

"A pond?" He scoffed. "Hardly a pond. Nothing like the sort. That would be a gross and unjust exaggeration."

"What would you call it?"

"A small holding pen for fallen logs." He smiled, revealing bright white, even teeth and one—no, two deep dimples in his cheeks. "Temporary, of course. Everything will be righted as soon as we finish the harvest." He snapped his fingers to emphasize the return of the flowing creek. Like a magic trick.

His smile was more than a little dazzling, and Lucy had to look away lest she forget the purpose of her errand. "But . . . what about in the meantime? She has crops and animals and . . . goodness, loads and loads of children." Just thinking of them made her feel an itch in the back of her head that took effort to resist scratching.

"Miss Wilson, I thank you for your concern, truly I do, but Mrs. Boling had no objections when she signed the contract."

"I don't think she understood that it would require altering the natural terrain."

"It was all spelled out in the contract with the lumber company. Your father's company, not that I need to remind you."

She didn't need reminding. A knot forming in her stomach made her drop her eyes, and she noticed the toes of her boots, now streaked with dust and dirt.

"Try to see it from the company's point of view, Miss Wilson. The weather hasn't been cooperating. There was very little rain this winter and many creeks have run dry. It gave us ample time to do the cutting, but we had no means to bring those logs down to the railroad station to be shipped out. We had to create a holding pen to collect the logs, and form a navigable stream to get those logs to town." He looked down the road and pointed. "And right on over to Jake Wilson's sawmill." He rubbed his chin in a thoughtful way. "If I'm not mistaken, I believe that Jake Wilson might be kin."

True, a distant kin. In the 1850s, Jake Wilson had built a water-powered sawmill and the town of Morehead grew around it. But Lucy recognized Andrew Spencer's deflection tactic and tried to get the subject back on track. "Mrs. Boling counts on that creek for her own crops."

He lifted his hands in a helpless gesture. "Mrs. Boling was fully informed of the process. It's all in the contract."

"Mr. Spencer, Barbara Jean Boling can't read! She didn't know what she was signing."

He coughed a laugh. "She knew enough to bargain for a better price for that choice stand of pines. She wanted full cash in advance, which isn't our usual policy. Normally, we pay half up front and half after harvest."

Lucy stilled. Andrew Spencer smiled in a conciliatory way, as if he realized her logic had been trumped. "Look, let's not worry ourselves about such unpleasantness. I'll have some of the boys deliver a few barrels of water to the Boling cabin."

"When?"

"Tomorrow morning, first thing."

"And every week until the creek is restored?"

"Done!" He lifted his hands in mock surrender. "I'll tell the boys to pick up the pace. Everything will be back to normal in no time. You can tell her that very thing."

"Well . . ." She was softening.

He took a step closer to Lucy. "Are all the girls in Lexington as pretty as you?"

She backed up a step. "I'd say they're much prettier."

He took another step toward Lucy and flashed that dazzling smile. "Impossible."

She blushed. Oh dear heavenly goodness, closer up, he was even more handsome. Straw-colored hair and sparkling blue eyes. As blue as the skies behind him. His cocky grin told her that he already knew his effect on her.

"Maybe I can show you around Morehead sometime."

She looked up and down at the sight of Morehead, a rather unremarkable valley town tucked between two ridges. Its one main street had a handful of brick and timber storefronts, the Normal School, the Gault Hotel, the freight station, the county jail, and narrow roads that stretched to who knew where. "I venture to guess that would only take five minutes."

He laughed. "Ah, but I suspect you haven't seen a few of my secret spots." He winked, then smiled. His eyes were full of merriment and caprice. Jaunty. That was the word for him. He would have been right at home back in Lexington. A sought-after escort for the many social events of the season.

She tried to remain deadpan, refusing to swallow his flirtatious bait, but there wasn't a girl in the world who could have resisted returning his smile. Infectious. That's how it felt. She refused to fall under his spell, but it was no small task to remain aloof to his charisma. "Perhaps, someday," she said, glancing toward Cora's office. "For now, I'll let you return to your work. And I'll return to mine."

As she crossed the road, she could feel Andrew Spencer's eyes following her, appreciating her. It wasn't an altogether unpleasant awareness.

DWARFING MISS MAUDE'S BREAKFAST TABLE was a large vase with a dozen long-stemmed red roses. All eyes were on Lucy as she carefully eased into her chair, staring at the roses. They were stunning. Exquisite. "Where on earth did someone find blooming roses in March?"

"What does it matter?" Miss Viola said. "All that matters is who sent them. They're for you!"

"For me? But . . . from whom?"

"Let's find out! Open the envelope, dear. The suspense is killing us."

"Speak for yourself, Viola," Mrs. Klopp said with a sniff. "I'm a firm believer in minding one's own grits."

Miss Viola shooed off such fussiness with a flick of her hand. "Do tell, Lucy."

Lucy took the little card from the bouquet and ran her thumbnail under the envelope's seal. The card read:

> *Water barrels are on their way to the Boling farm. As a gesture of good will, allow me to take you to lunch today. I'll pick you up at noon.*
>
> *Andrew Spencer*

"Who?" Miss Viola said. "Who sent them?"

Lucy felt her cheeks grow warm and her mind grow blank. "I . . . um . . . um . . ." All she could do was stammer. Then a suitable response came to her. "They're from a business acquaintance of my father's." She tucked the card back in the envelope and set it by her napkin.

Miss Lettie peered at her over a cup of steaming coffee. Her sparse eyebrows were lifted as if waiting to hear more.

"Andrew Spencer," Lucy said, instantly regretting that admission.

Mrs. Klopp's cheek twitched. "In my day, roses were a sign of a gentleman caller announcing his intentions."

Miss Viola clapped her hands in delight. "Our Lucy has a sweetheart!"

"I only just met him yesterday afternoon." Lucy tried to quell the rising color in her cheeks. "He's certainly not my sweetheart."

"Not yet, perhaps," Miss Viola said with a satisfied smirk. "Soon, though."

Miss Maude swooped in with a fresh pot of coffee, and Miss Viola looped her into the conversation about Lucy's roses, which was not difficult. Lucy listened as she ate her breakfast. She wasn't going to say one more word. Not one word.

Listening. Watching. Waiting. Such familiar roles for Lucy. So often she felt like a supporting character waiting offstage. Waiting for what? She didn't really know. She was glad for Cora and her endless tasks for Lucy. Even—and it shocked her to admit so— those arduous trips up into the hills on Jenny. Cora made Lucy feel useful. Purposeful. Being useful was an idea that kept having more and more appeal to Lucy. Maybe, just maybe . . . it was the answer to that clawing emptiness in her life.

Sipping her coffee, listening to the elderly ladies chatter and bicker over her roses, she realized that maybe she had come to Morehead to stop living a life of just waiting, waiting, waiting.

She fingered the card sent by Andrew Spencer. She smiled. No more waiting. She was starting fresh. Act one, scene one.

FINLEY JAMES WAS ON HIS WAY TO TOWN, thinking of ways he could cross paths with Miss Lucy without actin' like a stupid lovesick puppy. Whenever he caught sight of her, his heart started poundin' and his palms got all sweaty-like and his stomach flipped and flopped so much, he was certain he would throw up right in front of her. He'd never felt this way about a girl before. She was different from any girl he'd ever knowed. She asked him all kinds of questions and listened for his answers. She had a way of making a man feel smart, plus she was pretty and smelled like a spring flower. On top of all them fine qualities, she was fancy. Heck, it turned out he loved fancy.

Fin wondered if Miss Lucy thought about him as much as he thought about her. He thought not, and it worried him. Jest yesterday, he saw Miss Lucy talking with that Spencer fellow from the lumber company. Laughin' and smilin' with him, and it gave him a case of collywobbles.

Sheila slowed as she was nearing Little Brushy School, thinking that's where they were headed, and they sure as heck weren't. Miss Norah was ailing again, which suited Fin fine. When he saw

Angie Cooper at the open schoolhouse door, yoo-hooing and waving to him, he gave Sheila a light kick in the side to giddy up. "I cain't stop."

"Shore you can," she said, arms on her hips jest like Miss Cora. "You jest hold up. I need a little holp in here."

Disgusted, he pulled back on Sheila's reins and turned her toward the schoolhouse. "What?" It came out like a bark.

"I cain't get no windows to open. They're stuck shut. Whoever did the painting in here didn't think about windows needin' to open."

That would've been him, which she knew full well. He'd done the painting for the new school after the old one burned down last summer. Angie enjoyed tweaking him every chance she could. Well, he could dish it out too. "Then jest prop the door open with one of them books."

She gasped, like he knew she would. She was crazy for books and would consider it a sin to use one as a doorstop. It'd be like standin' barefoot on a Bible.

"It's hot in there. I need an open window to cross-ventilate." She said it very distinctly.

He scowled, instantly irritated whenever she tossed them big words at him. "Why do ya have to be hanging out in a schoolhouse when there ain't no school? Something's wrong with you."

"Ain't nothing wrong with me. I want an education. The books are kept in the schoolhouse so that's where I'm gonna be."

He stomped past her to head into the schoolhouse. "You don't need no more book learning."

"Yes I do. And so do you. You're missing days upon days of book learning." She hurried to catch up with him, like a little dog nipping at his heels. "I could holp you git caught up."

"Caught up on what?"

"On learnin'. On readin' and writin' and sums. You're smart, Fin. You could be sailin' through them exams, same as me, if you'd only give learnin' the time you give workin'."

"Don't need no exams. What I do need is work. My maw needs the money."

"If you learned to read and write better, you could make lots more money. Miss Cora's always tellin' us to read newspapers and keep informed of the world. Of events in the United States and the whole wide world."

"What . . . ," he said, jerking the stuck window open, ". . . for?"

"Because it's important."

He jerked another window open, then turned to face her, frustrated and annoyed. "Yeah? How so? Why do I need to be like you? Puttin' my beak in peoples' business?" He watched her happy face dissolve into something he couldn't quite define. In a second, however, it changed into something he could define very well. He'd made her mad.

"Because . . . ." Her face was turning red and he knew she was riled. "Because if you could read, you wouldn't have gotten cheated by the fine print in them loblolly contracts. You could've protected your maw and your land and your creek, instead of having to do odd jobs to make up for whatcha lost." Her voice dropped low, became gentle. "If you could read, you wouldn't be such an easy mark for scoundrels, Finley James. You ought not to be. You're too smart for that."

Furious, he stared at her, then brushed past her to leave.

By NOON, Lucy's bold resolve had weakened. By half past noon, it had fizzled out. Those terrible self-doubts had returned in full force, and she decided to decline Andrew Spencer's invitation to lunch. Assuming he might show up at all, which was looking increasingly doubtful. Twelve o'clock had come and gone, with no sign of him.

Cora had ridden up in the hills to have a talk with the elusive Miss Norah, whom Lucy had yet to meet and wasn't even sure she wanted to—not after seeing the reading material she'd given to Angie Cooper. Even Cora was horrified when Lucy told her about those cheap dime-store novels, and she didn't shock easily. Cora said she would take care of it, and she was doing just that.

The more time Lucy spent around her second cousin, the greater her admiration grew for her. Cora had dozens of schoolhouses to tend to in the hills, ones just like Little Brushy, each of which had dozens upon dozens of pupils, yet her energy seemed to never flag. She spent at least one day per week visiting different schools, checking in with the teachers, providing guidance and direction. Or, as Finley James would put it, chasing down children and driving them back to the schoolhouse like a shepherd with its sheep.

As the clock ticked to half past twelve, then past one, Lucy sat at Cora's big desk, tackling a stack of letters that needed answering. She had just finished one letter when Andrew Spencer bounded through the office door, his face flushed from running.

"Hello there, Lucy Wilson. Why, aren't you as pretty as a picture."

"Thank you." She felt herself flush, partly from the compliment, partly from feeling annoyed by his tardiness.

Andrew sat on the corner of Cora's desk and leaned in, mischief in his eyes. "Did you get my roses?"

"I did. They're quite lovely." Mercy! But he was a fine specimen of a man.

"What do you say to a picnic lunch?"

She hesitated, glancing down at the paperwork on the desk.

After a beat or two of silence, he added, "It won't take all afternoon. Just a picnic. I promise." He made a crossing sign over his heart with his hand.

She did love picnics. Still, she hesitated. "In Lexington, chaperones are required."

He grinned. "In case you hadn't noticed, this isn't Lexington."

So true. Social mores didn't seem to hold much weight here. "I suppose . . . it would be fine," she said, trying very hard not to be captivated by his irrepressible charm.

He hopped off the desk and bowed from the waist with a flourish, waiting until she passed by him, then followed her through the door. They took a path through town she'd not taken before, downstream instead of upstream, following a narrow dirt road until they came to an apple orchard. The trees were all in bloom, flowering in delicate shades of white and pastel pink. She could hear the buzz of countless bees, hovering overhead around the blossoms. Andrew pointed to a particularly beautiful tree; underneath sat a basket on top of a worn quilt. So *that's* why he was late! He must have come here earlier to prepare everything. She was touched.

She followed his lead and sat down on the quilt, knees folded under her like she'd been taught in finishing school. She lifted her head to look up at the cover of blossoms. "Oh Andrew, this is a beautiful place!"

"Please. Call me Andy. I'm glad you've come to Morehead." He handed her a sandwich wrapped in wax paper. Real white bread, not corn bread. Slices of meat inside. Lettuce and tomatoes! Lucy hadn't had either since leaving Lexington. She inhaled the orchard air. It was distinctive—soft, sweetly perfumed.

One delightful aspect of Andy she was discovering was that he was easy to be with, easy to talk to, and—unlike the mountain people—volunteered much about himself. Where he'd been raised—Tennessee. His family—two sisters, one older, one younger. "I started in the timber as a teen, then worked my way up to foreman. That's when I met your father." Apparently, Lucy's father had heard of Andy's diligence and offered him a job as sales agent. "It's been over a year now," he said with a satisfied smile. "Valley View Lumber is back on top. I hope to get out of this one-horse town soon and get transferred to company headquarters."

"Lexington?"

He nodded. "That's the plan."

Swallowing the last bite of sandwich, she said, "So when do you expect the creek on Barbara Jean Boling's land—"

Andy gave her a look of mock horror. "No business talk now!

It'll give us indigestion." He leaned toward her. "On Sunday morning, I'm going to take you to Limestone Knob. Highest point in Rowan County."

"I . . . can't. I plan to attend church." When he looked disappointed, she added, "You could come. If you'd like to. Brother Wyatt invited me to come."

He shook his head firmly. "Had my fill of those as a boy." He stretched out his long legs, one ankle over the other. "Limestone Knob will have to wait for another time, then." He took a deep breath. "Besides, can you imagine a more romantic setting than this one?"

Frankly, she couldn't. It was perfect. Everything was perfect. He was perfect.

LATER THAT NIGHT, as Fin lay in bed staring up at the roof rafters, he thought about what a terrible day he'd had. Arthur Cooper didn't need his help at the livery, and he couldn't scrounge up any other odd jobs. The only glimpse he caught of Miss Lucy was watchin' her disappear down the road with Andrew Spencer.

And then his thoughts bounced to Angie Cooper and her big ol' mouth. Mostly, he wondered if she could be right. If'n he had more schooling, could he have better protected his maw? Could he make more money? Would it improve his chances to court Miss Lucy?

Heck. What did Angie know about real life, anyhow? He hated school. He hated reading and writing and ciphering numbers. Hated how it made him feel, like he was dumb.

Eventually, he drifted off; when he woke, his head ached and he was in a foul mood. Then his spirits brightened. He recalled that he'd overheard Miss Cora tell Arthur Cooper she needed her horse and Miss Lucy's pony saddled and ready to go early Sunday morning. Fin grinned, all cheered up. That meant they'd be goin' to the brush arbor. Plenty of fried chicken and plenty of time with Miss Lucy.

NINE

LUCY HAD BEEN WAFFLING on attending the brush arbor until Cora insisted on it, and then there was no chance of backing out. Early Sunday morning, Cora's horse led the way up the trail, with Lucy and Jenny, as usual, struggling to keep up. Cora kept up a steady stream of conversation as they rode, using the time to "talk shop," as she phrased it.

"Whenever I get the chance to hear Wyatt sing, I jump at it," Cora said. "I like hearing from the circuit riders too."

"Father is quite critical of itinerant preachers."

Cora slowed her horse, waiting for Lucy to catch up. "That's because they're Baptists or Methodists, and your father, true to his Scottish roots, thinks being Presbyterian is the only approved means to get to heaven."

"Why aren't there any Presbyterian circuit riders?"

For this, Cora pulled her horse to a stop. "The Presbyterians didn't have enough educated preachers to send to the unchurched, but the Baptists and Methodists did. That's why they're the most prevalent churches in Appalachia." She looked up at the blue sky, peeking through the treetops. "When I was a child, I used to love attending camp meetings under the sky. They were filled with white and black and red faces, and so many souls were converted." She dropped her chin, eyes laughing. "People did all kinds of things to show they had the Holy Ghost in them. Once, during a particularly rambunctious revival meeting, a man climbed a tree and barked like a dog." She laughed. "True story. Your father witnessed it too. Ask if he remembers."

Lucy would rather not. "Was the man inebriated?"

"Not with moonshine. At least, not *during* the meetings." She gave her horse a little kick to start moving up the trail again, but she shifted slightly in the saddle to continue the conversation. "As soon as the meetings ended, someone would always bring a few jugs along and start passing them around in the shadows. We knew when it happened, because the menfolk would get happier by the minute." Cora turned to face forward again. "Oh, Lucy, it gives me great pleasure to ride into the hills on a beautiful Sunday in spring and see the tent meeting tradition live on. So much easier to worship the Almighty up here than in town where I'm often the recipient of a wagging finger."

Lucy wasn't sure how to phrase her next question, but she didn't need to. Cora seemed to read her thoughts. She held up two fingers in the air. "Two reasons. For one, I'm divorced. Thrice. And I have a career that traditionally belongs to men." She stopped her horse and turned around again in her saddle. "Lucy, you're going to discover, if you haven't already, that there are some who oppose me in Rowan County. They think I'm a bad influence on womenfolk."

"But you won the election to become superintendent." Won by a large margin!

"So I did." She grinned, then faced forward. "But each time I introduce something new or progressive, I know I'm in for a battle." She shrugged. "I have found in life that there are some things that are worth the fight."

Cora was quiet after that.

Not much later, they arrived at the site of the brush arbor, and it was quite a sight to behold. A large lean-to structure made up of tree limbs, tightly tied together with twine. The brush roof protected the very rustic pews: chunks of tree logs topped by benches of sawed lumber. A pulpit stood up front. Finley James saw them, waved, and bolted over to meet them.

"Yor here! I been lookin' for ya." He took hold of Jenny's reins to help Lucy climb down.

Lucy couldn't stop gazing at the brush arbor. "It's . . . like a plein-air sanctuary."

Fin's face wrinkled in a question. "Huh?"

"She means an outdoor church," Cora said. "And I can help myself down, thank you, Finley James. Not that you were concerned about me."

He colored slightly at her gentle scold. "I was gonna help you next, Miss Cora. It's jest that Miss Lucy still ain't sure which side of a horse to get herself down off."

Cora was already down by the time he finished his apology. "Finley James, how many times do I have to remind you to stop saying ain't?"

"One more time, I reckon." He shielded his eyes from the sky. "It'll be time to start soon. Better go claim yor seat. It's already fillin' up."

Lucy marveled again at how he seemed to tell time by looking up at the sky. Her childhood home in Lexington had clocks in every room, and the bells never synchronized, despite Father's conscientious and determined efforts. Cora made her way to the brush arbor, stopping every few feet to greet people.

"Best keep goin' and not wait on Miss Cora," Fin said, "or there won't be no seats left."

Fin was right about that. Cora seemed to know everyone and everyone knew Cora. Lucy walked over to the brush arbor to find a place to sit as Fin led the horses to a makeshift pen. Up front, Wyatt stood next to a man with a fiddle. Engrossed in conversation, he took no note of Lucy. She watched him for a while, noticing details. Black hair curled over his neck collar, and he kept pushing back a few strands that fell across his forehead, which Lucy found, for some reason, oddly endearing. He needed a haircut, and she wondered if there was a woman in his life—a sister, an aunt, a sweetheart—who looked after him. Who in his life would tell him such an ordinary thing as needing a haircut? He seemed to be a solitary soul.

Then he glanced up and noticed Lucy. He took a first slow step, then another, coming toward her in the aisle, eyes never wavering from her.

"So you came," he said, as he took her elbow to escort her to an open bench.

"Well, you said something about fried chicken," she said with a grin.

"Best you'll ever have," he said, grinning right back.

Fin stuck his head between them. "Brother Wyatt, they be wantin' you up front."

Seemingly unhurried, Wyatt went back to the front, gave a nod to a man with the fiddle, who picked up a bow and ran it along the strings to provide a note. People hurried to find a free spot on a bench, and Cora joined in, squeezing Finley James closer to Lucy. Excitement was nearly palpable, as if people were waiting for something to happen.

Wyatt closed his eyes and took in a deep breath. His mouth opened in a round O, and his voice filled the little makeshift sanctuary, soft and mellifluous, as if it had been dipped in honey. His mouth opened wider, lifting the notes to the sky.

One by one, men and women stood, swaying in time with the beat. Feet stomped, hands clapped, voices rose. The air in the brush arbor lifted with them, almost vibrating.

Mercy. Church was never like this at home.

Lucy took it all in, the warmth and music flooding her heart, filling it to the point of bursting. She felt something give inside her, something she hadn't known she could feel.

There was a place for everything, Father had told her, even religion. But this moment didn't feel like a compartment. It felt like her whole being was involved in worship.

Her gaze kept returning to Wyatt. Perhaps conscious he was

being watched, he turned to her at first with a smile, then his eyes grew full of concern. She was so lost in her thoughts that she hadn't realized tears were sliding, one after the other, down her cheeks.

NOT TEN SECONDS after the preacher gave the benediction, Wyatt was at Lucy's side, steering her away from others. "Is anything wrong?" he asked gently.

"I was just . . . moved by the music," she said, and surprised herself by realizing it wasn't a lie. "I've never heard church music played quite like that before."

"Mountain music? The style's been around a long, long time."

"You've a fine voice, Wyatt." What a beautiful voice he had. Deep and low, yet mellow as warmed butter. Truly memorable.

His cheeks grew rosy pink as he looked away. "Came from my granddaddy. I inherited his love for it."

Lucy had had years of chorus throughout her school years. She knew that to sing well, even to one with natural born talent, took hard work. She'd worked hard at it, but she'd never had a love for it.

"You'll stay for the singing school, I hope?"

"Unfortunately, no. Cora needs to get back to town. I'm still not confident of making my way back to town, especially when I'm in an area I've never been to before." Frankly, the hills and hollows all looked alike to her.

"Stay. I'll take you back."

"Goodness, no." Her voice came out an octave higher than normal; it didn't even sound like her own. "Honestly, Brother Wyatt— Wyatt—you've been so very kind already and I don't want to put you to more trouble. Really. I don't—"

"Stay," he said firmly and changed the subject. "Let's go get some fried chicken."

Suddenly Finley James was between them. "Yes, let's."

HECK. WHO SHOULD be doling out the fried chicken but ol'
Angie Cooper. When Fin approached the picnic table with Miss
Lucy and Brother Wyatt, Angie fixed her beady eyes right on him,
like a hawk about to pounce on an unlucky mouse. "Hello there,
Finley James."

"Where'd you come from?" It might have come out sounding
tetchy.

Angie frowned. "I been here the whole time."

"Angie, how pretty you look," Miss Lucy said. "Such a lovely
dress. Doesn't she look lovely, Fin?"

"This old thing?" Angie managed an expression of astonishment.

Fin realized it was the first time he'd seen Angie in a new dress.
A white frock with blue trim around her neck. He rubbed the back
of his neck and thought what he might say, then decided to fall
back on the truth. "Not as bad as usual."

Angie snapped Fin a look, then clapped her hands. "How many
pieces of chicken do you want? I cooked it myself."

Brother Wyatt, who seemed to be at Miss Lucy's elbow a heckuva lot today, interrupted. "I see Cora waving us over. Please excuse us."

Fin frowned, watching the two of them walk off.

"She's too old for you."

He turned back to Angie. "What are ya talkin' about?"

"You!" she hissed. "Yor makin' a dang fool out of yorself."

"Is that supposed to be a joke?"

"No it ain't." She held out a tin plate with two pieces of chicken.

"Don't say ain't. Don't ya know no better?" He grabbed his tin
plate of chicken—after all, despite how annoying she was, Angie
Cooper did cook up some mighty fine fried chicken—and made
his escape. He muttered beneath his breath as he walked around
the brush arbor, looking for Miss Lucy and Brother Wyatt. They'd
vanished. *Oh heck.*

CORA COULDN'T BE PERSUADED to stay on for the afternoon singing school, though she was delighted to hear that Wyatt had offered to escort Lucy down the hill. "You're in for a real treat, Lucy!" she said, as she swung a leg over her horse. "I'd stay if I could, but I have a frightfully busy week ahead and I need to prepare a talk."

She bent low in the saddle to say something to Wyatt, something that made him laugh. He patted her on the boot and off she went with a wave of her hand.

Wyatt shielded his eyes from the sun as he watched her disappear into the trees. "That woman is one of a kind."

"How do you mean?" Lucy said. "I've always thought so, but she's my kin."

He dropped his hand and turned to her. "Cora's a natural champion for the hill people. She knows the lifestyle firsthand, and knows what needs to change . . . yet she's able to instill pride in others. You've probably already been able to see that she's making strides."

"Yes, of course I see." But not really. Still overwhelmed by all she was absorbing in this new place, Lucy felt ignorant about so much. "Such as?"

"Well, for example, she's a believer in vocational training, so she started clubs . . . for boys as well as girls."

"What kind of clubs?"

"Farming clubs," he said, taking her elbow to lead her toward a stand of trees. "Poultry clubs, carpentry clubs. Did Fin tell you about the cabinet he's making for Miss Maude?"

"No. I'll be sure to ask him."

"He's doing a fine job. Borrows every tool he can get his hands on." Once they reached the trees, he led her up a steep trail.

"Where are we going?"

He glanced at her and smiled conspiratorially. "There's a place up yonder I'd like to show you."

This time, "up yonder" actually meant close by. When Wyatt

reached a small waterfall that dropped into a fast-running stream, he finally paused and sat on a large boulder. "Here we are. Thought you'd enjoy this spot. I call it nature's cathedral."

It was beautiful. Tranquil and peaceful. She leaned her elbows against the boulder. "You love these mountains, don't you?"

"I think I might like them better than anywhere on earth." He put one ankle over the other. "Whenever I'm away from these hills, I feel like I can't take in deep breaths. Like I can't fill my lungs completely. Up here, you can breathe. It's just you and the creeks and the birds and the trees and the sky."

They stayed there for a long while without talking, just listening to the waterfall, basking in the warm sun. Wyatt seemed to feel no need to make an effort at small talk, and to Lucy's surprise, the silence was very comfortable. Now and then she stole a look at him, wondering all that was running through his mind.

Too soon, he peered up at the sky, then over at the trees. "We should return and get you some of that fried chicken I boasted about before its gone. Singing school will start soon."

"How do you know the time? How does everyone seem to know what time it is without a timepiece?"

"By the shadows of the trees." He started down the trail, then stopped and turned. "Coming?"

She pushed herself off the boulder, a little sorry to leave this hallowed place.

When they returned to the brush arbor, Lucy saw men moving the benches to form a hollow square. Wyatt left her at Angie's picnic table and hurried away to prepare for the singing school.

Angie glowered at her. "There's only scrawny little wings left."

"That's fine. I'll take a wing."

Angie jabbed a fork into a chicken wing and held it out to Lucy. "Plates is all gone. Napkins too. Jest have to use yor fingers."

Gingerly, Lucy slipped the wing off the fork with her fingers. "When in Rome, do as the Romans do."

Angie gave her a curious look. "Where's that?"

"Rome? It's in Italy. Surely you've heard of Italy."

That familiar scowl returned to Angie's face. "There's a line behind you." Move along, she meant.

Lucy stepped aside to find two small boys, holding out their hands for a chicken wing.

"Here you go, boys. Toss them bones in the basket when you're done so Paw's dog don't choke." Angie's voice had turned sweet, motherly.

Lucy watched the boys head off. "Are they your brothers?"

"Yup. Twins. Double the trouble."

"I can tell they're twins. Goodness, they even walk alike." She glanced at Angie. "They don't resemble you. My sister and I . . . we didn't look alike, either."

Angie's face remained stoic.

"Is your father here?" He was at that dramatic hand-stitching crisis with Fin, but she hadn't taken note of him.

"Jest over yonder." Angie cupped her mouth to create a megaphone. "Paw! The fancy city lady wants to meetcha."

Lucy saw a man lift his head at Angie's shout, set his tin plate on a bench, and walk toward them. As he neared, he looked younger than he had from a distance, his beard dark against a sun-browned face. She could sense his authority, as well as his gentleness. "Hello, Mr. Cooper. I'm Lucy Wilson, Cora's cousin."

He gave a nod. "I've heered about yor coming. Glad yor able to bring some relief to Miss Cora's heavy load." He glanced at Lucy's hand, holding a chicken wing. He frowned at Angie. "Angel Eleanor, go find a plate and napkin for our newcomer."

Angel? Angie's formal name was Angel? Lucy swallowed a laugh. Arthur Cooper seemed like a kind and good man. What made his daughter act so cross all the time?

Just then, a bell rang to gather everyone for the singing school.

Lucy gave up on a plate for the chicken wing, ate it quickly, and dropped the bones in the basket as she walked past. Most of the benches were already filled, so she sat in the back. Fin left his spot on another bench to sit beside her. Most everyone from the morning's service joined in except for little boys and girls, allowed to play tag on the meadow.

After Wyatt passed out well-worn pamphlets, he stood in the center. Everyone stilled, and Lucy wondered what to expect next. Wyatt sang a line, but not in words. In syllables: *fa la la la la.* One by one, each section followed his lead, singing back to him that limited scale in syllables. It sounded more like babbling than singing. Wyatt occasionally shot Lucy a look, checking if she was okay, but despite being thoroughly confused, she was oddly content to sit back and take it all in as the outsider she was.

After all four pew sections had gone through the scales, Wyatt sang a line which Lucy recognized from an old hymn. Each section sang the line, this time in words, one after the other, so now it became four-part harmony. The woman next to her nudged her and shared the open pamphlet with her. It looked like musical notes on a staff, but the notes were different shapes, not circles.

Lucy stared at the pamphlet for a long time, until its meaning dawned on her. Each shape represented a different musical note: quarter note, half note, whole note. If a person couldn't read music, he or she could still sing along. But then Lucy realized there were no words written, either. Brother Wyatt provided the words to the songs, verse by verse, then each section would chant the line.

Her head bobbed up. *Mercy.* This entire group of people . . . they couldn't read.

ON THE WAY DOWN THE HILL, Lucy peppered Brother Wyatt with questions about the singing school. "Who first thought of it?"

"Shape note notation? Dates back to the 1700s, I believe. It spread quickly throughout the mountains. It's a way to help folks who love music but can't read. By looking at the shape of the notes, they can participate."

"The scale doesn't have a wide range."

"Good ear, Lucy. You're right. It's a limited scale." He shrugged. "But enough for most hymns and ballads. I adjust what I can."

"So, then, you print up those pamphlets?"

He nodded.

An offering had been taken at the end, which she assumed would provide payment for him. A pittance.

"So that's what a singing school master does with his time." She wondered what kept him so busy. He was rarely in town, and always seemed to have some errand or task on his mind. Always seemed to be on his way somewhere.

"What about you, Lucy?" He slowed Lyric so that Lucy could draw level with him. "I know how Cora is keeping your days full. But what was your life like in Lexington?"

Lucy told him a few things about her life in Lexington. About graduating from the Townsend School for Girls, about returning home to discover her father was engaged to a former classmate. When she stopped, he seemed to be waiting for her to go on, but she said, "That's about it." She leaned forward and stroked the pony's neck.

"That's it?"

"Well, when Cora asked if I would come to Morehead to be her stenographer, it seemed propitious timing."

He looked at her with such a mixture of interest and concern that suddenly she became self-conscious. "Is that why there were tears in church?"

"No," she said, surprising even herself. "That's not all. I had a little sister."

"What happened to her?"

Lucy never knew how to tell people about her sister, so she studiously avoided it. Guarding herself from others was such a deeply engrained habit that it overruled the nearly overwhelming urge to share her aching heart. But there was something about the look of kindness in Wyatt's eyes that made her want to tell him about Charlotte.

The words tumbled out, unchecked. "I was supposed to keep watch of her one day while we were at a train station, but I got absorbed in a book. She wandered off. Father and I searched everywhere. The police were involved. We looked for weeks but she was never found. There was no sign of her. Nothing. Not a single trace. Charlotte was simply gone. Father offered a large reward, but there was never any lead of substance. Lots of crazies, but nothing that led to our Charlotte." And as much as Lucy told herself over and over that it just didn't make sense, that it wasn't possible, that Charlotte couldn't have vanished without a trace, she had.

Wyatt let the words settle. He waited, as if to check that he had heard right. "How old was Charlotte?"

"She was only two-and-a-half years old."

"What do you think happened to her?"

"I don't know. I've never given up hope that she is . . . alive. Somewhere." She looked away. "I think it would've been easier if we'd known she had died. If her body had been found." She covered her mouth with her hand, as if horrified that she was even saying the words out loud. Saying it aloud made it so real.

Quietly, he said, "How you must miss Charlotte."

Something broke inside of Lucy and a wave of grief rose up. "So much," she said, her fists pressed tightly to her cheeks. "I miss knowing her. The feel of her and the touch of her and the sweet smell of her and the way she curled up with her stuffed bear and a hundred other things, like the way she used to try to say my name. I miss *having* a sister. I miss *knowing* her." Her voice choked with tears and she struggled to contain them. "I miss *her*."

"All these years," Wyatt said softly, his gray eyes filled with sorrow, "you've been living with that tragedy. That uncertainty."

Stalling to allow her emotions a moment to recover and stuff them back into place, Lucy studied the tips of her boots. They no longer looked new but were scuffed and scratched. After a long silence she stole a look at Wyatt. "It's better now, I suppose. With the passing of time."

"Better begins within." Lyric reached out to eat some grass and Wyatt let her stretch her neck. "There's a verse in the book of Isaiah, in which God declares that he knows the name of every star he set in the sky. Not one is missing, he says."

She watched the horse nibble the grass, not wanting to look at Wyatt. Not trusting herself to keep from tearing up. "What does that have to do with Charlotte?"

"He is the All Mighty, Lucy. Mighty over all. And if the All Mighty knows the whereabouts of each and every star, do you not think he knows where your sister is?"

A breeze came up and Lucy shivered, or maybe she shivered because of the topic. "If he knows . . . then why doesn't he say?" She crossed her arms tightly against her middle. "Wyatt, I know you mean to offer comfort. But I prayed and prayed and prayed about Charlotte. First, that she would be returned to us. Then, later, that at least we would know what happened to her. There was never any answer from God. Nothing. Not ever."

"Or maybe . . . not yet."

Please don't. Don't try to dig up buried hope. Don't try to over-spiritualize this tragedy. Bad things just happened. There was no explaining them. Lucy worked to get the conversation back to a more comfortable place. "We'd better get a move on," she said, startling him with her abruptness. "The sun is dropping." And her heart was too.

TEN

ANGIE COOPER TOSSED AND TURNED in bed that night, unable to sleep. She'd seen how often Finley James sidled up next to Lucy Wilson at the brush arbor. She'd seen how often he stole looks at her, gawkin' at her like she was a visiting queen from . . . Rome, Italy.

Stupid boy. Stupid, stupid boy.

Why did she have to love him so? As far back as she could remember, Angie had been head over heels in love with Finley James. She felt a devotion to him that had never wavered, not once, even though he could barely read and write. Even though he paid her no mind a'tall. His intelligence wasn't the schooling type, it was the heart type. Fin had a noble heart, like the heroes in the dime-store novels Angie loved to read. Time and time agen, she'd seen him go outta his way to take care of people in the holler—chopping wood for Miss Mollie, plowing a field for Sally Ann, hauling water for Barbara, then have to stay up late to finish his own chores. And then there was his knowledge of nature. He could identify every bird in the sky, knew which plants to eat and which to avoid, and was considered the best fisherman on this side of the mountain.

Most importantly, Angie was convinced the Lord had set Finley James aside jest for her.

Until the city lady showed up.

Angie had never known jealousy before; she'd never needed to. Her brothers adored her, her father depended heavily on her. He was always tellin' her that she was the best catch around, that it was only a matter of time until Fin figured that out. Angie believed him. But Lucy Wilson changed things. She was prettier than Angie, and smarter, and knew more, and talked fancy and dressed fancy. *Bother!* Even Angie could see why Fin was smitten.

Did Lucy return his feelings? Was it possible she was growing sweet on him? She smiled and laughed plenty around him today.

Angie rolled on her back and stared at the ceiling. Every problem had a solution, her paw often said. Mebbe . . . Angie could find somebody older to start paying attention to Lucy Wilson. Mebbe then she'd act her age and leave Fin alone. But who?

Brother Wyatt? No. He was too holy a man for Lucy Wilson, too fine and good. City ladies needed city men.

Angie smiled. *Andrew Spencer. Slick, polished, smooth talking, handsome as the devil. He's jest the one.* One dandy man for one dandy lady.

CORA WAS SELDOM IN HER OFFICE, and seldom relaxed. Moments like today, when no interruptions came at the door to pull her away from her desk, were a luxury. But when Lucy did have time alone with Cora, she felt as if she were starting to understand her, inside and out. Her father's cousin was such a unique individual. Cora was a traditional woman in a man's world, using every tool she could—charm, knowledge, enthusiasm, determination—to bring the light of learning into people's lives. The more she was around Cora, the more inspired she was to try and be more like her.

On this foggy morning, Lucy finished a few letters and handed them to Cora to sign.

"While I look these over, might I ask you to make some tea?"

Lucy smiled. That was Cora's invitation to sit a spell and visit.

Those moments topped Lucy's list of all-time favorites. When she returned to the office with two cups of hot tea, Cora had already pulled up Lucy's chair next to her desk.

She accepted the cup from Lucy gratefully and took a sip. "Tell me, how did you enjoy the singing school?"

"I thought it was quite clever. And the mountain people certainly enjoyed themselves. You should have heard them moan and wail when Wyatt announced the last song." Lucy sat back in her chair and blew on her tea to cool it. "Cora, it dawned on me that the reason the singing school is necessary, or at least the shape note notation, is because those people are illiterate."

"Most are." Cora sipped her tea. "Some are semi-literates. They might have had a bit of schooling here and there."

"I'm a little ashamed to realize how I've taken for granted my education."

"You and everyone else. Most Americans don't realize what a privilege it is to read. It may shock you to know that two-thirds of the world cannot read."

Lucy set her teacup on Cora's desk. "But if they can't read, how can they take part in the world? How can they vote? Or pay for goods and not get cheated?" She rose and paced the room. "I don't mean to sound callous, but two-thirds of the world is an overwhelming statistic to grasp. What I do understand is that Barbara Jean Boling has six boys to raise and she can't even write her own name. She had to scratch out a wobbly X on that letter to Valley View Lumber. Finley James struggled to make change from a dollar. Miss Mollie can't even read a note from her own daughter."

Cora's eyebrows lifted. "I can tell you're learning much about the people."

"So far, what I've learned is that their day-to-day lives are incredibly hard."

"True, but don't pity them, Lucy. Don't even think it. They'll sense it from you and their pride will be wounded." She picked up her pen to start back to work, then paused as a new thought came to mind. "The real pity boils down to illiteracy. It renders the mountain people victims."

"How so?"

Cora put her pen down and leaned back in her chair. "It takes an effort of the imagination to put oneself in the place of the illiterate. To picture what life is like for one who must get all his information by ear. If a man cannot read or write or vote, he cannot speak. He is mute. He is forgotten. You might think it's a pity they cannot read, but the real tragedy is they cannot *speak*." She picked up her pen. "That, Lucy, is the real tragedy of the twentieth century."

LATER IN THE WEEK, Paw asked if Angie would bring the boys to the livery after school and she agreed quickly. It gave her a chance to watch for Andrew Spencer. When she heard the jangles of a horse and wagon, she hurried to the front of the livery. There he was, at the railroad station looking over a load of freshly delivered lumber. Paw and the boys were in the back, so she hurried toward the station. She waited until Andrew Spencer finished talking to the wagon driver.

"Do you happen to know where Miss Lucy Wilson is? I been looking for her everywhere."

He stopped and turned to face Angie. "Miss Lucy? Have you tried the superintendent's office?"

"No, I haven't. I'll do that. I jest thought you might know her whereabouts, seeing as how she speaks of you so often."

He preened like a rooster. "She speaks of me often, does she?"

"Oh my goodness, yes. She never stops talking about you. Your hair—"

His hand immediately smoothed his hair.

"—your sense of humor."

He grinned.

"And then . . ." She glanced at the poster on the railroad bulletin board ". . . there's the dance coming up on Saturday." She lowered her voice and leaned in. "Jest between you and me and the fencepost, I think she's hopin' you might ask her to go."

"Is that right?"

"Well," Angie said with a shrug. "What do I know? I jest listen a lot."

ANDY SPENCER SEEMED to be everywhere at once. Lucy could barely turn around in town and there he was, smiling at her with his magnificent smile. Today, he appeared in Cora's office with one hand behind his back, and whipped his hand around to reveal what he'd been hiding—a bouquet of spring flowers. "Come to the dance with me on Saturday night."

She held the blossoms to her nose to inhale their scent. "Saturday?" Stalling, she started rooting through a cupboard for an empty mason jar. She thought she'd seen one, tucked away.

"Saturday night. You like music, don't you? It's supposed to be a real humdinger."

"Of course I like music." She found the jar and put the flowers in it. "I suppose that sounds fine."

He leaned a little closer. "You could sound more excited."

"I'm sorry, Andy. I am excited." And she was, especially with him just inches away from her. He was an exciting man, dashingly handsome and full of life. She knew how delighted her father would be to hear that she was being courted by Andrew Spencer. If Hazel were to know, she would start addressing wedding invitations.

"Then why do you seem as if you're a million miles away?"

She arranged the flowers in the jar. She didn't want to tell him that Finley James had just delivered a letter from her father, telling her to expect him on the train tomorrow evening. It unsettled her. Her father rarely came to Morehead. "I just have a lot on my mind."

Andy didn't seem to know what to say next—and neither did Lucy—so she went out to the bathroom to fill the jar with water and when she returned, he had left. She found a note on her chair to be ready at half past seven for the dance on Saturday evening. At the bottom, he added an XO.

Her heart beat faster with excitement, her stomach flipped once or twice in nervousness. She looked again at the XO he'd scribbled. Everything about Andrew Spencer was made to order. So why did she feel such mixed emotions about him?

FATHER HAD ASKED Lucy to meet at the Gault Hotel for dinner at seven o'clock. When she arrived in the dining room, she found her father—and Hazel—at a corner table, holding hands and whispering to each other. Lucy tried not to recoil, but there was something uncomfortable about seeing your father act like a silly schoolboy in love.

Her father spotted her first and jumped from his seat to greet her. "Lucille, come sit down."

Lucy brushed cheeks with Hazel and sat down. As she spread the napkin over her lap, she smiled. "Hazel, you look quite well."

"Do I?" She touched the hairs on the nape of her neck and gave a sideways coquettish look at her husband.

"Indeed, you look lovely, dear," he said, kissing the back of Hazel's hand. "You always do."

Lucy took a sip from her water glass, trying not to cringe.

"Your father tells me that Andrew Spencer is squiring you around."

"Squiring? Hardly that! We've only just met."

"Your father thinks the world of him. A genius in business, he says."

Lucy could see the hope in Hazel's eyes and had a suspicion what was behind it: If Lucy were married, that would take care of her new husband's former life. Check. Done. In the past.

"So what's new in Lexington?"

"Well, I've convinced your father to redecorate the house."

Lucy looked to her father for a response. He had never wanted to change anything. He kept his eyes lowered, buttering his bread as if it was the most dangerous task in the world.

"The décor is outdated," Hazel said. "It needs brighter colors, some original and surprising elements—it needs personality."

Oh, it had plenty of personality, all right. But that personality had belonged to Lucy's mother.

"And . . ."

Lucy looked up.

"Your father is allowing me to redecorate Charlotte's room."

Lucy stilled. Her father hadn't let anyone in that room, other than the housekeeper, who was permitted to dust it once a week.

Hazel reached over to stroke her father's cheek. "We're going to turn it into a nursery."

"Oh, I see." Slowly, her meaning dawned on Lucy. "Oh!" She looked at her father, whose eyes were fastened on his bride's.

"Isn't it wonderful news?" Hazel was glowing. "The baby is due in September, the doctor says."

Lucy sat there, stunned. Yet she shouldn't be stunned. Hazel was a young woman. She deserved to have a family of her own. Still . . . her father was no spring chicken.

Spring chicken. *Oh my goodness. I'm starting to talk like the mountain people.*

Fortunately, Hazel and her father were oblivious to Lucy's shock. They were too busy staring into each other's eyes.

"It is wonderful news," Lucy said, trying to sound more cheerful than she felt. They both turned to her, as if they'd almost forgotten she was there. "Perhaps you'll have a son, Father."

He smiled, Hazel smiled, and Lucy couldn't help but smile. They seemed so . . . happy.

But then Hazel's smile faded. "There's another reason we've asked you here tonight."

More news? Lucy wasn't sure she could stomach much more. Is this what it felt like to be afflicted with collywobbles?

Hazel placed her hand over Lucy's and looked intently in her eyes. "I learned a very troubling thing. Your sister has never had a grave marker."

Lucy looked to her father, who said nothing, just sat looking down at his plate. "I suppose . . . ," she said, "that's because there's always been a hope that we might find Charlotte."

"Oh Lucy, it's been over eleven years now. It's time. With your father's permission, I've ordered the marker. It'll be ready on Saturday. We plan to place it next to your mother's grave. A small ceremony."

A long, painful moment passed.

"We want you to be there for the ceremony," Father said.

"But . . ."

"No buts," he said, and then, "we . . . I . . . want you there."

Lucy kept her expression stoic, but inside was swirling the old and terrible question: What had happened to Charlotte?

LUCY LEFT FATHER AND HAZEL at the Gault Hotel and walked slowly, deep in thought, down the road to Miss Maude's boarding house.

There was no dissuading Hazel from insisting that Lucy return to Lexington for the ceremony of placing the headstone over Charlotte's empty grave. At the heart of Lucy's reluctance was that it meant all hope was lost that her sister would ever be found—something she and her father never had wanted to admit. Hazel, both pragmatic and forward moving, realized the time had come. Hazel wasn't wrong. It just hurt so much to face that fact.

She was so absorbed in her thoughts that didn't realize Brother Wyatt was behind her until he fell into step beside her.

"Must be something powerful going on in that head of yours.

Called out to you so loud that a flock of birds took off." He peered into the sky. "Frightened 'em clean off to another county."

She stopped. "I'm sorry. I didn't hear you. So you're staying in town tonight?"

"Yes. Here to get my mail. I'm hoping my new music pamphlets have arrived." He looked up the road toward the ridge. "Heading back up into the hills tomorrow. There's another singing school on Sunday. Same place. Same brush arbor." He turned to face her. "You'll come?"

Sunday? "No. I don't . . . think so."

Wyatt took a step toward her. "Lucy, are you all right?"

Lucy shook her head. "No," she confessed. "No, I'm not."

"Can I help?"

"No. No one can." She left him at the front door and hurried upstairs before she burst into tears. As soon as she reached her room, she flopped on the bed, in a bit of a state. The conversation with her father and Hazel had left her with a harsh recollection that, once begun, was nearly impossible to stop.

Staring up at the ceiling, she remembered that terrible day . . .

As Lucy and her father searched the railroad station, she was scared but certain Charlotte could be found. Her little sister was always sneaking off, getting into something she shouldn't. Surely, she was hiding somewhere. It would be just like all those other times when Charlotte slipped away, oblivious to the alarm she had created. Every railroad employee stopped to help Lucy and her father search for Charlotte. With all of them looking, they would find Charlotte in no time at all. Surely, she would be found.

But as darkness descended, there was still no sign of her. The police arrived, interviewing Lucy, and Father. Search parties were created to scour the surrounding area, with lanterns held high. By morning, nearly everyone in town was out searching for little Charlotte. Yet there was not a single trace of her whereabouts.

In the days that followed, Father posted a reward. He and Lucy went to each town on the rail line, knocking on every single door, asking if anyone had seen any sign of the lost little girl. Churches held prayer vigils. Newspapers ran the story on their front page. Still, not a single clue turned up. Charlotte was simply gone. As much as Lucy told herself that it just didn't make sense, that it wasn't possible, that someone, somewhere must have seen her, that Charlotte couldn't be gone without a trace . . . yet she was.

After a week of searching, the police told Father—who hadn't slept more than an hour here and there in seven days—to go home, that they would contact him if something turned up. Lucy overheard one police officer tell another that the child must be dead.

At last Father agreed to go home and wait for word. When they reached the house, he locked himself in Charlotte's room and wept. Lucy sat outside the door, helpless, unable to say or do anything, guilt settling over her like a thick and heavy mantle.

When he finally emerged, he never spoke of Charlotte again.

ELEVEN

FINLEY JAMES HAD FINISHED cleaning out the last stall at Arthur Cooper's livery and lay down on a haystack for a little shut-eye jest for a moment or two, or mebbe a little longer, when he suddenly heard someone yoo-hooing for him. He jolted up when he realized Miss Lucy had come looking for him, and in his scramble to get up, he fell right off the haystack. He jumped up, ran a hand through his bushy hair, and wiped his face down with his old handkerchief before he showed hisself. "Howdy, Miss Lucy," he said, walking toward the front of the livery, trying to act as calm as a man could be when his heart was beatin' double time.

"Fin, are you all right? Your face is bright red."

"Is it?" He put a hand against his face. "Jest working hard, I reckon." To be truthful, Fin felt downright dizzy. Miss Lucy was beautiful. Flawless. Like a porcelain doll.

He scratched his face. Mebbe he should start to shave.

"I found these two letters on my chair with a note from Cora to deliver them to Miss Mollie today. Cora's gone to Cranston to check on a school." She walked over to the pony's stall. "Would you mind getting Jenny's saddle and bridle on? Last time I tried, I put the saddle on backwards."

Fin grinned. "I'll deliver the letters for you. I'm going right by."

"Oh thanks, Fin, but Cora wants me to transcribe for Miss Mollie and bring down letters to post in the mail."

And Fin couldn't write. Not much, not in a straight line, anyhows. Unfortunate shortcoming on his part, but it did present a sweet opportunity to spend time with Miss Lucy. "I'll ride along with you. I'm about done here."

"Oh, would you, Fin? I'd be ever so grateful." Her lovely face brightened like the sun had come out, and for a moment he felt dazed. Stunned. It reminded him of once coming across a delicate wildflower in the dark forest, such an unlikely place for beauty to bloom.

After Fin saddled Jenny up, he was pleased to see that Miss Lucy finally knew which side to mount her on, though she still needed a boost. As they made their way upstream, a few raindrops fell and Miss Lucy asked if they should turn around.

"Won't be any problem a'tall," Fin said, not wanting to miss a chance to be alone with his sweetheart. "Asides, a little rain never hurt no one." Though he had to admit, the clouds were dark and low, lying heavy as a thick gray blanket.

They rode along, Fin stealing an occasional glace at Lucy, jest to prove to hisself that she was really there. He wished he were better at sweet-talking a woman, like Andrew Spencer was. Fin hadn't learned much about women, not yet. His paw had passed on before he'd got around to that lesson.

"Won't the horses slip in the rain?"

"Naw. They's surefooted." The sporadic drops of rain had now turned to a steady drizzle. "This ain't much. It'll pass soon."

"I guess the rain is good for the crops."

"Yep. We need every drop." And with that, as if ordered up, the drizzle changed to fat drops. Thunder rumbled. Not much later, rain hit with a fury. "It's turning into a real gully washer!" He glanced back at Lucy and saw the fear in her eyes.

"Are you sure we should be out when there's thunder and lightning going on?"

"Jest a minor squall."

"More like a hurricane!"

"Miss Mollie's is jest over yonder."

Lucy groaned at that but kept following behind. Even Sheila was getting jittery with the thunder, her ears pointed flat back, so he nudged her to go faster. Thunder cracked again, this time much closer, so close his ears hurt. The rain beat down in waves, sharp and falling sideways in the wind, and he knew he'd underestimated this storm.

As soon as they arrived at Miss Mollie's, he helped Miss Lucy down and grabbed Jenny's reins. "You go on in," he shouted. "I'll get the horses in the barn." Thunder and lightning flashed and boomed as he darted toward shelter, holding the horses' reins. He closed the barn doors and led the horses into a stall. They'd have to share for now, but it was better than being stuck outside. They'd have to take shelter at Mollie's until the storm passed, so he stripped the horses of their gear, shook the leather so it would dry, and hauled a bucket of water for the horses. He noticed an empty feed sack and used it to dry them off. His paw had taught him that a good man always took care of his stock first. Hisself second.

Fin made a run for the house and jumped over the steps in one leap to reach the porch. At the door, he wiped his face down with the now wet handkerchief and tried to make himself presentable. He was actually kind of pleased with this storm. The land needed the rain and he needed time alone with Miss Lucy to woo her. The door opened wide and he saw that Mollie and Miss Lucy weren't alone, as he had hoped. Brother Wyatt was at the table with Miss Lucy and Miss Mollie, and who should be at the door but ol' Angie Cooper with a great big grin wreathin' her face.

IF THERE WAS one thing Lucy was discovering about the mountain people, it was that they could turn any event into a party. And even better, a reason for storytelling. *So* many stories. Lucy could listen all day. And how Miss Mollie loved to tell them. Lucy didn't mind hearing one more, especially if it meant she could sit for a while longer. "So what happened then?"

On this rainy afternoon, over cinnamon tea and dried-apple cake, and fat hens roosting in the rafters—something Lucy still thought was odd—Miss Mollie told stories about the holler from years ago. She spoke of Angie's mother, Aria Cooper, quite a few times, and Lucy realized she must have died, long ago. Angie listened wide-eyed, hungry for every memory. Lucy understood *that.*

Miss Mollie told one story of Aria Cooper as a little girl, caring for an orphaned raccoon, until one day that critter bit her and her paw wanted to kill it. She wouldn't let him but insisted on setting it free. "It's jest its nature to be wild," was Aria's defense, and finally her paw relented. "And then that critter got in the henhouse and her paw shot and killed it. My oh my, Aria carried on weepin' and wailin' for days. Even had a funeral for it." Mollie smiled her gappy smile. "She shed tears over every lovely, sad, happy, holy thing in the whole wide world. Wouldn't eat no meat or fish or fowl . . . nothing with eyes that could look back at her."

Aria Cooper sounded like a gentle soul. Lucy wondered when she had passed, and why, and if Angie had memories of her. Lucy made a mental note to herself to ask Cora more about her. She dared not ask Angie, who had glowered at her most of the afternoon.

Lightning flashed and thunder struck at almost the same time, and Lucy jumped in her chair, half expecting the roof to cave in. Wyatt noticed her discomfort and clasped his hands together. "Let's roll up the rug and have a little fun." He crossed the room and bent down to pick up a fiddle. "Mind if I use Angus's fiddle?"

"That's what he'd want ya to do," Miss Mollie said.

Wyatt pulled it out of the case and held it close to his heart. "This belonged to Mollie's grandfather. He brought it across the ocean with him. The most important instrument any Scotch-Irish brought over was the fiddle."

"And the music," Mollie said. "There was jest enough room on the ship to bring along memorized songs."

Wyatt laughed, Fin and Angie, too, and suddenly Lucy caught the joke.

"Let's show Miss Lucy some of our beloved music," Wyatt said.

Fin had moved the table against the wall, and right behind him, Angie kneeled on the floor and rolled up the rug. Then Angie, Fin, and Mollie, too, stood in the center of the room, arms by their sides, faces solemn, as Wyatt tuned the fiddle's strings, turning the keys and cocking his ear until satisfied that he had each string just so.

"I have a feeling this is going to be good. Lucy, you're in for a real treat." Wyatt's foot tapped a beat, and he started to fiddle, and they started to kick their legs in rhythm. Back and forth, side to side, heel, toe, heel, toe. Why, even Mollie kept up! At a slower pace, of course, but she was thoroughly enjoying herself, relishing the moment. In her enthusiasm, Lucy could see hints of the girl she once was.

Any sounds of thunder were drowned out by the fast-moving bow against the fiddle's strings, the pounding beat of feet as they stomped. Now and then, Wyatt would drop the fiddle to his side and half sing, half talk a verse or two in his fine, deep baritone voice, then lift the bow to the fiddle and carry on without missing a beat. Lucy stared, transfixed. She wasn't sure what was more astounding—the many musical skills of Wyatt, or the clog dancing. Both, she decided.

Fin pulled Lucy by the hand to get her to clog along with them, and she tried. But she was terrible at it, truly terrible. Clumsy and confused, she gave up and stood against the wall, shaking with laughter. Besides, she'd rather just watch them! After a while, Mollie sagged down next to her in a chair, breathing hard, but Fin and Angie kept up to the end of the song, which was quite long.

And when it was over, the storm had passed by, and the clouds were breaking up.

Brother Wyatt set the fiddle into the case and closed it up with a satisfied pat. "Miss Lucy, if you'll finish up your work with Miss Mollie, I'll see you back to town."

"Oh, I'll see her down the hill," Fin said.

"No, Fin, you need to give Angie a ride home. Her paw must be worried sick about her."

Fin scowled, and Angie grinned, and Miss Mollie patted the chair next to her for Lucy to sit down and start writing down her dictations.

THIS AFTERNOON had turned out to be sweeter than cornbread dunked in sorghum. Angie'd gone to Miss Mollie's to take her a jug of buttermilk from their cow, and next thing she knew, she was dancing with Finley James. And riding behind him on Sheila, to boot. He'd hoisted himself up, then reached down to give her a lift, which she thought was chivalrous. She told him, too, but he only snapped at her.

"Stop showing off."

"I ain't. I cain't holp it if I like them big words." When he didn't say anything more, she added, "You could learn big words, too, Finley James. They ain't so hard, and you're plenty smart enough. Stubborn as a mule, that's yor problem." She could feel him tense up and she eased off from tweaking him. "Yor shore a good dancer."

"Anybody who don't know how to clog to that song don't know nothin'."

"Miss Lucy don't know it."

"That's different. It's all new for her." He kicked Sheila's sides so she picked up her pace, and Angie had to cling to him more tightly. "Don't wampish," he snapped.

"I ain't trying to wriggle! I'm hanging on for dear life." But she

135

was enjoying the ride immeasurably. That was another big word she'd learned this week. "Miss Lucy don't belong here."

"Why do you keep getting your knickers in a twist over Miss Lucy? She's book red. She knows lots of things. I mean, amazin' stuff. And she's a real fine lady."

"Her clothes? Why . . . they're jest fanci—"

"I don't mean her clothes. It's more than that."

"Well, what *do* you mean?"

"She's not childish. She don't go shootin' off her mouth."

Unlike you, that's what she was sure he was thinking. If God gave her a mouth, how could it be wrong to use it? What did he think a lady was meant to be, anyhows? Dumb and docile, meek and mouselike, that's what it sounded like. When Fin remained quiet, she changed the subject. "You going to the dance on Saturday night?"

"Don't know. Doubt it."

"Miss Lucy's going. With Andrew Spencer. He's works for the lumber company and I'm pretty sure they're sweet on each other. They make a fine-looking couple too. Why, jest the other day—"

The words were barely out of her mouth when Finley James stopped Sheila short and said, "Here's where you git off."

"But . . ."

"Quicker for you to head through them trees than for me and Sheila to go around. Off you go." He practically shoved her off, made a clicking sound, and Sheila took off.

"I take it back!" she shouted at his disappearing back. "You ain't chivalrous. Not at all!"

As Lucy took dictation from Miss Mollie, Wyatt stacked wood on the porch, and fed and watered her animals. It was touching to see the care everyone gave Miss Mollie, such a quirky old woman, yet she was working her way into Lucy's heart. Even the stench of the cabin was not as bothersome to her, at least not as odorous as it had been on her first visit.

Brother Wyatt walked alongside Lucy, who sat on Jenny's back, as they headed down the hill beside the rushing creek.

"This rain should help end the drought," she said.

"You'd think so, but the rain came down too fast and hard. Ends up just running right off the hill. Doesn't have a chance to saturate the ground. Better a rain that is slow and steady."

Something else she'd never considered. She hadn't had to. Weather never really mattered before. "That clogging . . . how in the world did Miss Mollie keep up?"

"She's been doing it all her life. But she's not as old as you might think. The hard life up here, it can age a woman mighty fast."

Lucy should have realized. Life up here must be so difficult for a woman. Babies, one right after the other. Scratching out sustenance on a hill took its toll. And their teeth! So many women she'd met, men as well, were missing teeth. There was so much she had to learn about this mountain life . . . starting with music. "Wyatt, that music—I've never heard anything like it."

"Mountain music?" He glanced up at her. "Music has a deep tradition up here."

"I didn't expect the storytelling."

He grinned. "Whatever happens gets written into a ballad. Love, murder, betrayal, you name it. Every detail. I know of one song that has over one hundred verses."

"So that's the style of mountain music? Storytelling?"

"Oh, that style goes back to Ireland. Most of the ballads made their way across the ocean and didn't die off in the mountains. Just the opposite, in fact. The mountains hold tradition in."

A sigh escaped her, and he took notice. "What is that about?"

"There's so much I still have to learn about this area. About these people."

"It's your history too."

"I suppose you're right, but my father never spoke much of it.

If I ever asked, he'd tell me that it was better to face forward in life, not backward."

"What about you, Lucy?"

Me? Lucy felt a jolt run through her. As many times as she'd heard her father make that remark, it never occurred to her that he might be directing it at her. She was always facing backward. Always sifting through the past, hanging on to it.

When she didn't say anything, Wyatt poked a little deeper. "What brought you here, Lucy? What made you agree to come?"

"I don't really know. Being here, coming back to my family's roots, I feel as if I'm living on the edge of two worlds. The past and the future."

Wyatt looked at her with his intense gaze. "Perhaps you're here to discover God's purpose for you."

"I don't believe God has a purpose for me."

After that Wyatt was quiet for a long time, until he stopped the pony and turned to Lucy. "Would you mind if I took the long way back to town? There's something I want you to see. It's just over yonder."

Over yonder. *Oh dear.*

NOT MUCH LATER, Wyatt led Jenny up a seldom-used trail in which Lucy had to duck several times to avoid getting whacked in the face. Then the trees started to thin, and he slowed Jenny to a stop. "Have you ever seen scalded land?"

"I've heard of tobacco fields that wear out the soil."

"That's not quite what I'm talking about. The lumber companies give it euphemisms. They say they've harvested the timber. Cleared the acreage. Or they say they've run it out."

She was well acquainted with those terms.

"I call it exhausted land." He tied Jenny's reins to a tree limb, low enough that she could nibble grass. "Follow me." He helped her off the pony, jumped the creek, then reached out a hand to help her across. Then he took her along a path, single file. "There," he said, stepping away so she could see around him down below at the side of the hill.

Shocked, Lucy took in the sight: a wasteland, littered with broken tree trunks. "What's happened?"

"Have you not seen what a forest looks like after sawyers and skidders have come through?"

"Yes, of course I have." Once, when her father took her along on a business trip. "But the stumps were cleared too."

"Not these loblolly pines." He looked at her, pained. "Woodsmen just take the trunk and leave the stump and roots. Straight and tall, without knots, strong, light in weight. Used for ship masts, for lumber, and the wood pulp is used for paper."

"Turpentine."

"Pardon?"

"Fin told me that the pitch is used for turpentine. He said these trees are in high demand." She gazed at the cutover acreage. It looked like a war had taken place on it.

"This stand had been here at least one hundred fifty years. Gone in just a few months."

"They'll grow back, though, won't they? Aren't pines fast growing?"

When he didn't answer, she glanced over and saw the disappointment in his eyes.

"But that's not the point, is it? You wanted me to see how the land has been ravaged."

"These trees need acid soil, full sun, lots and lots of water. Yes, they can grow quickly, if all those conditions are met. But look up." He pointed to a few tall trees standing along the edges, as if forgotten. "You can see a lot of seeds in their crowns. That's a warning that the trees have become stressed. They put seeds out to try and keep the next generation going."

"So why would they be stressed?"

"This forest used to have many streams crossing through it," Wyatt said quietly, his eyes watchful. "But . . ."

She held up a hand to stop him. "The water was diverted"—she took in a deep breath and finished her sentence—"by the lumber companies." She turned to him. "Who owns this hill?"

"It belongs to Finley James's mother." He looked up at the sky. "Used to be you'd lose count of the bald eagles soaring overhead. They build a nest and return to it every year to hatch their fledglings. Not this spring. No place for them to nest. No creeks to hunt for fish."

"Why did Fin's mother sign the contract?"

He raised an eyebrow.

Oh. Because she needed the money.

He gazed out over the hillside. "Sometimes, you just have to see it for yourself to truly understand it." He stood and offered her a hand to help her up. "We'd best keep going. It'll be dark soon."

She gave the hillside of sawed-off stumps one more long look. It did look worn out, beaten down, scalded. Exhausted.

As ANGIE COOPER reached home, she saw her paw over by the open barn door and waved. He beckoned her over, so she veered through the cow yard to see what he wanted.

"Where y' been, daughter?"

"Over at Miss Mollie's," she said, adding quickly, "helping out." Her paw was always pleased when she did a good turn for others.

"I saw Miss Cora in town. She said Miss Norah's been getting sick too much."

"Finley James sez she's mooning after the postman. He sez she's always ailing after he comes through."

Paw frowned. "Fin needs to respect his teacher and not go shootin' off his mouth."

Angie's father, Arthur Cooper, was a kind and fair man, highly regarded by all, and a stickler for respecting one's elders. "Miss Cora sez she's gonna have one more talk with Miss Norah, a warning talk, 'bout not missing any more days of teaching school. But she also said she thinks I need to start looking around for another teacher."

"I can teach Little Brushy. I can read better than any teacher we've ever had. I'm faster and better at sums too."

"Daughter, I knowed that and you knowed that and Miss Cora knowed that . . . but you got to git through your grade 8 exams before you can teach. That's jest the way it is."

"Miss Cora's in charge of every school in Rowan County. She could make a new rule."

"The law is the law. Time to stop yammerin' on 'bout it."

"Then who's she gonna git?"

He closed the barn door. "If needed to, she sez her cousin could fill in."

Angie's eyes went wide. "Miss Lucy? She won't do, Paw. She jest won't do."

"Why's that?"

"For one thing, you cain't hardly understand a word she sez. Sounds like a foreigner. All clipped and proper and fussy."

"She might holp fix yor grammar."

"Don't need no fixin'." Angie frowned. "Miss Lucy's nigh on scared to death o' most everything. Like that little bit of thunder today. You shoulda seen on her on top of Jenny, clutching the horn like that ol' pony was a bucking bronco."

Paw's eyes danced with amusement. "My oh my, she does sound dreadful." He cocked his head. "What was she doin' all the way up here?"

"Fin's been taking her into the hollers to do letter writing for folks. But see, Paw, I can do that too. I understand our people. She don't." She crossed her arms against her chest. "She's a highfalutin fancy pants. Everybody who meets her will agree t' that." Angie looked down at the tops of her two bare feet. At her dirty toes. The grandly lady's boots were so shiny you could use them as a mirror.

"Seems like a green-eyed monster is shapin' your opinion of Miss Lucy. Any chance Fin be smitten by Miss Cora's cousin?"

Angie snapped her head up with a scowl. She didn't take kindly to any teasing about her feelings for Finley James, even from her paw. Those feelings ran deep to her bones.

"We're hoping Miss Norah will stay put, but if not, then Miss Cora's hoping to have her cousin stay with us."

Angie snapped her jaw shut and marched toward the house. She knew what *that* meant. She would have to not jest share her special loft—her only private place in this whole world—but she would have to share her bed with the city lady. No, no, no. She was fond of Miss Cora, and grateful for all she'd done for her, but there were some things a girl had to put her foot down on.

"Angie!"

She stopped and turned toward her father.

"If Miss Lucy does come to teach at Little Brushy, she *will* stay here. That school needs a good steady teacher. You do too. I know you think yor smarter than anybody else, but you still got plenty to learn 'bout life."

She started to stride toward the house.

"Angel Eleanor Cooper!"

She stopped abruptly, but this time she didn't turn back.

"Yor to keep this conversation jest between us. Is that understood?"

She gave a brief nod, then made her way to the house. There was a tone in Paw's voice that even Angie, his favorite and only daughter, knew not to cross.

TWELVE

YESTERDAY'S RIDE TO MISS MOLLIE'S left Lucy distressed. Or maybe it was seeing that exhausted land that made her feel worn out, unsettled. Or maybe it was knowing she had to head to Lexington for her sister's grave marker service on Saturday. Or maybe it the way Judge Klopp's wife wrinkled her nose when she arrived back at Miss Maude's—asking if she'd been rolling in the mud with hogs.

Then again, it might have been the sheriff's dismissive remarks at breakfast this morning. The sheriff of Rowan County was a jowly cheeked man, triple-chinned, round-bellied, short and stout. Every once in a while, he'd drop by Miss Maude's for coffee and stay for breakfast. Today, the judge's wife pointed out that Lucy was kin to Cora.

The sheriff gave Lucy a frowning, narrow-eyed look. "I know Cora Wilson Stewart all right." He held out a cup for Miss Maude to fill with coffee. "So long as Mrs. Stewart minds her place, doesn't stir things up, we get along jest fine."

"Stir things up?" Lucy said. "How so?"

"Well," he said, drawing out the word to sound like *whale*. "That Mrs. Stewart, she's always wanting things to change."

"The judge had a saying about the Orient," Mrs. Klopp said. "You can't hurry the East."

The sheriff laughed and his belly jiggled like a bowl of gelatin. "Ain't that the truth? And you cain't hurry Rowan County, neither."

Mrs. Klopp and the sheriff smiled and nodded at each other, as if they had a much better understanding of the county than anyone else. Especially Cora.

Their condescending attitude unnerved Lucy. It shook her a little and she didn't know what to make of it. By the time she reached Cora's office, she felt even more out of sorts. Flustered and anxious.

And then came Cora's odd reaction when Lucy told her that Andrew Spencer had invited her to the dance on Saturday night. Cora's left eyebrow had lifted halfway to the heavens. What was *that*? "Well, I can't go, anyway." She told her about the graveside ceremony that Hazel had planned. It was the first chance she'd had to tell her.

Cora was genuinely sorry to not be going with her. "Oh Lucy, dear girl. I should be with you. If only I could. I'm giving a talk on Saturday to the Daughters of the American Revolution. That's what I'm putting my finishing touches on now."

"It's fine," Lucy said. "I'm fine." But she wasn't. Not really. She was thoroughly dreading Saturday. They each went back to their tasks at hand, though Lucy had trouble concentrating. Finally, she looked up. "Cora, why the look of warning when I told you about Saturday's dance?"

"Men are complicated creatures. Often spurious."

"All men? Or Andrew Spencer, in particular?"

"All men. But . . . a man like Andrew Spencer has the looks and charisma that can hide flaws. Like soft spots on a seemingly perfect apple. You don't realize they're there until you bite into them." She set down her quill to rub her forehead. "Don't mind me. I've a nagging headache today. I can sound a bit bitter when it comes to the toll that love and romance gone awry can take on a woman. I've come to accept that the roles of wife and mother were not to be my lot. Instead, I've come to believe that God has called me for service to others. I'm a public servant. It replaces any personal need." She lifted one finger in the air. "That's not entirely true. My work has become my only true love. It's faithful, too, something I can count on, unlike most men."

"But don't you get lonely?"

"There's a difference between loneliness and aloneness. I've grown accustomed to aloneness and find I rather like it." Cora leaned forward and pressed her palms against the top of her desk. "As I've told you before, Lucy, and as I hope you'll remember at the graveside service, you're stronger than you think."

Was she? She wasn't so sure. She wished she had Cora's confidence. Just being around her made Lucy feel sturdier, stronger. As Cora's chin tucked down to return to her speech, Lucy went to make some tea for the two of them. When she returned, she handed Cora a cup.

"She's not coming back, you know." Cora lifted her teacup with two hands, sipping thoughtfully. "Charlotte, I mean."

"I know."

"Lucy, I hope you won't mind if I speak frankly about your father. Even as a boy, he dished out blame rather freely . . . except when it came to himself. The truth of the matter is that he had no business leaving two little girls alone at a railroad station for hours on end while he carried on with his business. He shouldn't have let you shoulder this loss alone."

Lucy looked down, swirling the tea in her cup, watching it whirlpool. "Cora, I know Father can be . . . somewhat cold. You might not believe it, but he's never once said that he's blamed me for losing Charlotte."

"Dear girl, he didn't have to. You blamed yourself enough for the both of you. Nor did he stop you," she added with enough force that Lucy looked up, "from accepting full blame."

DURING HER LUNCH BREAK, Lucy went to find Andrew at the lumber office to tell him she couldn't go to the dance on Saturday night. "I need to return to Lexington for a family matter."

He seemed hugely disappointed. "Just when I find the girl of my dreams, she up and leaves me."

She smiled at his flair for the dramatic. "I'll just be gone for the day."

"Just for the day? Well then . . . why don't I go along with you?"

She blinked. "Would you?" She would love to have someone by her side at the graveside ceremony. And Andrew would distract Hazel, which would be an added bonus.

"As long as I wouldn't be interfering with a private family matter, it would be my pleasure."

She told him then about Charlotte, gone missing, and for the reason for the day's journey. It was easier the second time, she discovered, and Andrew offered just the right amount of sympathy. Different from Wyatt, who brought God into the story, and that only reminded Lucy of how God had refused to answer her prayers for Charlotte.

On the way back to Cora's office, she couldn't help herself from contrasting Andrew's lightheartedness with Brother Wyatt's solemnness. The two men were different in every way.

Unlike Andrew, Lucy had often observed Wyatt's restraint to speak up or tell jolly stories about his childhood. Instead, he always wanted to hear her story, her news, her concerns. He held his cards close to his vest, which, of course, made him intriguing. But his eyes were not filled with merriment and caprice, not like Andrew's. Though . . . they were kind eyes. Possibly the kindest eyes she'd ever known.

Saturday morning started out gray and drizzly, with a steady mist that caused Lucy's hair to go unruly and frizzy. Her spirits lifted when she arrived at the train and there was Andrew, holding a big bouquet of flowers. Just the sight of him made her hold her breath like a crush-stricken schoolgirl. And then her spirits took a nosedive when he told her that something had come up with work and he wasn't able to go with her to Lexington, after all. "I brought the flowers for your sister's grave."

She assured him that she understood, though she didn't, not really, and thanked him for the flowers. And then the train arrived and she hurried to board. Her eyes were stinging with tears and she didn't want him to see how disappointed she felt.

There was no reason to feel let down by Andrew, and yet she did. And later she forgot the bouquet of flowers on the train.

HAZEL MET LUCY AT THE LEXINGTON STATION, engulfing her in an enormous hug, with effusive apologies for Father's absence. "He had some important matters to attend to. You understand, don't you?"

"All too well." Hazel had just described Lucy's entire childhood.

"I told him you'd wouldn't mind," Hazel said. "And it's wonderful that you've come, that we're all together. It feels like an embarrassment of riches, doesn't it, Lucy? All of us together during this important time." She stopped suddenly. "Where's Andrew? Your father insisted that he accompany you."

Lucy tensed. So it was Father's idea, not Andrew's. "Something came up at the last moment."

Hazel frowned. "Oh, I am sorry. You shouldn't have to be alone during a time like this." She linked her arm through Lucy's. "Well, you certainly know all about a man and his ambition, don't you? It won't be a surprise to you."

Lucy wanted to ask Hazel why she assumed Andrew Spencer was her destiny, but what was the point? Hazel thought the ultimate goal for every woman was to find a husband, and then her life would have substance and meaning. There's a lid for every pot, she was fond of saying.

Lucy followed her to what she thought would be the horse and carriage, the very one in which Father had taken her to the station in March. In its place was a sleek automobile.

"Look! Isn't it divine? It's a Halladay Touring Car. Your father

went on a business trip to Streator, Illinois, and brought this home
. . . just to surprise me! Isn't he the sweetest? He'd had it all planned
out. I'm just now learning how to drive it. I'm not terribly good
at it yet, and you know how bumpy our roads are, so say a prayer
and hold on tight!"

The shiny black automobile had a fabric roof, a deep and wide
windshield, and leather interior—front seats and back. No windows, so Hazel wrapped her perfectly coiffed hair in a scarf. "It's
a four-cylinder," she called out happily over the roar of the engine.
"Whatever that means."

Hazel kept up a steady chatter on the entire bone-jarring, teeth-
rattling ride home, honking as she went to warn people and children and dogs to move out of her path. Lucy gripped the sides of
the seat, a terrified passenger. Whenever there was an empty stretch
on the road so Lucy could catch her breath and relax, slightly, she
studied Hazel, and to her surprise, she felt the stirring of admiration. Hazel floated along through life on the top of a river, safely
on the surface, blissfully unaware of the murky waters below. It
wasn't such a bad way to approach life.

Lucy had trailed two years behind Hazel at the Townsend School
for Girls, a highly regarded finishing school in Louisville known for
churning out young women prepared to take their role in society,
with all the required social graces. The ultimate goal was to find
suitable husbands.

Throughout their years together at boarding school, up until the
last two years, Hazel never took notice of Lucy. She was everything
Lucy was not: popular and pretty, extroverted and enthusiastic.
During Hazel's final year, she was in danger of not graduating
because she was failing a class in English Composition, and Lucy,
who was passionately devoted to proper English, was asked by the
headmistress to tutor Hazel. For the first time, Hazel noticed Lucy.
And during a subsequent Parents' Weekend, she noticed Lucy's
father . . . who noticed Hazel right back.

Hazel graduated from the Townsend School for Girls, prepared to return to her parents' home in Lexington and make her grand entrance into upper-class society. By the time Lucy had graduated and returned home to live, her father and Hazel were engaged to marry.

Their winter-spring romance thoroughly baffled Lucy. Father, while not unattractive, was forty, staid, and stoic. It seemed he was born old. Hazel, beautiful and lively, flitted about like a hummingbird. At first, Lucy thought Hazel was attracted to Father's bank account, which struck her as ironic because he could be a tightfisted spendthrift. But time proved her wrong. Hazel seemed truly head over heels in love with Father, and he acted like a smitten schoolboy. Their romance was genuine, charming . . . and a bit stomach turning for Lucy to be around for too long.

The car swerved sharply to avoid hitting a dog, jolting Lucy back to the present.

"Oh dear. Sorry!" Hazel glanced at her. "Everything all right?"

"Hmm?" She tried to remember what Hazel was talking about.

"Your new life. The new and improved Lucille Wilson. Is everything all right?"

"Fine, just fine."

Hazel let out a deep breath of relief. "Wonderful! Just wonderful. Your father and I had so hoped you'd find happiness."

Suddenly they pulled up at the house, and a wave of nostalgia washed over her.

She was home.

THIRTEEN

LUCY HAD BEEN GONE only a little over a month, yet it felt like years. Already, she no longer belonged in the life she'd left behind.

She took a moment when she was alone to go into Charlotte's room. It was the last time it would ever look this way. Already, change was afoot. Swatches of wallpaper were tacked to the wall and fabric bolts were on the bed, as if Hazel had been interrupted in the middle of making decisions. She noticed the stuffed bear Charlotte had loved to play with, Mr. Buttons, the one she had left behind on Father's coat when she wandered off. A memory of her sister, in this very room, floated through Lucy's mind like a motion picture. Charlotte was sitting on the floor with this bear in her lap, the sun streaming through the window and onto her curly blonde hair. She seemed nearly . . . angelic. No wonder Father didn't want anything changed. It was a way to keep the memories alive.

As Lucy bent down to pick up Mr. Buttons from the shelf, the door opened.

"We should go to the cemetery," Father said in a tight voice. "Hazel is waiting." He looked strange, as if he was trying to hold back tears.

Lucy hugged the bear tightly against her chest. "Father, I'm so . . . terribly, terribly sorry . . . I lost Charlotte."

There was a moment of such profound silence that Lucy felt like the world had stopped. Father was probably deciding how to respond. Then, finally, he opened his arms, and she entered them.

AT THE CEMETERY, a small gathering huddled around Charlotte's tiny grave. The Reverend William Blythe officiated. He read Psalm 23, then said a few words. More than a few words. He went on so long, in his wheezing, wandering way, that Lucy's thoughts drifted off. She wondered what her father was thinking but couldn't tell by looking at him. Then again, his expressions had always been inscrutable. Hazel stood beside him, tears flowing down her cheeks in great sympathy.

Lucy knew this was a symbolic gesture of closure, but it still felt strange to stand in front of a gravestone that marked an empty grave. More than strange. She hated being here, hated admitting that Charlotte was dead. Because, from this moment forward, she *would* be dead to them. All hope was gone.

It was so hard to accept such finality.

Lifting her head, Lucy took in a deep breath. A man had arrived, standing under a tree at a polite distance. Lucy squinted, aware that he seemed familiar. *Mercy be blessed.* Brother Wyatt! Wyatt, with his chiseled features and his quiet strength. She couldn't believe the feeling that overcame her. When he saw she had spotted him, he gave her the eyebrows. Lifted them a few times, a wordless hello.

She ducked her head so no one could see she was smiling.

LATER, AS THEY WAITED at the station for the afternoon train returning to Morehead, Lucy looked at Wyatt, in his neatly pressed suit coat. "But you never said anything about coming."

"It came up rather suddenly." He cleared his throat, shifting his stance. "I hope you don't mind that I showed up unannounced."

"No. I don't mind at all. I wish I could change your mind and encourage you to stay over. You're more than welcome at the house."

"Gotta get back. Singing school tomorrow afternoon."

"Oh, I forgot. I'm sorry to miss it." To her surprise, she truly was sorry not to be there for it. But she wanted to stay the night in Lexington, hoping for a private moment to talk to her father about Valley View Lumber's contracts. The whistle of the approaching train broke her thoughts.

As other passengers started moving toward the platform, Wyatt didn't budge. He held out a hand to say goodbye and she took it. "So, did it help? The ceremony?"

She looked down to see their fingers intertwined, her hand slender and small in its white glove, his large and brown. A workingman's hand. "Candidly, no. To think of an empty grave . . . it just seemed . . . like utter foolishness."

"She's not really there."

"Exactly." And then, "Wait. How do you mean?"

"Empty graves . . . are exactly why the Lord Jesus went to the cross and rose again. To offer each one of us a chance for an empty grave." He tilted his head. "'Whither shall I go from thy spirit? or whither shall I flee from thy presence? If I ascend up into heaven, thou art there: if I make my bed in hell, behold, thou art there. If I take the wings of the morning, and dwell in the uttermost parts of the sea; Even there shall thy hand lead me, and thy right hand shall hold me.'" He looked Lucy straight in the eyes. "Wherever your sister Charlotte may be, she is not alone. She's never been alone. The Lord is with her." He grinned. "Amen. Sermon over."

And just like that, the burden lifted, the heavy stone that had settled on Lucy's chest since Charlotte had gone missing. Where had it gone? She stared at him, frozen in place, until a man waiting behind them cleared his throat. Wyatt dropped her hand like a hot potato, as if he just now realized he'd never released it, and turned to climb up the steps to the train.

The train whistle blew and she watched the train get underway, at first slowly, then with gathering speed. She stood beside the train tracks until the train disappeared from view and the little white wisps of smoke from its engine vanished.

In the end, this day was what she had needed to finally let go of her guilt and remorse and sorrow over Charlotte: coming home again, the grave marker, the comforting words from Wyatt. Her body felt light, nearly buoyant, as she walked back to the waiting carriage.

AFTER A LIGHT SUPPER, Lucy went into the drawing room to sit by the fire, hoping Father might join her. There'd been precious little time alone with him today, as Hazel was ever present and quite talkative. Lucy couldn't stop thinking about Finley James's quick defense for the loblolly trees, or that exhausted land Brother Wyatt showed her, nor that look of discouragement in Sally Ann Duncan's delicate face, or the despair in Barbara Jean Boling's eyes.

Against the far wall of the drawing room, Lucy noticed a new wooden cabinet. When she crossed the room to study it, she noticed the cabinet's edges were trimmed in gold, and inside was a Victrola phonograph. A recent purchase of Hazel's, no doubt.

After just one full day back at home in Lexington, Lucy felt discomfited, as if she were wearing a dress two sizes too small. Almost shamed from the life of comfort—of luxury, of excess— she had lived, knowing much of it came at the expense of those in the mountains.

By the fireplace were her parents' sitting spots. Father's chair was big and overstuffed. Mother's low and snug, with a high back. Lucy wondered how long before Hazel had these two chairs replaced. Or the Oriental rugs, the velvet draperies.

She sat in Mother's chair and watched the licking flames, tired from the long day. Just when she was about to give up on her father, the door opened and in he came, book in hand. "I thought you'd retired for the night. Aren't you exhausted?"

"No, not really." She pointed to his chair. "Please come and join me. I'd like to talk to you."

He settled into the chair and watched the fire. "So, how's it going up there? Ready to return to civilization for good?"

Where to begin? There was no point in trying to tell her father what life was really like up in the mountains—the hardship, the poverty—because he knew. He would try to explain it all in a voice that suggested this was simply how it was.

What he didn't seem to want to acknowledge was the stark beauty of the mountain peoples' life—the fierce loyalty to each other, the reverence of holding on to beloved traditions from the old country.

"Actually, I've been learning quite a bit about the lumber up in Rowan County. The loblollies, in particular."

Now *that* pleased him. "The end of logging virgin timber in Rowan County devastated the county. They depended heavily on logging. Other counties have coal, but not Rowan County. All it has are those trees. By harvesting the loblollies, we've been able to bring relief back to the county." He opened his book and started to read.

"Yes . . . but, Father, I've discovered discrepancies . . ." Her voice stuck. This was harder than she thought it would be. "It seems"—she cleared her throat—"Valley View Lumber might have an unfair advantage over the mountain people."

"Unfair advantage?" he said in a calm voice, though she could sense his defensive reaction from the narrowing of his eyes.

"By altering the landscape. Diverting creeks away from farms to create holding pens. Those families depend on the water."

He scoffed. "Blame the drought for that. Valley View Lumber can't be held responsible for the weather. After the trees have been

harvested, the woodsmen will remove the dams to open the ponds."
He waved a hand in the air, reminding her of Andrew's similar attitude. "The rains will return. The creeks will start flowing. Land
is very forgiving."

"It's not just the ponds. What about the roads you've put in?
They crisscross peoples' fields. Fields needed for farming."

He abandoned his book to stare at her. "Lucy, those roads could
be—should be—seen as a gift."

"How so?"

"The world could open up to them with those roads. Instead,
they choose to remain hidden in those forsaken hollers." He slapped
his book on the table. "Business goes up into those hills to bring
jobs and opportunities. It's never the other way around. Those
hillbillies refuse to join the rest of the world."

"They can't read or write. They didn't know what they were
signing their X to. Father, don't you see? They don't understand
what they're signing."

"It's all perfectly legal. No one forced their hand on the quill.
We've done nothing wrong."

"Nor nothing right. It's like they're getting tricked." As soon
as the words left her mouth, she wished them back. Too accusing,
too insulting. The air in the room seemed to vibrate.

He rose to his feet, glaring at her. "That's a despicable thing to
say. You've been there what—just a month or so? And you think
you know everything about those mountain people? You don't."

There was no backing out of this now. "I'm trying to make you
see that people suffered at what your company has done. You've
taken resources out and left nothing in return. These are families.
Fathers and mothers and children."

"Suffered? Because of my company?" He thumped his chest
with his fist once, then twice. "My company?! I'll tell you what
has caused suffering. Isolation! It's proved disastrous for those
people. It's kept them poor and ignorant. Even the Indians used
to call it a dark and bloody ground."

"There's another side that you refuse to see." Lucy remained seated and tried to keep her voice as calm as possible, though her heart was pounding. She had never challenged her father before. "That same isolation has created rich pockets of culture. Isolation has meant they're forced to rely on each other for survival and for entertainment too. I think nearly everyone I've met, young or old, can sing or dance or play an instrument."

"Clogging to fiddle music," her father said stonily. "Some wouldn't consider that to be entertainment."

"Perhaps not in Lexington, but it's beautiful music. Songs that tell stories. Father, what I'm trying to say is that the land has shaped the people and the people have shaped the land. You can't separate the two. Lumber companies have taken advantage of innocent families and stolen livelihoods, all for the sake of a profit."

"Spare me the dramatics, Lucille," her father said. "What you call 'profit' is what I call progress. Valley View has created jobs and opportunities for more people than the few left in those decrepit hollers. The lumber has built houses and shops and courthouses. And schoolhouses. It's the way of the future. You can't hang on to the past."

"But surely you can see what happens when bright young children get a chance. Children like you, and Cora."

"Exactly. I know what those hills are like. I went to those schools. The only way you can tell who's the teacher and who's the student is that the teacher has shoes on. Those school trustees will hire whoever they like or know. Nothing to do with qualifications. And I'll wager that hasn't changed, even under Cora's watch."

"She's trying, though. She's creating interest and enthusiasm, and she's bringing the schools up to a higher standard. You should see the correspondence she gets from other teachers and principals, from all over Kentucky, asking her for advice about improving schools." Lucy folded her hands in her lap. "Father, please sit down."

Slowly, he lowered himself into his chair.

"You make your upbringing sound quite severe. Cora has an entirely different view."

"Oh really? Well, both of our parents had the wisdom to get us out of the hill country during the Rowan County War. There's no way to help those people, Lucy. They're too isolated. Their thinking gets isolated. They resist progress. They prefer to hang on to violent feuds and old ways."

"It's also their home. Their land. Valley View Lumber has a responsibility to be fair and reasonable."

"If Valley View is so despicable in your eyes, then why don't you read through all the contracts? Isn't that why you're there? To be Cora's personal assistant?"

"I never said despicable. I said that these people don't know what they're signing their names to."

"Their *X*, you mean." He crossed his hand in the air in an exaggerated gesture. "And I suppose you're accusing my sales agent of intentionally wronging them."

This was not going well. She had never assumed that Andrew Spencer was to blame. But wasn't he? "I . . . I'm not accusing anyone."

"Well, if you're going to judge, don't forget Cora. She isn't blameless here."

"Cora?"

"She's the county superintendent. It's her job to educate these people."

"To educate the *children*. Her campaign slogan to become superintendent was 'the children's friend.' And she's doing all she can to see that every child is in school."

He closed his eyes tiredly, inhaled deeply, and when his eyes opened she could see his fight was gone. "See here, it's been a long day. A hard day. I don't want to end it on a sour note. If you know of young men who are willing to live in the city to work at the lumberyard, then I'll give them jobs." He pointed a finger at her. "Assuming they're able workers."

Lucy barely held back from an eye roll. As if they weren't able workers! Why, she'd never seen men and women work so hard to scrape out a living.

Her father rose and went to the door, then paused to turn back. "You never used to be truculent, Lucy. Cora's influence, no doubt. This was a bad idea."

Interesting word choice, Lucy mulled, as she heard her father's footfalls down the hall. *Truculent* originated out of the Latin word *trux*, meaning "fierce."

She felt fierce. It infuriated Lucy that her father's answer to educate the mountain people was to leave the mountain. To leave their home, their families, the very place that made them who they were.

Lucy sat back in her mother's chair. A little smile tugged at her lips. Today she'd had a brutally honest conversation with her father and also shared a raw moment in Charlotte's room—the most vulnerable they'd ever been with each other. She would never have imagined someone, especially her father, calling her truculent. Other labels given to her by teachers came to mind: meek, mild, passive, compliant, deferential, docile. But truculent? Never!

She rather liked it.

FOURTEEN

FIRST THING ON MONDAY MORNING, Lucy told Cora everything about the weekend, including the uncomfortable conversation with her father. He'd been cool and distant when she said goodbye at the train station the next day. Still, she didn't regret bringing the topic of those dishonorable lumber contracts to his attention.

"Tell me what he said again?"

"He said that you're partly to blame. That it's your job to educate these people."

Cora frowned. "He can't expect me to wave a magic wand so that everyone is suddenly able to read. It will take a generation to change that." She stood and walked toward the window.

"What bothers me most is the way Father lumps mountain people together, as if they're all dumb and lazy and deserve what they get."

Cora turned to Lucy. "Don't be too hard on your father. He's a tough businessman, but he's not a dishonest one. And as much as he tries to hide it, he has a soft heart."

"Does he? I'm not always so sure."

"Trust me on that. I think your conversation with him will nettle him. Good will come out of it. Eventually." She sat down at her desk. "So Wyatt came to the cemetery during the service for Charlotte?"

"How did you hear that?"

"I was able to attend the singing school yesterday afternoon. He told me he'd been in Lexington."

"Yes, but he didn't say why, only that he had a meeting." She hoped Cora might elaborate, but she volunteered nothing more. Lucy felt again that nagging suspicion that Wyatt had come to Lexington only because he was concerned about her. Pity was not what she wanted from him. Not from anyone.

Cora studied her for a moment, then said, "Wyatt is a fine man. None finer, in my opinion." She said it with the emphasis on *fine*, as if comparing him to someone else.

Lucy knew little of Cora's ex-husbands, but she did know that the first one was an alcoholic, and the second one—whom Cora remarried and divorced again the following month—was abusive.

"Five, six years ago, when I returned to Rowan County, I was at a school function, and a tall mountain lad stepped up to sing one of the most beautiful pieces of mountain music I've ever heard. It was astonishing. His deep voice, the lyrical words. Afterward, I went up to the young man and asked for a copy of the song. I told him it was worth publishing. He said he'd had hundreds of such songs, all in his head, but was unable to write down a single one because he could neither write nor read."

"How old was he? Why hadn't he gone to school?"

"He was probably about Finley James's age. Fifteen or sixteen. And his story was not unique, Lucy. Getting to school just wasn't possible for a boy needed on the farm." She leaned back in her chair. "So I found a sponsor to provide schooling for him at a boarding school in Louisville. One in which music was encouraged."

Puzzle pieces started floating into place. Lucy's eyes went wide. *Oh my stars and garters.* "Brother Wyatt?"

Cora nodded. "And the sponsor, Lucy, was your own father."

AT THE LIVERY, Fin gave a carrot to Sheila, who nickered with pleasure. He saw Miss Cora and Miss Lucy walk past, with hardly a notice of him other than asking why he weren't in school. Miss Norah had gone ailing again, he explained, so Little Brushy School was shut down and Fin was jest fine with that. Though it did pain his heart some that Miss Lucy did not linger at the livery but hurried after Miss Cora along to the meeting. Women.

Fin hadn't seen Angie Cooper for days and days. That suited him jest fine. But then, he did wonder where she was keeping herself. Most likely, she was up at Little Brushy right now, standing at the chalkboard, trying to jam knowledge into them poor little uns who couldn't read the No School Today sign.

Not having school suited Fin jest fine, too, especially because he could work at the livery for Arthur Cooper, who needed to get his crops planted after last week's rain. Fin settled down against the building, on its shady side, scratched his back against the wooden building, folded his hands behind his head and closed his eyes, drifting off.

"Son, don't you want to do something with yourself?" A jab poked him in the side.

Fin startled awake, blinking, then jumped to his feet. "Hello, Mrs. Klopp." Miss Cora might scare him, but Mrs. Klopp terrified him. She had a way of pinning a man to the wall with her piercing stare. He rubbed his side where she'd poked him with her cane. "Somethin' I can do for you?"

"Yes. You can join the United States Army."

"Huh? We gone to war?" How long had he been asleep?

"You're going to waste away up in those hills, live a life that amounts to nothing. Just like everybody else up there."

Fin stiffened.

"The only option for a mountain boy like you is to join the military." Then she started reading from a brochure and showed him the uniform he could wear, boots included. Dapper, she called them. And then she pointed out the big rifle he'd be carrying, and the fine horse he'd be given. By the end of Mrs. Klopp's recruitment lecture, Fin was giving some serious thinking to joining the army. He wondered what Miss Lucy might think about *that*.

Would she miss him? Pine for him? Beg him not to go? He smiled, thinking she shorely would.

THE LAST WEEK OF APRIL brought nothing but fast-moving storms. Gully washers, to quote Fin. Today was a rainy morning, a tranquil moment in Cora's office. Lucy was organizing files while Cora worked at her desk. These quiet moments, working side by side, were Lucy's favorites. Teatime was even better. Lucy would serve tea and the two would sit and talk about all kinds of things. Important things, mundane things.

Those were the times when she could ask Cora questions about the peculiar traditions of the mountain people she kept encountering. "I've noticed that some beliefs are a strange mixture of superstitions and religion. Finley James got a fishing hook caught in his hand the other day and had me clean out the wound with moonshine. But then he was in a fit because I threw out the fishhook and he couldn't find it. He said he had to stick the hook in a piece of wood three times, one each for the Trinity, so the wound wouldn't fester."

"He's half right. The moonshine disinfects the wound." Cora sighed. "Frankly, Lucy, I don't even bother to try and dissuade the people from their superstitions. Most are harmless. I suppose . . . they provide comfort. Even entertainment."

"I thought that was what their music was for."

"Yes, true. Their lives are woven into music."

Cora polished off the rest of her tea and set the cup on her desk. Lucy knew enough to bring a pot of tea now, to prolong their teatimes. She refilled Cora's cup quickly. "And stories. Everybody in Rowan County seems to have a story. At least half of my visits end up as story-listening." Lucy breathed in the earthy scent of the tea. "Are they all true?" She never could tell.

Cora smiled, peering over her teacup. "My father used to say, 'Some folks can spin quite a yarn out of a little piece of thread.'"

A laugh burst out of Lucy. "Finley James! You just described him."

Cora rose and looked out the window at the livery. "Now there's a prime example of a boy who's smart as a whip but hasn't had near enough schooling. I fear the time is coming when it will be too late for him. He's already chafing at the bit to stay out of school and I barely got him into it."

"Sometimes I think it's unfortunate that you can't chase down all those illiterate adults in the hills and get them into school alongside their children."

Cora turned, her eyebrows lifted in surprise. "The accepted wisdom of the day claims that there's a window, as children, for the mind to acquire language. When the window is shut, that opportunity is lost." She sat down in her chair and picked up her pencil, signaling the end of teatime.

As Lucy picked up Cora's teacup, she said, "Cora, do you believe that?"

"I'm not sure." Cora leaned back in her chair. "I have to admit that in all my years in education, I've never known an adult to learn to read. Not a single one."

"I suppose the parents would be too proud to go to school alongside their children."

"Too proud, too busy, too old," Cora said in a vague and distracted tone. "Too everything."

LATER THAT AFTERNOON, a gentle knock came on the door to Cora's office. Peeping through the crack in the door was Mollie McGlothin, clutching a paper poke.

"Miss Mollie!" Cora jumped up from her desk to greet the old woman. "Come in, come in. What brings you down the mountain on a day like today?"

"Came down with Brother Wyatt on a jolt wagon. He's practicin' his preaching at the church on Sunday. Fillin' in for the preacher." Miss Mollie settled into Lucy's chair and fished through her poke. "I come down the hill cuz I got me a letter to post." She had a pleased look on her face, like a cat that just caught a mouse. "Wanted you to read it first." She held the unsealed envelope out to Cora.

Cora unfolded a paper and silently read it, then handed it to Lucy.

Deer Daughter,
　　This be my furst lettur. I pray it will not be my last.

　　　　　　　Luv, Maw

After reading, Lucy looked up. Cora's eyes were fixed on Mollie. "Who wrote this for you?"

"Me, m'self, and I." Miss Mollie smiled her big toothless smile. "I lurned m'self."

Cora and Lucy exchanged a look of astonishment. "But how?"

"I'd always figured that it was too late for me. Y' know . . . y' cain't teach an old dawg new tricks. But then I thought some more on that. My papaw Angus had an old dawg once, and that dawg kept on learning new tricks, right up to the day he died. So I got thinking that mebbe I could be like that old dawg o' Papaw's. Mebbe I could try."

Lucy glanced at Cora. Her eyes, she noticed, were shiny.

"So I asked Angie Cooper for help, and she brung me a book of letters. Jest a little children's book. I worked on them letters, worked and worked on them. At first they jest seemed like scribbles to me. Angie helped me figure out the sounds them scribbles

164

made. Lo and behold, one day them scribbles started to make sense." She couldn't stop smiling. "I cain't stop m'self now. I'm reading everythin' I git my hands on. Labels on jars. Ol' magazines. I found a newspaper stuffed in between some logs used for chinking. Dated 1891, if ya can believe that. Did ya know that the first basketball game was invented then? And they used peach baskets for hoops." She chuckled. "I have a great-grandson who loves to play basketball. I'm gonna send him that torn piece o' newspaper." She grinned. "That'll be m' next letter to write."

One tear, then another, started to trickle down Cora's cheeks.

Miss Mollie watched her, concerned. "I know it's a mite gaumish. That quill pen is hard to hold. And I know my letters are shaky. I redid it three times, but then the inkpot went dry."

With that, Cora's tears started streaming. Lucy handed her a handkerchief and she mopped up her face.

Distressed, Miss Mollie said, "Aw, no. I didn't mean to make ya weepy, Cora. And here I thought you'd be proud o' me."

"Oh, Miss Mollie. These are happy tears. I am proud of you. So proud." She mopped her face once more. "And you have taught me something today. Something powerful. You're never too old to learn."

Miss Mollie laughed, sounding more like a cackle. "I'd best be on m' way." She picked up her poke handles and, with Lucy's help, eased out of the chair. "Gotta go post that letter."

Lucy handed her the envelope to tuck in the poke. "I guess this means I'm out of a job as your scribe."

"Mebbe so," Miss Mollie said. She stopped at the door and turned back.

"Miss Mollie," Cora said, "your daughter should frame that first letter of yours."

Miss Mollie shook her head. "No need." Her eyes twinkled. "But I do look forward to hearin' back from her." As she opened the door, Lucy heard her repeat to herself, "Oh yes I do. I do, indeed."

Arms crossed, Cora went to the window, deep in thought. Lucy went back to where she'd left off with the filing. She set a file on Cora's desk and noticed she was still staring out the window. She came up behind Cora to peer over her shoulder. Miss Mollie was slowly making her way down the road.

"Amazing, isn't it?" Lucy said. "A woman of her age, teaching herself to read."

"It's more than amazing," Cora said. "Your father . . . he was right in what he told you. Absolutely right. I've made a terrible blunder."

"How so?"

"Just like everyone else, I've accepted the thinking of academics. What do they know? Heavens, they live far away in their ivory towers. Mollie has just proved that theory wrong." She clapped her hands, like a thunderbolt just hit her, and her eyes grew animated. "Lucy . . . we are going to prove everyone wrong." She grabbed her shoulders and gave them a squeeze. "We are going to set them free."

"What do you mean?"

"*What* do I mean?" Cora sat at her desk and reached for a pad of paper and a pencil stub. "What do I *mean*? We are going to teach illiterate adults how to read."

"How do you propose such a thing?"

Cora answered her as she kept writing, not even lifting her head. "They'll come to the schoolhouse by night."

"Night school?"

Cora finished scribbling and slapped her pencil down. "By the light of the moon. So they can find their way."

Lucy had experienced a bit of how dark those hills could be. Even on a cloudless day, the thick trees blotted out the sun and left her in a stygian inkiness. Imagine what a moonless night would be like. The very thought made her shiver.

Cora's thoughts were running on an entirely different track. "How could I not have thought of this long ago?" She looked up.

"I need Brother Wyatt here, right away. He's over at the Disciples of Christ Church. We don't have a moment to waste."

Lucy reached for her sweater. She'd been around Cora long enough to know that she'd just been issued a fetching order.

LUCY HEARD WYATT IN THE CHURCH before she found him. She paused at the open door that led to the sanctuary, recalling Miss Mollie had said he was practicing a sermon, so she stepped back to wait in the narthex and leaned her against the wall, listening.

"Jesus said to seek and we will find." Wyatt's rafter-raising baritone voice resonated through the empty church. "We usually find what we seek."

Was that true? Lucy wasn't so sure. Some things just couldn't be found, no matter how hard you tried. Some people just couldn't be found. But she did enjoy the sound of Wyatt's fine deep voice. He had a way of stretching her thinking, to dare her to believe there might be more purpose in this world, in her life, than she thought possible. Her eyes slid shut as she listened to him finish his sermon. She wished she could believe, the way Brother Wyatt did, and Cora did. Life seemed easier for them. Not so much in their circumstances, as she knew Cora had weathered some hardships and she suspected the same of Wyatt, but in how they handled those difficulties. That's what seemed easier.

"Lucy?"

Her eyes opened and there was Wyatt, peering down at her.

"Is something wrong?" he asked gently.

"I'm . . . I was . . . just listening . . ." She stammered away, blushing profusely. "Cora sent me to fetch you." She stumbled to explain Cora's idea but did a poor job of it. She didn't really understand it herself. "She'll have to tell you more. All I know is that she wants you in her office, lickety-split."

Wyatt gave her another odd look. "Did you just say lickety-split?"

"Did I? I meant, right away." She shook that phrase right out of her head. "Cora's got me all tangled up. Miss Mollie came to the office to show us she has taught herself to write, which is remarkable, and after she left, Cora started scribbling and tossing out ideas and said she needed you right away. It was like a tornado swept into the office."

"I've been caught in that tornado before." He grinned, holding the church door open. "She's never happier than when she's facing an insurmountable challenge."

Moments later, Cora beckoned him at the door of her office. "Hurry! What's taken so long? Wyatt, sit down. Sit! Lucy and I have the most remarkable plan. And we need you too."

He gave Lucy a curious glance, but she only lifted her shoulders in a shrug.

Cora didn't notice their silent exchange as she plopped down in her chair and slapped her palms on the desktop. "We are going to open the schoolhouses on moonlit nights for adults to learn to read. All fifty-one schoolhouses will be opened. Each one."

Wyatt put his hand behind his neck and rubbed it, a gesture, Lucy thought, of confusion. "What makes you think they'd come?" From the tone in his voice, Lucy could tell he doubted they would.

"Because I think they want to learn to read and write. And I'm going to make it worth their while, with a swift literacy."

"A swift literacy," Wyatt repeated. "Cora, I don't mean to douse your enthusiasm, but let's be practical for a moment. Who is going to teach them?"

"My teachers, of course."

"Do you mean to say that you would ask your teachers to teach all day long, and then expect them to teach at night too? Do you have the budget to pay the teachers extra?"

Cora paused. "No," she said in a drawn-out way. A kink in the plan. "Leave the teachers to me." She bit her lower lip. "Besides . . . opening the schools on moonlit nights will only happen for a few weeks. Five or six, until the weather turns cold."

Wyatt crossed one leg over a knee. "Just when are you thinking these night schools will take place?"

Cora's eyes went to her paper pad. "I was thinking . . . after harvest and before the frosts set in, when the farmers and their wives have time to spare." She cast a furtive glance in Lucy's direction. "We're going to canvas the hills and find out exactly how many illiterate adults there are—"

Lucy's eyebrows shot up. She had grown accustomed to Cora's use of the word "we." She meant Lucy.

"—and how many would be willing to come to night school. Then, I think we'll all have a sense of how this could be . . . monumental." She finished writing down a few more notes, then set her pencil down and leaned back in her chair. "Wyatt, what are your thoughts? Go ahead. I'm listening."

His chin had been tucked down, almost as if he had been praying. He lifted his head and looked straight at Cora. "This might be the only chance for those men and women to read the Word of God for themselves." He glanced at Lucy. "If there's any way I can support you, then you can count on me."

Cora gave him a tender smile. "Thank you, Wyatt."

Then, as if rehearsed, both Cora and Wyatt turned to look at Lucy. She had the sense of being caught up in a purpose she only dimly understood.

"Of course . . . you can count on my support as well."

Studying Cora, Wyatt crossed his arms against his chest. "Many will think you're attempting the impossible."

"Fools rush in where angels fear to tread," Cora quoted with a laugh. She was beaming.

Brother Wyatt rose to his feet. "I'll be praying, Cora, that your dream for these . . . moonlit schools . . . will be blessed by the Lord for his purposes—beyond anything you could imagine."

"Moonlight Schools." Cora smiled. "I like the sound of that."

Fifteen

When Lucy arrived at Cora's office the next morning, her mind was on Andrew Spencer, who'd met her outside of Miss Maude's boarding house, holding a handful of bright yellow daffodils, waiting to walk her to work. It was something he'd started doing after she returned from Lexington, and Lucy enjoyed the habit. She looked forward to seeing Andy each morning and took extra care with her hair and clothing . . . because he noticed that kind of thing. Noticed and appreciated.

"I have an idea," Andy said as they neared Cora's office. "Let's you and me go on a picnic on Sunday afternoon. How about it?"

"Yes," she said, dismissing any thoughts of requiring a chaperone once and for all. "Yes, I'd like that." She glanced up and noticed the steeple of the Disciples of Christ Church. "Right after we attend the church service."

Andrew's smile faded. "Church?" He cleared his throat, and his smile returned. "Lucy Wilson, I do believe you're a good influence on me."

As he was on her. Lucy felt so happy when she was with him. Andy was lighthearted, affable, pleasant to be around. Even after she asked him if she could read future loblolly harvesting contracts aloud to any prospective property owners. He readily agreed, though none had been brought to her attention. Despite some reservation, she found she liked Andrew Spencer. Quite a bit.

After saying goodbye to Andy, Lucy found Cora at the big desk they shared, scribbling away on a thick pad of paper with a fevered pitch. She barely glanced up as Lucy greeted her with a cheery "Good morning."

Distracted, Cora mumbled a greeting.

Setting her things down at her chair, Lucy noticed Cora was wearing the same clothes she had on yesterday. She stilled. "Don't tell me you've been here all night!"

Cora paused, a surprised look on her face. "Is it morning?" She set her pencil down and stretched, straightening her arms and rolling her shoulders. "Oh Lucy . . . I think I've got it all worked out!"

"What?"

"What else? How to make Moonlight Schools work."

Uh oh. Lucy braced herself.

"Here's the plan. The *first* thing, the *very* first thing the teachers will work on is to teach the adults to write their own name. Symbolic, I think. Foundational." She clasped her hands together. "And they should not have to use children's readers. Far too demeaning. So we're going to create newspapers."

"Newspapers?"

"Yes! I'm going to call it . . . let's see, where did I put that?" Cora pushed some papers around on her desk until she found what she was looking for. "The *Rowan County Messenger*. It will be filled with news about the county."

"A newspaper?" Lucy repeated duly. "Cora, it's not easy to read a newspaper."

"Ours will be! Because it will be directly applicable to the lives of our adult students. Full of simple sentences, with everyday words they use. Words that mean something to them. Easy to memorize, easy to practice. It's called the whole-word approach—different than the way Mollie taught herself . . . going through letters sound by sound. What I want is for these illiterate adults to have a sense of success, right from the start. And to get them interested in the process of reading."

Lucy sat in the chair across from Cora, growing intrigued. "So, then, you're not trying to give them a complete education."

"No. No, though I thought about it. But I think that's an impossible goal."

Now *there* was a shock. Nothing ever seemed impossible to Cora. Lucy was relieved that she recognized some limits.

"The goal of the Moonlight Schools is to teach illiterates to read and write. And semi-literates too. There's plenty of those up in those mountains." She pointed to Lucy. "As soon you'll find out."

A sinking feeling began its familiar swirl in Lucy, dropping her stomach. What did Cora mean by that?

Cora picked up another paper and held it out to Lucy. "I've been doodling some ideas. Tell me what you think of that sketch. It's a pad to help with writing. My thought is that it would be made of wood, with the alphabet carved into the wood as grooves, so they can practice tracing their letters. They can *feel* them."

Lucy looked at the sketch. "It's quite an interesting idea. But . . . how many of these wooden pads would you need?"

"At least a few per schoolhouse."

"Who could make them?"

Cora winked, smiling. "Brother Wyatt. His carpentry skills are exemplar."

"But they're intricate. It will cost him to make these wooden pads. Time and money. He should be paid for his efforts." After all, he was so terribly poor.

She scoffed. "I have no budget. Not for this or anything else." She pushed a lock of hair behind her ear. "But it did dawn on me that Andrew Spencer has been receiving quite a bit from our community. I thought he might be willing to give back. Donate to the Moonlight Schools campaign." Her eyes were fastened on the daffodils in Lucy's hand.

"Oh no. You can't mean . . . you can't expect me to ask . . ."

"He won't turn you down, Lucy. He seems rather smitten with you."

Lucy sighed.

"Is that a sigh of ardor? Are you equally smitten with Mr. Spencer?"

Smitten? Lucy picked at a piece of thread on her skirt. "I'm not entirely sure what I feel for him."

"No? Well, time will tell." Cora lifted a finger in the air. "Let's get back to Moonlight Schools. That's much more fun than talking about men. First things first. Your job is to get a complete count of illiterates and semi-illiterates in the mountains of Rowan County."

Dread filled Lucy. She wanted to help Cora's project . . . but *this*? "You can't expect me to ride up to these mountain peoples' cabins, knock on the door, introduce myself, and say, 'By the way, can you read and write?' The mountain people are leery of strangers."

"Just remind them we are kin." Cora smiled. "That should take care of any general suspicion when they find a pretty young woman at their door. Oh, and don't be surprised how many people don't know how to read but won't admit it. You'll have to find out without offending them."

"Oh, that should be easy," Lucy said. "Trying to not offend a moonshiner toting a loaded shotgun."

Cora ignored her sarcasm. "You have a lovely way with people, Lucy. I'm not at all worried about your personal safety."

No, she never was! Lucy worried plenty about her personal safety. "I suppose I could start with the families I've already met. Sally Ann and Barbara Jean." Just thinking of Barbara made an itchy feeling creep up her scalp.

"That's the spirit! Start with what you know and go from there."

"Just how many hollers are there?"

"Plenty. Brother Wyatt will help. I'll ask him to reach out to those living in the back country. They know him." She glanced up. "You shouldn't be wandering alone way up there."

Lucy couldn't agree more. "How do I know where to stop?" The last thing she wanted was to encounter a wild beast. Or a wild moonshiner.

"Just keep going until you hit a county line."

Of course. As if Lucy would happen across a big white fence that encircled a county of thick wilderness.

"And don't forget to tell them to come to the Moonlight Schools in September. Don't ask. Tell them to come. Monday through Thursday nights, seven o'clock to nine o'clock, for say . . . let's start with four weeks. No, scratch that. Six weeks."

September? "But, Cora . . . it's nearly May!"

"And a good thing, too, because you'll have lengthening days of sunlight to help you through those mountain trails. We have a very large county to cover. While you do that, I'll get the school-teachers on board."

"Isn't that the most important thing to do first? I feel as if you're getting the cart in front of the horse."

Cora waved that worry away with a flick of the wrist. "I've learned enough in my life to move forward with the snowball approach."

"How's that?"

"Just start rolling the ball." Cora cupped her hands together, as if packing a snowball. "It'll all come together in the end." She started scribbling something down, a thought captured before she lost it. Her mind moved so fast! Lucy could barely keep up.

Cora finished writing, then looked up. "Dear girl, why are you still here?"

"Why? Because . . . I am overwhelmed."

Cora smiled. "Oh . . . my sentiments exactly! It's such a thrill! Lucy . . . I do believe this venture is going to be the highlight of our lives."

Lucy went to the door, reached for the knob, and turned back, thinking of more objections. Reasons as to why this crazy notion couldn't possibly work. But Cora's head was tucked down, and she was feverishly writing, and she seemed so . . . happy. Full of joy, all because of the light she hoped to bring to others. How could Lucy say no? How could anyone?

SLOWLY, LUCY WALKED out of Cora's office and toward the livery, wondering how in the world she was going to be able to accomplish what Cora asked of her. She heard hoofbeats and looked up to see Wyatt ride down the road. She watched him dismount at the livery and hurried to meet him. He had started to unbuckle Lyric's girth when he heard her call his name. He stopped and turned, smiling as she approached, and she found herself smiling in return. "Do you have a minute to spare?"

"Always." He finished unbuckling the girth. "Something on your mind? Let me guess. Cora's handed you an impossible task for her moonlit school campaign."

"Yes! Yes, exactly that. And to be perfectly honest, Wyatt, I need a little help. And you're just the person."

He lifted the saddle and set it on the ground. "How can I help?"

"How will I ever be able to get an account of the illiterates in Rowan County? That's what Cora wants me to do."

"Ah, but you don't need to talk to everyone. Just find the right person who knows everybody else."

"But who?"

He grinned. "Miss Mollie, for one. Me, for another. Arthur Cooper. And then there's his daughter Angie. She seems to know just about everybody's business."

Lucy was feeling great relief . . . until Wyatt offered up Angie's name.

ANGIE WAS FURIOUS WITH HERSELF. She kept thinking about Finley James, which was precisely the wrong thing for her to do. Well, she was done with that boy. "I hope I never see Finley James again," she decided, even though he was due to arrive at her cabin any minute to help her paw finish up the planting.

It was only midmorning and the day was already hot. Angie made up a big jug of cool spring water to take to her paw out in the cornfield. To her paw . . . and to Finley James.

She whipped off her apron and hurried up the ladder to her loft. She grabbed her hairbrush, then twisted her hair into a bun and stuck some pins in it. She stood back and looked at the small mirror that Paw had hung by her washstand. Strands of her hair straggled on each side of her cheeks, down her neck. Pins stuck out of her bun, so she jammed them down again, but they kept popping out again. She sighed.

These were the moments she wished her maw were still here, and even more so, that she coulda been like other mothers. She loved her dearly, but her maw seemed more like a child than a grown woman.

Once Angie asked her paw about it and he grew silent. He wouldn't speak a word against Maw. So she went to Miss Mollie.

"Your maw," she said, "she's always been the sweetest gal on earth."

"I know, but . . ."

Miss Mollie held up a hand to stop her. "There's jest some things in life that shouldn't be looked at too close. You might not like what you find."

Out the window, Angie heard Fin's voice calling to her paw, so she smoothed out her dress, pinched her cheeks once more, added a dap of sheep's lanolin to her lips to make them shiny, and hurried to take the jug of cool water out to Paw and Fin. When she reached the field where Paw said they'd be, she didn't see any sign of her father. But there was that boyfriend thief Miss Lucy on poor ol' Jenny, and there was Fin, holding the reins to the pony, laughing and smiling and having a grand old time. Her happy mood frizzled like a damp squib.

Angie watched them for a while. Whenever Finley James was

around Miss Lucy, he turned into a different boy. He stood tall and stiff, talked slow and careful. This was the same Finley James who taught Angie to ride a horse and skip a stone over a creek and hunt for mushrooms. The same one who'd once given her half a penny and kept the other half for hisself. Two halves of one soul, that was her thinking. But mebbe he was jest being nice to share a found hay penny with her.

She should turn tail and leave. She should. But Angie, unable to stand being left out, had drifted in to listen. She might have watched them longer, but Jenny noticed her and snorted a howdy. They turned. Miss Lucy smiled, but Finley James jest stared at her.

She held up the jug. "I brought some water." When there was an entire second of silence, she asked, "Cat got yor tongue, Finley James?" trying to conceal her pleasure at his gawking.

Too soon, he was back to his ol' mean self. "Wonderin' if somethin' might be the matter with your hair." He grinned, and scratched his head dramatically with both hands. "Got cooties, mebbe?"

"I do not!" Angie said. "It's hot. I jest . . . pinned it up."

"You look very grown-up, Angie," the boyfriend thief said, and Angie scowled at her.

"Is that for me?" Fin didn't wait for an answer but took the jug from her hands.

Angie pulled two tin cups from her apron pocket. "There's an extra cup," she said in a mumble. It took every ounce of kindness she had to offer water to Miss Lucy, but she knew she had to. She was her paw's daughter. Still, she was disappointed that her time alone with Fin was ruined by Miss Lucy, and sore vexed that he didn't like her hair after she'd worked so hard to pin it up. Cooties. *Rude!*

Also in her apron pocket was a chunk of carrot. She held it out to Jenny, who nickered her pleasure. She shielded her eyes from the sun to look at Miss Lucy. Even on silly-looking Jenny, she looked as pretty as could be. It was a warm day, but her cheeks were barely rosy. Angie could sense her own face was bright red from the heat.

Miss Lucy's eyes darted to the house. "Angie, you read so well that I'm guessing your parents like to read."

What business of that was hers? "My maw could read. Not Paw. But he's the trustee for Little Brushy."

"Yeah," Finley James said, wiping water from his mouth, "but that don't mean much. Most of the trustees of the schools cain't read."

Miss Lucy looked and sounded a mite nervous. "Angie, I wonder if you might know of any in this area"—she swept her arm toward the hilly woods—"who can't read or write?"

Angie narrowed her eyes. "Why?"

"Cora's come up with the idea of providing schools at night on moonlit nights. To teach the adults to read."

Angie shook her head. "They won't come."

Fin rolled his eyes. "They might."

"They won't," she repeated.

"Don't listen to Angie. She thinks she knowed everything there is to know." Finley James put the cup on top of the now empty jug. "Miss Lucy, you gots to go to Miss Mollie. She's the eyes and ears of the hollow." He wiped his forehead. "I better git back to work."

Now Angie was steamed. Really furious. "And I gots to go meet up with Bobby McLean." Why did *that* pop out of her mouth? It was a bold-faced lie. For all she knew, Bobby hadn't gotten back from his mamaw's funeral. "He wants to teach me how to fish."

"Bobby McLean?" Finley James said with a scoff. "He don't know squat about fishing."

At least she finally got a rise out of Fin. He couldn't tolerate Bobby McLean. "Sez he knows more than you."

"He said such a thing?" Fin roared. "Then jest go on and see what ya can learn from a fella who's a-scared of putting a worm on a hook." He thrust the jug at her, picked up his hoe, and stomped back to the field. Suddenly, he stopped, pivoted, waved, and tipped his hat like a proper gentleman. "Nice talkin' with you, Miss Lucy."

Not a goodbye to Angie, not even a thank-you for the jug of

water. And now she had to leave the farm for a few hours to pretend she was fishing with Bobby McLean so she weren't caught in a lie. She'd made a mess of things, all because of that stupid Finley James, whom she hated. And loved.

"To tell you the truth," said the boyfriend thief, "I always get a bit lost after I pass your cabin. Is Miss Mollie's far from here? And please don't say it's just over yonder."

"But it is jest over yonder," Angie said. *Oh, bother.* "Hold up. I'll git my bonnet and take you there myself."

"Oh, you don't have to. Especially if you're meeting someone to go fishing."

Angie swallowed a scowl, not wanting to give away her fib. "I got me some time. And no doubts you'll get hopelessly lost." She ran up to the cabin with the jug, set it on the kitchen table, grabbed her calico bonnet from the wall peg, hurried down the porch steps, then stopped suddenly as she caught sight of Fin, watching her from the field. She spun around and went back up the porch steps, taking them two at a time, to grab one of her brother's fishing poles off the rack, then rushed off to join Miss Lucy. She had to bite her lower lip to keep from smiling at the sight of Fin's frown.

FOR ALL ANGIE'S PRICKLINESS, there was something about her that Lucy found endearing. Something she couldn't quite put her finger on . . . perhaps it was Angie's quick mind, or the way she darted around, or her defiant stance of claiming her territory— Finley James. So bold! So charming. Maybe she felt drawn to her because everything about Angie was the very opposite of Lucy.

They found Miss Mollie out on her porch in a rocking chair, a bowl of spring long beans on her lap, and in her hands were needle and thread. "Come," she said, delighted to have company. "Sit a spell. Angel girl, go git that tarred pony out of the sun and git her some water."

While Angie led the tired pony to the lean-to for some shade and water, Lucy sat on the porch step, facing Miss Mollie. "What are you doing with those?" She couldn't fathom why anyone would sew a bean.

"These leather breeches?" Miss Mollie said, holding up a row of beans. "That's what we call 'em. Jest string beans together and hang them soz they dry out. They won't be near so long. Then next winter I'll put them back in water and they'll plump up agen real nice." She smacked her gums. "Cut 'em up, add onions, pour some lard over 'em. That's some fine eating with fried corn bread."

It sounded dreadful. "What was it like for you, Miss Mollie? Growing up on this mountain?"

"Been a wonderful life."

"It seems so isolated. So far from . . . others." Lucy was going to say "civilization."

"Do ya know the history of our people?"

"A little," Lucy said. Not as much as she should know.

"Most folks can trace back more than two hundred years. Mebbe more. My own granddaddy came over on a cattle boat, right into Phillydelphee. They came to the New World lookin' for land to call them's own."

"But why here? Why such a remote place as the hills of Appalachia?"

Miss Mollie rested the string of beans in her lap. "Bein' far away from the cities, mostly from the gubbermint, holped us keep our own traditions."

"Miss Mollie, have you ever thought about moving to town?"

"Goodness, no. I cain't leave 'em." She pointed a finger off toward a hill.

Lucy turned and tented her eyes, but she couldn't see anyone.

Angie walked toward them and plopped down by Miss Mollie's feet. "She means the graveyard," and then Lucy realized the hill was a little family cemetery plot.

"It's a lovely site," Lucy said.

"Planted east to face the sun," Miss Mollie said. "Asides, I don't like town life. Too crowded. Makes me feel squirrely each time I go visit Cora. I jest feel better in the mountains. When you live in the country, you can do about anything you like. No one's puttin' their nose in your business, tellin' you how to live." She waved a hand in the air like she was shooing a fly. "If'n you don't like your neighbor . . . jest don't speak to 'em." Her eyes crinkled with humor. "I like most o' mine."

Lucy brushed some dirt off her skirt. "Cora says most young people talk of moving to the cities for better jobs. Have you ever thought of joining your daughter in Chicago?"

"Well, you got a point there. It can git lonely without the young. They take care o' us ol' folks." She smiled at Angie. "But I gots my girl here. She takes real good care o' me."

Angie beamed from the praise, and Lucy realized what a beautiful woman the girl would be one day. Then Angie changed the subject to explain why they'd come to visit, for which Lucy was grateful. Even when told she was kin to Cora, Lucy knew others viewed her as an outsider, and was well aware of how the mountain people opened up, acted more like themselves, whenever she had a local with her—Finley James or Angie or Wyatt or Cora—than when she was alone.

Once Miss Mollie started on her rambling about the locals, Lucy pulled paper and pencil from her pocket to take notes. It felt like trying to capture water in your hands from a gushing waterfall. That woman seemed to know just about everyone in Rowan County, and everything about them too.

Angie was a help in keeping Miss Mollie on subject, for her thoughts had a tendency to wander. Out of the blue, Miss Mollie would turn the tables and ask Lucy about growing up in Lexington. Lucy would answer . . . and Angie would clear her throat, and then she would veer the conversation back to Miss Mollie and her vast knowledge of the mountain people.

It felt like minutes, but an hour or two, or more, must have passed, and Lucy realized they'd stayed too long. Miss Mollie was slowing down in her storytelling, and then nodded off.

Lucy and Angie tiptoed away, leaving the dear woman sound asleep in her rocking chair. Holding Jenny's reins in one hand, her fishing pole in the other, Angie led Lucy to the creek and pointed the way toward town, then disappeared into the woods before Lucy could even thank her. Angie had stayed for the entire visit with Miss Mollie. Lucy wondered about the boy who was waiting to go fishing with Angie, until it dawned on her there was no boy waiting.

As Jenny plodded her way back to town, Lucy thought about all she'd learned today from Miss Mollie. Far more adults were unable to read than she would've thought.

And then there was Miss Mollie's casual mention of the Wilson clan. Lucy had numerous distant cousins in various hills and hollows, unknown to her, most of whom were illiterate.

With a jolt, Lucy realized this could have been her life.

She thought of how important education had been to Father. She appreciated it now with a different view, after seeing the world from which he had come. She understood so much more about him now, especially how he wanted to distance himself from relations, how he hadn't brought Lucy back to where he'd been raised. She'd always assumed he wanted nothing to do with the poverty of Appalachia. Now she recognized his avoidance as a revulsion of its intellectual poverty.

She gazed up at the trees that towered above. Not being able to read would feel like being born blind, aware there was a world you were left out of, but completely unaware of how beautiful it was.

She pulled papers from her pocket and counted up the number of adults in this hollow who couldn't read, or couldn't read well. Then she did it a second time. Over fifty. And this was just one hollow. Just one. There were dozens of hollows and coves all over this mountain.

She blew out a puff of air. She felt as if these mountain people had been hindered from a full life, stymied, thwarted. Robbed.

182

Now she understood what Cora meant when she said that illiteracy was a type of social evil. In this modern age of automobiles and radio broadcasting, it was unconscionable.

And suddenly, Lucy felt a stirring inside her. Something was changing in her, something fundamental, deep down, altering the very core of her being. She cared about these people, she wanted a better life for them, and she knew Cora was so right. So very right. Literacy was the start of that path.

Sensing they were getting close to town, nearing a supper of hay and oats, Jenny picked up her pace, and in a flash, they were out of the gloomy woods and into the bright sunlight. She seared that moment in her memory, never to be forgotten.

Lucy Wilson was emerging from a life in the shadows.

Sixteen

A NGIE HAD LISTENED CAREFULLY when Miss Lucy told Miss Mollie how she'd been taught to walk at her fancy girls' school by balancing a book on her head. She had to admit, Miss Lucy walked different than mountain women. Her head was held proud, her shoulders back. So one afternoon, when the boys were in the barn with Paw, she took his Bible and walked around the house with it on her head.

It wasn't easy at first, and she dropped it once, twice, thrice . . . which slowed her down because Miss Mollie always said if you dropped a Bible, you had to kiss it one hundred times. She wasn't sure why the kissing was necessary but figured it would put an end to any curse she might have invoked after dropping a Bible. It took time, but she finally got the hang of it. It required slowing down, which was not an easy thing for Angie to do. She liked the feeling of holding her head high, especially after she caught a glimpse of herself in Maw's hand mirror and thought she looked downright regal.

Until those bothersome little boys burst into the house and caught her in the act.

Wide-eyed, Mikey asked, "What are you doin' *now*?"

She grabbed the Bible off her head and held it to her middle. "Bible study."

Gabe, a mite slow, looked confused. "By puttin' the Bible on top o' your head?"

"Never you mind."

Mikey jabbed Gabe with his elbow. "Bet it's got something to do with copying Miss Lucy." He grinned. "She's trying to walk straight and fancy, just like Miss Lucy." He tried to mimic a woman's walk in an exaggerated way, walking on tiptoes, swinging his arms, hips swaying from side to side.

Angie moaned. "Why couldn't the Lord have brung me sisters instead of troublesome little brothers?"

Mikey lifted a finger in the air and spoke in crisp diction, like Miss Lucy. "I do believe *brung* ain't a word."

Angie swatted the air like she was shooing a fly. "Go on and git. Both of you."

"We be starvin'."

"Ya always say yor starving. And you both eat enough for a horse."

"Yeah, but this time, it's true. My tummy's been growlin' since breakfast."

Gabe sniffed the air. "Is that fresh-baked bread I smell?"

Angie frowned. "Go git yourselves a hunk of bread, and take one to Paw too. But don't make a gaum of it."

Both boys walked tiptoe first to the little stovetop, arms swinging, hips wiggling. Then they bent over in laughter, and even Angie had to laugh at their silly antics. Them boys! She corrected herself. *Those* boys.

FINLEY JAMES was on his way home from town and decided to go the long way. After all, it was spring in the mountains. Birdsong filled the forest, and the rhododendrons were in full bloom with blossoms as big as dinner plates. There weren't no place more beautiful on earth than this mountain in the springtime. It was like the Lord God was showing off, letting folks in on a hint of what's to come in heaven. That's what his maw said, and he believed her.

He heard someone call his name and hoped it might be Miss Lucy, but heck if it was only Angie Cooper. He shoulda known not to go so close to the Cooper cabin. She could sniff him out like a hound after a fox. He reined Sheila to a stop and waited as she splashed across the creek, one hand holding onto the hem of her dress so it wouldn't get wet. In the other hand was a wrapped bundle.

"What do you want?"

"I made an extra loaf of bread. Thought you might like some." She held it up to him.

It did look good, and he was mighty hungry. But first, he had a bone to pick with her. "How did fishin' work out with Bobby McLean?" He fixed his eyes on her, delighted to see her squirm after he caught her in a lie.

"Fine. Jest fine."

"Mebbe ya told a bold-faced lie and yor goin' to burn in hell for it."

Her eyebrows almost met in the middle.

"Jest saw Bobby get off the train, not an ahr ago. Said he'd been at his mamaw's funeral. Said he'd been gone over a week."

"You sound mad." She looked hopeful. "Were you jealous?"

"Nope. Besides, women are nothing but a nuisance." As far as Fin was concerned, Angie could play her games with somebody else.

"I only lied to you because you said I wasn't pretty."

"I didn't say nothing o' the sort."

She grinned. "So then . . . you think I'm pretty?"

"Mebbe," Fin snapped, "but ya also make me crazy."

"Well, you make me crazy too!" Angie smiled. "Do ya really think I'm pretty?"

He gave her a serious looking over. Her bonnet had slipped off and hung loose down her back, showing off her feeble attempts at pinning up her hair. Blonde curls escaped every which way, and if she hadn't vexed him so, he might admit she looked a mite fetching. "Well, I'll be. I hadn't noticed. I shorely hadn't. But you ain't nigh as ugly as ya used to be."

Furious, she waded back across the creek, feet teetering carefully across the slick rocks.

"Hey! What about the bread? I'm hungry!" He wasn't sure he heered her exactly right, cuz it sounded like something that might peel the paint right off the walls.

ON SUNDAY MORNING, Lucy sat in church next to Andrew Spencer and thought he looked unreasonably handsome, even for Andrew. He wore a trimly tailored suit, a new style of cut that Lucy had seen in Lexington, with a freshly starched shirt and collar. He was a smart dresser, standing out in sharp contrast to any other man in Rowan County. Especially Brother Wyatt.

Standing on the dais, hymnal in hand, Wyatt opened the church service. As he gave a warm welcome, she appraised him objectively. His face was lean and angular, such high cheekbones that gave him an almost severe look. He wore his black hair, which had a tinge of auburn to it in the right light, far too long. He wasn't particularly tall nor small, he wasn't particularly handsome. Frankly, his appearance wasn't notable. Certainly nothing like Andrew. But there was something about Wyatt that made him quite memorable.

Wyatt said a prayer and Lucy bowed her head, offering prayers for Charlotte as she always did. At the amen, she lifted her head and her eyes caught with Wyatt's. She saw something light in his eyes—warmth? tenderness?—but it vanished before she could put a name to it. When his eyes traveled to Andrew beside her, it left her mildly unsettled. Where in the world had that come from? She had nothing to feel guilty about.

Wyatt led the choir in a hymn Lucy didn't recognize, but she knew the second one. The entire church rose, with the sound of rustling pages in open hymnals, to sing "A Mighty Fortress Is Our God." Andrew sang along, woefully off-key, as if he didn't care. Lucy glanced at him sideways, slightly mortified.

He caught her look and grinned, then leaned toward her to whisper, "I used to be called the jailhouse singer. Always behind bars and missing a key." He nudged her with his elbow. "In case you hadn't noticed, I'm tone deaf."

Lucy clapped her hand over her mouth to keep from laughing out loud.

The sermon that followed expanded on the piece that Lucy had heard earlier in the week, when Wyatt was practicing in an empty church. "Seek and ye shall find," he quoted from the Bible, in a voice firm with promise.

What happened when you sought and didn't find?

After Charlotte went missing, after hope for her return grew dim, Lucy's trust in God had also faded. She had a vague belief in the Almighty, but it made her uncomfortable to hear those kinds of promises flung from the pulpit.

Wyatt always pronounced Almighty as two words. All Mighty. He said it made a difference.

She looked down at her hands in her lap to avoid Wyatt's gaze, which she felt was directed at her, though it probably wasn't. It reminded her of being at the brush arbor.

What had made that moment of worship at the brush arbor so different than anything she'd ever known? Or felt? For a short time, her entire being—mind, body, and soul—had been caught up in something she couldn't explain. Something that felt much bigger than herself. Was it just a result of the lively toe-tapping music, the unbridled enthusiasm of those around her? Or maybe it came from a church service held out in a breathtaking slice of nature. Such a different experience than in a staid church building.

She exhaled. Who knew? Maybe that moment was just her imagination. Maybe it was one of those experiences that Father had warned her about when she came to Morehead. After all, he had probably seen a good number of brush arbors. Perhaps those hard-to-explain experiences were why he found it best to keep his thoughts unencumbered of religious philosophy.

Or maybe it was her soul, reaching out to God, in spite of everything. A buried part of her that longed for God, even though she didn't know him or even trust his goodness.

She shook that thought off and shifted in the pew. Andrew, misinterpreting her squirm as an effort to draw close to him, reached over and took her hand in his. She looked down at his hand covering hers, and her first thought was that her hand all but disappeared in his larger one.

An hour later, Andrew was still holding her hand as they made their way to a grassy niche off Triplett Creek. She let herself be led by this strong, bold man and listened to him as he told her about funny things that had happened during his week. She had been with him enough times now to expect his accountings of the week, and she looked forward to them. Or maybe it was the way he had of telling stories that she enjoyed so much, for he had a gift for mimicry. "A treeman fell thirty feet but somehow landed in a soft bed of thick branches. Got up and brushed himself off." Andrew slipped into the mountain accent. "'Not heardly a scratch,' he said, and then he climbed right back up the tree. Like a boomer, he was!"

And then there was the granny who sold jugs of mountain dew to the crew cutting her timber, and when the foremen went to check on the work, he found the men in a drunken stupor. "That was less funny," Andrew said, though his eyes danced his with amusement. "To the foreman, anyway. He was going to get a bonus if he delivered on time." He chuckled and added, "I think the granny was the only one who got a bonus on that job."

Happy. Andrew was a happy man. Lucy kept thinking about the emotion, about getting used to it. *I feel happy when I'm around Andrew.* She wondered if this might be what it felt like to fall in love. Was it possible to always be this happy? Is this what it would be like to be married to him? What a silly thought! She'd known him for only a month or so. She decided to change the subject, at least from the one circling in her head.

"Andrew," she said, as they spread the blanket. "Cora wanted me to ask if you'd consider donating to her adult literacy campaign."

He stilled. "The what?"

She explained Cora's concept of opening the schools to adults on moonlit nights. Half listening, occupied with emptying the contents of the picnic basket, Andrew passed her a napkin.

"So would you?"

He found what he was after—deviled eggs, wrapped snugly in a container. "Would I what?" He held the container out to Lucy to offer her an egg.

"Donate to the Moonlight Schools campaign." She declined a deviled egg, needing to get this topic off her chest before she could eat. "Cora felt that you've gained such success from those mountain people, that naturally you'd want to give back."

With one bite, Andrew finished off an egg. Then another. Taking his time to chew and swallow, he finally said, "Valley View Lumber has benefited from Rowan County." He took another egg. "Ask your father for the charity."

"It's not really charity, Andrew. It's a campaign to help the mountain people help themselves."

"I wish I could help, Lucy. Really I do, but I have a lot of expenses to cover. One or two debts. You understand, I'm sure." And he polished off the last deviled egg.

As he lifted his arm, she noticed again his suit. The cloth, the tailoring, the crisp white shirt, it all looked new. Expensive. Flashing through her mind was an image of Brother Wyatt's threadbare shirt cuffs. "Of course I understand," she said, nodding. She didn't, though.

"You have to remember, Lucy, that I'm just like those mountain folks."

"How so?"

He grinned. "Like them, I don't have a trust fund to dip into."

She stiffened. A dig at her upbringing? Even more nettling was that he had guessed correctly. She was provided a generous monthly allowance, and she'd never wanted for anything. Never had gone to bed hungry. She crossed her arms and rubbed her elbows, suddenly cold.

He noticed. He picked up a small blanket and placed it around her shoulders. "It's turned chilly out there."

Yes, it had.

He sensed her withdrawal. "Luce," he said in a soft, coaxing voice as he wiggled close to her. "You're so serious . . . about being so serious."

A variation on a theme she'd heard most of her life. And it was true.

"Just ask your father for a donation. He'll give it to you." He gave her a gentle nudge with his elbow, first one, then another, until she smiled, in spite of herself. And then he wrapped his arms around her, and kissed her on the lips, once, then twice more. "I seem to be falling head over heels in love with you, Lucy Wilson."

She enjoyed his kisses, and he didn't seem to expect a declaration of love from her, which was a relief. Love? Andrew loved her?

It was too soon for that.

SUNDAY AFTERNOON was the one time when Fin allowed himself some time off. His maw took a long nap, and he would wait till he knew she was out cold, and then he'd grab his pole and hop on Sheila, and off they'd go to a favorite fishing spot, of which Fin had plenty. If'n he got lucky today, he might bring home an eel or two. His maw loved the taste of cooked eel, said it had a hint of sweetness to it. Fin didn't much care for it. His maw said you had to develop a taste for it.

He remembered his paw's rules about how to catch an eel. "At night, catch 'em feedin'," his paw had said. "At day, catch 'em hidin'." Eels fed by scent, so it required a stinky bait. Nightcrawlers or herrings. They'd go after bait tied to a string, and once they latched on, they could be dragged right out. It occurred to Fin that he hadn't brought a bucket to hold them, nor salt to douse them. The salt gave two gifts: a quick death to the eel and it got rid of their slime. He would have to make do and keep 'em in his net. It would be a slower death for the eels, and for that he was sorry. He wondered if they felt any pain, if they suffered, and he hoped not.

Wading along the creek, pondering all that he knew about eels and their hiding places, he found one, then another. He was hoping to come across a third eel, one his maw could cook real soft for Miss Mollie's gums, when Sheila nickered a warning. He straightened and spun around to find Angie Cooper, sitting on one of her paw's spare ponies, looking down on him from the top of the creek.

Fin groaned. *That girl.* Always looking down on him.

ANGIE RODE ALONG, stealing an occasional glance at Finley James, jest to prove to herself that he was really there, that they were racing horses together like they used to when they were children.

Angie's pony broke into a fast trot and Sheila paced her easily. "I'm givin' ya fair warning," she said. "This pony may be old, but she can surprise ya."

"Not as fast as Sheila," Finley James said. "Only horse that can beat her is Brother Wyatt's Lyric."

"Let's have a bet!" *The way we used to.*

"Depends," Finley James said, looking over his shoulder. "What's the bet?"

"I'll tell you after I've won!" Angie touched her heels to her pony, clucking, to get her into a canter.

She heard Fin laugh, and suddenly Sheila stretched out, bolting down into the creek and leaping up the bank. Angie's pony did her best to keep up, as if she sensed their fun. When they came to the opening in the woods that led to the Coopers' cornfield, the pony took off, surprising even Angie, startling a flock of black crows in the field. Angry, the crows rose to follow them, screeching insults. Fin was laughing so hard he had trouble hanging on and Sheila slowed. For a short stretch, the two horses were neck and neck, their eyes alight, coats glistening, frothing a bit. But then the pony lost her steam and Sheila bolted past. Fin slowed Sheila to a walk, then turned her in a circle to come alongside Angie.

"You lose agen," he said on a note of triumph.

Angie bent over to pat the pony's neck. "I weren't really so sure she still had such fire in her." She was blowing hard, poor girl, after giving all she had.

"Jest out of curiosity, what'd ya bet?"

Angie sat up straight. "That you'd take me to the top of Limestone Knob." It was where all young lovers went to be alone.

"Serves ya right," he said, bending over to check his net full of squirmy eels, tied to the back of his saddle, "for makin' a bet on the Lord's Day." Satisfied the eels were safe and secure, he looked straight at her. "Besides, I plan to take Miss Lucy to Limestone Knob to watch the sunset. Any day now." He straightened his hat. Smugly, Angie thought. "I'd say you could come along with, but it jest ain't the kind of place you want an extra body taggin' along." And with the lightest touch from Fin's heels, the big mare lunged forward and the two of them disappeared into the woods.

Thinking of Finley James and Miss Lucy on top of Limestone Knob together made Angie's gut wamble. She had to do *something*.

SEVENTEEN

BROTHER WYATT stayed at Miss Maude's boarding house on Sunday night and left a note pinned on Lucy's door that he planned to head into the hills tomorrow and she was welcome to join him if she wanted help with her census taking. The note said to be ready to leave right after an early breakfast.

Apart from promising to have lunch with Andy, Lucy had planned to spend Monday in Cora's office to keep up with day-to-day responsibilities, which were piling up on top of the Moonlight Schools campaign. But she knew Cora would prioritize the census, and Lucy did indeed need Wyatt's help to complete it. And she could have lunch with Andy on another day. She'd leave a note for him with Miss Maude. As she reread Wyatt's note, she felt a growing excitement about the day ahead.

The more Lucy knew Wyatt, the less she knew.

He seemed to be always busy, but what did he do? He traveled frequently by train, but he didn't volunteer where he'd been, or why. If she asked him, he just mumbled something about meetings. Cora, when asked about Wyatt, would only shrug and say, "There's a lot on his plate."

Yes, yes, but what?

As Lucy pinned up her hair early Monday morning, she decided that today would be the day to find out more about Brother Wyatt.

THE MORNING STARTED out gray and foggy, with a mist that wet Lucy's face and hair and clothes. As they rode along the creek, Lucy didn't let Wyatt turn questions onto her, like he usually did. Instead, she was blunt. "I'd like to know more about you."

The horses were side by side, and Wyatt turned to her with a quizzical look. "What exactly would you like to know?"

"To start with, your last name. I've never heard it. I've only heard you referred to as Brother Wyatt." It seemed like an easy answer, but Wyatt didn't respond. They approached the creek and Wyatt led Lyric through it first, almost dancing like she was stepping on hot coals. Jenny followed, plodding. As Lucy reached Wyatt, she watched him run a hand down Lyric's withers. She had started to notice such small things about him: the calming way he stroked his horse, the confident grace in his movement.

By now, Wyatt seemed to have decided to answer her. Or maybe he just decided what he wanted to tell her. "Lucy, have you heard much about the Rowan County War?"

Many times, she thought, and none favorably. Over the years, her father had referred to the feud as evidence of an uncivilized society. "Fin has mentioned it. Cora won't speak of it at all. She says she wants to wipe it from the county's history like it was a stain or a blot."

"No one wants to remember it, much less be associated with it," he said. "It began in the summer of 1884, between two families. The Martins and the Tollivers. A dispute over the election of a county sheriff that escalated into a feud. During the election, things got out of hand—hard drinking and hot opinions—and Floyd Tolliver wounded John Martin at the Morehead Tavern. Several months later, John Martin killed Floyd Tolliver and the Tollivers swore revenge. And they meant it. The Tollivers killed John Martin. That set off a feud that lasted three years. When it finally came to an end, more than twenty lives were lost. Rowan County's reputation was in ruins. Settlers left in search of a safer land. In the eyes of the country, Kentucky was filled with violent and vengeful hillbillies. And it all started with two men, moon-shine, and politics."

"Tolliver and Martin." Lucy still wasn't sure what any of this had to do with asking Wyatt about his name.

Lyric shifted her weight from one back hoof to the other, swish-ing her tail, eager to keep moving. Wyatt loosened the reins and let the horse have her way. As they moved up the trail, Wyatt turned his head to the side so Lucy could hear him. "Floyd Tolliver had a number of siblings. Brothers, mostly, who swore to avenge his death. Wesley Boyden Tolliver was a younger brother to Floyd and became one of the casualties of the feud. He was murdered in a gunfight to avenge the death of Floyd. He died in 1885, the year I was born." He leveled his gaze at Lucy. "That's why you haven't heard my surname. Wesley was my father. I'm a Tolliver. And my mother . . . she was a Martin. They never married. You can imagine how a boy like me was viewed with suspicion. Both Martins and Tollivers considered me an enemy."

Brother Wyatt? Of all the mountain people she had met in Rowan County, he would be the last one she assumed would have been born and raised amidst violence and vengeance.

When she didn't say anything, he turned in his saddle and smiled when he saw Lucy's face. "Shocked?"

"Me? Oh, my. I—" she stammered.

"Those big blue eyes of yours, Lucy, they give you away."

Oh, they did. She could never hide her feelings well. "So, you grew up not even knowing your father?"

"No. My mother's father took me in. Raised me as his own son. It was a remarkable act, and it stopped the feuding. Most of it, anyhow. A boy in these mountains could have no better man to guide him. My granddaddy taught me everything I know about music, and about the Lord, and about not letting the past deter-mine the future. He had a great, unwavering faith, as tall as the mountains, as deep and wide as the valleys. He believed that prayers and work were wedded, like a man and a woman. 'Boy,' he would say." His voice deepened dramatically. He turned slightly around in the saddle to say, "And if you think my voice is deep, you should have heard his." He faced forward and began again, "Boy, farm with your hand on the plow, your eyes on the furrow, and your mind on the Lord."

Wyatt slowed Lyric to a stop, stilled for a long moment, then exhaled a deep breath and turned in his saddle to face Lucy. "I was only fifteen when he died, suddenly and unexpectedly. It was a fork in the road for me. A hinge. Either I would trust in the promise of Romans 8:28, or I would go my own way."

He surmised from her blank look that she was unfamiliar with the verse, so he said it aloud, quoting it from memory: "'All things work together for good for those who love God.'"

He gave Lyric a slight kick and away they went up the trail, Lucy following behind. She was enjoying this immensely and had so many more questions to ask him. She felt as if the pump had been primed and water was pouring out. "So is that when Cora took hold of your life? She told me that she heard you sing a beautiful ballad and discovered you had written it."

He didn't answer, and she worried she had asked one question too many. But as they came to a level spot, he stopped Lyric and waited for Lucy and Jenny to catch up. "I'll get to Cora. First I must explain how the Lord took hold of my life." He gave Lyric a word, and she lunged forward, Jenny trotting to keep up. The trail had widened so they could ride side by side, and Lucy realized Wyatt had waited for this stretch to tell her more.

"You haven't been to a funeral in the mountains yet, have you?" She shook her head.

"Folks come from all over to show their respect, and stay on for days. It's one of the things I love the best about our people. They come alongside and mourn with you." He pressed his fist against his heart. "On the night of my granddaddy's burial, I needed some time to myself. I took a very long walk and ended up at a certain vista point, a place that's become my favorite. I remember it was a clear, cold night. One brilliant star above the ridge sparkled down on me like a diamond set in velvet. Just one, but that was all I needed. I knew, at that moment, that I must rest on the sovereignty of the All Mighty in this deep sadness. That I would claim the promise of Romans 8:28 and trust that 'all things,' even those that appeared to be a stark tragedy, would 'work together for good.' All things."

"So . . . has it?" Jenny was lagging, so she gave her a little kick with her heels to speed up. "Have things worked together for good for you?"

Wyatt looked over at Lucy, almost as if surprised by the question. "Far beyond my wildest dreams could have ever imagined."

Yet Wyatt was still as poor as a man could be. Nearly a vagrant, as far as Lucy could tell, a man who seemed to be heavily dependent upon the generosity of others. No career, no real future. And yet he was the most content, settled person she had ever known. Just being around him made her restless, unhappy spirit feel still and quiet. Different from Andrew. Better than Andrew.

Oh my stars and garters. She had completely forgotten to leave a note for Andy to let him know she had left early. No doubt, he would've arrived at the boarding house expecting to walk her to work and she wouldn't have been there. She'd forgotten all about him.

ANGIE GLANCED AT THE CABIN and didn't see no sign of Paw or the twins, so she ran up the hill to visit Miss Mollie. She needed to seek a remedy for her heartache before it ate up her innards. Miss Mollie was sound asleep when Angie arrived, resting in her rocker by the cold fire. When Angie told her what she'd come for, Miss Mollie squinted at her as if she couldn't hear her right, or mebbe she was still startled by Angie's sudden appearance in her cabin.

"Ya want another love potion? Oh honey." Miss Mollie rocked

back and forth for a long while. "When you be jest a littl'un, ya used to stand o'er by that windowpane and try to put the streaks of light into yor pinafore pocket to take on home. I played along with ya. But now that yor older, you know you cain't hold on to light. Same with love, idn't? It's there or it's not. You cain't hold it."

"It ain't for me. I want ya to make someone fall out of love. Shorely ya got something for it. During the Rowan County War, you was making all kinds of potions to keep gals from loving fellas from the wrong families."

The old woman sniffed. "I misremember doing such a thing."

"Miss Mollie! You tol' me stories about fixing love potions for as long as I been alive! Shorely you can figure out a way to make someone fall out of love jest as easy as it would be to make them fall into love." Angie let out an exasperated sigh. "Mebbe you can send lightning to strike 'em." When Miss Mollie's sparse little eyebrows shot up, she added the reassurance, "Not enough lightning to kill 'em. Jest to shock 'em a little."

"I cain but I won't. Twouldn't be right to make meddlin' mischief. The Lord sees all." Miss Mollie scratched her thinning scalp. "Asides, it always takes two sticks to make a fire, idn't?"

Angie wasn't sure exactly what that meant, but it left her feeling even more nettled than when she arrived.

Bother!

WYATT TOOK LUCY to four different cabins, to families who knew much about their individual hollows and were willing to share their knowledge. Lucy knew they were forthcoming only because Wyatt accompanied her. These people didn't just have a great regard for Wyatt, they adored him. Children shouted happy greetings as they caught sight of Lyric coming through the trees. Lyric and Jenny were spoiled with carrots and apples. Gifts of bread or hoecakes were tucked into Wyatt saddlebags as he prepared to leave; not a farmer nor a housewife allowed him to refuse them. So, Lucy realized, *this* was how a singing school master made a living. Her father would be horrified.

And yet, after today, she was horrified by her father. By Valley View's actions, and other lumber companies'. All through the hills, they rode through harvested loblolly stands, now scalded land. She could see for herself how the recent rainstorms had created new rivulets of water that had already begun to erode the hillsides. More than a few times, they found holding ponds for lumber, now abandoned, that hadn't been un-dammed. The pen near Barbara Jean Boling's property, the one that had diverted water from her creek, had indeed been reverted. Andy had been sure to let her know, and Lucy had assumed he meant all the pens were returned to their original state. She squeezed her eyes shut. So naïve!

She wondered if Wyatt intentionally led her past these pens, or if they were just that plentiful. He said nothing as they passed each pond or traveled up or down harvested hills. Maybe there was nothing to say.

Toward the end of the day, Wyatt led them to Sally Ann Duncan's cabin. Facing the snug home, Lucy had the same feeling as the first day she'd arrived in Morehead: something about Sally Ann, about the cabin, the setting . . . it touched her heart, deep, deep down.

Sally Ann not only knew quite a bit about the families in her holler, but also had her newborn baby girl in her arms and was eager for company. Hungry for it. While Wyatt watered the horses, Lucy sat at Sally Ann's kitchen table and took notes, just like she had at Miss Mollie's. After they finished, Sally asked if she'd like to hold the baby, and Lucy was so pleased.

She gazed at the newborn in her arms with a sense of awe. "Sally Ann, would Roy be interested in working for my father's lumber company in Lexington?"

Sally Ann spun around. "But . . . are there any trees left in Lexington?"

Lucy swallowed a smile. "A few. But your husband could also get some training for work in different areas."

Sally Ann set a dishrag on the counter and walked toward Lucy. "Think it might pay . . . a fair wage?"

"Oh my, yes. He'd make much more working in the headquarters than he could make working in the timber."

Sally Ann's eyes filled with tears. "I'd be ever so obliged t' you, Miss Lucy." One tear after another started streaming down her face, so much so that she wiped her face with the corners of her apron.

Lucy smiled. "Roy will earn his wages. And perhaps you could join him soon. You and your little one." It didn't seem right that a man wasn't at home with his wife and daughter. Sally Ann hadn't even named her baby yet. She said she needed to wait for Roy.

The baby stirred in Lucy's arms, lifting her arm and splaying her tiny fingers like a little starfish. Lucy stroked the small hand. So perfect, so miniature. "If you have embroidery scissors, I could trim her nails for you."

When Sally Ann didn't respond, Lucy looked up, startled when she saw the look of fear in the young mother's eyes. And in the next moment, Sally Ann whisked the baby out of Lucy's arms and asked her to leave.

IT WAS OBVIOUS Lucy had said something to offend Sally Ann, but she didn't know what and Wyatt didn't either. He told her not to worry herself. "Perhaps she needed to rest."

Perhaps. Still, one moment the friendship with Sally Ann seemed to be growing, and then suddenly it was snuffed out, like someone blew out a candle. It was one of those experiences that sharply reminded Lucy she was an outsider.

Wyatt led them off the trail and through an opening in the trees. "Let's pause for a moment here. There's something I'd like to show you."

He tied Lyric's reins to a bush, did the same with Jenny's, and beckoned Lucy to follow. "Come see. A sight to behold." He led her to an open, flat, rocky area. Beyond him, the sun was sinking behind a ridge.

"Goodness, it's so beautiful," Lucy said. She stared at the thick trees that laddered the hillside, the jagged edge of the ridge, the cloud mist that drifted along top, backlit by the setting sun with rims of fire.

They watched the sky change colors, deepening in hues until it looked like someone had painted vibrant reds and oranges with a thick paintbrush. It was magnificent. Anyone would be hard pressed to find a place more beautiful. Or peaceful. For a moment it was just the two of them. Everything else receded and all she could feel was the steady thumping of her heart.

"Nature is God's voice," Wyatt said. "Every sunrise and sunset is a word from the All Mighty, a reminder that he is with us. Every flower and tree, river and lake, mountain and sunset, 'tis God speaking."

In a deep baritone voice, he began to sing, "'This is my Father's world, and to my listening ears, all nature sings and round me rings the music of the spheres.'"

When he paused, she hurried to say, "Please don't stop." So he continued, and her thoughts drifted to her dormitory room at the Townsend School for Girls. Her desk was under a window that faced west, and she had observed countless sunsets. Never once did she think of how a sunset, as lovely as it often was, could be connected to God. Not once. Yet it was like a new canvas getting painted, each evening. How *much* she had missed in her life.

"'In the rustling grass I hear him pass, He speaks to me everywhere.'"

As he sang the last verse again, Lucy felt acutely aware of her surroundings. Every sense came alive: the musty scent of the forest, the cold hard rock that she sat on, the silent glide of the red-tailed hawks circling overhead, the swish of the horse's tail, a distant sound of a dog barking. The feeling reminded her of worshiping at the brush arbor. Every part of her was paying attention.

Brother Wyatt took in a deep breath and swept in the valley with a fond gaze. "I have found it vital to acknowledge the glory of creation aloud, each time I encounter it. Whether it's a sunset or a dogwood in bloom."

"Why?"

He turned and smiled in that patient way. "Lest I become immune to it."

Eighteen

That frightened look on Sally Ann's face, almost as if Lucy had threatened her newborn baby, continued to niggle her. The next day was so rainy that Cora insisted the census be on hold until the skies cleared and the ground had time to dry out. That suited Lucy just fine. It gave her a chance to catch up on paperwork in the office. And it also provided an opportunity to ask Cora about Sally Ann when they took their tea break.

"Cora, help me understand something. Sally Ann Duncan seemed happy to let me hold her baby. I noticed that the baby's fingernails were long, so I offered to trim them. Sally Ann gave me the strangest look, and then she practically snatched the baby out of my arms. She made it clear I had overstayed my welcome." That, too, seemed so odd to Lucy. The mountain people loved for visitors to linger. Normally, it was a challenge to depart.

Cora took a long sip of tea. "Sally Ann believes it would bring bad luck to her baby if nails are cut before she turns one year old." Her face grew soft as she beheld the shock on Lucy's face. "They hold tightly to their superstitions up there." She set her teacup down. "If someone speaks of illness, knock on wood." She rapped twice on her desk. "My granny wouldn't throw water outside after sunset." She chuckled. "I still have no idea what fear that was based on."

Tracing the top of the teacup with her finger, Lucy considered such things. Her father, for all his love of logic and reason, held a few odd superstitions. The night before she was to leave for Morehead, he and Hazel had given Lucy a new pair of boots—the very ones she was wearing now. She had opened the box and set the boots on the tabletop. Father bolted from his seat to grab them. "Never *ever* put new shoes on a table! It's a death warning." He was wholly serious. Hazel and Lucy had looked at him as if he'd lost his mind. Embarrassed, he'd quickly changed the subject.

"I don't even try to untangle superstitions." Cora finished the last swallow of tea. "They're too deeply embedded in the culture. Omens and signs and sayings—they all have something to do with how uncertain life can be, how much the mountain people feel they're victims of fate. I suppose they consider superstitions to be precautions."

Lucy refilled Cora's teacup. "I told Sally Ann that my father might be willing to give Roy a job in Lexington."

Cora paused. "And is your father willing?" She sounded doubtful.

"He said that if I sent him hardworking young men who could read and write, then he would give them jobs."

"Roy Duncan is a hard worker. And he's literate." She smiled. "Good for you, Lucy. I know that it's not easy to get your father to see a situation from your point of view." She tapped the desk with her fingertips. "But it's not impossible. As hard a shell as your father has, he has a soft interior."

"It couldn't have been easy to convince him to sponsor Wyatt's education."

Cora snorted. "Not easy, but once your father gives his promise, he does not renege."

"I would think that Father would have been gravely disappointed when he learned that Wyatt returned to the mountains."

Suddenly, Cora stilled, and her expression became unreadable. "Has Wyatt told you much of his life?"

"Yesterday, I learned more than I ever had. I had to ask, but he did tell me about his upbringing. About how his grandfather broke a pattern of vengeance."

"It's quite a story."

And that opened the way for Lucy to ask what she had been longing to ask. "Cora, what kind of a career is a singing school master? It seems a man like Wyatt could have a real future."

"Out of the mountains?"

"Yes. Yes, I suppose that's what I mean."

"Perhaps . . . from the world's point of view. God, I believe, has a different view of a man's future." She handed Lucy her empty teacup. "And thereby what constitutes a worthy ambition, as well."

BREAKFAST AT MISS MAUDE'S had a distinct pattern. Judge Klopp's wife would summarize her list of physical ailments as if anyone had asked. Her back gave her trouble, her right toe throbbed in the rain, and she couldn't sleep more than a few hours at a time.

Miss Viola, who had a touch of vinegar in her veins, enjoyed provoking her. "Sounds like cancer to me, Beulah." Or cholera. Or bubonic plague. Each morning, Miss Viola came up with a new diagnosis, spoken with authority, in hopes of flustering Mrs. Klopp. And it always worked.

"Do you really think so?" Mrs. Klopp would say, her expression worried. "Could it be cancer?"

Miss Viola and Miss Lettie would exchange amused looks behind their teacups.

Lucy felt the judge's wife just needed more on her mind. So on this morning, before Mrs. Klopp could launch into her list of ailments, she brought up Cora's Moonlight Schools campaign. Miss Viola and Miss Lettie listened with rapt attention, as did

Miss Maude, whenever she bustled in and out of the dining room. Miss Viola peppered Lucy with questions, fascinated by Cora's bold concept. Mrs. Klopp listened, but without any questions.

"Everyone has to admit," Miss Viola said, "that our county would be better off if there were more women like Miss Cora."

"Not everyone," Mrs. Klopp sniffed. She neatly folded her napkin, rose from her seat and said, "No one should get above their raising. The judge was always firm about that."

After she left the room, Lucy looked at Miss Viola. "What does *that* mean?"

Miss Viola waved a thin, blue-veined hand in the air, shooing the fly. "Beulah Klopp, as did her judge husband, believes everyone has a fixed place in this world, decided at the moment of birth. There are those who are high borns and those who are low borns."

"And Beulah Klopp," Miss Lettie said, "is a high born."

They heard a click of the front door closing. Miss Lettie exclaimed softly under her breath. "Oh dear."

Miss Viola raised a hand softly to her cheek. "Oh dear."

AFTER ANOTHER FULL DAY of canvasing hollows and glens and hills and coves, this time with Finley James's help, Lucy plopped down on her chair in Cora's office. "Census completed. Over eleven hundred."

Cora watched her with a curious look on her face. "Twelve hundred people?"

"No. Twelve hundred illiterates."

She'd been inking a quill and paused, midair, a shocked look on her face as ink dripped onto her paper. "You must be mistaken."

"One thousand one hundred and fifty-two, to be exact. Illiterates and semi-illiterates." Lucy had counted and recounted, until she recognized each and every name.

"You're sure? You're absolutely sure?"

"As sure as a person can be. Brother Wyatt helped a great deal. Miss Mollie too."

Stunned, Cora dropped her pen and leaned back. "It's a third of our county." Slowly, thoughtfully, she rose from her chair. She had her face turned to the window. "I do hope some will come. All I need is six weeks of evenings. I'm absolutely convinced the results will be astonishing."

"Cora, are you sure you're not setting your sights on, well, a nearly impossible goal? After all, how can adults learn more quickly than a child?"

With that, Cora pivoted to face Lucy. "A man of forty can learn more quickly than a child because he has a larger speaking vocabulary and he's learned how to reason. He doesn't have to rely on memory alone, like a child does." She pointed to a stack of papers on her desk. "As long as they can relate to what they're learning. That's why I've started a plan to create Country Readers, as well as newspapers."

"Country what?"

"Country Readers. Curriculum. Disguised as stories. We'll use them instead of primers. They'll be filled with short, informational articles about things adults are interested in. Using common, everyday words." She sat back in her chair and let out a sigh. "And that raises the question—who will write these stories and articles?" She looked straight at Lucy.

"Me?" It came out like a squeak. *Not me.* That's what she should have said.

Too late. Cora misunderstood her squeak as volunteering for the job.

Gratitude filled Cora's eyes. "Oh dear girl, sometimes I think you are an angel, sent to me straight from heaven." She lifted the pile with both hands and pushed it to Lucy's side of the desk. "You're such a fine writer too. A legacy from your sweet mother. These won't take you any time at all."

Lucy looked at the pile, papers thick with notes. *Lucy, keep*

*vocabulary minimum. Simple one- or two-syllable words. . . .
Lucy, add in some mountain jargon. . . . Lucy, use this one to
expand on the previous story.*

She let out a longsuffering sigh. Her name was written all over
this project from the beginning.

ON SATURDAY AFTERNOON, Lucy took a break from writing
for Cora and saddled Jenny to head up the hill on a now familiar
trail. She wanted to see Sally Ann Duncan. She brought along a
tin of shortbread, flowers from Miss Maude's garden, and a little
pink hat knitted by Miss Viola. Sally Ann must have seen her coming through the trees, for she was already on the porch, waving a
dishcloth overhead to welcome her in, and Lucy released a deep
breath. Their last visit had ended in such an awkward, unpleasant
way, and it still nettled her. Cora's advice was not to mention it
again. Just move on, as if it never happened. "You can't change
superstition by explaining it away," she told Lucy. "Doing so would
only muddy the waters."

As Lucy approached the Duncan cabin, her eyes swept over the
lovely farm. So different from most of the homes in this holler.
The carefully tended garden patch, the potted flowers, the meadow
grass trimmed. There was something about this tidy setting, some
kind of connection Lucy felt to it, that she couldn't quite put into
words. It just spoke to her, whispering deep to her heart.

Sally Ann met her at the gate with a big smile. Relief! It seemed
Lucy was forgiven for her gaffe. She slid off Jenny in one smooth
move and tied her reins to the gate post. "I brought you a letter
from Roy. Some treats from Miss Maude. And something for the
baby."

Sally Ann beamed, practically bouncing on her toes with excitement. "The baby's sleeping in her cradle. Mebbe we can read
Roy's letter, out here, afore we go in."

Smiling, Lucy reached into her saddlebag and riffled through it to pull out Roy's letter, plus the other items. She followed the young woman, struck again by how young she was—hardly more than a girl!—to the porch, where they sat on rockers with soft rush seats. Sally Ann had a look on her face like a cat that swallowed the canary. As Lucy opened the envelope, she reached out and took the letter from her. "Lemme try. I might need a mite holp here and there." She cleared her throat. Brows furrowed, she began. "Dear wife. I met . . . with . . ." She stole a look at Lucy, a silent plea.

Lucy peered at the letter. "I met with Mr. Wilson at Valley View Lumber."

Sally Ann nodded earnestly. "Mister Wilson at Valley View Lumber . . . and the . . . job is mine." She let out an audible shaky sigh and stared at the words on the paper. "Miss Lucy! Roy got the job!"

Lucy grinned. Her father had sent word to tell her the news, and of course she was thrilled. But even more exciting was listening to Sally Ann *read*. Slowly, haltingly, the young mother made out the last sentence, about joining him in Lexington. He included train fare and told her to send word. "I'll be the one . . ." She held the letter to Lucy to finish.

"I'll be the one standing on the platform with the big smile and wide-open arms. Love, Roy."

Sally Ann took the letter back and repeated the words, a shy smile covering her pretty face.

Lucy reached out to cover her hand. "Tell me. How did you teach yourself to read?"

"After I heard about Miss Mollie learning to read, I thought to myself, 'Why, if an ol' lady can learn to read, so can I.' So I talked to Angie and she's been comin' over in the nights to holp. I been working hard at it."

"So I see." Lucy squeezed her hand and released it. "I'm so proud of you, Sally Ann."

"I always wanted to be book red, but Paw wouldn't let me go to school. Didn't believe in book learning, no matter how much

Maw begged. Then I married Roy . . . and figured it got too late for me." Her eyes flickered to the letter. "I cain't thank you enough, Miss Lucy, for Roy's new job. I knowed you had a big part in it."

"No thanks are needed, Sally Ann. Roy will earn his keep, and Valley View is fortunate to have him." She gazed around the farm, her eyes resting on two fat red hens and their baby chicks, all pecking at the ground. One of the hens lifted a wing, protective of her chicks. "I'll miss you, though. Do you think you'll ever come back?"

Sally Ann turned to see what she was looking at. "O'course. Shore we will."

But they both knew they wouldn't be back for good, only for visits. Once the young people left for the cities, they didn't return to the hollows. Through the open door, they heard the baby start to stir, and Sally Ann went in to check on her. She came back out with the baby in her arms and sat down in a rocking chair to nurse her. Lucy looked away; she still wasn't accustomed to women unbuttoning their shirts and pulling out a naked breast for a baby to nurse.

"What will happen to your farm?" She cast a sideways glance at Sally Ann. "Until you come back, I mean?"

Sally Ann shrugged. "Arthur Cooper sez he'll look after it. Angie'll take good care of my hens." She sighed. "Life is all howdies and goodbyes, ain't it?"

Lucy looked down at the baby's little round downy head, nuzzled against her mother. "Yes, it certainly is."

"My mamaw always said, 'Sometimes you have to give something up to make room for something new.'"

Lucy sat silent for a long time, pondering the startling truth in that simple adage. By giving up her ever-present sorrow for Charlotte, her hope that her sister would one day be found, she had made room for a new life. It was like she'd opened doors and windows and released all the stale air, allowing fresh air in. "Your mamaw is quite wise."

"Would you like to hold the baby?"

"No! Um . . . thank you, but no." Not again. Lucy didn't trust herself not to say or do the wrong thing. There was still so much she didn't know about these people. But she was learning. She *was* learning.

THE NEXT MORNING, Andy was outside of Miss Maude's, waiting to walk Lucy to work. She hadn't seen him all week and, pent up, the first words out of her mouth were about the abandoned holding pens she'd seen in the hills with Wyatt. "Why hasn't the water been released?"

He flinched slightly, as if she'd struck him a physical blow. "Because . . . my crews aren't finished yet."

"I didn't see any lumber crews working at all. Not one."

"My crews are up north, near Waltz. We still need those ponds."

Oh. She and Wyatt had gone west toward Elliottville.

He took her hand in his, entwining their fingers, and started down the road. "Everything will get fixed, Lucy, don't you worry."

"Do you promise?"

"I don't have to, Lucy. It's standard procedure for Valley View Lumber."

"But—"

He pulled her behind a large shade tree and silenced her with a kiss. "Leave the lumber business with me, Lucy," he said, touching his finger to her lips, "and I'll leave the education business with you."

One more tender, lingering kiss and she felt a little dazed, nearly forgetting about those pens. Not quite, but almost.

"I've been missing you something fierce." He wanted to take her up to Limestone Knob on Saturday. "It's where all lovers go." His eyebrows wiggled in a way that made her laugh. "And," he said, his voice dropping low to a whisper, "maybe we can talk about what comes next. After our hardship duty in Rowan County is over."

She froze. She'd told him once that she had planned to stay in Morehead only for six months, and he had told her he had the same plan.

The church bells chimed the hour and she slipped out of his arms with a breezy, "I'm late!" She hurried down the road to Cora's office, turning to wave at Andy as she reached the door. He blew her a kiss and she pretended to catch it, but her smile quickly faded as she walked down the hallway to Cora's door. Andy was always ahead of her, rushing her.

She wondered what was wrong with her. Why wasn't she more eager? He was everything a girl could hope for in a man. Father and Hazel would be thrilled if she ended up as Mrs. Andrew Spencer. Ecstatic. She could imagine how they would congratulate themselves on their matchmaking. Maybe Hazel would stop pitying her. Maybe everyone would.

Something kept Lucy's feelings reserved about Andy, but then, she could hear Hazel's voice say, tinged with exasperation, "Oh, Lucy, something keeps you reserved about *everything*."

As she opened the office door, she was surprised to discover Wyatt and Cora, heads together, studying something on the desktop.

Cora looked up, beaming. "Lucy, come! Come see what this brilliant man has done."

Lucy set her things down on her desk and crossed the room. On Cora's desk were two wooden slates with carefully chiseled letters, polished until they gleamed. "Wyatt, you made these? They're perfect! Exactly what Cora had imagined." She glanced up at him and he looked away quickly, as if he didn't want to be caught watching her reaction.

"Nearly forgot the stylus." He patted his pockets and pulled out a wooden stick, chiseled down to a point. "Pick which slate you like best, and I'll get working on them."

"They're beyond my expectations, Wyatt. I don't even know which one would be better than the other."

"This one"—he picked a slate up—"would be my choice." He glanced at Cora. "Just how many folks do you expect?"

She lifted her shoulders in a sigh. "I wish I knew. Lucy's census revealed over one thousand illiterates."

Lucy raised a hand to interrupt. "One thousand one hundred fifty-two, to be exact."

"I'd love to have everyone come, oh how I would! But there seems to be some growing resistance in town to Moonlight Schools. I fear its trickling into the mountains."

Wyatt picked up the two slates. "I've heard a rumble or two." He put them in his satchel. "I'll make one hundred."

Cora smiled. "I would be . . . over the moon if one hundred people came."

Wyatt swung his satchel over his shoulder. "Cora, have faith."

"I have plenty of faith in the Almighty. It's people . . . that's where my faith falters."

"All Mighty means just that. Mighty over all." Wyatt said it often. He didn't just say it. He believed it.

ON SATURDAY, all the schoolteachers came to town for a special meeting by Cora's request. They met in the Disciples of Christ Church, and Lucy was shocked to realize she was older than most every teacher by quite a few years. They all looked to be barely out of school themselves, boys and girls of the mountains. The girls reminded her of Angie Cooper. The boys of Finley James.

Cora knew each one and welcomed them with warm hugs. She started out the meeting by enthusiastically telling them to prepare themselves for the highlight of their life. Then she rolled out her plans to launch the Moonlight Schools campaign. The room, which had been full of chatter a moment ago, was dead quiet. You could have heard a pin drop.

Cora carried on. "The main goal is not to give each adult a complete education but to interest them in reading and writing. Better still, I want them to have an appreciation and love of learning for its own sake. They shouldn't have to read primers designed for children. Instead, we're going to create newspapers that will have stories of interest to them. Stories that relate to Rowan County, filled with simple news."

One teacher, a wisp of a girl barely five feet tall, raised her hand. "Miss Cora, let me get this straight. You think maws and paws are gonna leave their homes at night and go to the schoolhouses, led by the moon?"

"That is the plan, Ellie."

"How many do you think'll come?"

Cora took a deep breath. "Perhaps just a few will show up at each schoolhouse. Hopefully many more. With your enthusiasm"—she swept a hand over the room—"with all of you spreading the word to invite the parents, I think we will have a decent turnout." Only Lucy heard her mutter, "I hope."

"How old can they be?"

Cora smiled. "No one is ever too old to learn, Ellie."

A male teacher seated a few rows behind Lucy spoke up, his voice cracking. "But we get paid whether they come or not?"

Cora held her breath for a long moment. "Unfortunately, the Moonlight Schools campaign has no budget."

Ellie remained standing. "Miss Cora, you mean to say we teachers ain't getting paid for night school?"

Cora cleared her throat. "No."

"You mean to say that we got to teach them children all day long, then teach their maws and paws at night?"

"That's correct, Ellie. And their mamaws and papaws too. From seven o'clock to nine o'clock. For six weeks."

Lucy watched the shocked looks the teachers exchanged with each other. She couldn't blame them. Teachers worked long days for little pay, and now Cora was asking them to work in the evening, as well.

A door opened and shut. Someone had left.

Nobody spoke. The silence stretched. The only sound in the room came from a fly, buzzing against the window. The teachers began to shift in their seats. Cora remained unfazed.

However, she did seem to realize she had made a serious mistake. "I know this is a formidable challenge. But I have no doubt, no doubt at all, that we will be changing the course of history for our county. And as I said at the beginning, this experience will be the highlight of your life. I guarantee it will be."

One by one, the teachers sat up a little straighter.

"You are all professionals. Each one of you have received a calling to teach. A *calling* from the Almighty! A *calling*. Imagine what will happen when Rowan County throws off its blight of illiteracy and leads the state in adult literacy. Not just the state, the entire country! Imagine the part you will have in this great moment of history. It's playing out, right before your eyes."

It was like watching Cora sprinkle fairy dust over the room. The teachers started to pepper her with questions, excitement grew, and then came the irresistible challenge.

"Young men and women, a mighty tide has begun to rise in our county. Nothing can stop it now."

A teacher, tall and thin, raised his hand. "Miss Cora, you got the lessons all planned out for us?"

Cora smiled. "Working on it now, Curtis. There will be plenty of things that will need to be planned as we go along, and adjustments made as needed. Flexibility is essential. Always our attitude will be—let's experiment and find out what works."

She detailed the curriculum, describing the "whole-word approach" to teach reading, but most of all, she emphasized the attitude she expected from the teachers. "Adults who can't read have a sense of inferiority. Never use a loud tone of voice, never a frown or rebuke. If a new reader feels timid, your job is to encourage him. If slow, never show impatience. Whatever these adult students do well should be praised."

She walked down the church's aisle, making eye contact with each teacher. "Remember how it felt to handle a quill pen when you were new to school? It's difficult! But the most important thing is to give praise, praise, praise. Every effort deserves a kind word. Shaky letters should be admired, not critiqued." Back up the aisle she walked, intentionally slow, as all eyes riveted on her. "And above all, dear ones, have patience. I can't stress enough the need for patience. And when the ink pot spills, as it will, and as it did for you as a new learner, you should respond with patience instead of anger. We want to create an environment that gives your adult students a sense of success."

Success. Somehow, Cora had swept away all objections to focus on that one powerful word. No, Lucy thought. It was more than a word. She had created a vision.

Up front, Cora held up one of the wooden slates that Brother Wyatt had created. "To teach writing, the students will be able to trace letters until they learn how to make them on their own." She passed the slates out to the teachers to examine. "These pads contain all the letters of the alphabet. After the students have mastered the grooved pads, I'd like you to encourage them to write a letter to me, telling me something about themselves. For each letter I receive, I'll send the writer a small Bible as a reward."

Lucy smiled, wondering who Cora had talked into donating the money to provide the Bibles. She knew it wasn't going to come from Andrew Spencer. He shut down the conversation each time she brought it up, which was often.

After the meeting came to an end and the teachers drifted out of the church, Lucy waited until only she and Cora remained. "After you said that there would be no salary, someone left. Who was it?"

"Who else?" Cora rolled her eyes. "Norah."

NINETEEN

CORA PLOPPED DOWN IN A PEW. "Before the meeting, she told me that she was quitting. I asked her to at least stay and listen to what I had to say. But it was clear from the start that her mind was made up."

Lucy slipped into the pew to sit down beside her. "Finley James will be happy."

Cora rubbed her temples, as if a headache was coming. "That boy needs schooling."

"What about Angie Cooper? She considers herself to be quite well qualified."

"Indeed she is, but she needs to graduate grade 8. Then I've got plans for her." She let out a sigh and dropped her chin, arms crossed against her cushiony chest. "If only Norah had waited for the end of spring term." After a long moment of silence, she snapped her head up to look straight at Lucy, like a bird of prey zooming in on an unlucky mouse. "Lucy, *you* can do it. You can teach at Little Brushy. You can fill Norah's shoes."

"No!" Lucy jumped up from the pew like she'd sat on a bee. "No, no. Cora, that's just not possible!"

Calm as could be, Cora said, "Why not?"

"Well, for one, I'm not good with children. It would be bedlam. Sheer chaos. I can never manage a schoolhouse full of them."

Good heavens . . . she couldn't even keep track of her little sister. She might lose them all!

"You're just lacking confidence, dear girl. It's always been what's held you back. But I have no doubt you'll rise to the occasion. There is no failure until you have failed yourself." That was a favorite phrase of Cora's.

"Please listen—"

"Besides," Cora said, not listening at all, "it's only through the spring term. You must help, Lucy, if for no other reason than to help Angie Cooper pass her grade 8 exams. She'll take the teaching spot for Little Brushy in the fall. I promise you that. This will just be a short stint. Why, I'd do it myself if I didn't have so much to do to get ready for the Moonlight Schools."

"Exactly how long?" Lucy could hear the weakening resolve in her own voice.

"A few weeks."

"Cora?" This time, Lucy's voice held a warning tone.

"The term ends in June." Cora clasped her hands together. "I don't what else to do, Lucy. I need you. Angie needs you. Finley James needs you. If we don't get that boy back in that classroom soon, he'll never learn to read."

Cora had found Lucy's Achilles' heel—the need to be needed. She let out a puff of air in resignation. "Fine."

Cora jumped out of the pew. "Oh wonderful! Simply wonderful! I'll go tell Arthur now that you'll be boarding with him. Hurry and go pack up from Miss Maude's, and I'll meet you at the livery."

"Wait. What did you say?" Boarding? At the Coopers? "Cora! Hold up!"

But Cora was out the door, far away from earshot. Lucy sank back down on the pew, covered her face with her hands, and groaned. How in the world had this happened? The thought of teaching school was terrifying. Boarding at the Coopers' small cabin, facing Angie's fierce scowls at her day and night, coping with a roomful of barefoot children who rarely bathed . . . it all sounded *awful*. Horrifying!

After a long moment of abject self-pity, she heard Wyatt softly say her name. "Lucy?"

She dropped her hands to look up at his kind, serious face.

"I bumped into Cora. She told me about Norah. About you stepping in to teach at Little Brushy."

Lucy's shoulders slumped. It really was happening. Cora's determination couldn't be stopped.

He sat in the pew in front of Lucy and turned to face her. "One of the things I've always liked best about Rowan County is that people come together when they're needed. It's been true for me, for Cora, and it'll be true for you now, as you step into a role you hadn't expected."

Hadn't wanted. Ever.

"You told me once that you didn't believe God had any purpose for you. I think you're wrong. I think you're seeing his purposes for you unfold."

She blinked back unexpected tears.

He dipped his chin to bid her goodbye and left her alone in the church. To think. To pray.

Lucy sighed and let the rest of her upset go. Wyatt always did that to her. Made her think. Made her think about praying.

ANGIE WAS IN A STATE. The worst nightmare—the very worst—of her life had come true. Paw came home from the livery to tell her to clear out a drawer in her cupboard for Miss Lucy, because she was comin' to stay with them 'til the school term finished up. The troublesome twins were thrilled and danced a little jig around the cabin. Angie sat at the table, sipping her coffee (mostly cream because Paw didn't allow her much coffee), steaming with fury.

Angie would not only have to sit in the classroom and observe

Finley James gawk at Miss Lucy all the livelong day, but she would have to share her private loft! She'd only had the loft since Maw passed on. Paw said it was too lonely for him, plus it was high time Angie had a mite of privacy, so he moved downstairs with the boys and Angie got the loft.

Angie started to give Paw all the reasons this was a bad idea, a *terrible* plan, but he silenced her objections with a stern look, and a reminder that if she wanted her grade 8 exam so that she could teach next fall, she'd better jest have another think. "And fast, daughter." He peered at the grandfather clock, the only ornate piece of furniture in the humble cabin. "Because Miss Lucy'll be coming tomorrow."

Angie flew up the loft ladder to throw herself on her bed, too angry to cry.

Her life be ruint.

ON SUNDAY AFTERNOON, Lucy packed the clothes she would need for the week. She had decided she would continue to let her room from Miss Maude and return to town on the weekends. That way, she could maintain a little space to recoup from close quarters in the Coopers' cabin, and she could see Andy.

She gave one last fond look around her spare little room with the corner windows and sighed. "Goodbye, little room." Bending down, she hoisted her saddlebags over her shoulder. How strange. It was now a familiar gesture to her. As she walked down the stairs, she found the sheriff and the judge's wife, deep in conversation in the dining room. They stopped talking as Lucy appeared in the doorway.

"What's that delicious smell?" Lucy asked.

"Hasenpfeffer," Mrs. Klopp said, as if everyone should know. "A German delicacy in these parts. Miss Maude makes it, at my request, at least once a month."

"What is hasenpfeffer?" Lucy was tempted to pop in the kitchen for a sampling from Miss Maude.

"Sour rabbit."

"Ah." Lucy's stomach, always a little dubious of mountain dishes—most of which were fried in lard—turned at the sound of that. She excused herself and stopped, hand on the doorknob, as she heard the sheriff mention Cora's name.

"Then you might be aware," she heard the judge's wife say, "that she's been working these last weeks to set up a campaign to teach those hillbillies to read."

By the sheriff's mumbled response, he knew of the campaign.

Then Miss Maude came into the dining room, talking a mile a minute, and Lucy left to get Jenny to head to the Coopers'. The pony nickered when she saw Lucy, a sign of familiarity. She was holding on to anything that lifted her spirits.

ARTHUR COOPER AND HIS TWO SONS couldn't have been more welcoming. The boys led Jenny to the barn while Arthur carried her saddlebags inside and up to the loft. Arthur said Angie had gone off visiting, but Lucy had a hunch she had purposefully absented herself. Sulking, no doubt.

Not much later, Lucy knew Angie was standing behind her as she hung a few dresses on the wall peg because she'd heard a deep sigh. She glanced over her shoulder at Angie and forced a sweet smile. "It won't be for too long," she said, keeping her voice light and chipper. "I'm here to help you pass grade 8."

"I could pass right now. Go ahead. Ask me anythin'."

Lucy hung her last skirt and turned to Angie. "Well, have you been studying grammar?" Wrong question! Wrong question!

Angie looked at her with that *look*, the one where she narrowed her eyes into the smallest slits possible and scowled at her. The one that said, "My grammar ain't got no problems."

Lucy had known she'd get a cool reception from Angie, but she hadn't expect snow and frost and ice. Angie told her to stay on her side of the bed, with a warning to not cross over the middle line. Adding fiercely that if Lucy dared to snore, to expect a hard kick. "And don't even think about trying to lady me up!" she snarled as she climbed down the loft ladder.

As if Lucy *could* "lady-up" Angie! As if anyone could. She was the most disagreeable, ill-mannered, peevish girl Lucy had ever known . . . and that was after ten years at the Townsend School for Girls, plenty of whom were disagreeable and ill-mannered and peevish. None came *close* to Angie Cooper.

Lucy should've been offended by Angie's snippy behavior. After all, she was the loser here. She was the one whom Cora had coerced into teaching at Little Brushy School, and she was the one who left her adequate but comfortable room at Miss Maude's to come to the Coopers' cabin. She'd been given no choice about where to stay.

But for all the girl's bluster, there was something endearing about her, something that touched Lucy's heart. She supposed it had to do with the fact that Angie watched her so carefully, tried to imitate her, copying her in numerous ways. As they prepared supper together tonight, she noticed that Angie made efforts to self-correct her own diction. A handkerchief was tucked into her apron pocket so that it peeped out, and her boots were polished until they shone. Why, just the fact that she wore boots seemed remarkable. Her brothers were barefoot.

During supper, Angie kept peering at Lucy's hairstyle and later that evening, she found her glued to a small mirror, clumsily attempting to pin her curly blonde hair up to mimic Lucy's hairstyle. And then, as Lucy brushed out her hair that night, she heard Angie softly counting to herself the number of strokes as Lucy made them.

"Why do you do that?"

Lucy stopped, midstroke. "To make it shiny. It's something

my mother taught me. Each night, brush your hair one hundred strokes."

For a fleeting moment, Angie's crossness softened, replaced by wistfulness. Then just as quickly it vanished and back came the scowl. "Sounds like twaddle."

Angie rolled to the far side of the bed, as if Lucy had a dread disease, and warned her again about snoring. She need not have worried. Lucy could barely sleep. She felt so anxious about facing a classroom of students tomorrow. Cora had spent all Saturday afternoon and evening with her, creating lesson plans to give structure to the days—much to Andy's disappointment. There was no time for a visit to Limestone Knob.

As Cora mapped out the school day with chunks of time given for each subject, it had seemed manageable to Lucy. Now, she could barely remember what to do first.

She lay stiffly in bed, counting the gongs of the grandfather clock below as it chimed the hours. How long would it take before the children realized Lucy had no experience teaching school? Five minutes? Ten?

How she *dreaded* the morning.

ANGIE ALWAYS FELT that special things happened in the schoolhouse, but the most special thing she could've ever imagined was happening right before her eyes. She could not have been more pleased to see Miss Lucy stammer and stumble and make a downright fool of herself, pretending she could teach. What a ninny! Miss Lucy was shaking like a tree limb in a storm. Her voice quivered like Miss Mollie's underdone custard. The children kept their worried expressions all morning long.

Perfect.

Lucy Wilson didn't understand mountain people, not their ways, not their talk. She had to ask Johnny what he was trying to say three times over, till finally Finley James stood up and interpreted for her. Fool boy. He stared at Lucy like he'd never seen a female before.

Angie let out a sigh. Finley James should be sitting next to her, but instead he sat up front with them littles, seeing as how he scarcely had nothin' but a grade 2 education. His seatmate was a seven-year-old named Belle, missing her front teeth, who hugged a dirty rag doll all the livelong day. The room was full of girls, jest a sprinkling of boys. Their help was needed at home. When Angie became the teacher at Little Brushy, she was going to figure out how to git them boys in the schoolhouse.

She'd hoped the luster of Miss Lucy's shine might be tarnished for Finley James after seeing her mess up so bad today, but the opposite happened. At the worst of the day, when a fight broke out between two boys and bedlam followed—girls screamed, boys cheered—Miss Lucy looked like she wanted to cry. Finley James grabbed the two boys who started the fight and tossed them outside like they was nothin' more than a sack of potatoes. Then he stood by the door and shouted, so loud it cracked a mite in the middle of his speech, "Who else wants to git on home? Who else wants a lickin' from your paw when he hears what you done to the new teacher? Better still, it'll save time if I jest give ya a lickin' right here and now."

Silence covered the classroom like a heavy fog had rolled in straight off Limestone Knob. One by one, children slipped back into their seats, facing forward, hands folded on their desks like model citizens. Miss Lucy gave Finley James a look of appreciation, and he gazed back at her with such fondness, and Angie felt so sickly she thought she might retch.

Not five minutes later, Miss Cora came visiting the Little Brushy School. All Miss Cora did was sweep the room with that piercing gaze o' hers, and Finley James cleared his throat, and all them children jerked to attention like puppets on a string. You woulda thought Miss Lucy was the finest teacher in the whole wide world.

Miss Cora stayed a long while, gave a 'rithmatic lesson, talked about how to grow fruit trees in the county cuz that's what our county done best, had a spelling bee—which Angie won, naturally—and then off she went to visit another school, pleased as punch.

Angie wanted to bang her head against the wall. *Cain't no one but me see that Miss Lucy got no business teaching Little Brushy School?*

As soon as the school day ended, Angie dashed out the door. She didn't want nothin' to do with walking Miss Lucy home. Happily, Paw's horse was gone from the yard, so she hurried inside the cabin and went straight up to the loft. In front of Maw's little mirror, she ran a comb through her tangled hair, stroking it one hundred times, fussing and fretting and tutting to herself as she tried to pin it into place.

"You tryin' to look jest like Miss Lucy?"

Angie spun around to see Mikey and Gabe staring at her from the top of the loft ladder, eyes wide. Unbelievable. She had no privacy at all. "Shush yor mouth. I am not."

"Yor hair's the same," Gabe said, climbing over the top of the ladder. "And ya musta worshed it." He came close to sniff her. "I can smell the soap."

She swatted him away. "Never you mind what I do with my hair. Besides, every grown woman wears her hair pinned up like this."

"Mebbe so," Mikey said, "but ya ain't grown. Ya still wear pinnyfores."

Angie pointed at him. "Don't say ain't." Angry and exasperated, she glanced down at her pinafore. "Git to the barn and milk that sorrowful cow before Paw gits home. I can hear her wailing all the way up here."

She turned back to the mirror to see half her hair had fallen from the pins. She threw the comb against the wall in disgust and yanked off her pinafore, bunching it into a ball and tossing it on the floor.

Bleak, bleak. Life was so bleak.

As LUCY CAME THROUGH the trees to the Coopers' cabin, she saw Angie taking laundry off the clothesline that hung from the porch to a tree. She slowed Jenny down, bracing herself for Angie's prickliness. Today held many surprises for Lucy, especially the discovery that Angie was sweet, tender even, to the other children in the schoolhouse. Someday, she would be a fine teacher for Cora. But . . . not if Finley James were still a student.

Sliding off Jenny, Lucy tied the reins around the hitching post and crossed the yard. "Can I help?"

"Worsh is done. Don't need no holp."

Lucy's perky smile began to waver. "There's a lot of clothes to take down. I'd like to help you with the house chores. It's a lot of work to take care of your father and brothers." When Angie didn't respond, she added, "I'd like to be friends."

"Don't need no friends."

"Everybody needs friends."

"Don't need no friends like you." Squinting her eyes, she hissed, "Ain't there a law about old maids chasing after boys? If not, there should be."

Lucy's smile vanished completely. She had to bite her lip to keep from snapping a harsh retort. She pivoted on her heels and returned to take care of Jenny, a much friendlier face.

LIFE SURE COULD BRING a man some interesting twists and turns. Fin had dipped in and out of school over his long life, mostly out, but no teacher had ever bothered to teach him how to write his front and back and middle names until Miss Lucy came along. *Finley James Randolph Cunningham.* "Such a *dignified* name," she had said in her singsongy voice, and that was all it took for Fin. He practiced writing his dignified name all the livelong day. And to his awe and wonderment, it *did* give a man his dignity to write his own name for hisself.

A spark lit Fin's imagination—he saw himself signing property deeds, buying back land that his maw had sold off. He saw himself voting in an election. Heck! Even better. He saw himself sitting in that big ol' White House, signing bills and laws and letters and whatever else a president signed. Something about writing his own name gave Fin a sense of power, of personhood. No more of them wobbly X's, which made a man seem like a mouse, shaking in his boots.

All the way home from school, whenever Fin saw a particularly toothsome spot on a tree, or a particularly inviting fence post, he stopped and carved his name. His full, complete, dignified name.

BY THE TIME FRIDAY AFTERNOON rolled around, Lucy felt as if she'd climbed a mountain. She had survived an entire week of teaching school! Not just survived, but she actually enjoyed herself. She had even decided not to return to town this weekend, as she had so much work to do to prepare for next week. Her spirits lifted with a sense of quiet accomplishment, and she wondered if this was what Wyatt meant when he spoke of the purposeful life.

But the week was hard all the same. There were so many things she'd felt anxious about, so many fears she'd anticipated. And every single fear came true! There was nothing glamorous about a room filled with children who needed bathing so badly that Lucy felt she was suffocating. Nothing admirable about standing at a distance from the Boling boys who scratched their heads endlessly, or yanking her hand out of the grasp of a cute little girl who was covered with signs of ringworm. Lucy knew she was no hero. She lacked courage. Despite everything, in spite of herself, she finished Friday afternoon forming a tender connection with the children.

Even Cora had noticed. She stopped in the classroom this afternoon and whispered to Lucy, "Those children care about you."

And she for them. These dear little ones had quickly found a place in her heart.

Now she understood why Cora championed these mountain children, convinced that only geographical boundaries kept the children from getting the educational opportunities that were due them. These children . . . they were different from any Lucy had known, or any she'd grown up with in Lexington. The best way to describe it was that they were thoroughly unspoiled. Hungry to learn, quick and bright, naturally imbued with poetry and an oratorical prowess that astounded Lucy.

The little girls—so many of them!—won her over on day one. Bright eyed, with round cherub cheeks and lisps from missing front teeth. Out on the play area, one or two would come and slip their chubby little hands into Lucy's and her heart would melt.

The boys, they were more of a challenge. Lucy wondered if the handful of boys that arrived each day were only sent to school because they were so much trouble to their parents. Were it not for Finley James's bold authority over them, Lucy would've ended each day in a puddle of tears.

And then there was Angie Cooper. She sat in the back row with a bored look on her face. The only time she seemed interested in school was when she had an opportunity to shine by showing off. And shine she did. Angie was smart, quicker than Lucy in nearly every subject. She would make a fine teacher for the school if she could just drop her arrogance. Much of it, Lucy knew, had to do with that big crush Finley James had on Lucy, and how threatened it made Angie feel.

Finley James was the biggest surprise of the week. As it turned out, that boy had quite an aptitude for learning. His reading ability grew at an astonishing rate. On Monday, Lucy had tested him to see if he knew the alphabet and the sound of each letter. He knew most, but not all. Tuesday, he had them down pat. By Wednesday, he was sounding out words in the speller. She would never forget the look on his face as letters and sounds passed from nonsense into sense. By Friday, he read through the grade 2 primer with a decent proficiency, and copied down a list of words he'd learned in an exact and careful penmanship—a vocabulary that seemed to grow exponentially with each passing day. It seemed like a miracle was occurring before Lucy's very eyes. Like the flowers on the rhododendron bushes she passed every day, unfolding from tight buds to big blossoms.

Every other day, late in the afternoon, Wyatt would stop by the schoolhouse. In recounting the day's events to him, she realized how much she wanted his approval. "I'm starting to see how Norah's frequent absences slowed down the children's learning."

When she described Fin's lightning streak progress, he listened with a knowing smile. "Goes to show you're just the right teacher for him, Lucy."

"Me?" She pressed her palm against her chest. "Quite honestly, Wyatt, it has nothing to do with me. I know copious amounts of Latin and can conjugate verbs, but I've never taught anyone to read before. I have no illusion about my teaching ability. Credit goes all to Fin. I think he's even inspiring the other students to pay attention. It's like . . . magic."

"When motivation meets opportunity, miracles can happen."

"Is that what happened to you?"

He looked up, surprised. "Indeed it did. Though I wouldn't give credit to magic, only to the All Mighty." Before she could ask another question, he turned the subject back to Fin. "Cora's instincts were spot on with Fin. He needs to catch up in his schooling before long. I hope you can take him as far as he can go in the next few weeks. I doubt he'll be back in the fall."

"Why not?"

"With Angie Cooper as his teacher?" He coughed a laugh. "There's a limit to Fin's humility."

"She'll do fine as a teacher. She knows just about everything there is to know."

A laugh burst out of Wyatt, and Lucy laughed too.

"Speaking of Angie," Lucy said, "this morning I noticed that in the Cooper family Bible there isn't a birth date for her. Why do you suppose that's so?"

"Most folks don't pay much attention to celebrating birthdays."

"How do you keep track of someone's age?"

"We round up." He grinned. "Or down."

"It just seems parents would've noted their own baby's birth date."

"Arthur can't read. And Aria . . . she was a mite different."

"How so?"

He lifted a shoulder in a shrug. "She had some troubles of her own."

Lucy jerked her head up. This week, she'd noticed that Aria was a shadowy presence in the Coopers' household. "What do you know about her?"

"Aria Cooper? Not much. Each holler tends to keep to themselves. Miss Mollie might be the one to ask." He picked up his hat, preparing to leave. "Lucy, have you considered teaching Angie some of your Latin?"

Hmm. Latin. Angie.

They exchanged a small smile. Wyatt lifted a hand and brushed a lock of Lucy's hair from her forehead. It was an intimate gesture, another surprise in this week of wonders, and Lucy felt her cheeks coloring.

"I quit!"

At the sound of Fin's voice, Wyatt and Lucy sprang apart. He stood in the open doorway, glaring at them.

"I'm quittin' school." He turned and ran.

TWENTY

FIN WAS DONE. Done with schooling. Done with women.

He shoulda never gone back to the school this afternoon, but he'd been struck by an idea to whittle a piece of wood he'd found for Miss Lucy to use as a chalkboard pointer. Or mebbe it could be a tool for her to smack some of them unruly boys.

Unruly. U-N-R-U-L-Y. That was a new word he'd added to his growing list. He liked to try out his immense vocabulary, especially if it meant he could stump Angie Cooper. Today, he'd beat her in the spelling bee on the word "cell." Angie spelled it like it sounded: sell. Fin knew better, but only because Miss Lucy had explained homophones to him jest yesterday morning. "If you sell moonshine," she told him as an example, "you might end up in a prison cell."

He'd said it over and over to hisself so he didn't forget it. Funny thing, the sheriff did most of the selling of moonshine in Rowan County. He didn't tell that to Miss Lucy.

There were jest a few weeks left of school, so Fin cooked up a plan. He was going to pass one grade level each week, mebbe two. It was a nigh on unscalable goal—unscalable was another word he'd learned this week—especially for a fella who'd never thought much past one day at a time. But Fin was determined, and whilst it didn't happen often, when he did feel that burden of determination, he would see it through. Besides, he knew he needed to buckle down and get serious 'bout getting book red. No way was he ever gonna step foot in any school taught by Angie Cooper, and this was his last chance to make sure Angie didn't have the upper hand on him for the rest of his livelong life. He had a few weeks left to go, and heck if'n he wasn't gonna give it his all. If nothing else but for the look of sheer delight on Miss Lucy's angelic face whenever he mastered a new grade.

But all that changed this afternoon when he saw the way Brother Wyatt and Miss Lucy were gazing at each other, inches apart, in the schoolhouse. All this time he'd thought Andrew Spencer was his competition. And all along, Brother Wyatt was sneaking around behind his back, winning her heart.

All day Saturday, in between feeding horses and cleaning out stalls at the livery, Fin worked out his plan to live a good long life and die an old bachelor, unfettered by the misery caused by women. Not his maw, but most other women. Such a plan cheered him, and he was almost back to himself as he pushed the last barrow out to the manure pile when he heard hoofbeats. He glanced around, hoping it might be Lucy Wilson, coming back to her senses, coming back to him . . . but heck if it was only Angie Cooper.

"Finley James?"

"I'm busy," Fin replied in as gruff a tone as he had ever used with her.

"What's got ya so riled up?"

If'n he would confide anything in Angie Cooper. He pulled a handkerchief from his back pocket and wiped his forehead.

She had a smile wider than a watermelon slice. It worried him, so he pointed at her and gave her a stern look. "Don't go thinking you've got me pinned down. You don't. No female does. Besides . . . I'm off to Mexico, soon as I turn sixteen."

"Mexico?! Do you even know where it is?"

"Shorely do. It's . . . near Texas." At least, he thought it was. "I'm gonna join the U-nited States Army's fight in the Border War."

"Whatever for?"

"Cuz they need vital young men."

"Who ya been talking to?"

"No one."

"Judge Klopp's wife, I'll bet. She's biggerty. Thinks she knows everything."

How'd she figure that out so fast? Judge Klopp's wife came by the livery earlier today and read aloud to him again from the "Join the Army!" brochure. She thought Fin needed some ambition.

"Did the judge's wife tell you that you'd have to pass a test to join the army?"

"What kind of test?"

"Reading and writing and numbers and such."

Heck. The judge's wife never said nothing 'bout no test. "Well, I'm still going to Mexico."

"But why would you go and do a fool thing like that? The border with Mexico ain't your fight."

"Because . . . because I'm going"—he rubbed his unwhiskered chin and tried to remember how the phrasing went in the brochure—"where the need is greatest. Where the ranks are thinnest and the battle hottest."

"Ya sound like yor readin' off a something."

Fin frowned. Sometimes, most times, Angie Cooper was jest too quick for him. He had trouble keeping up with her. He tore off his hat in frustration and came near to throwing it down but decided to hang on to it. Good hats being hard to come by. He plopped it back on his head. "Well, like it or not, I'm going."

"How're you gonna make it all the way to Mexico when you cain't speak a lick o' Spanish?" Angie smiled smugly, pivoted around, and sauntered off, her head held high and shoulders stiffly back like she thought she was the queen of Mexico. Then he scratched his forehead. Did Mexico even have a queen?

AMBULO, AMBULABAM, AMBULABIT. I walk, I was walking, he will walk. Angie lay on her back in bed, listening to the sound of the howling wind in the trees. "I still don't know what parsing Latin verbs gots . . . er, *has* to do with passing the grade 8 exam."

Miss Lucy lay next to her on her side. "It will improve your understanding of grammar. In Latin, verbs include a lot of information about the sentence. The verb tense can tell you the time frame. The verb can tell you who the subject is, even if there's no pronoun in the sentence."

Angie let out a deep sigh of exasperation, but jest for Miss Lucy's sake. In truth, she was captivated. Parsing Latin verbs felt like a puzzle, and she was good at figuring out puzzles.

"Do you get many storms like this? All wind, no rain?"

Angie turned her face toward Miss Lucy. "Now and then, by and by. These storms is, uh, *are* the worst kind. Knock trees down and create havoc and nothing to show for it." Feeling restless, she flopped to her stomach. "Miss Mollie sez these storms be . . . um . . . *are* the work of the devil."

"I can appreciate that thought. This wind has a different sound to it."

Angie flipped on her side to face the wall. It was easier talking this way. "How'd you talk Finley James into coming back to school? He tol' me he was running off to Mexico."

"I asked him to come back, to help me get through the term. He's been a wonderful help."

Angie frowned. Finley James was making a fool out of hisself— she squeezed her eyes shut—himself. He lost all reason around Lucy. When would that boy come to his senses? When would he realize that Angie was the one who was meant for him? The whole thing irked her to no end. What frustrated her even more was that as angry as she was with Miss Lucy for stealing her boyfriend, she felt even more intrigued by her. Fascinated by her polite manners and show-off fancy talk and fine clothing. It pained Angie to admit it, and o'course she'd never say so aloud, but her world seemed a little brighter since Miss Lucy had started to teach school. "Finley James said you went to a school for lady lessons."

"Lady lessons? Oh, he means finishing school." Lucy chuckled. "The Townsend School for Girls. It was a boarding school."

"What's that?"

"I stayed there most of the year," she said, yawning, "and only came home for holidays."

Angie flipped over again to face her, bending her arm to rest her head in the palm of her hand. "Your paw sent you away?"

"Not like *that*. Boarding school . . . it's what most everyone does in the city."

Angie plopped on her back. "Then I'm glad I weren't . . . *wasn't* born in the city. I couldn't go to that finishing school to learn to be a lady. My paw would miss me too much."

"You're right," Lucy said, glancing over at her. "He would." Her voice held a sadness to it.

"And the troublesome twins . . . they'd turn into holy terrors without me here to make 'em mind." The very thought of them without her influence made Angie shudder.

After a long moment of quiet, Lucy added, "You don't need finishing school to learn how to be a lady, Angie. You're already learning. Every day, I see new signs of your maturity. Like a flower that's starting to bloom."

In the dark, Angie smiled.

TWO WEEKS HAD PASSED and Lucy hadn't seen or heard from Andrew Spencer. She was too busy to dwell on his absence—and surprisingly content in her role as teacher. A role she hadn't wanted, and a role in which she looked forward to its end, for it took every ounce of her and she fell into bed at night, thoroughly exhausted. But the challenge of teaching was a stimulating one, and it occurred to her that she rarely thought of Charlotte anymore.

Thoughts of Andrew would push aside other thoughts. Especially when Angie reported, smugly, he'd been seen riding past the Cooper house on his way to Licking River. Lucy responded nonchalantly to Angie, but the information did bother her. She wondered about those strong feelings he'd confessed for her. If he loved her like he said he did, wouldn't he have stopped by to see her, to check in on her?

And then one day, after the children had gone home from Little Brushy, Andrew burst into the schoolhouse holding an enormous bouquet of flowers. "There's my girl!"

She stared at him. "I've been right here. For two weeks now."

"You can imagine how busy we are, with all this rain. And besides, when you didn't come to town last weekend, I figured you needed time to get settled."

True, both.

He set the flowers on her desk and held his arms open wide. She hesitated. "I'm just offering you a hug," he said.

Softening, Lucy took a tentative step toward him. His hands went to her waist and drew her to him, wrapped his arms around her. She fit into him perfectly, like a glove.

"I have exciting news."

She had to smile at his little-boy delight. She pulled back to face him but remained in his arms. "Tell me."

"I'm getting a promotion! A big one."

She couldn't help but hug him again. "Andrew, that's wonderful news! Father never said a word."

When he didn't say anything to that, she stepped back and looked at him. "What is it?"

"Actually, this opportunity is with another lumber company."

Her eyes went wide. "A competing company?"

"You know how it is in the business world, Lucy. Dog eat dog."

She didn't know such a thing. She didn't understand such a thing.

She squirmed out of his embrace and went over to the window. The clouds were breaking up and sun rays were streaming through.

"I'm hoping I'll get transferred soon to Lexington, to the company's headquarters." He came up behind her and put his hands on her elbows. "We'll be together, Lucy. You've always said this job was only for six months."

She did. She had said it and thought it often, though less so lately.

"There's something you need to know." When she turned to face him, he said, "There's pushback brewing in town for this moonlit school notion."

"What do you mean?"

"Not everyone is in favor of it. Apparently, there's been a call for a town meeting."

"What? Surely you jest."

He lifted his shoulders in a shrug. "I thought you should know."

"But . . . what is there to object to?" She studied his face. "Why wouldn't the people in town want the mountain people to be able to read and write?"

He took her hands and pulled her to him, slipping his hands around her waist. "It'll all work itself out," he said, smiling. "It's just a meeting to give people a chance to air their grievances. These people love to complain." He kissed her on one cheek, then another. "Darling, you're so serious. Can't you see the humor in it all?" He bent down to kiss her on the lips, and for a moment, she forgot how annoyed she was that he hadn't come to see her these last two weeks, or that he had accepted a job with her father's competitor. As he kissed her again and again, murmuring how much he missed her and loved her, she even forgot all about the hullabaloo brewing over the Moonlight Schools campaign.

Then the wind slammed the school door shut, and it was like something shut down inside her. Lucy pulled out of his embrace. "Andy," she said, "I'm sorry. I can't do this."

He grabbed her hands and held on. "It was just kissing. That's all."

"You're right," she said after a moment of thought. "That's

all it is." Because that's all everything was to Andy. Everything and everyone. Nothing more than stepping-stones on his climb to the top.

He squeezed her hands. "Let's go out this Saturday evening. I'll take you someplace special! We'll celebrate my promotion."

She hesitated, glancing at her desk. "Thank you, but I think I'd better say no."

"You're tired. You've been working too hard." At the door, he turned and smiled his most charming smile, the one she found hard to resist. "If you change your mind, just sing out and I'll come running." He gave her a wink. "I think you will."

Would she? She wasn't sure.

ONLY THREE WEEKS of the school term remained. Finley James had asked Lucy if she knew any Spanish. She didn't, but she did start him on Latin. Same roots as Spanish, she told him, and that satisfied him. This week, he found he was able to out-memorize Angie in parsing Latin verbs. His interest in conjugating Latin suddenly skyrocketed.

Lucy was doing all she could to shore up Fin's learning before he quit for good. She doubted he'd make it through the grade 8 curriculum before the school term ended, but at the rate he was going, he could definitely plow through sixth grade. Maybe seventh.

Late one afternoon, as Lucy returned to the Cooper cabin after a long day of school, she saw Angie at the clothesline and asked if she could help.

Angie barely gave a glance in her direction. "Don't need no holp."

Lucy rolled her eyes. There'd been a little thawing out in Angie, it seemed, but not after Fin started beating her in Latin. Angie was peeved. Too bad, Lucy thought, turning to head to the cabin. *That's just too bad if you don't win at everything.*

"If you want to help, then take that basket into the house and put them—*those*—clothes away."

Lucy pivoted and picked up the basket of folded laundry. Inside the cabin, she put the boys' clothes away in their cupboard. Some of Angie's clothing was folded in the bottom of the basket. She carried the rest of the clothes up the loft. The dress she hung on a wall peg, but she wasn't sure what to do with Angie's undergarments. Such things could make her so touchy! But Lucy knew she shouldn't always react to Angie's ridiculous overreactions. She opened the drawer to set the undergarments inside. The top drawer was full of sweaters, so she closed it and opened the bottom drawer. Stuffed in the back corner was something pink. Lucy pulled it out, thinking it belonged in the top drawer. It was a toddler's sweater, made of soft pink wool, and as she unfolded it, a small sack fell out. She picked it up, thinking she should put it away before Angie came in and snapped at her, but as she fingered the sweater, something vague and unsettling stirred inside her.

She glanced out the window and saw Angie cross the yard to head to the barn. Setting down the undergarments on the bed, she took the sweater and sack over to the window to look at them in brighter light. Her heart started beating as she fingered the buttons of the little sweater. She held it to her face, breathing in deeply. With trembling fingers, she opened the sack and shook it upside down. In the palm of her hand rested a woman's ring made of ruby red chips. She felt something shoot through her, a jolt, a shudder. It took a moment before she registered what she held in the palm of her hand, what it could mean, and the shock was so severe that her shoulders began to convulse.

Her mind swirled with confusion. How? How could that even be possible?

She tipped her forehead against the windowpane, eyes closed. She wasn't sure what to say, what to do, what to think. From the first moment she had met Angie, in spite of the blatant hostility of the girl toward her, she sensed some kind of connection to her. A tender feeling for her that defied explanation.

She shook her head. "No. Impossible. Angie Cooper is not Charlotte."

Her fingers closed in a fist, wrapping the ruby ring in its hold. But she could be.

Twenty-One

"PUT THAT DOWN!"

Lucy spun around to see Angie glaring at her from the top rung of the loft ladder. She stared into the girl's face and was met by steady, blue eyes. Even while Lucy stared, she tried to read familiar features. Her own, or her father's or . . . was that her mother's face? Perhaps. Maybe. It could be. She uncurled her hand and held her palm out. "Where did this ring come from?"

"None of yor business." Angie stomped toward the window and grabbed the ring out of Lucy's hand. "I'll thank you to stay out of my things." Eyeing her coldly, she practically hissed the words.

In as calm a voice as Lucy could muster, she repeated, "Angie, do you know where that pink sweater and ring came from?"

"They be mine."

"You wore that sweater as a baby?"

Angie ignored her, tucking the ring carefully back into the sack and folding it up into the sweater.

"Angie?"

She looked up at her with an expression pinched with distrust. "The ring came from Maw. She said it belonged to me." She lay the sweater into the bottom drawer of the cupboard. "Didn't expect you'd stoop so low as to go pokin' through my things. You're more trouble than the boys." She slammed the door shut and stood, fists on her hips, as if waiting to hear more.

"You asked me to put these clothes away." Lucy's voice, even to her own ears, sounded shaky.

"Then how come you look so guilty? All white faced like you'd jest—I mean, *just*—seen a ghost."

Maybe she had. She took another look at Angie. No, she couldn't be. She wasn't Charlotte. Or was she? She needed fresh air. She needed to think. Dazed, she climbed down the loft ladder, her head spinning with what-ifs.

IN THE DIM LIGHT OF THE BARN, Arthur Cooper looked older than he was, which was forty-one. Lucy knew that to be a fact because she'd seen it written in the Cooper family Bible. He was bent over a barrel, scooping oats into a bucket, as she interrupted him, and he straightened up in surprise. "Howdy, Miss Lucy."

"Arthur, I happened to notice that there's not a birth date entered for Angie in your family Bible. The boys have one, but not Angie. Her name is entered, but without a date of birth. I just wondered why."

He seemed baffled, as if such a thought never occurred to him. But then, he couldn't read nor write. Perhaps he didn't know it was missing. Slowly, he covered the barrel with a wooden lid. He took his time responding to Lucy, as if gathering his thoughts, sifting through them to decide what he wanted to say. "Angel's adopted. Aria couldn't have no more children, not after the first one."

"The first one?"

He dropped the scooper in the barrel and wiped his hands on his overalls, then sat on a hay bale. "Our first baby died. A little girl. A stillborn. It was a hard birthing, and afterward, the doc said Aria couldn't have no more babies. That was real bad news for Aria to hear, and she didn't cope well." He paused, his chin tucked to his chest.

Lucy held her breath, willing him to continue, worried he wouldn't.

"One day I found her up on the slope, digging away at the baby's grave. She kept saying she didn't want to live no more, and it scared me, the way she was talking. So scared, I went to her folks, and they sent her to a place to get some rest."

"A sanitarium?" There were a few sprinkled around Kentucky. A large one in Louisville.

Other than a curt nod, Arthur didn't pick up where he left off for another long moment, and Lucy thought he might not finish the story. But then he began again, and this time he sounded weary. "She was gone for a long time. When she came back, she brought Angie home with her. Said she was an angel, sent from heaven, meant jest for us. That's what we named her. Angel."

Lucy's heart started to pound so loud she was sure it could be heard in the rafters. "But . . . what had happened to Angie's parents?"

He rubbed the back of his neck. "I don't exactly know."

"You never questioned your wife?"

He shook his head and looked away. "Aria told me that this little angel needed our love."

"That's all you knew about her? Nothing more?"

"No need."

"Arthur, did it occur to you that Angie might have had a family of her own?"

She saw the Adam's apple bob in his throat. "Aria said she was a motherless child."

"And you believed her."

"O'course I did. Why wouldn't I? Aria weren't capable of telling a lie." He pushed himself off the hay bale. "Angie and the boys don't know they's adopted, and I'd like to keep it that way."

"But . . . there must be others who know. Friends and neighbors."

"Mebbe so, but people of the mountain know to keep themselves to themselves."

"May I ask, what is the background story to the boys?"

"They's my brother Bob's boys. He got kilt in a timber accident, and his wife couldn't manage them two. They's the littlest of twelve. At Bob's funeral, she asked us to take 'em and raise 'em as our own. So that's what we done."

"So you never formally adopted Angie or the twins? No legal documents?"

"Those children belong here. I'm their paw. Don't need no documents to tell me that."

"But did it ever occur to you that someone might have been looking for Angie?"

"No," he said firmly. "I don't think so." He frowned. "If someone was careless enough to lose a child, well, I think mebbe they deserved to lose her."

Trembling now, Lucy felt a chill, though the day was growing warm. She pulled her shawl around her. "I had a sister. I was supposed to watch her, but I got distracted. She wandered off while I was reading a book. We never found her. She just . . . disappeared at the train station in Louisville. She'd be about Angie's age."

He sucked in a deep breath. "You must miss your sister something fierce."

"I do remember one specific moment on that fateful day. There was a woman at the train station who had noticed my sister Charlotte. She kept staring at her." Lucy was clutching her shawl so tightly that her fingernails dug into her palms. "I can't help but wonder if that woman could have been . . . your wife."

He stared at her. "Miss Lucy . . . that's jest crazy talk. My Aria could never, *ever* do such a thing."

"I wonder if you might have a photograph of your wife. I'd like to see for myself if she might be the woman I remember staring at Charlotte."

Too much. She'd said too much. Too soon. He was overwhelmed

by her accusation. She could see the shock, the denial in his eyes. "Mr. Cooper," she said softly, "What if I had proof?"

He narrowed his eyes. "Like what?"

"A pink sweater. A ring that I remember as once belonging to my mother. I found both of those items in Angie's cupboard."

It was plain as day that he had no idea what she was talking about. "You talking about something you *remember* . . . as solid proof?"

Put like that, it did sound dubious. It would end up being Lucy's word against Aria Cooper's word . . . a woman who was long dead. "When a mother is grieving, isn't it possible she might do . . . anything to relieve her pain. Even take someone else's child."

She watched him for a while, twisting and twisting a piece of hay in his hands until it snapped. He was angry.

"Miss Lucy, I'm sorry 'bout your sister. I'm sorry for what I said, 'bout deserving to lose her. No one deserves such a thing. What I do know is that Angie's meant for us. Aria got well cuz of Angie, and Angie got a family who watched out for her. She got a maw and a paw who love her, and she's got brothers. And she got Finley James." Ever so slightly, the corners of his eyes crinkled. "Though the boy don't know he been got yet." He started for the door, then flung over his shoulder, "We'll not speak of this again."

"Wait! Please, wait. May I ask you one more question?"

He stopped, and turned, a pained look on his face as if he was bracing himself for something hard.

"Who were your wife's parents? Or are they still living?"

"Jest one. Judge Klopp's wife." His eyebrows lifted at the shock on her face. "I'm surprised you didn't know. It ain't no secret."

Beulah Klopp? *She* was the mother of Aria Cooper? That stern, cold woman? Lucy couldn't have been more stunned if Arthur Cooper had slapped her in the face.

Lucy walked to the porch and sat in a hardbacked rocking chair, watching Angie hanging more laundry on the clothesline, looking for any resemblance to her own parents. To herself. The long, tapered fingers, though rough from use, reminded Lucy of her own hands. The high forehead, the stern set of her mouth, the cheekbones, all could be rearranged in Lucy's mind to form a female version of her father's face. And that long torso, those full lips . . . . . . weren't they just like Mother's? Yet, those same features might be formed in other ways too.

The more Lucy watched, the more she thought of it, the more her hopes rose that indeed, her lost sister was standing only fifty feet away from her. Right here, right now. Flashing dark scowls at her.

Lucy had to go find Wyatt, who always seemed to have the right answer.

LUCY KNEW WYATT was somewhere in Morehead, but it took some hunting before she finally found him waiting for a train at the station. It didn't even occur to ask where he was going or why. Instead, as soon as she drew close, she blurted out, "Do you remember Aria Cooper leaving the hollow and returning with a two-year-old child? A girl?"

"Well, hello to you too, Lucy," he said in his patient, deliberate way. "I'm just fine, thank you for asking."

She blew out a breath. "I'm sorry. I just have to talk to you."

"Let's sit down. The train is late, anyway." He led her to a bench and turned to her. "Now then, what's on your mind that's so important?"

She repeated her question about Aria Cooper coming back to town with a two-year-old.

"I don't remember." He shrugged. "I didn't pay much attention to the coming of babies." He gave her a puzzled look. "What are you getting at?"

"As I was putting some clothes away in Angie's cupboard, I found a ruby ring and a baby's sweater."

"Go on."

She took a deep breath, cupped her hands on her knees, and fixed her eyes on her hands. "Wyatt, I recognized them. A little pink baby sweater that my mother had knit. A ruby ring that my father had given my mother for an anniversary gift."

He still seemed confused. "Why would Angie take them from you?"

Lucy took a breath, in and out, trying to stay calm, and kept her eyes fastened on her hands. "No, no. She didn't. The pink sweater was . . . it was what Charlotte had been wearing the day she went missing. And she'd been playing with the ruby ring the day before. In Mother's writing room."

She paused, chancing a glance at him. Though his gray eyes were looking at her unwaveringly as ever, she hoped for some kind of reassurance, but none came. But he remained quiet, which was good in a way. She couldn't handle hearing doubt voiced aloud. She was struggling enough with disbelief, and trying very hard not to cry, trying to keep her voice from not sounding as shaky as she felt. "If you remember, I'd already noticed that Angie didn't have a birth date entered in the Cooper family Bible—"

"I remember."

"So I asked Arthur about it. He said that Angie had been adopted. Aria Cooper had lost their first child, a stillborn, and was unable to have more children. She suffered greatly, and her parents sent her to a sanitarium. And when Aria returned home, she brought a little girl with her."

She rose from the bench and took a few steps toward the train platform, then pivoted. "I know it seems incredulous, it does to me as well. But I tracked down the timing of these events. The gravestone of Aria and Arthur's baby indicates the baby died in the summer of 1898. Arthur said Aria returned home with the child in January, which was exactly when Charlotte went missing. Exactly."

His eyebrows lifted. "So you told Arthur about your suspicion?"

"I did. He refused to believe that Aria would—or could—steal someone's child."

"Lucy, I would trust my life on Arthur's word."

"I'm not saying he lied. I think he felt protective of Aria and chose to accept her explanation about Angie."

"So what did she tell him?"

"That Angie was a child in need of their love. He said he trusted Aria. And he also said that she returned home happy. He didn't want to risk her happiness. He said that after she lost her own baby, she was overwhelmed by despair. I got the impression that her sorrow was so great that he feared she might take her own life."

Wyatt reached out and put a hand on Lucy's arm, and his touch calmed her. "Lucy, the chance of Angie Cooper being your lost sister Charlotte, well, the chance is highly unlikely."

She nodded. "I agree. Highly unlikely."

"It would be an odd chain of circumstances. You coming here, staying at the Coopers', putting away things in a cupboard that held those particular pieces."

"Yes. Very odd." She nodded again. "Improbable coincidences."

He inhaled a deep breath. "But then again, I've seen some strange coincidences in my life."

"Surely not as strange as this?"

"Even more so. After all, is anything too impossible for God? Not one sparrow falls without his noticing, the Bible tells us."

Lucy darted a glance at him. She envied Wyatt's bold faith, absent of doubts. She was forever plagued by doubts. There were times when she even suspected that, depending on how you read the Bible, you could make it say anything you wanted it to say. Verses could be twisted and turned to suit the speaker's intent. Not Wyatt, but plenty of others seemed to pluck verses out of thin air and jam them onto circumstances.

Wyatt watched her with a concerned expression. "You told me once that God had not listened to your prayers for Charlotte. Could it be possible that your prayers *were* being answered?"

"How so?"

"Perhaps Charlotte *was* receiving love and care."

Lucy's mouth dropped open. "Receiving love and care? By whom? Not by her family! Not by her father and her sister."

"Prayers aren't always answered the way we want them to be. God's timing . . . and his ways . . . they're a mystery. But I do believe that God cares about your sister, wherever she may be now. Whoever she may be now."

Lucy allowed a sigh. When Hazel had the tombstone set in place for Charlotte, she thought she had finally come to terms with the realization that her sister was long gone. Presumed dead. Until today.

And here Charlotte was. Or was she?

It was not outside of the realm of possibilities, but even Wyatt called it an odd chain of circumstances.

What if there was never anything to confirm or deny that Angie Cooper was Charlotte Wilson? What if there could never be proof beyond *any* doubt? What would happen then? It was too much to think, to ponder. To hope for. "Charlotte is dead," Lucy said at last. "It's best to accept that as a fact."

A whistle pierced the quiet, announcing the arrival of Wyatt's train. "Seek the Lord on this matter, Lucy," he said, with a squeeze of her hand. "Don't do or say anything to anyone until you hear clear guidance from him." And then he left her to catch the train.

She felt let down. Even more muddled, as if she were stuck in a thick fog and didn't even know which way to go. She had hoped for clarity from Wyatt. She wanted a plan of action. But waiting? Expecting God to provide clear guidance? Answer a prayer? That was the last thing she wanted to do.

As the train pulled away, she saw Wyatt wave from the window, a concerned look on his face, and she lifted her hand in return, wondering where he was going. And when he would be back.

THE VERY NEXT AFTERNOON, Cora paid a visit to Little Brushy School. The children cheered when they heard her familiar yoo-hoo at the door. Lucy breathed a sigh of relief. Whenever Cora arrived, she'd step in as teacher, or help a child who was struggling, or create a game that drove home a difficult lesson.

On this day, Cora asked Angie to teach long division to the fourth graders. Angie couldn't have been more pleased and bolted to the chalkboard to grab the chalk. Cora made a suggestion or two, but let Angie carry the lesson to completion.

While Angie taught, Cora walked around the room, desk by desk, to check on each child's work. Always, she left them with an encouraging word, a pat on the shoulder. Fin, who was sailing through fifth grade curriculum, received a warm hug. Lucy waited on a bench at the back of the room, correcting papers, observing Cora's affirming way with the children, of the way they looked up at her with expressions of respect. It was like watching a master at work.

Cora came to the back of the room and sat down next to her. "I do believe Little Brushy is my favorite school," she said with a satisfied smile. Lucy had a sneaking suspicion she said the same thing at every school. And sincerely meant it.

As they listened to Angie explain how to carry over figures, Lucy decided to stick a toe in the water. "I learned recently that Mrs. Klopp is . . . was . . . Aria Cooper's mother? That they were estranged."

Cora nodded. "She wasn't in favor of Aria marrying Arthur."

"Why? Arthur Cooper has the livery business, and a farm."

"The Klopps are town folk. Learned. And they're . . . German. Arthur is Scotch-Irish." As if that explained everything.

"Why would that matter?"

"The Germans look down on the Scotch-Irish. They assume they're not as intelligent, not as hardworking, not as religious. People oppress people. It's their nature." She lifted her palms. "And you know how folks love their grudges. Nurse them like they're babies." She shifted her attention to the class, letting out a deep sigh. "My goodness. Just look at her. Angie's a natural. This, *this* is where she belongs. Just think of the impact she'll have when she finally gets her own schoolhouse."

Lucy turned her head. Angie was helping a boy at the chalkboard who was making a mess of a math problem. In a surprisingly gentle way, she corrected the boy by straightening his column of figures from a sloppy zigzag. The look of sudden understanding on his face was priceless.

Yes. Yes, Lucy could see it. Angie was born to teach.

Lucy swallowed once, then twice, and decided to stick a whole foot in the water. "Cora, does Angie remind you of my mother?"

"Your mother?"

"As a young woman, I mean."

She squinted her eyes, focused on Angie. "Perhaps a bit, in the face. The eyes, maybe. But then, I didn't know your mother very well. Now, your father's stubborn determination, *that* I see in Angie." She looked at Lucy with a smile, then it faded. "Why do you ask about your mother?"

Lucy smoothed out a wrinkle in her skirt, her heart pounding. "I suppose . . . so much time has passed that I can't always recall her appearance."

Cora sighed. "Time is like a fast-moving river. Moves along whether you want it to or not."

What if it could be stopped? What if time could roll back? What if Charlotte could be brought home to Lexington, brought back to the family fold where she belonged? Assuming, of course, that Angie was indeed Charlotte.

She imagined the moment of bringing Charlotte home to Father in Lexington, walking into the grand house, sitting in the parlor together the way they used to. Father would be in his high-backed chair near the fire, Lucy and Charlotte would sit on the settee. Slowly, carefully, Lucy would unveil the astonishing discovery, savoring the look of wonder and amazement and relief on Father's face. The lost had been found! Would he pick Charlotte up and twirl her the way he did when she was two years old? Would he reach an arm out to pull Lucy close, into the warm circle, as he used to?

Dreamlike, her gaze shifted to Hazel, standing at a distance, a puzzled look on her face, one hand protectively holding the top of her rounded belly. Hazel's attention wasn't on Father, nor Lucy, but on Charlotte. Lucy's musing took another unbidden turn and she peered at her sister's face, expecting to find the same happy emotions as Father. But her sister seemed bewildered, distressed, confused. She looked frightened.

And then a startling thought broke through this reverie. Would Charlotte even want to come home again?

COME SATURDAY MORNING, Lucy went to town. She had taken Wyatt's advice and prayed about what to do next, and still felt confused, off-kilter. There was no way that Angie Cooper was Charlotte Wilson. It was too farfetched to be probable. And yet . . . and yet . . . what if she was?

Stuffed in Lucy's saddlebags were clothes that needed washing. She was conscious of not creating additional work for Angie, so she brought her worn clothing to Miss Maude's and paid a hired girl to launder them. Avoiding Angie's longsuffering sighs was only part of the reason. It embarrassed Lucy to have so many clothes when Angie had but a few dresses. More than once, Lucy had caught Angie trying on her riding gloves or touching her clothing that hung on the wall pegs, running a hand gently down the fabric as if made of silk. Hardly that, but a much finer, more tightly woven cloth than Angie's worn calicos.

Lucy opened the door to her room at the boarding house and stopped for a moment, watching dust motes float in the sunlight streaming through the window. She dropped her saddlebags on the floor and emptied each side, tossing her clothing on the bed for Miss Maude. Then she bent down to pull her trunk out from under the bed and knelt, opening the lid. It was full of skirts and shirtwaists. She pulled out two skirts and two shirtwaists, and noticed the Mr. Buttons bear, tucked in a corner. On an impulse, she pulled him out and stuffed him in the saddlebag.

Heading down the stairs, she saw Miss Viola and Miss Lettie in the sitting room. Stopping for a moment to say hello and exchange pleasantries and hear the latest news, she left feeling anything but pleasant. She marched past Jenny at the livery, who watched her with mild curiosity, and went straight to Cora's office, where she knew she'd be. Sitting at her desk, Cora lifted her finger in that now familiar hold-on-and-wait-a-minute gesture.

She finished what she was doing and set the quill in the holder. "Dear girl, how good it is to see you!"

"Cora, there's talk of a town meeting to discuss the Moonlight Schools campaign."

Cora sighed. "So I've heard."

Lucy sat down on her chair, facing Cora. "What could anyone object to? You're only trying to help people learn to read."

"Oh, I can think of many objections. Starting with"—she pointed her thumbs at herself—"me."

"You? Why, you've always had the best interest of others at heart." Cora was beloved. Her warm personality and concern for others had endeared her to the community.

"That's very loyal, Lucy, but keep your eyes wide open. A female in a man's traditional role is an uphill battle. In Kentucky, women are expected to stay home and tend the hearth."

Lucy could hear her father's voice in Cora's words. A disdain for women in the workforce wasn't unique to Kentucky. "Father has a saying. 'All ships rise when the tide comes in.' It seems as if everyone in Rowan County would benefit if the mountain people were literate."

"I agree, it seems so. Unless it's to someone's advantage to keep people ignorant. That way, all power remains in their hands."

Into Lucy's mind popped an image of the sheriff, huddled in

conversations with Judge Klopp's wife. And then . . . she thought of Andy.

"Don't give that silly town meeting a second thought. I certainly don't. I have no patience with those who spend their time drumming up problems, discussing them ad nauseum, and ultimately doing nothing about them." She clapped her hands together. "Let me show you what I've been working on for the Moonlight Schools curriculum."

As Lucy came around the desk, she noted that Cora seemed supremely untroubled by the town chatter, which, according to Miss Viola, was quite troubling. She said it was gaining momentum by turning the Moonlight Schools campaign into something quite unrecognizable.

Lucy wished she had more of Cora's single-minded focus. By contrast, the information given to her by Miss Viola only added to the swirl of worries in her head, mostly spinning around Angie Cooper.

ANGIE HAD BEEN IN A CROSS MOOD all Monday afternoon, after she'd come into the schoolhouse at lunchtime and found Lucy and Fin together. It was unfortunate timing. Lucy had been standing on a chair to erase words off the chalkboard and taken a step backward, tumbling right into Fin's arms.

Watching them, Angie's eyes narrowed until they formed slits. "I guess you two want to be alone!" She stomped out, down the steps of the schoolhouse, and off into the woods.

Lucy wanted Fin to go after her, but he refused. "Serves her right. She thinks she owns me and she don't." He gave her a big grin. "And besides, she's right. I do want to be alone with you."

"Fin, I'm flattered, but I'm much too old for you."

His face clouded over. "If you be the man and I be the girl"—he shrugged—"t'wouldn't be no problem a'tall."

"I suppose you're right on that account, but that doesn't change the facts. You're still a young . . . man"—Lucy nearly said "boy" but caught herself just in time—"and I'm a grown woman." Though at this moment, Lucy felt like anything but an adult in this silly triangle of misunderstandings. "I don't have romantic feelings for you, Fin."

He blinked, trying to make sense of her meaning. "So there ain't no hope for us? None a'tall?"

"I'm sorry, Fin. But . . . no." It hurt her to be so blunt, actually pained her, but it was better for him.

Crushed, he turned and left the schoolhouse, shoulders slumped.

Later, at the Cooper cabin, Angie hardly spoke to Lucy all through preparing supper, eating supper, nor afterward, while cleaning up. Lucy had tried coaxing her out of her foul mood, but to no avail, so she gave up. Upstairs in the loft, she noticed her saddlebags by her side of the bed. She paused, then yanked the stuffed bear out of one of the bags and set it in the middle of the bed.

Moments later, Angie climbed the loft ladder and stopped at the top rung to glare furiously at Lucy. She stomped across the small room to grab her nightdress off the peg, spun around, and stopped abruptly, staring at the bed with a startled look on her face. She reached out to pick up the bear. "Mr. Buttons!"

TWENTY-TWO

A FTER A SULKY DAY OR TWO, Fin's good spirits returned, largely because he was starting to best Angie Cooper in just about every subject. This morning, as Lucy gave Fin a new list of Latin verbs to conjugate and memorize, he happened to mention that Wyatt was back in town and working on some project for Miss Cora in the livery. As soon as school let out, Lucy saddled up Jenny (all by herself again!) and rode straight to Morehead. She found Wyatt in the back of the livery, chiseling small numbers on wooden slates. He had done a double take when Lucy had knocked on the door of the tack room, and she felt pleasure spiral through her.

She shook off such a distracting thought. She had interrupted him for a very specific reason, to tell him exactly what had happened last evening.

He leaned back against the barrel top. "Did you ask Angie why she called the stuffed bear Mr. Buttons?"

"Yes, of course I did. She seemed puzzled at first, then said it was because his eyes were made of buttons." She held up a hand. "I know what you're going to say, Wyatt. It's true that the bear has buttons for eyes, but if you could've seen the look on her face when she saw him on her bed. Why, that look was *all* Charlotte! She adored that bear. They were inseparable."

He looked down at the carving tool in his hands, turning it over

257

and over, and she could tell he was thinking this all through. *That was why she had come to him this afternoon.* She needed Wyatt's help to sort out the mess in her mind.

Finally, his hands stilled and he gave her a level look. "Lucy, what do you plan to do?"

She took a step inside the tack room. "I wrote a letter to Charlotte . . . I mean, to Angie. I told her everything that had happened. About to whom she really belongs."

He crossed his arms over his chest. "You haven't given it to her?"

"Not yet."

"What's stopping you?"

"Nothing." Everything. "I suppose I want to wait for the right time."

"You do realize this will change her life profoundly. How she views her father, her brothers, her life in the hollow. Her place in the world."

"Of course. Of course, I realize that." But what about how Angie would view Lucy? And Father? And her place in the Wilson family?

"What about sharing this information with Cora?"

Lucy shook her head. "She's terribly distracted with the Moonlight Schools campaign, and besides that, once she knows, everything will change. I fear she'll feel compelled to tell Father . . . and I wouldn't blame her. They're almost like siblings."

"And your father? What are your thoughts about telling him? Or not telling him?"

She clapped her hands on her cheeks. She'd gone round and round on that very question. "Not yet. He's so . . . happy right now. His marriage to Hazel, the coming baby. I feel hesitant to stir up feelings of grief and regret."

Wyatt set down his tools and came close to her, taking her hands in his. "Lucy," he said softly. "Is it so much better? The life you came from?"

Lucy looked away. She thought of the heavy silence of the Lexington mansion. Of being sent off to boarding school before she was ready to leave home. Of the crushing loneliness that accompanied her childhood. "Not . . . necessarily," she admitted.

"And has it been such a bad life for Angie?"

Lucy thought of the important role Angie played in the Cooper household, the way her father and brothers depended on her. The noisy happiness that filled the little cabin. "If you'd asked me that months ago, I would've said yes. That it's been a terrible shame to grow up in poverty and ignorance. Yet the more I see of these people, of their lives and their hearts, I wonder if I'm the one who grew up in poverty and ignorance. Poverty of spirit. Ignorance of heart."

His eyes grew tender. "Lucy, sometimes what we choose not to do is just as important as what we choose to do." He squeezed her hands and released them, and returned to his work.

BROTHER WYATT HAD FINISHED the wooden slates for the Moonlight Schools, all one hundred of them, and stacked them neat in a jolt wagon at the livery. Fin picked one up to admire it, running his finger along the sanded edge, soft as silk. "You shore do good work."

"You helped, Fin. Getting that wood for me was a big help." Brother Wyatt raked a hand through his hair and fixed his hat jest so. "You never did tell me where you found it."

"Some things is best not to know," Fin said, grinning. He had rummaged through scrap wood at the lumberyard to collect enough for Brother Wyatt, and he might not have bothered to ask anyone for permission. He saw the concern taking shape in Brother Wyatt's eyes, and he worked quick to redirect him. "Ain't you late for the town meeting? Jest saw Andrew Spencer strutting toward it." Come to think on it, Andrew Spencer did remind him of a strutting peacock. Always dressed in his Sunday best.

"I'd better get going. You coming?"

"I'll be along shortly." Fin wanted to check Sheila's hooves and make sure no stones were jammed in her frogs. As he ran a hand down her leg and lifted her hoof, he noticed ol' Angie Cooper sniffing around the jolt wagon.

Angie picked up one of the wooden slates out of the wagon. "What's all this?" That girl poked her nose into everybody's business.

Fin barely glanced at her as he cleaned Sheila's hoof. "Don't touch 'em. Wagon's heavy. Don't want it tipping over."

"But what are they?"

"Something for Miss Cora's Moonlight Schools. Miss Lucy and I are going to take 'em to each of the schoolhouses."

"Together?" She squinted, and then her expression turned angry. "That don't seem like a job that takes two people. Why cain't she jest do it alone?"

"Because . . . jest because." Because Miss Lucy had asked for his help, and he'd do anything for her. "Asides, what I do ain't no business o' yours."

He turned away to check Sheila's other hooves for stones, for this fine horse wasn't a complainer. Not like most women.

He half expected Angie to start up with another objection to spending his time with Lucy, but by the time he finished checking the last hoof, she was gone. He cleared his thoughts and got back to business.

WHEN LUCY ARRIVED at the town meeting, she was shocked to see the room was packed full, people standing shoulder to shoulder. Andrew had been watching for her and he lifted an arm in a friendly wave, smiling his dazzling smile, pointing to an empty seat next to him.

She ignored his gesture, slipping through the crowd to take a spot near an open window. The room was oppressively warm, that stuffy, heavy air thick with the scent of unwashed bodies, and she feared it would get only worse.

The sheriff stood in the front of the room to address the gathering. "Folks, we come here today to talk about Mrs. Stewart's Moonlit School notion. The real truth behind this . . . campaign o' hers . . . is she wants to turn us into a *progressive* county." He made it sound like a dirty word. "And you know what that means, don't you?" He surveyed the sea of faces. "The government'll start interfering in your very home, telling you what to do and how to do it. It's happening all over the cities."

"How so?"

Everyone turned to Lucy. The words had come out before she could stop them. She felt her cheeks start to flame. "I, um, I've lived in cities all my life." Unlike everyone else in this room. She cleared her throat and raised her voice. "I haven't noticed the government coming into our homes to tell us what to do just because people have learned to read."

Frowning, the sheriff ignored Lucy's objection and carried on. "They'll be poking around your stills."

Finley James spoke up. "You're the only one poking around stills." He brought his hand to his mouth like it was a bottle and made a *glug, glug, glug* sound.

The sheriff pointed a finger right at Fin, scowling. "Boy, I been getting complaints about you. Cease and desist from carving your name all over public and private property or I'll toss you right in jail."

Fin's eyes went wide as he sunk down in his chair.

Satisfied he'd put the fear of authority into Fin, the sheriff turned back to the matter at hand. "Now, where was I? Oh yes. Once the government starts poking around, they'll be raising taxes."

A low buzz of murmurs started around the room. The sheriff had hit his mark. Nothing raised ire more than taxes.

"The government will have to start raising taxes. You know as well as I do that Mrs. Stewart don't have no budget for this campaign." He crossed his arms against his chest. "Reading ain't necessary for everyone. Womenfolk, for example. There's an old saying among the Indians, 'Will learning help a woman to blow the fire?'" He swept the room with his gaze, and Lucy was astounded to see how many men were nodding in agreement. "I think not."

"That is outrageous!" The words suddenly exploded out of Lucy, surprising even herself with her vehemence. Heads swiveled in her direction, wide eyes staring at her, and she nearly faltered. But this prevailing attitude toward women couldn't, shouldn't continue. The education of women was one of the most basic problems of Rowan County. Cora had told her that only 4 percent of the county's women could read and write. "That kind of ancient thinking about women," her voice lifted in frustration, "belongs in another century."

Somehow, her outburst fed right into the sheriff's argument. "Men, do you want your daughters to act like that little gal?" He jabbed his thumb at Lucy and her mouth dropped open. "Not knowing their place in the world?"

Lucy stared at Cora, wondering why she was being so calm. Why wasn't she defending the literacy campaign? Speaking out? Why wasn't she flustered, upset, angry—the way Lucy felt? Cora sat in the front row, hands folded on her lap, relaxed and at ease. She could have been in church.

Before the sheriff could ratchet up another notch, the door opened and he stopped to see who it was that had come. Heads swiveled. There stood Angie Cooper at the door, an odd expression on her face. When nobody said anything and continued to stare, she said, "Am I late?" Ears turning pink, in the continuing silence she added, "I guess I lost track of time."

"You come right on in, Angie," the sheriff said.

From where Lucy stood, she could observe how Mrs. Klopp's

eyes followed Angie as the girl moved to a spot across the room, and she realized she'd never seen them in the same room before.

"Now, folks," the sheriff continued, "Angie's given us a prime example of what I been talking about. Females . . . they jest don't have the same kind of brains that menfolk do."

Nobody spoke. Lucy bit her lip, furious.

"Have females not lived many years without knowing how to read and write? And it ain't hurt 'em at all. Jest the opposite. Womenfolk need our help and guidance."

A sprinkling of clapping started through the room. Men only.

"You old buzzard!" Shakily, Miss Viola rose to her feet. "Why, if women could vote, you'd never been elected in the first place."

Lucy saw a smile tug at Cora's lips. Finally! Some outward sign of her fighting spirit. She scanned the room, noting those who nodded along with Miss Viola's bold declaration and those who shook their heads. Finley James glared at the sheriff. Angie seemed preoccupied, as if she hadn't heard what the sheriff had said about her gender. She stood against the door, not reacting to the heated discussion, in a way that was very un-Angie-like.

Lucy scanned the room and noticed Wyatt on the far side. When their eyes met, he gave her a reassuring smile. *Don't give up*, was what his smile conveyed.

"There's clearly another issue here. I'd put a dollar to a dime that grown folks jest can't learn to read. It's a fact. Some folks are born to be educated, and others are born to till the soil." He sent a smug smile at Mrs. Klopp. "As our late judge was fond of saying, 'Folks need to not get above their raising.'"

Mrs. Klopp nodded in agreement.

"Mrs. Stewart means well, I do believe that, I surely do. But she's asking for something that just ain't possible. She'll end up embarrassing folks, making 'em feel like they ain't worth a plug nickel."

Pride. It was the mountain people's most cherished value.

"I don't have to remind you that as soon as your boys and girls git educated, they'll run off to the cities to find better-paying jobs.

They'll leave y'all behind to fend for yourself in your old age. You'll never see 'em again."

Lucy stilled. That prediction was hard to refute—after all, look at Roy and Sally Ann Duncan. Or Miss Mollie's daughter and son-in-law. They did leave for better-paying jobs, never to return. The sheriff had just thrust a dagger into the heart of the Moonlight School campaign. Heated whispers traveled across the room, and it seemed as if plans for literacy among the mountain folks would die then and there.

But then Cora stood up. "So, Sheriff, let me get this straight. You are against the Moonlight Schools because you care so deeply about the pride of the mountain folks. About the next generation staying in the hills."

"Exactly right." He folded his arms across his wide chest. "And I'm against raising taxes." He eyed the assembly in a wide sweeping gaze. "I am *for* preserving the family and not letting the government butt itself right into your homes." He walked back and forth, looking through the rows, shaking his head. "No doubt it's as obvious to you as it is to me that we got to shut this campaign down."

Cora, undaunted, continued. "What's obvious to me is that you don't want things to change because the system of ignorance works so well for you."

He pointed a chubby finger at her. "That is slander if I've ever heard it!"

"The reason you ignore repeated requests to follow up on complaints with lumber companies' selective harvesting contracts is because you're benefiting from an arrangement with them. I believe it's called . . . ," she paused for emphasis, " . . . a finder's fee. Otherwise known as a kickback."

His mouth opened and shut, opened and shut. "Why, I never . . ."

Ah! So *this* was why Cora had waited to let the sheriff spin his web. She was absolutely right. How did Lucy miss that? Spinning through her mind were all the families she had met during the census, and how many spoke of their harvested loblollies. She

264

looked over at Wyatt and realized this was no surprise to him. Her mind flashed back to the first time she met him, in Cora's office, when he had seemed deeply concerned about something. Had he known, months and months ago, or suspected of this finder's fee arrangement? Lucy cast a sideways glance at Andrew, seated a few rows behind Cora. Staring at his profile, Lucy could tell he was angry. His mouth, tight and pinched. His hands, tight fists on the tops of his knees.

"Hold on a minute." Finley James rose to his feet. "You been collecting money off my maw's loblolly pines?" He looked around the room. "From all our loblollies?" He locked his hands on his hips. "Ain't it your job to protect us, idn't? Ain't that the reason we pay taxes, idn't?"

The sheriff sputtered. "I never . . ."

"You know exactly what them lumber companies done to us. Divertin' creeks and puttin' roads in where they don't belong. You said there weren't nothing you could do about it. A contract is a contract. Well, you never said nothing about gittin' money for them contracts." Fin pointed a long finger at the sheriff. "You are one heckuva worthless lawman."

The room erupted.

"Settle down, settle down!" Then the sheriff's face turned red as he tried to regain control. "Hold on. You're getting me all confused." His voice took on a desperate plea. "This meeting is about putting an end to Mrs. Stewart's Moonlight Schools."

Cora rose to join him in front and his eyes went wide in panic. "The sheriff is proving exactly why we need to eradicate illiteracy from Rowan County. Our illiterates have been the victims of educated scoundrels, who have taken advantage of their ignorance. The only way to lift people is to teach them to lift themselves. Literacy is the only road to true freedom. And that does *not* mean a road leading your loved ones elsewhere—as the sheriff would have you believe—but to a better life right here, in Rowan County." She had the crowd in her hands now, and she knew it. "Literacy is the means to many good ends. And these ends are not just the immediate practical ones, but literacy gives a voice to the silent." She cast a sideways glance at the sheriff, who was practically whimpering. "Only a literate people can have a truly democratic government."

Her gaze swept the room. "Together, we can do this. We can teach all the illiterates in our county with this Moonlight School campaign. Why would we not do what we can to help others? Indifference is our only obstacle, and Rowan County is not indifferent. Not at all. We take care of each other."

Miss Lettie lifted her birdlike hand. Slowly she rose to a stand. After hesitating a moment, she spoke with a quiet certainty. "Well, I think it's a fine idea. I believe all right-minded people here should support it." She lowered her head so she could see over her half-moon spectacles as if she dared anyone to contradict her. "That's all I have to say." She sat down again.

One person clapped, then another, and another, and the sheriff's shoulders slumped. The meeting was over.

In her own brilliant way, Cora had done the impossible. The Moonlight School campaign was safe.

Lucy looked over to Andrew, but his chair was empty.

TWENTY-THREE

FINLEY JAMES LEFT THE MEETING as soon as it ended to feed the horses at the livery. It chapped his hide to find out the sheriff had been dippin' into the lumber companies' purse, which meant he was taking money from his maw. Never again. Never again would he let his maw get taken. He could read now, sailing through sixth grade books, and no one could ever take him being book red away from him.

Ol' Angie Cooper was right. If'n he coulda read better, he coulda protected his maw. *Oh heck.*

Fin went around back to the lean-to where the feed was kept, and stopped abruptly. He couldn't believe his eyes. Someone had pushed the jolt wagon filled with Brother Wyatt's wooden slates into the creek that ran behind the livery, and flipped it over.

Fin bolted over to the top of the creek and looked down. The slates were scattered below—some broken into pieces as they hit rocks, some floating in the water, some on the edges of the creek, some downstream. He skidded down the creek bed to gather as many as he could. He scrambled back up to get help. When he reached the top, he saw someone watch him from across the road, then turn on his heels and leave.

Andrew Spencer.

LUCY REMAINED IN THE TOWN HALL, chatting with Wyatt, as they waited for Cora to finish talking to her many fans. The door burst open and in flew Fin, breathing heavily from running, or panic, or both.

"The slates!" he yelled. "They're down the creek!"

They bolted from the town hall and followed him to the creek. Wyatt and Fin made their way down the creek bed, gathering the slates. Lucy stationed herself on a level spot, halfway down. They created a human chain. Fin handed them up to Lucy, who in turn handed them to Cora, and a few others who came to help. She remained at the top of the creek, next to the uprighted jolt wagon. When Wyatt and Fin finished, they climbed back up to join Cora. Wyatt examined the slates in the wagon.

Cora picked one up to brush mud from it. "Are they salvageable?"

Wyatt, calm as a man could be, sorted through the wagon. "The wet ones will dry out." He took broken ones out of the cart and tossed them in a pile. So many were beyond repair.

"Fin," Cora said, "tell us again what happened."

He pointed to the front of the livery. "I left the jolt wagon over yonder, then I went to the meetin'. When I come back, the wagon was here, flipped over. Someone done this." He rested his hands on his hips. "I shoulda put the wagon inside the livery afore I went to the meetin'. It's my fault."

"Not your fault at all." Wyatt put a hand on Fin's shoulder. "Can you find more lumber?"

Fin lifted his head to look down the road at the lumberyard. "Not a problem."

"Good, that's good," Wyatt said. "I'll clean up those that are worth saving and tomorrow we'll get to work on new ones."

How could Wyatt be so calm, so resilient? He'd spent hours and hours working on those slates. "But who could have done this?" Lucy said. "We should find him. Make him responsible. Make him pay for this!"

Wyatt stopped rifling through the wagon to answer her. "Vengeance is mine, saith the Lord."

Lucy blinked. "You don't think we should seek justice?"

"If I take revenge into my own hands, then I am no better than the one who did this."

She turned to Cora with a question on her face.

"I agree with Wyatt," Cora said. "The town hall meeting resulted in our favor. This . . . mischief . . . is the result of someone who didn't like its outcome. I don't think we should waste time and create any more animosity by seeking the perpetrator."

"Asides," Fin said, scowling, "the sheriff wouldn't do nothin' 'bout it."

Cora sighed. "Well, we know it wasn't him. He's still in the town hall."

Lucy noticed the light was on in Andrew's office at the lumberyard. She rinsed mud off her hands in a bucket and went across the road to talk to him. She found him packing up his office. He didn't smile when she came in.

"You've been giving the sheriff a finder's fee to locate loblollies?"

He set the box he'd been packing on the floor and plopped in his desk chair. "Everyone does. It speeds up the process." He leaned forward and rested his elbows on the desktop. "Let me remind you, Lucy, that those contracts have provided cold hard cash to those landowners."

"Loblolly stands are everywhere in Rowan County. Valley View Lumber contracts happen to all be with illiterates. The sheriff fed illiterates to you."

Andrew rose to his feet and banged his palms on the desk. "I was just doing my job the best way I knew how. Lucy, you've got to believe me."

The funny thing was that she did believe him. Andrew just wanted the contracts. Nothing else mattered to him . . . but him. It made her pity him. To think of only himself, all the time.

"You need to direct your woodsmen to return every single holding pen in the county to their original state."

"What?"

"Every single one. This very week." She notched her chin up a bit. "Or I will see to it that you never work in the lumber industry again. Have I made myself clear?"

He stared at her, a standoff, but she held his gaze—not even blinking—until he dropped his eyes. He nodded once, a jerk of his head. "I'll take care of them. This week."

She turned to leave, then pivoted to face him. "Do you have any idea what happened to that wagon load of wooden slates over by the livery?"

"What wagon?"

"Wyatt had made slates to be used in the Moonlight School campaigns. He left them stacked in a jolt wagon by the livery. You left the meeting early. I just wondered if you might have seen someone push them over the edge of the creek."

"Are you accusing me?"

"Just asking if you might have seen someone." At the door, she said, "Goodbye, Andrew." It was more than a goodbye.

Heading back up the mountain on Jenny to return to the Coopers' cabin, Lucy thought of how far she had come in the last few months. It was embarrassing to think she had once needed a mounting block to hoist herself up on this small horse, even more so to think of how frightened she'd been by the gentle animal. Riding Jenny felt natural to her now. They understood each other. They'd become partners. She stroked the pony's neck.

Before the turnoff in the trail to the Cooper place, Lucy paused for a moment and dropped the reins so Jenny could drink from the creek, clear water murmuring and bubbling over the stony bed. On an impulse, she detoured to the overlook spot that Wyatt had once shown her, and inhaled the sight of the tree-lined valley below. It might just be the prettiest sight she'd ever seen. She couldn't believe she thought so, but she did. She couldn't believe she was teaching school, but she was, and enjoying it. While she still didn't relish being in front of a classroom all day, and she still felt like she was not at all gifted at teaching—not like Angie or Cora—she did care about the children.

And she also knew that whenever Cora mentioned that "we" would spend the summer writing up the newspapers and readers, she meant Lucy. Knowing that didn't bother her anymore. In fact, Lucy looked forward to the coming summer, and especially to the Moonlight Schools in the fall.

TWO NIGHTS IN A ROW, Angie had tossed and turned. Her stomach hurt and her appetite was gone. When Paw and Lucy asked what was wrong, she jest shrugged and said her monthlies. But that weren't it. It was something else entirely. Paw had a saying, "Sin is sweet in the mouth but bitter in the belly." *That* was it. *That* was what was wrong with her.

On Saturday afternoon, when Paw asked her to go to town to get something he left at the livery, she jumped at the chance. Brother Wyatt was in the back, crafting another batch of wooden slates for Miss Cora. He looked up and smiled when he saw her, that kind smile of his where the corners of his eyes went all crinkly. She figured he wouldn't ever smile at her again, not after she told him.

"Howdy, Angie."

"Howdy," she said softly, her smile wavering.

He kept whittling away at a board, glancing up at her once or twice. "Looking for your paw?"

"No." She walked around the edges of the small room, touching the harnesses hanging on the wall.

"Something on your mind?"

She stopped. "Brother Wyatt, I got something to tell you." She lowered her face into her hands and let out a shaky sigh. A long moment passed before the words would come. "I'm the one. I did it."

"Did what?"

She dropped her hands. "I sent your wooden slates tumbling down the creek."

There was a long silence. "You? Why, Angie?"

"Jealous. Terrible jealous." She couldn't look at him. "The devil's done got hold o' me. Twistin' my innards. Makin' me think and do dreadful things." Wiping away tears, she told him the whole story, how she'd pushed and pulled and yanked that jolt wagon all the way to the top of the creek and dumped those beautiful wooden slates right down into the water, then hurried to the town hall meeting acting like everything was right as rain. She'd scared herself with how mean and ugly and deceitful she could be—that's how awful she was.

"All because Finley James is so fond of Miss Lucy?"

She nodded, tears starting to spill down her cheeks. "And it's my own fault too. I put a spell on him. I jest cain't figure out how to unspell him." She wiped away tears with her arm, swallowed and raised her chin. "Devil's gotten hold of me, I'm afreared." Her shoulders slumped. "Happened to my maw now and then. She'd have bouts when she'd have to wrestle the devil. I remember. She'd lie in bed all day and all night, sad and sorrowful." She sighed. "Devil turned Maw inwardlike. Devil turns me mean and hateful." She lifted her shoulders in a defeated shrug.

He didn't say anything for a frightfully long while. So long that she chanced a peek at him and realized he still had that kind look in his eyes. "Angie, there's something important you need to know about the devil. 'Greater is he who is in you than he who is in the world.'"

She tilted her head. "What's that mean?"

"It's a verse from the Bible. As much as the devil would like you to do wrong and think wrong and act wrong, if God lives in your heart, then there's no room for the devil."

"The devil goes?" She snapped her fingers. "Jest like that?"

"Just like that. He has to go. God is greater, and bigger, and mightier. He won't tolerate the devil."

A flicker of hope began. "How do I do that?"

Wyatt smiled. "Just a simple prayer, Angie. Invite the All Mighty into your heart."

"And then the devil be gone?"

"He goes, and with him goes jealousy, worry, fear, anger."

Angie bowed her head and asked God to move on in and kick the devil out. And when she finished that prayer, her heart didn't feel quite so heavy anymore.

Brother Wyatt, waiting beside her, was watching her like he'd been praying too. "Angie, as far as anyone knows, the jolt wagon rolled into the creek all by itself."

She stared at him. "But I know better. And you know better."

"And I'm already halfway done with a new batch of slates. Better than the first batch." He blew some wood shavings off the bench. "Some things are best forgotten. Makes it easier to move forward." He gave her a wink. "I do believe this is one of those things."

FIN HAD FOUND a nice fishing hole to spend his summer afternoon, and some sweet honeysuckle to chew on. School was out, he was done with it—and he had done it well, if he did say so himself—the sun was shining, Arthur Cooper didn't need him at the livery, and Maw was off visiting her auntie. For a few hours, he was a free man. Unfettered.

U-N-F-E-T-T-E-R-E-D. He grinned, imagining himself beating Angie Cooper in a spelling bee over *that* half-dollar word.

Fin jammed the fishing pole up his overall pants leg so it could keep workin' while he lay back for a little shut-eye. The soft summer air swirled around him, as did mosquitos, so he plopped his hat on his face and, drowsy, soon dozed off.

"Finley James, you can jest keep on loving Miss Lucy. It's fine by me."

He startled, eyes blinking. "Huh?" He whipped his hat off his face and found Angie Cooper standing there, blocking the sun, staring down at him. Rubbing his eyes, he pushed himself up, leaning back on his elbows.

Angie crouched down, leaned in, and gently touched her lips to his, jest a whisper. "So long, Finley James." She rose and disappeared into the woods.

Fin was about as confused a man as there could be. Muddled. He'd never had thoughts like that before. What was happening to him? He scratched his head and spat out a new cuss word he'd heard at the livery. If Angie Cooper was saying goodbye to him, that meant she was saying hello to somebody else.

As Lucy packed her saddlebags, Angie had sat cross-legged on the bed. She was unusually quiet, lacking her spit and fire, so much so that Lucy asked what she was brooding over.

Angie looked at her with blue eyes wide, and she reminded Lucy so much of Charlotte that her breath caught. "Did I pass my grade 8 exam?"

Lucy had wanted to let Cora give Angie the news . . . but . . . why not just tell her? "You passed. With flying colors." And she meant it. Not a single mistake, not in math, not in English, nor civics. Not even in conjugating basic Latin verbs. She knew, from Cora, that Angie would be offered the chance to teach at Little Brushy School in the fall. Cora had also told her that Finley James would be teaching one of the bigger schools. Somehow, he had passed his grade 8 exam. His marks weren't quite as high as Angie's, but his progress was astounding.

Lucy felt Angie watch her every move, noticing each skirt and shirtwaist. She thought of the clothes waiting for her at Miss

Maude's. "Angie, these skirts just aren't fitting me right. Too much of your good cooking, I suppose. Any chance you could use them? You'd be doing me a favor."

Angie gave a nonchalant half shrug of a shoulder, though Lucy knew she was pleased. "I suppose so," she said, already hanging them up on her wall pegs. The gifts of clothes seemed to chase away Angie's low spirits, and she hopped off the bed to help Lucy pack.

Later, long after supper, as Arthur rose from his chair to bring the horses into the barn for the night, Lucy stopped him. He looked so tired. "Let me do it."

Surprised, Arthur responded with a nod.

They had an amiable relationship, Lucy and Arthur, though he'd never brought up Angie's adoption again. That discussion, as far as Arthur Cooper was concerned, was closed.

But not for Lucy Wilson.

The letter she had written to Angie was tucked in her pocket, safely away from snooping eyes. She was still undecided about whether she should share it. Still waiting for a word from the Lord, the one Wyatt had promised would come. She wasn't quite so sure.

One by one, she led the horses into their stalls in the barn. Jenny, being the stubborn cuss she was, wouldn't come to her, so Lucy grabbed a rope and crossed the yard. As she slipped the rope around Jenny's neck, she glanced over the pony's head at the house. Dusk had come, and a soft buttery glow spilled from the kitchen window. Seated at the table were Angie, Arthur, and the twins, playing a game.

Jenny's nose pushed against Lucy and she heard the crinkle sound of the letter. From somewhere, somehow, a question emerged: Are you going to rip her out of this happy home?

She looked up at the sky, at the first evening star near the moon, and answered back, loud and clear. "God, did you not rip Charlotte from her home? Did you not ignore my desperate prayers?"

She scanned the skies, waiting for an answer, demanding a response. And suddenly she realized she was not going to get the answer she wanted. But she also realized she was, indeed, getting *an* answer, and the thought made her shiver, for she felt so unwilling to accept *that* answer.

Without any warning, she dropped to her knees, overcome by emotion, by despair. "How? How can I keep this from Father? Angie Cooper is his daughter Charlotte, his baby girl." The tears began to flow, and she could barely choke out the words that were on her heart. *It isn't fair. It isn't right!* Aria Cooper had *stolen* someone's child. *My sister! Father's daughter.*

Wyatt's piercing question kept buzzing around Lucy, like a bee around a rosebush. *"Has it been such a bad life for Angie?"*

Lucy exhaled, unaware she'd been holding her breath. Had it been such a bad life for Angie?

Just the opposite. She's had quite a lovely life. She couldn't deny that her sister had been loved, cherished, and well cared for. She held an important place in this family, in this community. Perhaps Angie had been given the greatest of all gifts: she had, to quote Cora's favorite word, a calling.

Has it been such a bad life for Angie?

Finley James came to mind. Teaching at Little Brushy. *There was more loveliness to come.*

Lucy looked up at the moon and its neighbor, the first evening star. "If I do this, if I walk away, I will need your strength. I will need your help with peace of mind."

At that, Jenny blew air out of her nose and gave up waiting for Lucy. The pony sashayed her way to the barn, the rope dragging behind her. A smile tugged at Lucy's lips, for she realized she'd been given another answer. *In the end, it will all turn out.*

She wiped her tears from her cheeks, rose to her feet, dusted off her skirt, and followed in the pony's tracks.

Early the next morning, before Lucy went down the loft stairs, she stood next to the bed where Angie lay sleeping with Mr. Buttons wrapped in her arms. Someday, she might tell Angie the truth, the whole story. She had once been lost, and then found. Someday.

But not now, and not for a very long time. She bent over her sleeping sister and whispered, "Goodbye, dear Charlotte."

There was one thing she wanted to do before she left the Cooper home for good. Arthur, she knew, had left the cabin long ago to feed the animals. He told her last night he would feed Jenny first and get her saddled up so the pony would be ready to go when Lucy came down to the barn.

She tiptoed past the sleeping troublesome twins, who weren't so very troublesome, and went straight to the Bible that lay on the kitchen table. Taking pains to be quiet, Lucy set her saddlebag on the floor, bent down to unlatch one side, and riffled through until she found the quill pen and ink pot she used to scribe letters for the mountain people. Kneeling on the floor, she opened the Bible to the first page. Alongside Angel Eleanor Cooper's name on the family tree, she carefully added, *born May 12th, 1896.*

Every girl should have a birthday.

TWENTY-FOUR

JULY PASSED AND ROLLED INTO AUGUST. Summer bore down hard on Morehead, yet as much as Fin longed for the cooler weather of autumn, he was hanging on tight to each and every day. September loomed large. Terrifyingly large.

As soon as Fin heered someone call out his name, his heart thumped hard. "Comin'," he shouted, as he wiped his sweaty face and neck with a rag. He even tucked his shirttails into his overalls, hoping the female voice might belong to Angie Cooper, looking to bother him like she'd used to, but heck if it was only the Judge's hoity-toity wife. That woman had more airs than a duchess. D-U-C-H-E-S-S.

"Boy," Mrs. Klopp said in that whiny voice o' hern, "rumor has it that you're going to be teaching school."

"Yes, ma'am."

"So you finally found some ambition."

"Yes, ma'am." Not really. It found Fin. In the size and shape of Miss Cora. That woman could talk the spots off a leopard and sell 'em to a tiger.

Happily, before Mrs. Klopp could start in on him about one thing or another, a fellow arrived to hire a horse. While Fin excused himself from Mrs. Klopp and hurried to the windowless tack room—hot as Maw's oven—to fetch a saddle and bridle, he

278

cheered himself with the thought that at least it was cooler in the hills. He winced, thinking jest how high up in the hills he'd be livin' come September. Sky high.

But it lifted his damp spirits to think of the pay he'd be fetchin' for his troubles. It was good, real good, much more than ol' Angie Cooper would fetch for teaching Little Brushy. Miss Cora warned him that was going to change. She said female teachers should be paid the same as man teachers. To Fin's way of thinkin', it was more than fair to get better wages, seein' as how he'd be having to board somewhere, plus teach a school that was double the size of Little Brushy. All things considered, he aimed to earn his keep and work hard at teaching, even do a better job at it than ol' Angie, despite the fact that he didn't really feel like he got the "call" to teach.

Miss Cora said to keep listenin' for it.

THE HEAT IN LATE AUGUST WAS OPPRESSIVE. Cora had been working long days to prepare for the start of the school year, late nights to complete the curriculum for the Moonlight School campaign. Lucy did all she could to help, but she could see exhaustion's toll on Cora. Tired eyes sunk deep in their sockets. Furrows of tension lining her forehead. Lucy could sense she was suffering from headaches, though Cora refused to stop.

Then came a blow: Some teachers had sent word that they were dropping out. They cited different reasons: two wanted to be paid, one said she "feared she might be too tarred to teach at night." Three more felt sure that no adults would dare come.

When Cora told Lucy and Wyatt about the dropouts, even her voice sounded weary. "What if they're right? What if no one comes? All this work, all this effort, and what if it's a complete and total failure?" Leaning on her elbows, she closed her eyes and rubbed her temples.

Wyatt's eyes sought Lucy's, and though he made no comment, she felt certain the same concern ran through his mind: They'd never known Cora to be discouraged.

"Things will work out, Cora," Lucy said. "Have a little faith."

At that Wyatt's eyebrows shot up, as if surprised by her boldness. Or her declaration. Or maybe she was too acutely aware of him, of the way he had of observing her. It was oddly discomfiting.

"Lucy's right," Wyatt said firmly. "It might take time for the campaign to be accepted, but we knew that, going into this. Mountain people need this campaign, Cora. Change comes slowly here. But it does come. It will come. We just need to have patience."

Lucy marveled at how Wyatt discussed the Moonlight Schools campaign as if it belonged to him as well as Cora, and to Lucy, and to the supportive teachers. Right from the start, he had taken hold of the campaign, offering suggestions or words of support. Crafting wooden slates, and then making them all over again. He never wavered from seeing this through. Lucy wished she were more like him, wished she could do more to help. Suddenly feeling completely useless, she folded her arms across herself to grip her elbows.

What if Cora's fears were right? What if the schoolhouses were opened and no one showed up? She loved Cora so much—she wanted this campaign to succeed for her sake as much as the sake of the mountain people. She couldn't bear to see Cora disappointed.

And then the unexpected happened. Thoughts filled Lucy's mind that came not from a swirl of panic, but from somewhere else entirely. Clear, guided steps, and along with them, a sense of calm and purpose. She stilled. What just happened? Had she prayed? Was this an answer to a prayer she hadn't even realized, consciously, that she'd asked? Could prayer be as simple as that—lifting up her hands with a cry for help?

Jumping out of her chair, Lucy bolted across the room and flew out the door.

STRIDING TO THE LIVERY to get Jenny, Lucy started a mental to-do list, knowing exactly what she had to do and how to do it.

"Wait," came Wyatt's voice, from behind her. "Hold up, Lucy. Where are you off to in such a hurry? You bounded out of Cora's office like fleeing from a fire."

She stopped and pivoted to face him. "Wyatt, somehow I want to . . . rally people. To sound the call for the Moonlight Schools campaign. Find volunteers who will visit every home in the hills and hollows. To have them extend a personal invitation to every illiterate adult in Rowan County. Every single one."

He ran a hand along the back of his head. "Volunteers."

"Yes. We need all the help we can get. Find every possible volunteer."

He bit his lower lip. "Preachers."

"What?"

His eyes lit up. "Preachers." He grabbed Lucy's shoulders. "They can spread the word from the pulpits. Storekeepers. They can tell their customers. Librarians can tell their patrons."

"Yes!" Relief—and enthusiasm—filled her as he caught her vision. "There must be others who will help. The Christian Women's Board of Missions . . . they might be willing to help. The Morehead Women's Club should be willing. For goodness' sake, Cora started that club."

"Lucy, this . . ." Wyatt gazed at her with such intensity that her thoughts started to tumble and roll and she nearly forgot what they were talking about. "*This* is a wonderful idea."

She smiled. "If you'll get started in town, I'll go talk to those teachers who dropped out."

His eyebrows lifted. "Are you sure? You could stay here and I'll go."

"No. No, I'll go."

"You *want* to go into the hollers?"

She felt the heat of his hands on her shoulders, and sensed her face starting to color. "I need to go," she said, plucking up her courage. She needed to start with the teachers. If they remained unwilling, she feared the entire campaign could start unraveling at the seams. Their damper would infect other teachers.

Up in the hills, accompanied only by Jenny, birdsong, and the dappled morning light of the forest, Lucy made her way to six schoolhouses, one by one, to call on those teachers who had dropped out. She asked each one to support Cora's campaign. "At the very least, give it a week. Monday through Thursday night. Just to see if some people might come to the schoolhouse. Most likely, only three or four will come." That was Cora's goal, anyway.

"And if they don't?" Each one voiced the same objection. One thing Lucy discovered today—the six reluctant teachers were kin to each other, as well as to Norah. These rural schools, her father often complained, were "cousined to death." Trustees preferred to hire kin as teachers, even if unqualified, over any qualified outsiders.

Lucy refused to give up. "If no one comes on the first night, then close up the schoolhouse and go home." She paused. "But what if they do come? And no one is there to help them in their quest?"

And then she delivered the pièce de résistance. "Give it a valiant try, for Cora's sake if for no other reason." Not a single teacher could deny that Cora deserved that effort. She was beloved.

Lucy left each teacher fired up. Maybe not *fired up*, not the way Cora could rally the troops. But these six teachers were committed and she prayed their enthusiasm wouldn't cool off before September 5. That was the night Cora had chosen to kick off the campaign because the *Farmer's Almanac* had promised a full moon.

She had grown familiar with the winding trails in the hollows, and even had a rough idea of a few cut-throughs. One led fairly close to Miss Mollie's, and Jenny stopped at the fork in the trail that led to her cabin. "You're in the mood to visit Miss Mollie?"

The pony flicked her ears back and forth, which Lucy took as a yes. She was getting used to Jenny's moods. So off they went to pay a call on the dear old woman, and Lucy smiled, pleased with herself. Not six months ago, had she been told she'd be riding a pony into the hollows to visit an old toothless woman who kept chickens in her house—a visit that was not requested of her by Cora—she would have said she must have lost her mind. Yet here she was, eager to see Miss Mollie, hoping to be entertained by a story or two, with hardly a worry for the pungent fug that filled her cabin. Today the stink came from a cast-iron pot hanging over the hearth, simmering with wild leeks and ramps. Miss Mollie offered her a bowlful, which Lucy declined, insisting she'd just eaten. She could never take food from a mountain home, but if offered stories, *that* she freely indulged in. A feast for the ears!

Two hours later, Jenny plodded down the trail, Lucy mulling over Mollie's recollections. They'd sat on rockers on the porch, and Lucy, just because she was in a celebratory mood after visiting those teachers, accepted a cup of Mollie's moonshine. Her entire mouth went numb, and for a moment or two, she thought she saw two Mollies. Apart from declining a refilling of shine, they'd had a fine time of it, and Lucy had learned more stories about Rowan County's mountain people than she imagined was possible.

Mollie's tales, she realized, were historical composites, re-creating life as it had been lived from one century to the next. In a region where there were few books and even fewer people able to read, accounts were handed down from generation to generation. Those tales revealed the heart and spirit of the mountain people.

If her father was right, those lives would soon be changing. The muddy, rustic logging roads that trickled throughout Rowan County would one day be full of automobiles. The roads would be laced with poles, stringing telephone and electric wires. Modernization was coming to the county, like it or not.

She looked up at the canopy of trees, aware of the deepening shadows cast over the forest floor. Cognizant, by shadows' slant, of what time it was. Her breath caught, overcome by an unconscious awareness that swirled up from somewhere deep inside her and filled her conscious mind. She loved this place. Loved the hills and the hollows and the people who lived there. She loved knowing she had a purpose to fulfill here. And for the first time in her life, she knew what it was.

Mollie's stories should be recorded for posterity. And others too. How had Lucy nearly missed realizing what a treasure she'd been handed? Gratitude bubbled up, and she found herself whispering over and over, "Thank you, Lord, thank you."

When she reached town, she handed the pony's reins to Fin at the livery and told him to add a little sorghum to Jenny's supper. He grinned, and she knew why. A few months ago, she didn't even know what sorghum was. Now she ate it nearly every day at Miss Maude's. Cane sugar didn't grow well up in the mountains, so the only way to sweeten food was with sorghum, honey, or maple syrup.

As Lucy walked into the boarding house, she started up the stairs, then stopped. There was one more task she wanted to complete before this day came to an end.

She went to the back of the house to Mrs. Klopp's room. She knocked on the door and waited. Mrs. Klopp opened it, surprised to find Lucy. Surprise turned to shock when Lucy asked her if she could see a picture of her daughter.

"Aria?"

"Yes, please."

"Whatever for?"

"I've heard so much about your daughter while staying at the Coopers. They loved her very much." With that, ever so slightly, Lucy could see Mrs. Klopp's countenance soften. "I would like to know what Aria looked like."

The door opened wider, and there, on the night table, was a picture of Judge Klopp in his black robes. Seated next to him was his wife; they both sat stiff backed, stern faced. Behind them was a young girl about Angie's age, her face was slightly turned in a different direction than her parents, as if she were looking elsewhere. As if she belonged elsewhere. That look in her eyes . . . *that*, Lucy recalled. Vividly. She held the picture in her hands. "How did you choose the name Aria?"

"The judge named her." Mrs. Klopp gave up a rare smile. "It means air. When she was born, she was such a tiny girl. Holding her, he said, felt like holding air." Her smile disappeared. "And then, it seemed to come true." Her eyes grew shiny. "We tried and tried, but we couldn't hold on to her." She took the framed picture from Lucy and set it back on the nightstand. A signal that this moment was over.

But not for Lucy. "Mrs. Klopp, you have a beautiful granddaughter up in those mountains. Angie is smart as a whip, funny and clever and bighearted. And you also have two fine little grandsons."

Mrs. Klopp looked away. "They're not my blood kin, after all."

"No, but . . . after all . . . your daughter loved them like they were her own. They need you. They need you more than you can imagine."

The judge's wife stared at her for a long while, her mouth opening and shutting and opening again like a fish out of water. At last she said, "What do they need *me* for?"

"Different reasons. Arthur does his best, but those boys need to be taught good manners, and Angie needs help to become a lady. They all need a woman's touch." She walked to the door. "One thing I know for sure, Mrs. Klopp. As much as they need you—and they do, they truly do—you need them even more."

Her voice trembled as she said, "It's too late."

"You're wrong," Lucy said with firm shake of her head. "It's never too late."

She left Mrs. Klopp to chew on that and walked slowly up the stairs. No one at the Townsend School for Girls would even recognize her as the same meek, passive, shrinking, nearly invisible Lucy Wilson. Was this really her? Had she changed that much? Yes, yes she had. A wide smile wreathed her face, without meaning to. She felt suddenly, unexpectedly happy. Truly happy.

IN THE MORNING, Cora welcomed Lucy back to the office with a surprise. She stood beside her desk, hunched over a Victrola phonograph, similar to the one Hazel bought but smaller, more compact.

Curious, Lucy tipped her head. "Where in the world did you find that?"

"Borrowed!" Cora said. "They're finally making an affordable version." She turned to Lucy with a triumphant smile. "There's something I want you to hear. A small thank-you for all you've done for me." Carefully, she set the needle onto the record and turned the crank. From the large trumpet came a man's deep baritone voice, singing a ballad.

Lucy walked closer to the Victrola, listening carefully. The song wasn't familiar to her, but that voice . . . That voice! She would know that beautiful baritone voice anywhere, she realized with a jolt. *It belongs to Wyatt.* Eyes wide, she looked at Cora.

Cora grinned from ear to ear. "He recorded it in Louisville a few months back. Whenever he disappears for a stretch, it's because he's off recording his music."

"But . . . he never said anything about recording songs. I mean . . ." Lucy's mind was spinning like a windmill. "He spoke of meetings. I assumed that it had something to do with his singing school pamphlets." She never thought to ask the purpose of those meetings.

"There was probably truth in that. But it's also true that he's been recording his music at a studio."

"Why didn't he say something?"

"He's far too modest. Though I have been encouraging him to tell you about his recordings, and he finally said that I could tell you." She smiled like a cat that swallowed a canary. "So, of course, I did."

"But Cora . . . why . . . is he here? Why do the singing schools at all? They seem like so much work for him. Why not just stay in the city and concentrate on his career?"

"Oh Lucy, after all these months, do you still not understand that man? Have you listened to his music? His ambition is not for himself but for others."

Lucy listened to the rest of the song, one she realized now that she'd heard Wyatt sing at a gathering, but she'd been so distracted by the clapping and the clogging that she hadn't paid much attention to the lyrics. She assumed it told a love story between a man and a woman, but now she realized that it was a love story between God and his people. Seeking them, calling them back to him, drawing them to his tender love and unfailing kindness.

The record finished and Cora reached over to pull the needle up, but Lucy asked her to play it again, so she did. Lucy plopped down in a chair, eyes closed, swept away by the song. When it finished for the third time, she looked at Cora. "Wyatt is your sponsor for Bibles as rewards, isn't he?" When Cora nodded, she added, "And here I thought you'd talked Father into providing funds."

"Your father is amenable to helping individuals, those who've already proved themselves. But he's a hard sell for blanket donations. Too difficult to see results, he says." She shrugged. "All business, that's your father."

"Wyatt is quite an unusual man, isn't he?"

"*That*, he is."

As Cora lifted the record from the Victrola and carefully slipped it back into its jacket, Lucy cupped her hands over her knees. "I've been thinking . . . after the Moonlight Schools campaign, I'd like to stay on."

Cora's mouth opened and Lucy raised a hand to cut off her thought before it was expressed. "*Not* as a teacher. And not as your assistant. I'm sorry, Cora. I've enjoyed both roles more than I thought I would, but they're not where my heart lies."

"And where is that?"

"I'd like to write down the stories of the mountain people. Miss Mollie's, Finley James, others. To capture them on paper."

She looked down at her hands. "Perhaps, one day, they might be published." Something like the dream her mother always had.

Silence. When she chanced a look at Cora, she saw her eyes were glittering.

"So," she said softly, "you want to write?"

Lucy smiled. "I do."

"I think that's a fine idea, Lucy." She reached for her handkerchief and dabbed at the corners of her eyes.

"I'm going to live in Sally Ann Duncan's cabin. It's all arranged. Roy is working for my father's lumber company. It seemed like an ideal arrangement. They can use the rent money, and I'd prefer to be up in the mountains." Did she really just say that aloud . . . and mean it? She did! "There's something about that cabin, that property. I just love it."

Cora smiled. "I don't doubt the connection. That property belonged to our great-great-grandfather. The first Wilson to immigrate from Ulster, long ago."

"Hold on a moment." Lucy tipped her head. "Are you saying that Sally Ann is kin to us?"

"Many times removed." Cora sighed. "Like most everyone up there. All related to each other, to some distant degree or another."

And then there are closer degrees than you might ever imagine, Lucy thought.

"Seems like this is the day for revelations. There's something you should know, Lucy. It wasn't my idea to have you come to Morehead. It was presented to me, and, of course, I loved it. But I had no budget for an assistant. You've seen for yourself how tight things are here."

She was well aware. Cora wrote and sold articles under a pen name just to make ends meet. All spare funds were used for publishing materials.

Confused, Lucy rubbed her forehead. If Cora was unable to pay her, that meant . . . someone else was providing her salary. Someone else was paying the fee to hire Jenny from Arthur Cooper's livery, to let the room at Miss Maude's boarding house. She dropped her head with a sigh. "Hazel."

"No," Cora said with a smile. "Not Hazel. It was your father. When I saw him at his wedding to Hazel, he told me that he worried you seemed to be lost. Growing invisible, were his exact words. He asked me if I'd take you on as an assistant for six months, and he'd provide the salary."

Lucy stared at her, shocked. "But Father acted as if he was against it. He told me he only acquiesced because you wouldn't take no for an answer."

"Self-contradiction." She wiggled her eyebrows. "A clever tactic to make it all the more enticing."

"But . . . he's never had anything positive to say about Rowan County."

"All bark, no bite." Cora grinned. "A teddy bear at heart, that's your paw." Her face turned facetiously stern. "But don't *ever* tell him I told you that."

A memory of Charlotte as a baby flashed through Lucy's mind—curled up in Father's lap, holding Mr. Buttons. This time, the sharp and lingering sting that usually accompanied those memories was missing.

Cora stood at the window, looking up the road toward the mountain. She rubbed her elbows tightly, as if holding herself together. "Less than a week away."

The Moonlight Schools campaign, she meant.

TWENTY-FIVE

IT WAS A GLORIOUS NIGHT with a great harvest moon—so close that a man might think to reach out and touch it. There was a breeze, just enough to rustle the leaves on the trees.

The first night of the Moonlight Schools had arrived. The skies were clear. Cora had hoped for one hundred people to show up, a few per schoolhouse. Recently she lowered it to fifty. "And if it catches on, then perhaps more will come as the week goes on." She tried to sound optimistic, but she was anxious and couldn't sit still all day long.

Late in the day, Wyatt stopped by Cora's office. "Are you excited?"

"I'm . . ." Cora paused. "I supposed I'm . . . uneasy."

"I'm going to head on up to Little Brushy School. Will you come?"

Lucy grabbed her sweater. "I'll go with you. Cora, come with us."

She hesitated, rubbed her forehead. "I fear a headache is coming."

"Cora, we have prayed mightily about this extravagant idea of yours," Wyatt said. "Let us have faith in the All Mighty's extravagant answer."

Slowly, Cora rose and followed them to the livery. Lucy had grown so accustomed to riding Jenny that she climbed on with ease, stroking the pony's mane with fondness. Wyatt on Lyric led the procession of Cora and Lucy, on their mounts, and as they passed the train station, Andrew Spencer waved, flagging Lucy down. She told Cora to go on ahead and tugged slightly on the reins to stop Jenny.

Andrew tipped his hat. "I wanted you to know I'm leaving Morehead."

"Off to bigger and better things?"

He grinned. "That's my plan." He took off his bowler hat and held it against his middle, a gesture of sincerity. "Lucy, I hope—sincerely—that you won't be too disappointed tonight."

"Nor do I," Lucy said and gave him a nod. She tapped her heels against Jenny's girth to catch up with Cora and Wyatt, who were waiting for her at the trailhead. She didn't mind leaving Andrew Spencer behind.

As they crossed the creek, she thought again of how much she had changed in these last few months. She was barely conscious of how thoroughly she had adjusted to Jenny: leaning forward as the pony extended her neck to climb the hillside or lowered her nose to pick her way through the rocky trails. The inside of her knees gripped the saddle and her hands allowed give and take with the reins. When had those responses become instinctive? She hadn't even noticed.

They walked the next couple of miles in silence. There was no talking tonight, not like they usually did. Each one, deep in their own thoughts. Cora held the reins tightly in her hands, evidence of her churning mind. Wyatt, Lucy had no doubt, was praying for a successful turnout. But what would be a success? A few people per schoolhouse, as Cora hoped for? Wyatt expected hundreds. Lucy hoped for something in between.

The shadows deepened as they went up the mountain, darkness descending as they rode, though the moon was round and bright, the sky cloudless. Lucy breathed in the familiar musty scent of the woods. She gazed up at the tall canopy of trees, at the twinkling stars above. How she loved these hills, so far, so remote from town life. The hills and hollows were becoming part of her. As if they'd always been a part of her.

Strange, so strange. These mountains and valleys were where her grandparents and had lived and were buried. Her father ran away from this place, and returned only to reap its harvest. He didn't realize what he had missed seeing in these mountains. Cora saw.

As they came around the last bend, a faint sound floated through the treetops. Wyatt lifted a hand to stop them. He glanced back at Cora and Lucy, curious, then turned around again and cocked his ear.

"An owl?" Lucy said, pleased with herself for being able to identify a night bird. Six months ago, she probably wouldn't have noticed.

"No, I don't think it's a bird." Wyatt tipped his head. "There. There it is again." It was the sound of a baby crying, wafting through the night air, followed by a murmur of voices. "Let's keep going."

As they came through the trees, Cora let out a loud gasp of shock, as if the wind had been knocked out of her. The door to the Little Brushy schoolhouse was wide open, revealing a schoolhouse packed with people. Cora made a clicking sound and her horse moved into a fast trot, then cantered over the field to the schoolhouse. She leapt off her horse, dropping the reins to run up the porch steps. She peered inside, then turned to Lucy and Wyatt as their horses approached the schoolhouse. "Every seat is full," she said, her face covered in relief and joy. "Men and women of every age." Her hands flew to her cheeks. "And then there's Angie . . . she's at the chalkboard acting like a seasoned general." Her gaze shifted past them and she pointed to the trees, as more people arrived. "Look! There's Martin Sloan, coming down the trail." She lowered her voice to a happy whisper. "Why, that old coot. He told me just yesterday that he's eighty-five years old and didn't I know that old dogs can't learn new tricks." Beaming, she clasped her hands together over her heart. "Oh Wyatt, you were so right. We serve an extravagant God. Why did I ever doubt?"

"Why, indeed?" Wyatt replied, but Cora had already disappeared into the schoolhouse. He swung a leg over Lyric's back and slid to the ground, saying hello to Martin Sloan and a few other people as they walked past them.

Lucy watched them as they paused at the schoolhouse door, looking for a place to sit. "Wyatt, do you think all of the schoolhouses will have this kind of turnout? Or most?"

"I do," he said, looking up at her. "I believe that all will be like this one."

"How can you be so sure?"

"There are just some things," he said as he reached out his hands to help Lucy down, "that a man knows without knowing how he knows." In one smooth move, he lifted her off the pony and into his arms. And then he paused for a moment, hands around her waist. "Cora tells me you're not leaving Rowan County."

"That's right. I'm staying put." Something welled up inside her and burst out. "There's no place else I want to be."

They were inches from each other, his eyes locked on hers. In those intense gray eyes of his were several emotions: confidence, contentment, serenity, hope. And there was something else in his look: love. Her breath quickened, her heart skipped a beat or two. He loved her. She could see it, sense it, feel it. And she loved Wyatt. She loved this fine and humble man. She knew, without knowing how she knew.

A jumble of sounds floated out of the schoolhouse, a song, voices high and low . . . and the spell was broken.

Wyatt lifted his chin to look over the horse's neck at the school. "Sounds like a party's going on. Shall we go in?"

But Lucy wasn't quite ready to go inside. She wanted to soak this moment up, to fix it firmly in her mind. The soft, buttery glow casting light out the schoolhouse door, followed by a hum of chatter. Being here, with Wyatt's arms around her, with Cora. With Angie. She knew she would never, ever forget this night. Cora was so right. The Moonlight Schools would always be the highlight of her life.

So . . . What Happened Next?

CORA WILSON STEWART declared September 5, 1911, as "the brightest moonlit night the world has ever seen." On that first night of the campaign, over 1,200 illiterate and semi-literate adults, almost one-third of the county, trooped through the hills and hollows to fill the rural schoolhouses of Rowan County, Kentucky.

Stewart described her observations in an interview with American journalist Ida Clyde Clarke called "Moonlight-School Lady":

> There were overgrown boys who had dropped out of school and been ashamed to re-enter. There were girls who had been deprived of education through isolation. There were women who had married in childhood—as so many mountain girls do—and with them came their husbands, men who had been humiliated by having to make their mark or to ask election officers to cast their vote for them. There were middle-aged men who had seen golden opportunities pass them because of the handicap of illiteracy—men whose mineral, timber, and other material resources were in control of educated men who had made beggars of them.[1]

1. Ida Clyde Clarke, "Moonlight-School Lady," *Pictorial Review*, January 1926.

Yvonne Honeycutt Baldwin, in her informative book *Cora Wilson Stewart and Kentucky's Moonlight School: Fighting for Literacy in America*, wrote,

> Ranging in age from eighteen to eighty-five, they sat on small benches in the little schoolhouses, confronted marks on the tablets in front of them, and examined chalked images on the blackboards. They sang songs and visited with neighbors, and took home that first night a vision of what it would mean to be able to read and write.[2]

According to Stewart's accounts, one young man's joy upon learning to write his name was so complete that he etched it in several trees on his way home from school, then carved it on numerous fence posts the following day, and continued to place his name on public property throughout the county until requested by the sheriff to desist.[3]

Sounds a little like our Finley James, doesn't it?

This was the schedule: Moonlight Schools met Monday through Thursday evenings from seven to nine o'clock for six weeks. Sessions began promptly at seven, with a fifteen-minute devotional that generally included singing. Reading lessons took twenty-five minutes, writing exercises another twenty-five, followed by twenty-five minutes of arithmetic. Teachers then led two fifteen-minute drills in basic history, civics, health and sanitation, geography, home economics, agriculture, and horticulture. Students left promptly at nine to head home.

In two six-week sessions, Moonlight pupils generally gained the ability to sign a document, make basic mathematical calculations, write simple letters, and read a few verses of the Bible. Stewart did not set grade-level equivalencies, perhaps thinking that to do

---

2. Yvonne Honeycutt Baldwin, *Cora Wilson Stewart and Kentucky's Moonlight School: Fighting for Literacy in America* (Lexington: University Press of Kentucky, 2006), 42.

3. Baldwin, *Cora Wilson Stewart*, 45.

so might insult or demoralize adult pupils; instead, completion of the second six-week session marked the point at which they moved from illiteracy to literacy. With no set standards defining literacy, such "functional literacy" (a term that was not introduced until World War I) came to mean a fifth-grade reading level.

Throughout the sessions, Stewart visited as many of the Moonlight Schools as possible, riding horseback or traveling in a small buggy throughout the county, to check on their progress and offer encouragement to pupils and teachers. One teacher even wrote a "fight song" for the moment, entitled "Onward Rowan County," to be sung to the tune of "Onward Christian Soldiers."[4]

Two years later, Stewart calculated that only twenty-three illiterates remained in the county. Six of these were blind or had defective sight, five were "imbeciles or epileptics," two had moved into the county as the session closed, and four "could not be inducted to learn." She loved to quote the old mountaineer who once remarked that the Moonlight Schools had taken his community from moonshine and bullets to lemonade and Bibles.[5]

Stewart's faith in humankind was almost as strong as her faith in God. She saw great potential for change in the movement to which she devoted her life. Better-educated adults produced better-educated children and demanded better schooling for them. She envisioned a world transformed by full literacy.

Stewart's Moonlight Schools caught on quickly, and when the state legislature created the Kentucky Illiteracy Commission in 1914, the Moonlight Schools were operating throughout all of Kentucky as well as in other states. From 1910 to 1920, Kentucky's illiteracy rate dropped by nearly 4 percent. The national illiteracy rate declined by only 1.7 percent during that same period.[6]

Just in case you're wondering, in 1911 in Rowan County, there was a schoolhouse set aside for African American children, yet it

4. Baldwin, *Cora Wilson Stewart*, 42–45.
5. Baldwin, *Cora Wilson Stewart*, 46.
6. Baldwin, *Cora Wilson Stewart*, 188.

remained empty, for various reasons. Not for long, though. Eventually, there were Moonlight Schools for African Americans and Native Americans, as the concept spread to other states.

Stewart received national and international recognition for her work with adult literacy. In 1923 she was elected to the executive committee of the National Education Association. Six years later, President Herbert Hoover named her to chair the executive committee of the National Advisory Committee on Illiteracy. She also presided over the illiteracy section of the World Conference on Education. On December 2, 1958, she died of a fatal heart attack. She was eighty-three years old.

Cora Wilson Stewart had a dream to eliminate illiteracy in one generation.

If she failed to completely eradicate illiteracy, she did make an important and long-lasting contribution. Playing a critical role in the development of adult education, she is now considered a pioneer in the field of literacy training.

Fact or Fiction?

ISTORY HAS "STORY" AT ITS CENTER. Narrative is assumed—a beginning, a middle, an end. And yet, while reading historical fiction, a reader has every right to wonder where truth ends and fiction begins. Cora Wilson Stewart's story was indeed factual and, I hope, her personality and determination were accurately represented. While the characters surrounding her (Lucy Wilson, Angie Cooper, Brother Wyatt, Finley James, and the others) were fictitious, I tried to remain true to Cora Wilson Stewart's spirit as I wove a story about her.

Mollie McGlothin, the elderly mountain woman, was also factual. There were three aha moments with mountain people that provided Cora Wilson Stewart with the inspiration for her life's work. Mollie McGlothin was the first incident and, most likely, the most profound. Mollie brought her daughter Jane's letters to Cora to read and to answer back. There came a day when Mollie told Cora that she no longer needed help. She had bought a speller for herself and had taught herself to read. For Cora, Mollie's accomplishment turned upside down the current academic presumptions of adult illiteracy. Academics assumed there was a window for a child to learn to read, and once that window was shut, the opportunity was forever lost. Inspired by Mollie McGlothin, Cora Wilson Stewart proved them wrong.

FACT: Singing school masters and shape note notation. Similar to itinerant preachers, these singing school masters would stay in a location for a while to teach a singing school. The first singing schools began in New England in the early 1700s as a means to spread the use of written music. The tradition caught on quickly in the rural South, including the use of shape-note hymn singing.

FICTION: Miss Norah and a handful of other teachers weren't enthusiastic participants in the Moonlight Schools campaign.

FACT: Right from the start, all the teachers under Cora's management were loyal to the campaign, extremely supportive. It was entirely a grassroots movement, made up of volunteers. Many years later, one teacher said it was the highlight of her life.

> The teachers were her strongest supporters, but she did not know if they would be willing to give up their evenings to teach adults after they had dealt with children during the daytime. She decided to appeal to their basic self-interest: she told them that teaching the parents would encourage interest in the public schools. If parents were interested in the schools, they would see that the children attended during the day, and they would support the county schools. With this inducement, the teachers volunteered without exception to teach the night schools.[1]

FACT: The speedy educational progress of Finley James in a month's time. According to Yvonne Honeycutt Baldwin, a highly motivated older student, in those days, could sail through grades.

BOTH FACT AND FICTION: The superstitious beliefs held by the mountain people. One example in the book was Lucy's father's reaction to boots on a table top as a sign of coming death. Odd old traditions, as illogical as they may be, are hard to let go of.

1. Baldwin, *Cora Wilson Stewart*, 35.

Recommended Reading about the Life of

Cora Wilson Stewart

Yvonne Honeycutt Baldwin, *Cora Wilson Stewart: Fighting for Literacy in America* (Lexington: The University Press of Kentucky, 2006).

Willie Nelms, *Cora Wilson Stewart: Crusade against Illiteracy* (Jefferson, NC: McFarland, 1997).

Discussion Questions

1. Cora Wilson Stewart was an unsung hero, a woman ahead of her time. The facts surrounding her life were all true—she was raised in Rowan County, she became the first female Superintendent of Education, she was divorced three times (twice to the same man), she created the Moonlight School campaign, and she had a remarkable, purposeful long life. What aspects of her life or personality did you find most inspiring?

2. How do you respond to Brother Wyatt's provocative question: "If it's not wrong, does that make it right?"

3. Cora, who did not have success with marriage, held a calling to a life's work in higher regard than matrimony. She gave Lucy a warning about men. "A man like Andrew Spencer has the looks and charisma that can hide flaws. Like soft spots on a seemingly perfect apple. You don't realize they're there until you bite into them." What is your reaction to Cora's advice?

4. Brother Wyatt divided Almighty into two words. All Mighty. Mighty over all. He said it made a difference. How so?

5. Sally Ann Duncan told Lucy, "Sometimes you have to give something up to make room for something new." How many times did you notice that adage coming true in this story?

6. "Try to picture," Cora said, "what life is like for one who must get all his information by ear. If a man cannot read or write or vote, he cannot speak. He is mute. He is forgotten. You might think it's a pity they cannot read, but the real tragedy is they cannot speak." Put yourself in the place of an illiterate. What privileges would you be missing?

7. Lucy's father was unlikable and likable, both. He lived by a basic philosophy: "Better to face forward in life, not backward." Given the circumstances of his life, from growing up in Rowan County, to losing his wife and daughter, what are your thoughts about his mantra? Was it a coping mechanism? Or wise counsel?

8. Put yourself in Lucy's polished boots. How would you have handled her discovery of Angie's identity? Do you think Lucy made the right decision? Explain.

9. Finding a life of purpose is a central theme in this novel. Lucy Wilson found purpose in Rowan County. Or . . . did purpose find her?

Read on for Chapter 1
of the First Book in
THE DEACON'S
FAMILY SERIES!

ONE

A YEAR HAD PASSED since Luke Schrock's exile from Stoney Ridge began. A very long year. He'd been in and out of rehab twice. Wait. Hold on. Make that three times. He'd forgotten the three-day holiday weekend he'd checked himself out and went on a bender.

The bus swerved and bumped on the country roads, stirring his stomach and ratcheting up his anxiety. The bus was stuffy and hot; it made him long for fresh air and cold, all at once. He was on his way back home.

Home. Luke had a feeling he couldn't name exactly, but one he'd never had in relation to home before. It used to mean security, belonging, unconditional acceptance. What he felt now contained that, all that, but to today was added a hint of desperation.

This was a bad idea. A terrible idea. He'd never intended to return to Stoney Ridge. The counselor had strongly recommended that Luke find sober, supportive living arrangements. What could be more sober than an Amish farm? he asked Luke.

Uh, well, that depends. Luke had been living among the Amish as he developed a dependency on alcohol.

But then David Stoltzfus, his bishop, agreed with the counselor.

He had told him to stop running away from his problems, that coming home again was the only road to manhood.

He recognized the fork in the road that would lead the bus straight into Stoney Ridge. Pulling the cord to hop off the bus seemed like a very appealing option. He could head right toward Lancaster, rather than left to Stoney Ridge. He could do it. He should do it.

But he didn't. The bus zoomed left.

David had promised he'd be waiting at the bus stop. Luke held out a sliver of hope that his mother might be there too, and maybe his younger brother Sammy. There was no chance that Galen King, his mother's husband, would be there. No chance. Not after what had happened to Galen's prized horse. Nope. No chance.

When Luke had asked David what he would do with himself once he was back in town, the bishop was vague. "One thing at a time, Luke. Let's get you home first."

Luke had wanted to ask him if home meant the Inn at Eagle Hill, where his mother and brother and stepfather lived, or if he was using "home" as a metaphor. But something inside held him back from asking, partly because he had a feeling David didn't know the answer.

David Stoltzfus had gone above and beyond the call of duty for Luke this last year. He'd come to visit him regularly, even when Luke told him not to bother. But David did bother, over and over again. He brought books to read, for he knew Luke loved to read. He read them too, and then they would discuss them. Conversation grew easier between them. Those visits, they meant a lot to Luke, and he hoped David had some idea how much. The reason David had never given up on Luke was, he said, because God never gave up on people.

The bus hit a pothole and jolted Luke against the window. He recognized the passing farm as Windmill Farm, belonging to Amos and Fern Lapp, and took note of the new mailbox. Not so long ago, he'd put a cherry bomb in their old one and blown it to smithereens.

Why had he done that? It was a circling discussion in group therapy—what were triggers that caused destructive behavior? The counselor encouraged everyone to identify those triggers, so they'd know to recognize them. And then, to redirect thoughts and feelings and behaviors toward something beneficial.

Luke had tried to identify his triggers, tried and failed. Why had he hurt people, like the Lapps, who had been so good to him? He couldn't find an answer.

For a short while, before blowing up the Lapps' mailbox, he'd even apprenticed for Jesse Stoltzfus's buggy shop at Windmill Farm. Like so many opportunities Luke had been given, it hadn't gone well. The counselor suggested that if anyone got too close to Luke, he would do something to push them away. Translation: self-sabotage. If anything went too well, he would find a way to ruin it. He saw that in himself. What he didn't know was *why*.

That was another reason the counselor had consistently encouraged Luke to return to Stoney Ridge. "Find out *why*," he'd told Luke. "You'll never move forward until you find out why."

"Moving forward." Translation for counseling code: *aftercare*. Luke had grown savvy to counselor code. The first time he was released from rehab, he was adamant that he would not return to Stoney Ridge. Moving forward, he was convinced, meant moving on. Make a fresh start.

He tried. He failed. Back he went to rehab.

This time, rehab lasted a little longer. Instead of sixty days, it was ninety days. "Better chance for long-term success," the counselor said. Not so for Luke. As soon as he was released, he went on that three-day bender. David bailed him out of jail and took him back to the clinic. This time, it lasted more than six months. Now *that* should give him a much, much better chance not to relapse. Added to that was the warning from David that this was the last rescue. If he relapsed, if he ended up in jail, he'd stay there. Three strikes was the limit, even for David, the most tolerant man in the world.

Luke had to agree with the counselor on one thing: he didn't seem to be able to move forward. "Why not go back and face your past?" the counselor said. "What do you have to lose?"

Nothing. Absolutely nothing. Absolutely no one. Grudgingly, Luke agreed to return to Stoney Ridge. It was one thing to say no to your counselor, but nearly impossible to say no to your bishop, especially one like David.

After making that decision, he'd had the first good night's sleep in . . . well, maybe in the entire last year. But that didn't mean he wasn't anxious about his homecoming. He was. These Amish, they had long, long memories.

At the turnoff to Windmill Farm, he noticed a woman standing behind a beat-up farm stand. Amos had fine orchards, old trees that had been lovingly tended. Luke remembered that very farm stand, topped with baskets of tree ripened fruit, jugs of cider, and an honest jar. He also thought of how often he used to dip into that jar when he was low on cash.

Ouch. Another stinging memory.

David called those stinging memories one of the greatest gifts given by the Holy Spirit. Convicting memories, David called them. Conviction was meant to turn us to confession. And confession brought us back to God.

Luke doubted David ever had much of anything to confess. If he did, he would know the sick feeling that came along with the stinging memories. The disgust and self-loathing.

The bus jolted again. He squinted, wondering if Fern Lapp was the woman at the farm stand, but quickly dismissed that thought. Fern was thin, wiry—small but mighty. A force to be reckoned with.

This woman looked young. She was tall and held herself erect, like a queen. She wore a Plain lavender dress with a black apron. A blue kerchief kept the hair out of her eyes. Luke leaned closer to the window to peer at the woman as the bus passed by. Who was she? Just then, she looked up and waved at the passing bus, and Luke felt a shock run through him. *Izzy Miller.* She'd been a patient at the rehab center during his first attempt to get clean and sober. He'd been in a group session with her once or twice. She hadn't talked much, but he did notice her. Oh yeah, he noticed her all right. She wasn't the sort of person you'd easily forget. He remembered thinking she was the prettiest girl he'd ever seen. High, wide cheekbones; snapping dark brown eyes; luxurious brunette hair. He also remembered her as being frustratingly aloof; he had tried, without success, to get her attention a few times. Why in the world was she at Windmill Farm, of all places? And why was she dressed Plain?

Well, well. Luke's grim spirits lifted considerably. Stoney Ridge was looking better already.

Acknowledgments

INSPIRATION CAN COME in the most unexpected ways . . . *if* you're listening for it.

I have a daily habit of listening to a local classical radio station as I write. A while ago, the radio host made a casual remark about this day in history: "On September 5, 1911, the Moonlight Schools began." The host explained a few brief facts about the campaign and mentioned Cora Wilson Stewart. A shiver went up my spine. I stopped what I was doing to research the Moonlight Schools. I knew I had to tell this story. That very day, I called my editor. Not much later, a contract was in the mail. And . . . if you're wondering, the answer is *yes!* I sent a big fat donation to the listener-supported radio show as a thank-you for the inspiration.

Thank you to Dr. Mattie Decker and Dr. Yvonne Honeycutt Baldwin, for sharing their enthusiasm, their vast knowledge on the subject, and their willingness to answer my questions. As Mattie said, "I feel as if Cora is my friend. I know her so well." Yvonne, whose dissertation about Cora Wilson Stewart was a goldmine of information, could not have been more generous with her time. Her well-researched book provided one dimension about Cora. Our phone conversations brought Cora to life, making her three dimensional. From Yvonne came little extra tidbits, such as Cora's headaches (possibly migraines), that made this woman so real.

To Rick Charles at the Railroad Museum at Morehead, thank you for your willingness to share your knowledge.

To the oh-so-talented Trent Smith, who answered some questions about the violin and fiddling.

To Lindsey Ross and Meredith Munoz, my first readers, whose input and feedback made this story so much better.

Research is my favorite part of the writing process. I spent long hours studying Rowan County in eastern Kentucky, its history, its topography, and what made it stand apart from neighboring mining counties. I also spent time studying the folklore and culture, the food and the fauna. And then there's the music! Learning about the tradition of music in Appalachia—fiddling and clogging, shape note notation, singing schools—became one of my favorite discoveries.

A book passes through so many helpful hands before it reaches its final stage. The Revell team are stellar at bringing the best out of a manuscript (first to Andrea Doering's wise initial editing, then passing it to Barb Barnes's eagle eye), gift wrapping it in a beautifully designed cover (Gayle Raymer), and delivering it to the right venues to catch readers' attention (Michele Misiak, Karen Steele, Brianne Dekker). And there are still others who play a quiet yet vital role: my agent, Joyce Hart, of the Hartline Literary Agency, for one, to whom I will always be grateful for cracking open that first door.

As I've studied the impact of literacy for this novel, my appreciation for the Author of language has only expanded. God is a communicator. I'm so grateful for his help to find remarkable people whose stories are worth telling.

Great stories move people. So do great people. I did the best I could in trying to bring to life the story of a significant year in the legacy of Cora Wilson Stewart's life, arguably her most defining year, and to provide an accurate historical context for the story. But this book is a work of fiction. Any and all blunders belong to me.

Suzanne Woods Fisher is an award-winning, bestselling author of more than thirty books, including *On a Coastal Breeze*, as well as the Nantucket Legacy, Amish Beginnings, The Bishop's Family, The Deacon's Family, and The Inn at Eagle Hill series, among other novels. She is also the author of several nonfiction books about the Amish, including *Amish Peace* and *Amish Proverbs*. She lives in California. Learn more at www.suzannewoodsfisher.com and follow Suzanne on Facebook @SuzanneWoodsFisherAuthor and Twitter @suzannewfisher.

"There's just something unique and fresh about every Suzanne Woods Fisher book. Whatever the reason, I'm a fan."

—SHELLEY SHEPHARD GRAY,
New York Times and *USA Today* bestselling author

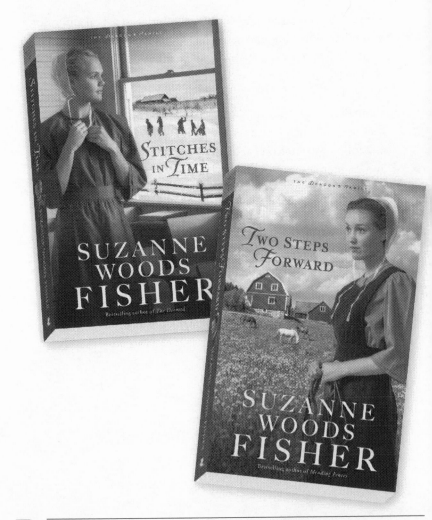

Revell
a division of Baker Publishing Group
www.RevellBooks.com

 RevellBooks

Available wherever books and ebooks are sold.

Don't Miss Any of The Bishop's Family

"Suzanne is an authority on the Plain folks. . . .
She always delivers a fantastic story with
interesting characters, all in a tightly woven plot."

—BETH WISEMAN, bestselling author
of the DAUGHTERS OF THE PROMISE and the LAND OF CANAAN series

Revell
a division of Baker Publishing Group
www.RevellBooks.com

RevellBooks

Available wherever books and ebooks are sold.

"Memorable characters, gorgeous Maine scenery, and plenty of family drama. I can't wait to visit Three Sisters Island again!"

—IRENE HANNON,
bestselling author of the beloved Hope Harbor series

Following the lives of three sisters, this brand-new contemporary romance series from Suzanne Woods Fisher is sure to delight her fans and draw new ones.

Revell
a division of Baker Publishing Group
www.RevellBooks.com

 RevellBooks

Available wherever books and ebooks are sold.

Connect with SUZANNE

www.SuzanneWoodsFisher.com

Be the First to Hear about New Books from Revell!

Sign up for announcements about new and upcoming titles at

RevellBooks.com/SignUp

@RevellBooks

Don't miss out on our great reads!

Revell
a division of Baker Publishing Group
www.RevellBooks.com

Printed in the United States
By Bookmasters